DARK DODGERS

C.P. JAMES

BOOKS

BY C.P. JAMES

The Reassembly Series

Rocket Repo
Trawler Trash
Ship Show
Xeno Xoo
Fleet Feat
Dark Dodgers

The Cytocorp Saga

Dome Six
Into the Burn
Out of the Seam

Vinci Books

vinci-books.com

Published by Vinci Books Ltd in 2025

1

Copyright © C.P. James 2023

The author has asserted their moral right to be identified as the author of this work in accordance with the Copyright, Designs and Patents Act 1988.
This work is a work of fiction. Names, characters, places and incidents are the product of the author's imagination or are used fictitiously. Any resemblance to actual persons, living or dead, places and incidents is entirely coincidental.
All rights reserved. No part of this publication may be copied, reproduced, distributed, stored in any retrieval system, or transmitted in any form or by any means, including photocopying, recording, or other electronic or mechanical methods, nor used as a source for any form of machine learning including AI datasets, without the prior written permission of the publisher. The publisher and the author have made every effort to obtain permissions for any third party material used in this book and to comply with copyright law. Any queries in this respect should be brought to the attention of the publisher and any omissions will be corrected in future editions.
A CIP catalogue record for this book is available from the British Library.
Paperback ISBN: 9781036701352

Printed and bound in Great Britain by Clays Ltd, Elcograf S.p.A.

CHAPTER 1
SLOW GIN FIZMO

Voprot, the colossal Kigantean who resembled an irradiated iguana, lifted the dice cup from the Fizmo's galley table and grinned. The moment he did, Geddy Starheart's stomach flooded with bile.

"Uguinok!" exclaimed the lizard, clearly having expected everyone to be happy for him.

"What the shit?!" Oz slurred, her nose wrinkling distastefully.

Denk gathered his scoring sticks in disgust and re-sorted them in the tray, shaking his head. "V, I love ya like a brother, but that ain't right."

"That not uguinok?" Voprot asked, genuinely confused.

"I mean that you keep winnin'."

Geddy slid another fifty-credit square into the kitty and rubbed his face, noting that his drink was empty. "Anyone else's glass have a hole in it?"

"On it." Oz teetered as she rose from the galley table.

— *She's hitting it harder than usual tonight.*
— *You noticed that, too?*
— *I wonder why.*

— You and me both.

They'd been at it for hours, yet Voprot's winning streak had only extended. He barely even knew how to play. Wasn't that always how it went?

Voprot's lucky streak contrasted starkly with their own. Since jumping into space over the reviled desert world Kigantu — the planetary equivalent of dry anal — the crew of the *For Sale Make Offer* had been killing time waiting for a massive sandstorm to clear. It followed a northeastern track, suggesting it originated in the south. It had engulfed Aquebba entirely, and Jel figured it would be at least another sixteen hours before they could even think about an entry. Everyone was getting on each other's nerves.

Oz returned with a fresh bottle of Kailorian gin and refilled everyone's cup as Voprot's claw swept the little pile of credit squares at the center into the growing mountain in front of him.

Denk also got up. "I'm starvin'. Who's up for nutrimush? Cap? Oz? Nutrimush? Jel?"

"I thought you said, 'food.'" Realizing his sour stomach had no buffer against the harsh liquor, Geddy added, "Yeah, okay."

"Nutrimushes all around." He gleefully removed a stack of bowls from the cupboard.

"I wish Doc was here," Jel mumbled. She rarely imbibed, but when she did, she often became sullen.

Doc Tardigan had taken Eveth, the Zelnad deserter, with him to Basoa to convince the reclusive genius Lestiko to help the Alliance. Lestiko was host to a Zelnad but had figured out how to regain control. In so doing, he had gained deep insights into their tech and the so-called original energy that powered it. That made him invaluable to Doc and the Ornean scientists who were studying it.

All Lestiko cared about was learning how to separate

himself from his nasty entity, Rai, without killing them both. He believed that the massive energy it released was being exploited by the Nads in order to create a weapon capable of destroying Sagacea. A weapon made of hosts.

Geddy's eyes slid from Jel over to the nutrimush spigot, where the greenish-brown paste had begun to emerge. It coiled lazily in the bowl before softening into it like an incel into a lounge chair. Its distinct smell, an earthy tang that stuck to your clothes, drifted through the galley.

"It's extra thick today, guys," Denk said, moving on to the next bowl. "We must be near the bottom."

"Please don't say bottom." Geddy turned away from Denk's labors and tried not to gag.

— *How is he always in such good spirits?*

— You saw Durandia. Anywhere else would seem like nirvana.

Having filled everyone's glass, Oz returned to her seat at the hexagonal metal table and took a swig directly from the bottle. The others exchanged concerned looks.

"Everything okay?" Geddy asked her.

"Don't I seem okay?"

"Just ... sad, I guess."

"Fuck sadness." Jel raised her glass to Oz.

Oz gave her a crooked nod and did likewise. "And fuck the damn Dans — er, Nads. Ha!" She took another guzzle and smacked her lips. "Ahhh."

Geddy felt a presence over his shoulder. Jel raised her eyes to the door and squinted. "Oh, hey."

Tretiak Bouche had entered the *Fizmo's* galley, joining Voprot as the only sober ones left. He'd been sitting at the comm station for hours trying to reach Krigor, his and Geddy's mutual friend, in Aquebba. Jel said the storm's iron-rich sand created too much interference, but he kept at it anyway. As hard as it was to believe that he actually cared about Kriggy, people could still surprise you sometimes.

Denk returned to the table with two full bowls, which he gave to the ladies. "Pretty girls first. Hey, Mr. Bouche. You want some nutrimush? It's only slightly fermented."

Oz made a show of scooping the stuff onto her spoon and slipping it into her mouth. "Mmm ... you can really taste the cricket meal today."

"A tempting offer, but no thank you. I came to say goodnight."

"Still no luck reaching Krig?" Geddy asked.

For three long weeks, the storm had raged, and they were no closer to Aquebba. But the moment it broke, they had to be ready. The Zelnad research ship they'd yanked out of Beebit Tompanov's greedy hands hadn't been sold after all. Tretiak had hidden it in the Double A's so-called Tomb, the location of which he alone knew. They'd come to Kigantu hoping that the mysterious empty ship had actually discovered Sagacea's position. If that was true, then the Zelnads would be equally desperate to find it.

Tretiak shook his head. "I'll try again in the morning. Let me know if the storm breaks." He disappeared down the hall.

Having distributed all the bowls to the crew, Denk returned with one of his own, bigger than even Voprot's portion, and settled onto the seat. "Well, everyone, better dig in before the skin forms!"

———

By the time the bleary-eyed crew stumbled into the bridge the next morning, the storm appeared to be dissipating. Still no luck reaching Krig, but Geddy had lived through enough sandstorms in Aquebba to know that the comm array on the mountain could become encrusted with sand. If that was the case, they might have to wait until it was safe for Krig to venture outside and clean the housing.

If the bars and brothels on Turduranto Street were lucky, a resupply ship had arrived shortly before the storm. Running out of booze with the galaxy's dregs cooped up inside would've created an entirely different set of problems.

Having just refilled his mug of coffee, Geddy returned to the bridge and stared down at the fading spiral of sand from the captain's chair. Oz's eyes were closed, her crimson tendrils spilling over the back of her seat by the weapons console as she loudly snored.

Jel sat next to Tretiak with her headset on, busily scanning recorded and current chatter on the Band of Thieves and emergency channels in hopes of learning what happened down there.

The last crew member plopped down onto Geddy's left shoulder, giving him a start.

"Dammit, Morph, how many times have we talked about sneaking up on me?"

— *Maybe you should tie a bell to him.*

Geddy laughed out loud, and so did Oz.

"Ha! Good one, E."

She'd begun picking up much of what Eli said, asserting that it was just her keen Temerurian empathy. It was getting to where his and Eli's conversation was no longer private when she was around. He wasn't sure how he felt about that.

Morpho seemed to give a shrug, then relaxed into his shoulder.

— *Perhaps the day will come when you can tune with Morpho without the ...*

— Aural sex? That would be nice.

Lestiko had taught Geddy how to tune, or psychically connect, to other hosts. He'd been practicing with Morpho here and there but hadn't made much progress. He needed more coaching.

"Hey." Oz opened one eye but didn't raise her head. "You sure you're feeling all right?"

"You of all people should know a hangover when you see it."

"That's fair."

She gave an impassive shrug. "Besides, what the hell else are we supposed to do?" He'd barely opened his mouth to reply when she added, "Actually, don't answer that."

"Ged, I might have something here," Jel said to his right. "Fair warning, it ain't much."

He swiveled the chair toward her. "Expectations set to low."

"It's a snippet of a conversation between a Zorran transport and a private Zihnian ship." She threw the recorded audio to the front screen.

"... just glad I got out of Aquebba when I did," said a gruff male voice.

Another male with a thick accent asked, "You mean the storm?"

"Well, yeah, there was that, but I mean the firefight."

"I heard it was a bar brawl that spilled onto the damn street."

"I dunno, man. I was already halfway up the spaceport steps when I heard the blaster fire. It sounded pretty heavy to me."

The recording stopped, and Geddy turned expectantly to Jel.

"Told you," she said.

Indeed, it wasn't much to go on. Bar fights were a daily occurrence in Aquebba. Sometimes, blasters were drawn, but only rarely fired. As rough as it could be, the city was surprisingly self-policing. Most altercations got shut down by owners before bolts began to fly. That an apparent gunfight broke out the same time as the storm rolled in made him suspect a correlation.

But this wasn't getting them anywhere. They had to see for themselves.

"How are winds in the lower atmosphere? Above the storm, I mean," Geddy asked Jel.

She switched screens and consulted her atmospheric data. "It'd be risky. High winds, particulates ... it's your call."

Geddy activated the speaker in the hold. "Denk, Voprot ... return to the bridge. We're going down."

CHAPTER 2
RAW-DOGGING THE ENTRY

Denk punched the *Fizmo* through the upper atmosphere at a shallower angle than Geddy would've, and he feared it would kick them back into space if it didn't tear the ship in half. But the kid had spent a good chunk of his young life at the controls of the old trawler. He knew what he was doing, so Geddy kept his mouth shut.

Of course, the big, boxy ship had the aerodynamics of a barn. As it screamed toward Aquebba, yellow flames licked the edge of the badly flickering front screen, the vibration threatening to liquefy their insides. Even so, in his blurry peripheral vision, Oz was still half asleep.

Tretiak, cinched tightly into the jump seat, wore an expression somewhere between disgust and terror. He surely wondered why they couldn't have taken literally any other ship to Kigantu. But he also must have understood that the *Fiz* wouldn't attract attention like an Alliance ship. That was valuable, especially if the place was crawling with Nads as they suspected.

Jel and Voprot sat opposite each other at the rear of the

bridge. As usual, Voprot looked like a kid on a rollercoaster, his tongue half hanging out over jagged rows of teeth. For Jel, this was just another day at the office.

The violent shudder tapered off as they dipped below the clouds and the city in the desert appeared. Denk eased back on the throttle, and the engines that operated at a faint hum in space settled into a throaty rumble.

Tretiak was the first to unbuckle and return to the communications console. His desperation to reach Kriggy surprised Geddy. The man was as inscrutable as they came. But the further away he got from his persona, the Auctioneer, the more humanity percolated through his cold manner.

For the millionth time, he donned the headset and said, "Merchant Niner, this is Sales Manager. Do you read?"

Tretiak didn't like anyone to know when he was coming or going, so employees referred to him in conversation as Sales Manager.

Still no reply.

The swirling storm, less opaque than it appeared from space, had largely moved past Aquebba and was on a northeastern track toward the mountains. Sand had piled up in massive drifts along the ranse wall, particularly at the southwest edge. When that happened, the dreaded ranses could, in theory, climb over the top. In such cases, drones would drop weights on a path leading away from the city so the infernal creatures would follow the vibrations.

Soon, everyone from barkeeps to madams would emerge with shovels and blowers to clear away drifting sand. By nightfall, it would be piled in the streets and bulldozers would return it to the desert through the main gate. Then the party would begin anew with the hope that the next storm was way off. Usually, it was. Sometimes only a week would pass. Such was life in a desert hellhole.

Denk dropped lower as he made a slow circle around the

city. Zooming in revealed signs of a fight, with fresh blast marks on buildings and dozens of sand-covered bodies in the streets. That wasn't entirely unusual for Aquebba. A pissing contest between a couple of pirates sometimes descended into a full-scale riot. Any unclaimed dead were launched far over the wall to be ranse food, and the city went about its business. Thinking about it now, it was pretty fucked up.

— *Where is everyone?*

— I'm wondering the same thing.

The look on Tretiak's face suggested he did, too.

"Sales to Merchant Niner. Come in, Merchant Niner, over," he repeated, again to no effect.

They were close enough to the comm array, perched atop the hill behind the Double A, that it was plainly visible. The housing appeared intact and clear of sand.

"Aquebba Station, requesting clearance to land," Denk squeaked.

No response. Denk quartered back toward Geddy with a bewildered look.

Even through the beige veil, he noted that maybe half of the oval spaceport's entrances were closed. Normally, they would've been sealed against the storm. The attack must've come before.

— *What do you make of this?*

— I dunno, but I don't like it.

"Jel, how are the winds at the surface now?"

She consulted her readout. "Gusting to thirty knots."

With a small ship, that was too much wind to land safely. Not as big a deal for the *Fiz*, though its flat sides would make her tricky to fly.

"Think you can bring her in?"

Ordinarily, landing at an intergalactic spaceport without clearance could get you shot down. But it was clear that no one was manning the cannons today.

Denk didn't hesitate. "No problem, boss."

"Are you sure about this?" Jel cautioned. "We might not be able to reach the fleet from down there."

Geddy shared her concern, but they'd already waited this long, and there was no guarantee their window wouldn't close again. "I hear you, but we need to know what happened here." He turned to Oz, who looked like death warmed over. "Weapons and suits. Take Voprot."

She saluted sarcastically and unfastened her restraints. "Aye aye, sir."

— *She's not okay.*

— No. Once she sobers up, I'm gonna find out why.

Denk brought them down, holding the big ship against the wind as sand buffeted the fuselage.

Fortunately, the large entrances were on the leeward side of the spaceport. Once Denk got low enough and squared her up, the wind became less of a factor. Drifts of reddish sand stretched across the open door. The interior was dark.

Geddy activated the landing lights to reveal an empty bay. Various pieces of equipment and loaders were intact but scattered as though hastily abandoned. No security force was there to greet them. In fact, there were no signs of life at all.

Once they were through, Denk extended the skids, eased the big ship onto the floor, and powered down. Oz returned from the hold with a thick scarf wrapped about her head and a pair of goggles, her energy blades strapped across her back. She handed Geddy a scarf and goggles of his own.

"Thanks." Geddy got up and tugged it on. "Oz and I'll do a sweep. Keep the ramp closed until we get back." His trusty PDQ blaster was strapped as always to his thigh.

"Be careful," Jel warned. "Whatever happened here might not be over."

"Can I come?" Voprot appeared through the airlock

wearing a hopeful look. He'd grown up here and didn't need a suit. "I am eager to breathe the Kigantu air."

It was still weird to hear the lizard use complete sentences.

"Like an alpine meadow, I'm sure. C'mon, then."

He excitedly fastened his electric whip to his belt and was the first to stand beside the exit. Once Geddy and Oz joined him, he activated the ramp. As it lowered, a puff of sand blew up through the gap. Voprot's clawed foot hit the floor the same time as the ramp stopped, and he marched confidently forward with Geddy and Oz in tow. The ramp closed behind them.

He placed a hand on Oz's shoulder. When she raised her eyes to him, he mouthed, *Are you okay?*

Please stop asking, she mouthed in return.

Their view of the hangar's yawning expanse was obscured only by the wide central support column. Still, it appeared completely empty. Not once in his eighteen years here had Geddy ever seen that.

"This place must've cleared out in a hurry," Oz noted.

If so, it suggested the attack came from the other end of the city, giving the spaceport time to clear out.

Voprot knelt to take a handful of sand from a sinuous pile on the floor and sniffed at it, letting it fall through his reptilian fingers. "It is good to be home."

"I couldn't agree less," Geddy said. "Let's check out the portmaster's office. The exterior cameras feed into there."

Geddy drew the PDQ as he brushed past Voprot and made a beeline toward the office at the back. Oz readied her blades, which hummed with power and cast the dust-littered concrete floor in a faint red glow. Voprot followed at a distance.

The remnants of the storm whistled through the open bay doors. A distant, rhythmic squeak of metal on metal. No signs of life. And yet, it didn't feel entirely empty.

Stacks of shipping crates and abandoned loading equipment made ample hiding places. Even with the wind, anyone still in the city would know they were there. Their footfalls echoed too loudly in the cavernous space. Geddy signaled to Oz that he'd take the left side of the column and that she and Voprot take the right.

Halfway around the column, a faint shuffle from overhead stopped him. Before he could raise his eyes, a shadow fell over him, and the PDQ was yanked away by a large, rough hand. Half a second later, his legs were swept out, and he hit the concrete so hard that stars filled his vision. A nearby commotion suggested the same had happened to Oz. His eyes cleared just enough to see a hulking figure growl and raise its foot to cave in his face.

As the muscles in its sinewy leg tensed, a sizzling blue cord coiled around it and yanked taut. Geddy barely rolled clear before its owner landed beside him with a bone-jarring thud. A moment later, Voprot drove his knee into the fallen assassin's chest, his full weight sinking into it.

"Do not move," he growled.

Looking down at his fallen foe, Voprot bent low and tilted his head curiously, blinking as though in abject disbelief.

"Father??"

CHAPTER 3
HERE, KRIGGY, KRIGGY

— Wait ... father? Eli asked. *— I mean, I figured he had one, but I thought maybe, y'know, eggs ...?*

— He'd still have a father. Unless Kiganteans reproduce asexually.

— Uf. That'd be a drag.

Voprot promptly removed his foot from his father's chest and extended a claw to him, ignoring Geddy as he rolled painfully onto his side. His powerful arm hauled the even larger Kigantean to his feet.

"Oz ..." Geddy wheezed as he scanned the floor for the PDQ.

"Be with you in a moment," she said.

"Voprot, it really you?" asked the burly Kigantean in a deep voice.

Geddy spotted his blaster a couple meters away and was about to retrieve it when a second Kigantean's hand picked it up. At the same time, Oz appeared from the other side of the column, her blades in the hands of yet another Kigantean pushing her ahead of him. Or maybe ahead of *her*? With the codpieces, it was impossible to know.

"It long time," Voprot said.

"Don't worry, I'm fine." Geddy slowly got to his feet but was instantly surrounded. Oz's captor shoved her inside the corral of giant, scowling reptiles with him.

"Who they?" demanded Voprot's father.

"That Geddy and Oz. My friends. Guys, this is my–"

"Father. We sorta pieced that together," Geddy finished.

"And my cousins! And two I not know."

More light had filtered into the hangar, making their captors easier to see. Unlike Voprot, who had recently completed another molt, the Kiganteans were more brown than green, bits of sand pinched beneath their scales. Their ranse armor bore the scars of numerous run-ins with the foul creatures. All carried the same whips as Voprot, but his father also had a tall metal staff wrapped in leather. Each end flattened to a double-edged blade that looked like it could slice through anything.

Voprot's father advanced on Geddy, his chest puffed out as the vertical slits of his orange-yellow eyes narrowed imperiously.

"*Friends?*" he sneered. "Kiganteans have no friends. Not even on Kigantu."

That was a hard point to argue. According to Kriggy, Aquebba was built atop an ancient Kigantean city. Its life began as a prison colony several hundred years ago, and now it was a haven for thieves and vice. Most visitors to Aquebba didn't even realize Kigantu had natives other than ranses. Vanishingly few had ever seen one.

"I get it, big guy, believe me. But Voprot actually has many fr–"

A blaster bolt cut him off, tearing a divot from the column

above their heads with a powerful sizzle. All seven Kiganteans whirled toward it, whips unfurled.

Tretiak, flanked by Jel and Denk, emerged from behind a set of crates, blasters leveled at the wall of lizards.

"I'd let them go if I were you," Tretiak warned.

Geddy raised both hands. "Guys, it's cool. This is a misunderstanding."

Voprot pushed his way through to stand in front of him and Oz. "Geddy is right. It cool."

Tretiak's eyes narrowed suspiciously. The rest of the crew tentatively lowered their weapons, but he only tightened his grip. "What happened here? Did you people do this?"

"You dare accuse Dheson of Kigantu of mass murder?" Voprot's old man hissed.

"They not enemies," Voprot asserted. "Only wonder what happen."

A tense moment followed, during which it seemed as though Dheson might lash out with his whip and relieve Tretiak of his arm.

"Before storm, strange ships fill the sky," he explained, sweeping his big hand overhead for emphasis. "Looking for what? We not know. Men ask us about some ship. We have no ships. Foolish young scout attack, and men destroy camp. Many dead. We come under cover of storm seeking revenge but everyone dead here, too."

Tretiak lowered his blaster and muttered, "Damnit."

Geddy frowned. "You know what they're talking about?"

He stroked his long, pointy beard and shook his head. "Those men weren't from Aquebba, Dheson. They were Zelnads. My guess is, they asked around here first and didn't like the answer."

Dheson seemed highly doubtful of this reasoning. "Zelnads? I not understand."

Voprot jumped in to reply. "People with other people inside." He tapped his head. "Like puppets but bad."

— *That's actually a very succinct explanation.*

— Is there such a thing as a good puppet, though?

"What ship they want so bad?" asked Dheson.

"The same one we're looking for," Geddy said. "And the only reason this place isn't a smoking crater is because they didn't find it."

"Yet," Oz pointed out. "Did the strange ships leave?"

Dheson blinked as he looked at her. "Woman ... allowed to speak?"

"She talk all the time," Voprot replied. "Never punished once."

"Okay, two things ..." Oz began through clenched teeth. Geddy touched her forearm and shook his head. *Not now.* Her face reddened with anger, but she settled for deep breaths.

"Osmiya's right," Tretiak said. "They know it's here. Once the storm breaks, they'll be back. That means we've got a few hours at most."

"Then let's get moving." Geddy turned to Tretiak. "And hope that Kriggy's still alive."

———

Jel decided to stay with the *Fiz* out of her growing concern that they wouldn't be able to call for backup. Meanwhile, Geddy, Oz, and Tretiak decided to see about Kriggy and any other survivors before making for the Tomb.

Before they even stepped through the threshold of the open bay door, Geddy realized he had under-appreciated the protection the hangar offered. He had to lean into the wind to stay upright, and visibility at ground level was ten meters at best. Morpho tightened his grip on his shoulder.

The Kiganteans' leathery multiple eyelids were perfect for

this harsh environment. And their hooded, deeply recessed nostrils acted as natural filters. They struck a streamlined shape on all fours that allowed the sand to sweep over them like a river over stones. At times, Geddy lost sight of them.

The suit's filtration system suddenly required greater effort to breathe. A flutter of panic quickened his heart.

— I love Krig like family, but if we don't find him in the next five minutes, I'm gonna have a full-on freakout.

— *Slow and steady. I'm right here with you.*

— Which makes it that much more cramped.

The wide-open gate in the ranse wall might've been a parting gift from the Nads. Fortunately, the whole city sat on a concrete slab, so even if they got in, they couldn't sneak up on you. The wall's chief purpose, then, was to take the sting out of the incessant winds and provide a sense of safety. Not that anything about Aquebba was safe.

Most of that concrete was coated in ripples of sand, giving the impression the desert was eager to claim it. As they'd seen on their approach, half-buried corpses dotted the streets. Mostly business owners, Geddy supposed, who didn't look kindly upon the Zelnads' interrogation.

Kriggy would have defended the tattoo shop and the Double A to his dying breath. Only if he was the last man standing would he ever dream of leaving. For reasons only he understood, Krig loved this place.

But his was among the very last shops on Turduranto, which dead-ended at the Double A on the opposite end of town. If the Nads went in through the front door, they would've had to go through Kriggy. But he likely didn't know where the Tomb was any more than Geddy did. He always figured it was somewhere beneath the auction room, but even that was a guess. The most valuable items sometimes wound up there. If nobody with the auction had ever seen an item before it went on the block, then it likely came from the Tomb.

A body lay in the middle of the street, its face half-covered by sand. Geddy and Tretiak exchanged a grim look. It was the owner and namesake of the bar on the left, Doo Doo's. He was a jolly, but rough character who never liked Geddy. The feeling was mutual.

He pointed down at the corpse and said, "That's Doo Doo."

Denk said, "Geez, Cap, have some respect for the dead."

"No, that's his name." He indicated the bar's sign behind where Denk stood. "Kinda fitting he wound up lying in the street, though."

Oz's exasperated sigh rang inside his helmet. "Let's keep moving."

With the Kiganteans still on point, they continued until they reached Kriggy's place. The tattoo parlor's lone window, bulletproof alycite like all the rest, was intact. Sand had piled knee-high in front of the door.

Geddy turned to the others. "Wait here for us."

They needed Voprot's help to get it open wide enough for Geddy and Tretiak to slip through. The moment it snapped shut behind them, he threw off his mask and panted, his face slick with sweat. He withdrew the PDQ and inspected it for accumulated sand. Outside, the others lined up against the wall of the bar across the street and out of the wind.

"Krig!" he shouted. "It's Geddy and Tretiak!"

Silence.

— Does he have a place to hide? Like a safe room or something?

— Not that I know of. He'd probably go to the Double A.

— What if he couldn't?

There wasn't much to the parlor — only a short counter, the chair, the cabinet that held his inks and needles, and the curtained door to the back room where he lived. Not exactly secure. However, a faint funk hit Geddy's uncovered nostrils that seemed out of place.

Everything was in its usual spot. With the gun leveled at

the curtain, he swept it aside and cleared the room. No signs of a struggle or anything amiss. Just the weird smell.

"Krig, if you can hear me, we have food and water. Remember that big, ugly trawler? We've got a lot to talk ab—"

A faint sound cut him off. Something between a whimper and a sob from the direction of the couch.

"Did you hear that?" Geddy whispered.

Tretiak nodded, wrinkling his nose at the room's sour smell.

Geddy tiptoed over and ripped off the cushions, which he never would've dared to do otherwise out of fear for what he might find. But it was only crumbs and candy wrappers.

The sound came again, louder.

"Krig? Is that you?"

"Lever …" returned a muffled, raspy voice.

"Kriggy! Where are you? What lever?" Geddy's eyes darted frantically around the couch in search of a lever or the source of the sound — whichever came first.

"The bandit," he croaked.

The whole time he worked at the Double A, Geddy only bid and won one thing — a working replica of an Old Earth slot machine. He paid three grand for it. Zirhof, who loved such artifacts, let him win the bid.

But despite hanging out with Kriggy often in this room, he'd never given it a pull until now. When he finally did, electric motors engaged with a springy sound, and the entire couch hinged open from the back. As it did, Kriggy rasped, "Oh, thank the stars!"

Geddy holstered the pistol and joined Tretiak before the opening. Kriggy lay at the bottom of a cramped crawlspace in his usual clothes, albeit stained with sweat and piss. His head lolled back and forth as though delirious, his phallic nose flopping grotesquely from side to side.

"Are you okay? What the hell happened?" Geddy asked.

"The latch ... wouldn't open ... from the inside," he croaked. "Water."

Morpho slung himself over to the little sink in half a second, filling the tallest glass he could find and returning to them without spilling a drop.

Meanwhile, he smiled at Tretiak. "Hey, Boss."

Tretiak allowed a relieved grin. "Good to see you, Krig."

Krig noticed Morph on Geddy's shoulder and squinted. "What the hell is that?"

"That's Morpho. He specializes in sticky situations."

Geddy climbed down the little steps and knelt beside his old friend. He shoved a cushion under his head and lifted the glass to his lips. Half of it spilled sideways as he drank. The smell was overpowering.

"We thought you were dead," Tretiak said.

"So did I," he sputtered, his voice already much clearer. "I knew the storm was coming. My left knee told me. So I closed up and crawled down here to wait it out."

"Without food and water?" Geddy asked.

"I didn't exactly figure on bein' here so long." He blinked, shaking his head, and tilted the glass once again to his friend's grateful, cracked lips.

"So you've been in here for like thirty-seven days?"

He stared up at Geddy, momentarily disbelieving. "If you say so. Is the storm gone?"

"Almost, but ... there was an attack."

"Attack?" Kriggy asked. Geddy nodded. "Who the hell would attack Aquebba?"

CHAPTER 4
THE WAY IS SHUT

Kriggy had just managed to sit up on his own when Tretiak entered, followed by Oz, Denk, and Jel. The look on Tretiak's face when they found him alive revealed a depth of concern Geddy had never seen.

Tretiak's eyes slid from Kriggy to Geddy and back. "You really don't know what happened?"

He shook his head as he finished the water, his pendulous nose going along for the ride. "I know a sandstorm hit." Morph snatched the glass away to refill it.

"Remember that Zelnad ship we brought in?" Geddy asked.

"I ain't *that* old, kid. Sure, I do. We bamboozled that big, dumb Kigantean before putting it on the block. Made out pretty good on it, too."

Tretiak said, "It never left here. I canceled the sale and moved it to the Tomb."

Krig was genuinely baffled. "Really? Why?"

"Because the Screvari Circle was behind the bid, and they were in deep with the Zelnads. I didn't like it, so I killed the deal. It seems the Z's came looking for it and got pissed off when they couldn't find it."

"Why do you want it back?" he asked.

Geddy replied, "Because it may point the way to their home world. The Alliance needs that information."

"Alliance — bah!" Kriggy said. "What do you care about those assholes?"

Tretiak exchanged a long look with Geddy. Much had happened since they were here last. Apparently, Krig knew nothing about the Committee or the fact that Geddy was Otaro Verveik's right-hand man. Now didn't seem like the time to explain.

"Look, we need to get into the Tomb," Tretiak said, ignoring the question. "Can you walk?"

"The Tomb?? I'd give all three nuts to know where that damn thing is." Kriggy extended his hand to Geddy. "Help me up, wouldja?"

Geddy hoisted him upright while Tretiak steadied him. He wobbled a moment until he found his balance, and then they carefully guided him up the concrete steps.

"Morph, see if there's any food in here."

Morpho leaped from his shoulder and opened all four cupboards at once. They were nearly empty save for a box of crackers, which he quickly returned with. Tretiak closed the couch-hatch, and Geddy eased Krig onto it.

"Crackers?" Geddy asked with a laugh. "They'll have to do until we get you back to the *Fiz*."

Kriggy looked at the package and pinched his face distastefully. "Is that the only flavor?" His goofy smile verified that he was kidding.

Geddy chuckled as he proffered a stack of herbed crackers. Krig shoved them all in his mouth and chewed, his eyes rolling back in his head between sips of water.

"Tastes pretty good right now, though." Crumbs tumbled

out as he ate, which helped explain how many were under the cushions. "So what's this attack you're talking about?"

There was no easy way to say it. Geddy explained exactly why they were there. "When the Nads didn't get the information they wanted, they shot the place up. And, apparently, a Kigantean settlement."

He paused his chewing while his baleful, bloodshot eyes searched theirs. "Shot it up? How bad?"

"Looks like most everyone got out," Tretiak said. "But not the stubborn ones."

Krig knew exactly what that meant. His expression darkened. He had no enemies in Aquebba — only friends he'd known for decades.

"The Double A?" he asked hopefully.

"That's where we're headed. You got a sandsuit in here somewhere?" Geddy scanned the room. Most everybody had one in case of emergencies. Not that you'd survive for long beyond the wall.

"I don't need one a' them damn things," he said, rising determinedly off the couch. He gave Geddy's steadying hand a grateful pat and tottered toward the closet in the near left corner.

Tretiak flared his eyebrows at Geddy. Getting around in the wind was tough enough without being half-starved. Besides, the streets were littered with Krig's friends. But once his mind was set, there was no changing it.

Working together, they helped Kriggy put on his jacket and heaviest pants. Then they affixed goggles to his eyes and wrapped his head in a scarf. After covering back up themselves, they helped him to the door. Voprot rushed forward to hold it open. Immediately, a blast of wind almost knocked Kriggy over.

The others taking shelter from the wind included the eight Kiganteans. On seeing them, Kriggy froze.

"What the hell are they doin' here?" His eyes traveled up and down Turduranto, noticing the sand-covered bodies.

"They came looking for revenge but found us instead. They're cool."

Voprot and the crew raised their hands in greeting, but the other Kiganteans only stared through the narrowed slits of their eyes.

"Is that supposed to make me feel better?" the question hit unpleasantly in Geddy's ear, betraying Krig's prejudiced view of Kiganteans.

"Let's keep moving." Tretiak braced determinedly against the gale as he led the retinue toward the Double A's arched entryway.

The burly front door was pinned to the wall. Ordinarily, it was only open on auction days. Not a great sign. They processed through and into the entry tunnel. Once they rounded the corner, they could remove their masks.

The main entrance to the Vault, the hemispherical auction hall carved out of the mountain, also stood open. Tretiak took one tentative step through it and stopped, his shoulders sagging.

Geddy drew even with him and released a long breath.

— Aw, hell.

— *Guess we don't have to wonder if they were here.*

The once-elegant room lay in ruin. Half the ceiling had collapsed onto the rotating auction stage. The hand-carved bar was now kindling. Divots had been taken out of the walls by some incredibly powerful blaster. The far door that led to the main warehouse and the holding cells where Geddy had once cooled his heels was obstructed by fallen debris.

It was a wonder the whole thing hadn't collapsed.

The normally implacable Tretiak's lips formed a thin line, and his eyes, however briefly, turned glassy. He was the high priest of the artifact and weapons trade, and this was his temple. What began as a literal smoky room where the rich and unprincipled traded rare or ill-gotten goods had become a haven for those who didn't want to be found. There were plenty of reasons to hate what the Double A did, but seeing it like this was just sad.

"I'm sorry," Geddy offered.

"It doesn't matter."

"How do we get to the Tomb now?"

He heaved a sigh. "There's another entrance, but nobody's gonna like it."

CHAPTER 5
WALK THIS WAY

Tretiak's secret entrance was half a click outside the main gate at the spaceport end of town. That meant taking Kriggy past all the bodies, most of who were people he'd known his entire life. Geddy couldn't wait to get him out of the storm and into the *Fiz* with Jel so he could have a proper meal and get cleaned up.

As expected, the long walk down Turduranto was rough for him. He stopped to identify the first couple of corpses, then just shuffled along between Geddy and Tretiak with his head lowered. By the time they reached the wall, his meal of water and crackers had seemingly worn off, because he was already gassed.

The windswept desert stretched endlessly through the open city gate. An oddly conical hill that locals called the Titty was the only significant topographical feature apart from the distant mountains. A handful of scraggly bushes dotted its surface, their very existence miraculous in a place where it literally never rained.

Tretiak extended his long index finger toward a boulder

near the base of the hill that looked like it didn't quite belong. "That's the only other way in."

"A rock?" Geddy asked.

"It hides a door. A tunnel leads back toward the city and into the Tomb, roughly below the Double A."

"Your backup entrance is outside the wall?"

"I didn't make it. It's—"

"Kigantean," Dheson finished, his tone dripping with contempt. Geddy thought Aquebba had always been a prison colony, but maybe not. "Ancients build many places deep underground."

"Us, too!" Denk slapped Voprot on the thigh. "See? We're pretty much twins."

"Hill above made from earth below." Dheson traced the Titty's outline with his long, bony claw. "Nobody know how. Old ways lost."

Geddy's first thought was to fly across in the *Fiz*. But it was challenging enough just to land in the spaceport. Holding her at a steady near-ground hover would be impossible in the unrelenting wind, even for him, and landing was out of the question. Besides, they didn't have the right gear. A skimrover would've been perfect, but he never expected to be outside the wall. Tretiak hadn't mentioned that little detail.

Oz, apparently, had already arrived at this unfortunate fact. To no one in particular, she asked, "The desert's crawling with ranses. How the hell are we supposed to get there?"

"We walk," Dheson answered.

"Ha! Yeah, right," Geddy laughed. But Dheson didn't strike him as a kidder.

His eyes drifted down to the Kiganteans' feet. They were wide and flat, with four long toes that could spread wider still. Clearly, they'd figured out a way to travel without alerting ranses or they wouldn't be here.

"How?" he asked Dheson.

The hulking reptile looked him up and down like he couldn't handle the truth. "Ancient Kigantean secret."

"No, it not!" Voprot argued, earning a glare from his father. "We use the eleven steps. Here, Voprot show."

He proceeded through a series of steps that called to mind a drunken tarantella. A big, but dainty step to the left. A short one to the right. Another, crossing his left foot in front. A turn. On it went, no two moves alike or in a straight line, until he'd covered five meters in about as many seconds.

"You out of practice," Dheson teased. "But that the idea."

"No pattern," Voprot said as he returned to them. "Confuses ranses."

"Of course. Their hunting evolved around predicting movement," Oz noted. "The pattern's too random for them."

Geddy turned from her back to Dheson. "Can you show us how?"

Dheson equivocated. "Steps take long time to master, but yes, I show."

He put his hand on Kriggy's shoulder and jutted his chin at the spaceport nearby. "Krig, my girl Jeledine's got food and clean clothes for you back at the ship. We'll catch up when we get back."

Krig wrenched his shoulder away. "Like hell, kid! I've gotta see this place before I die."

"But—"

"I know what's waiting for us out there, Ged. Better n' you, even. If I get et, I get et."

Geddy heaved a sigh and gave a helpless shrug. *But you're a liability for the rest of us* was what he couldn't quite bring himself to say aloud.

The crew spread out in front of the wall so the Kiganteans could critique their sand-walking technique. They pressed their palms to the ground to feel the vibrations. Geddy just pretended he was drunk-dancing and moved accordingly, though it was tiring to stay light on his feet. Every time someone's heels hit the ground, took a heavy step, or fell into any kind of pattern, Dheson would shout, "Dead!"

Not surprisingly, Oz picked up on it immediately, constantly changing up her patterns as she glided across the sand like a specter. Tretiak wasn't half bad himself. Denk moved in nearly a straight line no matter what he did because of his stubby legs, which made it difficult to be dainty. Geddy fell somewhere in between, but after thirty minutes of practice, they became adroit enough to satisfy their teachers.

Then there was Kriggy.

Even out of the wind, he was simply too weak and clumsy to make it more than two or three steps without hearing, "Dead!"

"Krig, let us handle this." Geddy put a friendly hand on his shoulder. "There's a full tank of fermenting nutrimush and a cabinet full of Kailorian gin on the *Fiz*. Well, maybe a third full."

An indignant scowl crossed his face and he jerked his shoulder away. "I just spent a damn month alone in that hole! I'm not goin' anywheres. Besides, if I die finding out where the Tomb is, it'll be worth it."

"I carry you," Voprot offered, extending his thickly muscled arms like a forklift as he grinned at Krig.

"Carry yourself, ya overgrown gecko," he growled, giving a dismissive wave of his hand.

As usual, Kriggy's stubbornness carried the day. At least he realized it might end badly for him.

"Cock-nosed little man want to lead way?" Dheson gestured through the gate with a bemused grin.

Kriggy blinked back at him. "What?"

Again, he nodded toward the distant rock.

It did make a certain amount of logical sense to put the weakest one first. But Krig had been like an uncle to Geddy when he had no family and few friends. The last thing he wanted was to see him torn in half by a ranse.

But, in classic Kriggy fashion, he drew himself up and marched defiantly to the edge of the concrete, seemingly reinvigorated by the danger.

"No, no," Geddy said. "That ain't happening."

"It's all right, kid. I ain't scared." Krig looked over his shoulder and winked. "Wish me luck."

His first step was soft and straight toward the rock. The next, ahead and left. The next, straight right. When he was fifteen meters clear of the wall, Dheson activated his electric whip, still coiled on his belt, and strode toward the gate.

Before stepping into the desert, he glanced back over his shoulder. "We go next. Ten paces apart. Voprot go last."

A lifetime of doing his particular eleven-step pattern made it beautiful to behold, like a piece of music only he could play. He covered the same distance as Krig in a fraction of the time.

Oz patted Geddy's helmet and smiled her effervescent smile. "Last one there's ranse food." She pivoted on her heels and strode toward the gate.

"That wasn't funny," he called after her.

On it went like this, Kiganteans and crew, until only he and Voprot remained.

"It okay, Geddy. I watch your flank."

He regarded his quirky reptilian friend with gratitude. "Fine, but don't get any ideas."

The sand swept across the ground like a river, instantly erasing their shallow footprints. How many times would he have to face this foe? He'd watched one turn Captain Bykite into a beverage holder before he sent it into space and barely escaped Zelnad-engineered super-ranses thanks to Voprot and his girl, Iondra.

He could still feel the sand boiling under him. One wrong step was all it took.

Geddy drew the PDQ and whispered Doc's old sesehlu mantra between a series of deep breaths as his left foot stepped onto the sand. "Maaah haaa kuuut …"

CHAPTER 6
RANSE DANCE

The thought that kept running through Geddy's mind as he did his goofy little dance across the sand was that they could cross the entire galaxy faster — much faster, in fact — than it would take to reach this fucking door. Every step invited a gruesome death. That they'd made it two-thirds of the way without incident was both heartening and portentous.

His calves ached from being on his toes, and he hadn't sweated so much since the bad old days in the geo tunnels on The Deuce. Despite taking only small and furtive sips from his hydration tube, it was more than half empty, giving him another reason to worry about the return trip.

Kriggy had put forth a Herculean effort, but his glacial pace was becoming an existential liability. Every second on the sand was an opportunity for somebody to die or for the Nads to come back.

The wind was lighter overall but still gusted hard. When it did, he could barely make out the boulder that supposedly marked the entrance. Kriggy's faint outline was no more than fifty meters from it, but he was struggling.

— *I can practically feel his footsteps, and I'm way up in your head.*

— He just needs to make it a bit further.

But a couple steps later, Kriggy stopped completely, shoulders stooped, his energy spent. Everyone else had to stop to keep their ten-meter padding.

They remained still for an uncomfortably long time. Oz cast back a worried look, which Geddy passed along to Voprot.

Dheson turned and signaled to the other Kiganteans to close ranks around Kriggy, then waved up Oz and Geddy. Again, they danced their dance, but before they could grab him, he took a big, clumsy step and toppled headlong into the sand. Like Eli, Geddy felt the deadly vibration in his very soul.

The moment Krig hit the dirt, the Kiganteans unfurled their whips. Dheson's left fist shot skyward. *Stop*.

A prolonged, anxious interval passed, during which the wind was the only sound. Dheson, as dainty on his giant feet as a ballerina, eleven-stepped up beside Kriggy and knelt to pick him up. At that instant, Dheson shoved him to the right and rolled left a millisecond before the first ranse blasted up through the sand like a geyser from hell, its scissoring jaws just missing Dheson's foot. The bright blue whip curled behind him and shot forward, wrapping around the ranse's armored thorax. One sharp yank, and the upper half of the giant centipede-like creature fell to the sand while the lower half sank into it.

The storm would've driven the ranses' usual prey, globzoiks, to take refuge in the rocky buttes and plateaus that dotted the planet. That meant they were starving, and Kriggy just rang the dinner bell. Sneaking was pointless now.

"Run!!" Dheson cried.

He threw Kriggy over his shoulder like a doll while Tretiak bolted up the side of the Titty.

Geddy had only taken a few steps when a giant hand

shoved him forward, sending him sprawling face-first into the sand. He whirled in time to see a large ranse rocket skyward from where he'd stood. Before he could raise the PDQ to fire, Voprot's whip wrapped around it and tore the cursed creature neatly in half. The head continued to snap even after it landed as though it didn't know it had just been bisected.

"Swarm!" Voprot shouted, hoisting Geddy to his feet by grabbing a fistful of his jacket. "More coming. Hurry!"

Denk and Tretiak had already scrambled up to the big rock, followed closely by Dheson and the other Kiganteans. Oz bounded up the short rise and spun around.

"Let's go! Move!" she shouted in his ear.

"Can't you see I'm fat and out of shape?!" Geddy yelled back.

"It's hard to miss!"

Tretiak was still fumbling with the door when Geddy and Voprot made it to the rock. Panting, he shot a glance over his shoulder and saw hundreds of tiny rises in the sand. Ranses were never so close to the surface except when they were desperate. They were barely safer here. Five seconds, and they'd be chum in a shrinking ocean.

"Uh, Tretiak …" Geddy began.

He was frantically trying to clean off an electronic keypad beside the door, repeatedly entering a code that only seemed to activate a red light.

"I don't know! Sand must've gotten inside!" he said.

The wave of ranses had reached the base of the hill, and it didn't stop.

"Forget it, we've gotta climb!" Geddy grabbed Oz's wrist and tugged her with him as he clambered up the slope.

One of the other Kiganteans hung back for Tretiak, who was still fruitlessly trying the door. No sooner did he yank Tretiak away than the ground under his feet exploded like a geyser of dirt, upending him. Before he could strike with his whip, two ranses coming from opposite sides cut him in half at the waist. Two more slammed his upper torso before it even hit the ground, the blood spray carried off by the wind.

At that point, Denk jumped into Voprot's burly arms, and they rushed up the colossal pile of loose rock and sand. It crumbled underfoot as their motoring feet struggled for purchase, cascading behind them as the wave of ranses gained ground.

The Kiganteans and their passengers opened a wide gap between Geddy, Oz, and Tretiak. At one point, Dheson looked over his shoulder, stopped, and leaped over them, unfurling his whip in midair as a ranse shot from between the rocks toward Tretiak. It lashed out, but only severed the rear quarter, which tumbled end over end down the slope while the rest of its body plunged, undaunted, back into the sand. Another one rose like a trout to snatch the tail section off the ground.

"Jel, do you read?!" Geddy yelled. "We need an extraction, now!"

No reply. On a clear day, the comm cuff's transmitter would have more than enough range to reach the spaceport. But with so much ferrous sand in the air, it was a long shot. Of course, Jel couldn't possibly manage in the wind either, and she'd know it. They were on their own.

He kept pumping his legs, his face shield fogging with his desperate breaths.

— *What happens when we reach the top?*

— *I guess we start shooting.*

— *Solid plan.*

The other Kiganteans gained the summit, forming a circle around Kriggy and Denk while Geddy and the others charged upward, his muscles and lungs searing from the effort. A few seconds later, they were all crowded together at the peak.

— *Would this be the Nipple, then?*

— *Kind of a nice bookend to my life.*

The advancing horde was plain to see, churning its way up all sides of the Titty like a ravenous tsunami. The Kiganteans were damn good at killing ranses, but at best, they'd only get the first few.

Geddy squeezed the handle of the PDQ to charge it fully, then swept it back and forth, trying to anticipate where the wave would crest. Hell, so much movement might cause the Titty to crumble entirely. Morpho gathered into a hard ball on his shoulder, though there was little he could do to a ranse.

His left hand found Oz's without looking. Their eyes met through their dewy face shields, and he managed a weak smile. Everyone's weapons were drawn. Kriggy was curled into the fetal position in the middle, his arms wrapped protectively around his helmet, just waiting for the end.

"Well, guys, it's been real," Geddy said.

"Thanks for believing in me, Cap," Denk sniffed. "At least we'll go out swingin'."

The nearest part of the wave was inside ten meters now. Geddy aimed at the edge and unleashed a full charge, cratering the hillside as the ruptured bodies of at least three living nightmares sprayed into the whipping wind.

Oz dropped his hand and readied her blades. "Well, this sucks."

"Yeah, but the view," Geddy winked.

She managed a weary smile. "I love you."

Geddy charged the pistol for another, maybe final, shot. "Baby, you have no idea."

Before he could release a final blast into the oncoming swarm, a deep rumble came from directly overhead. They craned their necks upward. Geddy squinted into the hazy disk of the sun, hoping to see the *Fiz*. Instead, a dark gray ship shaped like a manta ray plummeted straight toward them, the fuselage still glowing red from its entry. He didn't recognize it.

"Who the hell's that?" Oz asked.

"I dunno, but duck!" Geddy cried, and they hit the dirt.

Barely twenty meters from them, however, the retros fired with a mighty roar, pinning them to the ground. A port in the underside opened, and a canister about the size of a small trash can dropped onto the ground beside Kriggy. Corkscrew legs shot into the sand and whirred as they anchored it firmly to the hilltop.

Before anyone could even react, a deep voice from overhead commanded, "Take a deep breath!"

Geddy turned away just as the canister exploded.

CHAPTER 7
DESCENDING OPINION

When Geddy opened his eyes, he expected to find himself flying through the air into the waiting mouth of a ranse. Instead, he only saw a cloudy, shifting image of the same landscape. Something obstructed his vision besides the fog inside his face shield, and he couldn't move his limbs.

Beside him, Oz was in the same state of suspended animation, her blades still glowing as her big eyes swiveled toward him. *What the hell?* she mouthed, suggesting she couldn't move, either.

It seemed they'd been enveloped in some kind of gel. But why? And by whom?

— *What's happening?*

— *I think we just got turned into a jello mold.*

— *I never imagined it would happen this soon.*

A faint pop met his ears, followed by a tingling sensation that traveled through his whole body. As his eyes swiveled down and right, the ranse leading the nearest wave shot up out of the sand and barreled toward him with its jaws splayed, countless rows of needle-like teeth bearing down at his face.

But before it even made contact with the gel, it burst into a cloud of red mist.

The shockwave rippled down the Titty, turning the tide of ranses into slimy goop that painted the slope red. Another powerful wave came, and another, each causing the same tingling sensation as their attackers turned to mush.

As joyful as it was to behold, it was offset by abject confusion.

Shortly, though, Geddy found he could move his legs a little. Then his arms. The gel softened, then dried and was whisked away by the fierce wind within a few seconds. Apparently, it had protected them from whatever sonic weapon had taken care of the ranses.

Oz was frozen in the same prone position, looking as bewildered as he felt.

"You okay?" he croaked.

She nodded, her eyes slowly rotating upward as she rolled onto one elbow. Geddy followed them up to a circular floating platform emerging from the belly of the ship. Two dark figures were visible through its force-field floor.

Geddy's fist was still closed around the handle of the PDQ, primed to be unleashed if he didn't like what he saw.

But even before the platform came to rest a meter overhead, he recognized the robes of one man and the Alliance-issued pants of the other. Doc Tardigan and Lestiko peered down at them through the translucent orange floor like savior gods.

"Doc?" Denk asked, incredulous.

A broad grin split Geddy's face. "Lestiko?"

"It is good to see you, my friend." He could barely hear his friend through the helmet.

— **Hello, Eli,** Lestiko said in Geddy's head.

— *Greetings, Lestiko. You sure know how to make an entrance.*

Doc allowed a Mona Lisa grin as he stepped off the platform, which was about as demonstrative as he ever got. Geddy wrapped him in a bear hug and squeezed hard.

"Uf! It seems we arrived just in time, Captain." Geddy released him, tears forming in his eyes as Doc nodded at the others in turn. "Osmiya. Denk." He paused. "Tretiak? Krigor?"

"We'll fill you in later," Geddy said.

When he took in the other Kiganteans, his grin only widened. "Voprot? Surely this isn't your family."

Voprot's face lit up at the recognition. "Yes, it is! This my father, Dheson, and my great uncle—"

"Later, perhaps," Doc cut him off. "We cannot linger."

"Ornean sky man is right," agreed Dheson. "We grateful to you."

Doc stepped aside and gestured for them to board the platform. "Come on. Let's get you out of here." Lestiko stood on the back edge, his hand extended to help the first person climb on. Doc frowned and scanned the hilltop. "Wait — where's Jeledine?"

Geddy nodded toward the dark outline of Aquebba. "Back with the *Fiz*. Look … we, ah … can't go just yet."

He wished to hell it wasn't true. Doc likely didn't know much, if anything, about why they were there.

"Why not?" Lestiko asked.

The so-called Titty was now a mix of sticky sand and viscera that had already turned gummy, the dead ranses unrecognizable save for the thick, chitinous exoskeletons that littered the slope. Some were hollow like straws. Lestiko's weapon had turned the soft tissue into liquid.

"Ugh, this is so gross!" Denk said, grimacing as he stepped in a gooey pile of viscera.

"Good cardio, though," Geddy offered.

The distant mountains were barely visible now, suggesting the storm had nearly cleared. He glanced up from time to time as they descended, half expecting the Zelnad armada to pop into view at any moment.

The floating platform glided silently down the hill beside him and Denk. Doc tended to Kriggy while Tretiak finished explaining why they couldn't leave yet.

"You're certain we can access the ship's navigation data?" Doc asked.

"No, but between us and Eli, I'm hopeful we'll figure it out," Geddy replied as he stepped in the remains of a small female ranse. "So how did you know we were here? Did you come straight from Basoa?"

"We'd just returned to the fleet when Commander Verveik relayed an emergency message that Jeledine had sent from an old TAC terminal. *'Trouble on Kigantu. Can't reach crew.'* We immediately jumped in and recognized your predicament."

It seemed his desperate plea to Jel had made it after all, but she couldn't reply. Apparently, only tachyon-accelerated communication could make it through the dregs of the storm and across the galaxy to the fleet. How she could've lined up the highly directional system in such a short timespan boggled the mind, but if anyone could do it, it was clever little Jel.

"Does it ever seem like you guys have to save my ass a lot?" he asked, grinning.

"I have noticed a pattern," returned Doc. "But that is what makes us a crew."

He nodded appreciatively. "I guess it does."

Twenty minutes of switchbacks and sliding through goopy sand finally landed them back at the uncooperative door. Tretiak stepped up to the access pad and tried the code again.

The well-hidden door immediately dropped down, revealing a set of stone steps. The look on his face spurred everyone to grateful laughter, though the sight of the dissected Kigantean lying beside them dampened their mirth.

Dheson sniffed at the air and knelt, working his claw under the sand as he closed his eyes.

"More ranses coming," he warned.

Tretiak expectantly regarded him and the Kiganteans, who only stared back. Geddy knew what the look meant. *You may go now.*

They didn't move.

"Chief Dheson, we're grateful for your protection and sorry for the loss of your tribesman."

Dheson scowled. "Zarnul a female."

Tretiak cleared his throat. "And what a lovely woman she was."

Voprot's father said, "We come with you."

He gave a pained grin, his eyes drifting over to Geddy, who could only shrug in return. "Of course you do."

CHAPTER 8
NAME THAT TOMB

The stairs ended in a lengthy corridor. It was trapezoidal in shape, and electric lights aside, it was clear it had been there long before Tretiak had. The stonework was impeccable, with no visible mortar and smooth seams. Everyone removed their protective gear.

They'd barely entered it before Dheson boomed, "I right. This made with Kigantean hands."

Indeed, surprisingly crisp painted images soon appeared on both sides, a timeline of sorts with shockingly artful depictions of the big lizards. Praying. Dancing. Building. And by the looks of one particular image, holding a very well-attended orgy.

Doc, who was just in front of Voprot in the middle of the procession, asked, "I do not know the language. Can any of you read it?"

"Very little," Dheson said sadly. "It as dead as ones who write it."

— Maybe this is the long-lost Tomb of Complete Sentences.
— *It probably not.*

The drawings took a darker turn as they went, clearly

depicting some kind of huge battle against ranses, the sand stained with blood. At the far side was a funeral procession in which the dead were carried underground. Its meaning was plain.

— *Wait — this is a literal tomb?*

— Looks that way.

Dheson, who was right behind Tretiak, grabbed his shoulder and spun him around. "This not a city! It for ancestors! Sacred! What you do here?"

Having dealt in ancient artifacts for much of his life, Tretiak had no problem with desecration if it paid well.

"Cool it, chief. I keep important things here. That's all," he said. "After this, you can move in for all I care. Aquebba's as dead as your ancestors."

Clearly having considered this the final word, he continued along the corridor while Dheson bristled.

"What more important than souls?" he demanded.

"Business," Tretiak said over his shoulder.

"The entire history of Kigantu is painted on these walls," Doc marveled, breaking the tension. The illustration that excited him depicted scores of X-shaped insects forming a cloud over a cluster of plants. "If I'm not mistaken, this depicts the great bone locust plague."

"Bone ... locusts?" Denk glanced nervously at Geddy.

"Scholars have always wondered if the term refers to their morphology, pale color, or their ability to strip animals down to the bone," he explained. "Thousands of years ago, parts of the southern valley were farmland, but a centuries-long drought took a terrible–"

Tretiak cut him off. "Take a picture if you'd like, Dr. Tardigan. We need to keep moving."

"He's right, Doc." It pained Geddy to agree, but this was no time to dawdle. "The sooner we get this done, the sooner we can get off this godforsaken ball of sh…" When the Kiganteans' elongated heads swiveled angrily toward him, he gulped. "I mean this ... garden spot."

Everyone else quickened their pace to keep up with Tretiak. Voprot briefly equivocated before joining Geddy and the others, leaving his relatives to bring up the rear.

"What's his problem?" Oz whispered, nodding at Tretiak.

Geddy drew even with her and leaned in. "His whole empire just crumbled."

"That's no reason to be an asshole."

Oz had a low opinion of Tretiak because of what she knew about Geddy's time here. To be sure, his relationship with his old boss was always fraught. Tretiak turned him, a scared orphan, into a calculating henchman who wouldn't hesitate to kill anyone who cheated the Double A. But intentionally or otherwise, he'd given Geddy other gifts that served him well. Courage. Independence. A respectable right hook. An above-average bullshit detector.

The corridor eventually became a bridge that crossed a high-ceilinged, vaulted chamber. The strip of bluish lights that had been overhead now marked its edges, and they didn't have much of a throw.

Geddy got out his flashlight and swept it around the space. More trapezoidal openings in the surrounding walls were filled with crumbled bones, accessed by narrow steps that jutted out from the smooth stone. The massive support columns reminded Geddy of a cathedral, with thick horizontal supports bridging the vaulted ceiling. The volume of material that had to be excavated was staggering, but it further explained the Titty.

"Whoa ..." Denk's squeaky voice echoed through the chamber. "This almost looks like Durandia!"

"Indeed so, Denk. And no less a feat of engineering," Doc said. "It seems there's much about this culture we don't know."

"Even Basoan architects would be humbled by it," noted Lestiko.

"If I'm not mistaken, this was a mausoleum for commoners," Doc said, then directed his question to Tretiak. "There must be another chamber for the ruling class, yes?"

"Through here," Tretiak said, disappearing through the doorway at the far side.

Dheson and his entourage had entered the room behind them and seemed equally awed by it. They engaged in a hushed conversation as they studied its features, glancing furtively at Geddy and the others as they moved into the next room.

— What're they whispering about?

— *Cultural appropriation?*

Kriggy followed Tretiak inside and gasped. The domed chamber had similar, but much fewer recesses in the curved walls. All but a handful had been bricked over, with depictions of what must be the dead Kigantean rulers entombed inside. Stone benches were set around the perimeter at four places, likely aligning with compass points.

In the middle of it sat a modern structure made of Gundrun steel, basically a large box twenty-five meters on a side. How it could've been constructed here, when, and how anything got from here to the Double A was known only to Tretiak. There were no obvious doors or elevators.

"I never thought I'd live long enough," Kriggy marveled, running his fingers along the Tomb's smooth wall.

"You nearly didn't," Geddy reminded him.

"We're right under the Vault," Tretiak said, referring to the demolished auction room.

He marched up to the gigantic metal container, which had no visible access panels, and pressed his hand to a spot about a meter from the right edge. A beep rang through the chamber, and internal locking mechanisms noisily released. The entire front side of the box popped out, then swung open with a soft hum. Kriggy excitedly joined the others as the gawking Kiganteans finally entered, falling silent as they took in the space.

Inside, as promised, was the Zelnad research ship.

Tretiak turned and said, "Your turn, Geddy."

Lestiko's jaw hit the floor. He placed his hand on Doc's shoulder as he beheld the Zelnad ship. "My stars, Krons. Look at it!"

It really was something to see, its iridescent skin made of some organic material that could heal itself. Now that they'd seen a Nad fighter up close, it was clear that this ship was a different animal. Geddy and Doc had come to believe that it was an experimental skin the Nads hoped could make it past Sagacea's barrier. But it seemed only shinium could do that.

Geddy, Doc, and Lestiko stepped through the open front of the box. Geddy touched his fingers to the ship's surface, again triggering the faint green ripples.

"It responds to touch?" Lestiko said, drawing closer.

"Not just any touch." Geddy smirked at him. "You need Big Sagacean Energy."

"Oh, good grief," Oz muttered.

"You mean …?" Lestiko asked.

Lestiko was the only person Geddy ever met who was like him. Ideologically, the entity in his brain, Rai, was a Zelnad, but they both had full control of themselves. Geddy's was given freely. Lestiko's was taken.

"You want to try?"

Lestiko splayed his fingers across the ship's outer skin, and the same ripples appeared. His fascinated smile widened to schoolchild proportions. Geddy pointed to a spot next to where he remembered the door was. "The control panel's right around here somewhere, if I recall."

He touched it again, and the spreading ripples revealed the edges of the circular panel. When he pressed his whole hand to it, the door slid aside. The inside of the ship lit up, and Lestiko took a small step back. After a quick check with Geddy, he stepped through the threshold.

The ship's basic layout was pretty conventional, with four stations along each side of the main level and two on the upper level, which appeared from the outside as a sleek bubble protruding from the roof. Last time, it was Eli who showed him how to disable the vessel's organic outer shell after it accidentally sealed them inside. That was as deep as his understanding of the bizarre holographic controls got.

Lestiko was like a kid in a candy store, his eyes sparkling with wonder as he took in the admittedly dazzling tech. "One must marvel at their ingenuity."

"So how do we figure out where the hell this thing went and what happened to the crew?" Geddy asked.

Lestiko's head swiveled toward him, his faint smile suggesting he'd heard the brief exchange with Eli. "It was found empty?"

He drew closer. "That mean something to you?"

"Perhaps. We have much to learn about this ... original energy as you call it. One possibility was that it got zapped into another part of space, or even another dimension before being returned as a warning."

"Another dimension?"

"Oh, Sagaceans almost certainly have mastery over inter-dimensional space. Perhaps even time itself," Lestiko said, staring off into his own inter-dimensional space.

"What's the other possibility?"

"That it was unmanned," Lestiko replied obviously.

"Gentlemen, need I remind you that these same impossibly

advanced beings would do literally anything to find this ship?" Tretiak stood just inside the ship's opening with his arms crossed.

Geddy clapped his hands. "Right. Well, before, I managed to turn off the outer shell using this thingy here."

He led Lestiko a couple steps over to the glowing spherical hologram. As before, he closed his hand around it as though its warm light had substance, and when he opened it, the schematic of the ship again spread out in his palm.

Lestiko leaned in close, studying the strange language. "Those symbols ... I've never seen anything like them."

— *Tap the snail reading a newspaper. Lower right corner.*

Geddy only saw a spiral shape eclipsed by a split parallelogram. He tapped it, and another diagram appeared, this time revealing two wide conical shapes stacked tip to tip.

Lestiko gave a little gasp and shook his head. "Snail, indeed."

"All right, then, Geddy," Lestiko said. "Let's figure out where this thing has been."

CHAPTER 9

DATA DAY

Eli explained that the cones in the diagram represented its data storage system. With Lestiko looking over his shoulder, Geddy eventually arrived at a spherical star map that expanded to fill the middle section of the ship. Lestiko made a slow circle around it, studying the various clusters and nebulae on display. The tiny points of light moved like viscous fluid as he passed through them.

Even at this unfathomable scale, no celestial features were recognizable. A massive green-blue nebula resembling a hook. Superclusters. Voids. No single thing was bigger than his palm. Entire galaxies were the size of a fingernail.

"What's this a map of?" Geddy asked.

Doc drew closer and took in the map with equal fascination. Denk, Oz, Tretiak, and even Dheson poked their heads inside for a closer look.

"It stretches far beyond the bounds of our known universe," Doc said. "Can you make it smaller?"

"Smaller? Why?"

"I do not believe we are seeing the whole image."

Geddy splayed the fingers of his right hand over the open

palm of his left and pinched them back together. It took half a dozen of the gestures before the map's edges were visible. By then, it was nearly a solid ball of light. Their galaxy was no more than a pinpoint.

"Incredible," Lestiko whispered. "We may be looking at the entire universe. To the extent it can be visually represented, at least."

"So where's Sagacea?"

— *Overlay the ship's navigational history. The upside-down condom.*

— Who the hell came up with this language?

— *Some bureaucrat. I dunno.*

He dutifully followed Eli's instructions, and a thin red line appeared inside the ball. Zooming back in, they saw it begin at one point and end at a supervoid, a vast area of nothingness between clusters of galaxies and star nurseries. Geddy only understood space to the extent sea captains did the ocean, which was to say, in concrete terms. The models he'd learned in school depicted the universe as a ragged sort of honeycomb, with walls of filaments separating bubbles of empty space thousands of parsecs wide. Even so, two things about this particular void struck him as odd.

The first was its spherical shape, which few celestial features had besides stars and planets. The other was its immense size.

"Why's it so perfectly round?" Geddy asked.

Doc squinted closely at the empty area in the light-generated model. "I wondered the same thing, Captain, until I remembered something Eli said."

"Who'd bother to remember anything Eli said?"

— *Just wait until I manifest my physical form and burst out of you.*

— Wait, what?

— *Nothing.*

He cleared his throat and blinked. "I mean, oh really? What was that?"

"That Sagacea was at the center of the universe," Doc explained.

"But it has no center," Lestiko noted.

Doc and his fellow Orneans had been studying the Zelnads' mysterious energy since Beebit Tompanov delivered Eveth to the fleet. Geddy suspected they already knew more than they'd shared with anyone, including Verveik.

"Now that we know how to detect it, we find it everywhere," Doc said. "According to both Morpho and Eveth, Sagacea is its source. It may mark the origin of our universe."

"Well, if Sagacea's in the middle of that void, then where's this barrier supposed to be?"

Supposedly, Eli's home world was protected by a barrier through which only Sagaceans could pass. Sagaceans drifting through the young universe sometimes became entrapped in molten tukrium as planets formed. The resulting alloy, shinium, had both the strength of tukrium and the so-called harmonic — the strange frequency that connected Sagaceans to both original energy and each other. Encasing a ship in it, as Geddy and Eli had done with the *Penetrator*, would allow it through. That's why the Nads needed it for their weapon. But nobody really knew what the barrier was or what would happen if an ordinary ship hit it.

"This navigation data ends here." Doc pointed at the spot where the red line ended, *near* but not *at* the spherical void's center. "Something must've happened right here that transported the ship to our galaxy. Almost like the ..." Doc and Lestiko's eyes met, and they both said, "Bubble drive!"

"Huh?" Geddy inquired.

"Yes, Krons!" Lestiko excitedly said. "What we've been calling the barrier may actually be the edge of a large bubble universe around Sagacea."

"So if you hit it, you're transported away?"

"It's just a theory."

"Transported where?" Geddy asked.

He hemmed and hawed for a moment. "It's impossible to know. It could be anywhere in any galaxy. Space, a planet, a star. That this particular ship was transported to our galaxy may be mere chance."

Geddy crossed his arms, staring intently at the tiny red line while he pieced it all together. "So, the Nads send this ship, probably unmanned, to find Sagacea. It hits the barrier and gets transported here. Wouldn't it have sent coordinates back to Nad Central by then?"

"It's likely they couldn't," Doc said. "The energy density around Sagacea would cause incredible interference. Besides, we believe their base is …" He made a slow circle around the map and pointed to an area quite far from where the red line ended. "… somewhere around here. It must be billions of parsecs. I cannot imagine any transmission reaching that far."

"If the ship was unmanned, it could've been looking for Sagacea for a long time, right?" Geddy asked.

Doc and Lestiko both flared their eyebrows. "You're absolutely right," Lestiko affirmed. "For all we know, this ship could be thousands of years old. It would explain why the design is so different."

"So the only record of Sagacea's location is right here. And we found it before the Nads did," Geddy gave Lestiko a self-satisfied grin. "How do we download the data?"

Smirking, Lestiko bent his left arm and raised his wrist to reveal a thick black bracelet. "We make a copy." Glowing orange particles spat from it and arranged themselves into an exact overlay of the dense star map. Lines of light popped in and out of view in between them as though measuring distances between the points, then they just as quickly sucked back into the bracelet.

"Got it," he said, self-satisfied. "And with it, the most extensive map of the universe anyone has ever seen."

The electric crack of a Kigantean whip came from the direction of the door, giving them a start. Denk fell as he backpedaled inside, followed by Oz, who raced in to haul him up. Her lips pressed into a thin line as she met Geddy's confused look with a less ambiguous one.

The Kiganteans were herding the others inside.

Kriggy and Tretiak entered with their hands raised, both looking equally unamused.

"Father, what you doing??" Voprot protested, standing defiantly in front of the door.

"This place Kigantean," Dheson grumbled. "We make it new home."

"You not understand!"

"I understand it a tomb."

— But not your Tomb of Complete Sentences, apparently.

— *It was a fool's hope.*

Voprot's muscles had just tensed when Dheson kicked him in the chest, sending him tumbling backward into the ship. Only his powerful tail kept him from landing on his ass.

"Morph, the door!" Geddy cried.

Morpho threw a tendril across the room, but before he could rubber-band himself into the opening, the door slammed shut, and the organic skin sealed it like plastic wrap.

CHAPTER 10
A FLY ON THE WALL

Either the Kiganteans didn't realize that the ship could be opened from the inside, or they planned to guard the door in perpetuity. It seemed unlikely that Dheson actually intended to entomb anyone, especially his son. His outrage over the desecration of this sacred place made him act without forethought. He'd taken the others' weapons, but not Geddy's, Lestiko's, or Doc's.

For a pregnant moment, everyone was dumbstruck.

An enraged Tretiak lunged for the door and pounded on it. "Stupid Kiganteans! We don't have time for this. Let us out!"

Voprot hissed, "Kiganteans not stupid!"

Tretiak spun and shot back, "Oh, please. Do you even hear yourself??"

Geddy stepped between them, pumping his hands up and down. "All right, let's all take a beat. We'd be dead if it weren't for them. Dheson's got every right to be pissed off."

"This place was buried for two thousand years!" Tretiak objected. "Until today, nobody besides me even knew it existed!"

"He head– er, *is* head of our clan," Voprot said. "Heritage matter to him."

"And getting out of here alive matters to me," Tretiak retorted. "Geddy, open the door."

"Voprot and I'll talk to him, okay?" Geddy was about to use the holographic interface to let themselves out when a sharp fluttering sound seized everyone's attention. They all froze.

"What the hell was that?" Oz asked.

It came again, the ship's acoustics making the sound's precise origin difficult to pinpoint.

"It sounds like an insect," Denk offered.

The flutter returned, this time distinctly from the direction of the door. Geddy pointed his flashlight in that direction. A flash of movement crossed it, again with the sound. A moth, maybe? He swept the circle of light slowly across the ceiling and immediately spotted the culprit. The pale insect was large, about five centimeters across with rounded triangular wings.

"Isn't that one of those insects in the drawings?" Denk asked, his voice shaking. "A bone locust?"

"That species is long extinct," Doc noted. "Although I don't deny the resemblance."

"Who cares what it is?" Tretiak said. "Just open the door."

— *I thought you were the claustrophobic one.*

The insect remained motionless as though held there by the light. "How the hell'd it get inside?" Geddy asked.

Not only had the terrible locusts been extinct for centuries, but Geddy had spent half his life here without seeing so much as a fly. Aquebba's water came from a very deep aquifer. Doc once told him that fewer than twenty native species still remained, plants included. Not an insect among them.

— *I am not certain it is organic.*

"What if it's not organic?" Oz asked, adding a wink to acknowledge she'd eavesdropped.

"Now that is an interesting question," Lestiko said, drawing closer to it. Again, he raised his black bracelet, and the tiny orange points of light formed a window that hovered in the air. "Anything living should appear red."

Though the insect's outline was clear enough on the screen, it was the same color as the metal surrounding it.

"It's a drone," Lestiko announced, the magical light dust returning to his bracelet. "And it just recorded everything we said and saw."

"We smash it!" Voprot said, taking a step forward to do exactly that.

"No!" Lestiko stuck his arm out in front of Voprot. "We don't know its defensive capabilities."

"Anyone got a pickle jar?" Oz asked drolly, her irritation rising. This wasn't the first time they'd been locked inside this ship. Back then, Voprot somehow managed to pry it open from the outside.

Lestiko was right. They had to assume it was dangerous. But if they couldn't kill it or let it out, where did that leave them?

— Any bright ideas?

— *The bridge has a bulkhead door. If you can corral it in there, you could seal it inside.*

"Of course!" Lestiko said. "Good thinking, Eli!"

"Could everyone please stop listening to the voices in my head?! Jeez!"

Lestiko held up his hands in a *mea culpa* gesture. "Sorry, force of habit."

"What'd he say?" Denk asked.

— *Don't say it out loud!*

Eli was right. The drone couldn't know their intentions. Only he, Lestiko, and maybe Oz did.

"Lestiko, I need a word in private. It's about Sagacea." He nodded his head toward the open door to the bridge.

He immediately understood. "Certainly." They shuffled together past the star map.

"I dunno what the heck's going on," Denk noted. Oz gave his shoulder a reassuring pat.

As they brushed past Doc, he whispered, "Good luck."

When he neared the door, Geddy heard the same soft flutter and felt the faintest tap on his back. Behind him, Oz gasped.

— It just landed on me, didn't it?

— *I believe it did.*

The plan was to lock the damn thing in the bridge and run, which wasn't possible if it was on him. Lestiko hadn't seen this happen, but maybe he'd heard Geddy and Eli's inner dialog. He went all the way to the very front of the relatively cramped two-seat bridge. When Geddy was past the bulkhead door, he silently gave a little jerk of his head to indicate his back, and Lestiko nodded that he understood.

Morpho snaked a tendril into Geddy's ear, causing him to wince. He really needed to learn how to tune.

— **I can remove it.**

— You sure about that? We don't know what this thing's capable of.

— **I am.**

— Then what?

— **Then you run and close the door behind you.**

"So what's this about Sagacea's location?" Lestiko asked mechanically, giving a nod to indicate he'd heard Morpho as well.

"Could be a red herring," Geddy replied with a wink. "Something to throw us off the scent. They've done it before. Clones, crypsids ..."

"I wouldn't put it past them," Lestiko said. "We should probe deeper into the nav data. Make sure there's nothing we missed."

— On three. One ... two ...

Morpho tensed on his shoulder. He whipped out a tendril so fast, it cracked. A faintly metallic *tink* came from the front of the bridge where he'd flung the drone, and Geddy bolted through with Lestiko right behind him. The moment they burst back into the main cabin, Lestiko slammed the door shut.

Everyone but Oz wore the same bewildered expression.

"Is it gone?!" Geddy asked Lestiko, craning his neck to see.

Before Lestiko could answer, a sharp but powerful hiss came from behind him. Everyone's heads spun toward the sound. A minuscule purple glow appeared at the inside seam. The drone was boring its way out with some kind of original energy beam. They had seconds before it succeeded.

"It's not going to hold. Geddy, unseal the door!" Doc urged.

Again, Geddy curled his hand around the glowing holographic sphere and he opened his palm to reveal the ship schematic. His eyes flew straight to the umbrella-looking symbol with three dots underneath, the same way he'd disabled the security protocols almost a year earlier when he was showing it to Kriggy. He touched it, and a soft *whumm* signaled that the ship's outer skin had unsealed.

"Voprot, get the door!" Geddy commanded.

The big lizard lunged forward and threw the latch just as the first sparks spat forth from the seam of the bulkhead.

"That's one strong bug!" Denk said.

"Everyone out! Go! Go!"

Voprot barreled through, bowling over two Kiganteans who had posted up in front of it. Denk ran out behind him. Oz herded Kriggy through ahead of her, then Doc, Geddy, and Lestiko. The Kiganteans were too surprised to do anything but stare. But just as Lestiko slammed the door shut behind him, the drone, now glowing purple, got stuck in the seam and was wriggling its way free.

"Stop that bug!" Geddy cried.

One of the Kiganteans shot out his long, forked tongue and snatched the drone out of the air just as it wriggled out. It swallowed, and for a moment, nothing happened. Then, the Kigantean's eyes widened to saucers, and the bug shot through his abdomen like a bullet. He could only stare dumbly at the hole it left before he crumpled to the ground.

CHAPTER 11
BUGGING OUT

Momentarily disoriented, the drone zigzagged drunkenly overhead for a few moments, its flapping wings casting off a fine spray of blood from the hapless Kigantean who'd swallowed it. He held the wound in his stomach as a couple of others attended to him.

Without thinking, which was how he tended to roll, Geddy drew the PDQ.

"No!" Tretiak lunged for the pistol.

But he was already committed to the shot and fired a low-power burst at it. It dodged it, and the bolt exploded on the chamber's domed ceiling, dislodging a basketball-sized chunk that turned to dust as it cracked onto the floor.

The bug's guidance system seemingly recalibrated, because it quite suddenly zoomed toward the exit with shocking speed.

"Damnit!" Geddy shouted.

The Kiganteans were so confused that Oz grabbed her blades and Voprot's whip from where they'd been dropped. Geddy was about to squeeze off another shot when Oz roughly clamped onto his arm from behind.

"Stop it! You want to bury us all in here?!"

"But it recorded everything! We can't let it leave!" he spat back.

But the opportunity had passed, and he seethed at Oz for intervening. The bug darted through the arched entrance to the antechamber.

"I catch it, Geddy!" Voprot bolted away.

"Don't do it the same way as your cousin!" Geddy shouted.

Oz took off. Geddy gave chase and shot through the doorway behind her just as Voprot snapped his whip at the drone, which had nearly reached the door across the bridge. He missed, and Oz raced past him. She leaped and swiped at it with her blades, but it easily dodged her and kept going.

— Screw this!

— *For once, maybe don't screw anything!*

— I won't miss this time. Trust me.

Geddy stopped dead in the middle of the bridge and raised the pistol, exhaling as he drew a bead on his target. He gave the handle a quick tap.

The cloud of dust that burst from above the far doorway made it impossible to know if he found his mark. But he couldn't see Oz, either.

The gut punch of horror had barely landed before Voprot spun and shouldered him with such force that it knocked him off his feet, the PDQ flying out of his hand. As he sailed backward, massive chunks of the ancient ceiling fell where he'd just been standing, slicing through an entire section of the narrow stone bridge.

He fell awkwardly, rolling to the left until his right leg came across his body and found only air. His momentum carried him over the edge, which he barely managed to grab before the rest of him flopped over the side. As he hung by his fingertips, his legs swinging back and forth under him, he cast a desperate look in the direction of the dust cloud, hoping Oz would appear through it.

"Morph, the gun!"

Voprot scrambled over and grabbed his forearms, yanking him up onto the bridge while Morpho retrieved the PDQ. Geddy's eyes never left the far entrance. The worst few seconds of his life finally ended when the dust cleared, and the glowing red tips of Oz's blades appeared again.

"Geddy!" she yelled. "Voprot!"

"Oz!" Geddy cried. "Are you okay?!"

"Yeah. You?"

"We okay!" Voprot yelled back.

"Go! Stop the drone!" Geddy urged.

The thing still had Tretiak's Gundrun steel door to contend with, but he couldn't know how tight the seal was or how long it would take the shockingly powerful little drone to punch through.

Oz's blades disappeared as she sprinted after it. Geddy spotted the PDQ teetering on the opposite edge of the bridge. He carefully picked it up and holstered it.

"Thanks, big guy."

"You do what Oz say not to do," Voprot said with a scowl.

He dusted himself off, willing his racing heart to slow. "Yeah, that's pretty on-brand for me."

A rush of footfalls behind him meant the others had come running.

"What the hell did you do?" Tretiak asked. "Are you guys okay? Where'd it go?"

"Oz went after it," Geddy replied. "We're fine, but I can't say the same for the bridge."

The dust had cleared enough to see the extent of the damage. The gap wasn't that large, but it was too wide to jump. Before he could even think of a way across, Voprot had wrapped his whole arm around his torso.

"We catch up."

"Whoa, wait — what are you–"

Voprot lashed out his whip, the end wrapping around one of the stone crossbeams. Voprot took a couple of quick steps, and before Geddy could explain why suspending five hundred kilos from the ancient stone was a bad idea, they'd left the ground and were swinging together across the gap. He gave a terrified squeak and shut his eyes tightly. A second later, Voprot set him down and reassuring weight returned to his feet.

"See?" Voprot gave a toothy grin. "Ancient Kigantean workmanship."

"Look out!" came Denk's voice from behind them.

Geddy spun in time to see Denk, Doc, Kriggy, and Tretiak rushing toward them with the Kiganteans, two of them helping the injured one limp through as blood streamed down his scaly leg. Behind them came a calamitous rumble as the entire roof of the Tomb surrendered to gravity.

Tretiak and the others paused just long enough to watch dust billow through the archway.

"Come on!" Voprot yelled, tugging on Geddy's sleeve.

"But ..." Geddy protested.

Without hesitation, Dheson grabbed Doc under his arms, coiled his whip around the roof support, and swung across. Another quickly followed suit with Lestiko, then Denk, Tretiak, and Kriggy. Only after they were all on the other side did Geddy finally sprint after Voprot, charging through the archway and back into the long passage.

Far ahead, Oz slashed away at the now-invisible drone, her blades slicing wildly in the half-darkness as she cursed. Voprot had closed half the distance between them before Geddy reached top speed, then Oz bounded up the steps out of view.

By the time Geddy caught up, a purple flicker was already visible at the top of the stairs.

He was halfway up before he even raised his eyes. The bug was boring its way through the seam of the door with its bright purple laser. Oz took frenzied slashes at it, but each strike only revealed the outline of a fist-sized shield.

Again, Geddy instinctively reached for his PDQ but stopped the moment his fingers touched it. That was their only way out, and Zelnad shields had proven to be impervious to anything they might throw at it. A wayward shot would block their only escape.

A breathless Tretiak came up the steps behind him. "That thing's shielded?!"

Oz unleashed all the anger she'd been carrying around, giving a primal scream as blow after blow failed to connect. She took one final, desperate thrust before the bug slipped through the still-glowing hole it had made. Her blade got stuck in it, a spiderweb of red lightning arcing against the Gundrun steel structure before she yanked it free.

Tretiak was already shoving Geddy and Voprot aside when Oz shouted, "How do you open this stupid thing?!"

"Move!" Tretiak growled, and she stepped aside.

He reached into the stonework around the door, and it again descended into the ground, freeing Oz's blade. She leaped through the narrow opening and into the blazing sunshine before it had even lowered fully. Billowing sand blew down the steps as Denk and the rest appeared at the bottom.

Voprot charged through after Oz, followed by Geddy. He jerked his head sideways, shielding his eyes as the light punched him in the face. Voprot's whip shot skyward, snapping haplessly at the tiny target as it climbed.

— *It's probably safe to shoot now.*

Squinting tightly, he drew the PDQ, hoping for a glint of sunlight that would reveal the drone's exact position. But even a direct hit at a full charge wouldn't penetrate that shield. His fingers relaxed.

"Bug get away," Voprot said sadly.

Lestiko and Doc came through the door behind him,

followed shortly by Denk and the Kiganteans. "Tell me you got it!" Lestiko cried.

Geddy shook his head, a thick red splotch lingering on his retinas. "It wouldn't have made any difference. The damn thing's shielded."

Doc drew even with him, looking to the sky. "There goes our tactical advantage," he gravely noted.

"Now we just have to hope they haven't found enough shinium yet."

"You!" Dheson snarled behind him, unbothered by the sun as he charged toward Geddy, his claws flared murderously wide. "You destroy sacred place!"

Voprot stepped between them, defiantly thrusting back his shoulders. Dheson pulled up short, apoplectic with rage.

"No, father! Geddy try to save the world. He my ... er, he *is* my friend!"

Dheson drew himself up, his snout clear above the top of Voprot's head. His eyes darted momentarily between him and Geddy, angrily baring his teeth. Voprot stood fast.

"Take your ... *friends* away from here and never come back," Dheson hissed.

Lestiko had reactivated the platform still floating outside and climbed on. Its force-field floor could accommodate all of them. It would be tight, but they'd be aboard his ship and back at the spaceport in a few minutes. With any luck, they'd never see Kigantu again.

Voprot managed a faint smile and put his claw on his father's shoulder, which seemed to surprise him. "We save you, too, Father. All of you."

Lestiko and Doc waited while the five of them onto the floating platform. Geddy boarded last, his feet disturbingly close to the edge. Before he got on, Lestiko reached in his pocket and withdrew a capsule the size of a lighter. He tossed it to Dheson.

"It's a docbot," he said, nodding to the injured Kigantean. "It'll close up that wound."

"We no need Basoan medicine," Dheson said flatly, and cast it aside.

"Suit yourself." Lestiko turned his attention to the platform's controls.

"Hey, what's the rated capacity of this thing?" Geddy whispered.

As the platform floated away, they all turned to look at the Kiganteans, who quickly disappeared behind a scrim of blowing sand. "We'll find out soon enough."

CHAPTER 12
DON'T TOUCH THAT DIAL

Lestiko sat across from Geddy at the long table in the containment room, which until recently had been the Orneans' primary research facility. Once Ornea formally joined the Alliance, they'd sent a fully equipped science ship, *Inquiry*, where they'd since moved operations. But owing to its thick, tukrium-reinforced walls, it was almost completely silent. Perfect for practice.

The side of the room with the original lab equipment was pitch dark. They preferred the other end nearer the door beneath a single light that was always on. Morpho had spread into a puddle on the table between them, which generally meant he was bored. Lestiko's hands were folded patiently in front of him.

"Let's try again." He'd been leaning on his hand for the past hour. "You're painfully close."

They'd just returned to Kigantu the day prior. Lestiko agreed to teach Geddy the delicate art of what he called tuning — a technique by which hosts could communicate telepathically. So far, it hadn't gone well. But as hosts to a Sagacean and a Zelnad, they shared something unique. You might call it a bond.

Lestiko still hadn't said what convinced him to change his mind about helping the Alliance. That was Doc's entire reason for returning to Basoa, but Geddy couldn't help but wonder how Doc flipped the switch. It seemed something was weighing on him.

"You sure you have time for this?" Geddy asked. "I thought you and the Orneans were balls-deep in your research."

"They're the researchers. I'm closer to a mad scientist."

Geddy gave a confused frown. "But aren't you here to help them with original energy?"

"I shared what I knew. They'll figure out the rest."

"Then why did you come? You were pretty resolute about staying."

He gave a helpless shrug. "What can I say? I guess I decided an Alliance battle cruiser was a better place to tinker than the Empty."

"You mean weapons." He nodded. "But if you're not working on the *Inquiry*, where are you working?" He jutted his chin toward the darkened lab area. "Here? Why?"

"Same reason we practice here. It's quiet. Plus, if I blow myself up, I won't hurt anyone."

Suddenly, the lesson had taken a backseat. "Can I ask what you're working on?"

A schoolboy grin fell over Lestiko. "Really, it's just a souped-up version of my black hole bomb — which I understand came in handy, by the way." He managed a weary smile.

Indeed, Lestiko's powerful gravity weapon had sucked a Zelnad destroyer into a temporary black hole, enabling their harrowing escape from The Deuce.

"Souped-up how?" Geddy asked, very intrigued.

"I call it a jump torpedo. Instead of an explosion, it creates a large jump bubble, transporting the target to whichever galactic coordinates you wish. From open space to the ... heart of a star." He winked knowingly.

"Like a bubble drive you can fire."

"Precisely."

"Why not just make more black-hole bombs?"

"Because the weapon is filled with innocent hosts. We have to take it off the board, but we can't just destroy it or suck it into a singularity. So, we'll have to jump it away. But we digress." He drew himself up and returned his full attention back to Geddy. "Now focus. You can do this."

Geddy gave his bearded face an invigorating rub and leaned in. "Right. Fiftieth time's a charm."

Lestiko gave him a look of paternal encouragement. "Patience, Geddy. It took Oraisa months just to have her first breakthrough."

That was of dubious comfort. Jel's sister was locked up in Lestiko's facility and force-fed his so-called Process before she developed the ability to tune, first with the Zelnad she'd fought off then later with Lestiko. But they didn't have that kind of time.

As Lestiko coached him to do, Geddy placed his palms flat on the table and closed his eyes, attempting to clear his mind of all distractions. No small feat in such times.

"Ready."

"Tuning requires absolute presence in the moment," Lestiko emphasized. "Only then can you open to the energy."

Geddy's mind had a maddening tendency to wander into the future. He'd already pictured the Zelnad bug drone fluttering into space and sending Sagacea's coordinates back to whatever they used as a base.

— *You're not being present.*

— Sorry, did you just say something?

— *Knock it off! Now come on — you talk to me, you can talk to him.*

Visualizing a big red RESET button, he pressed it, and his mind briefly quieted.

"Imagine fibers connecting you to me and Morpho. Hair-like filaments playing the music of the universe." He closed his eyes and took a couple of rhythmic, deep breaths. "See them vibrating, then try to *feel* them."

"Music. Hair. Good vibrations. Got it."

Per his instructions, Geddy envisioned gossamer bundles connecting him to both Morph and Lestiko in a weird little triangle, pulsing with vibrant purple light.

"Now, play a note. Any note you like. Let it ring, and then allow your consciousness to ride the sound right into Morpho."

Had this conversation taken place just a few weeks earlier, Lestiko's guidance would've struck him as woo-woo bunk. But since his experience on Basoa, he had opened himself to new ways of thinking.

He played his note, imagining a rainbow-colored wave traveling down the threads. For some reason, the image resonated as strongly as the note he played. When the wave crashed into Morph, he said,

— **Geddy? Are you in here with us?**

"Cap'n Starheart, please report to the *Gallant*." Denk's boyish voice over the *Stalwart's* loudspeakers blasted Geddy's ears like a plasma cannon.

"Gah!" Geddy slapped the table out of frustration. "If the Zelnads win, at least I won't have any more fucking meetings!"

Just like that, the spell was broken. He was barely in his own head now, let alone Morpho's. Still, something had happened. Maybe he could replicate it later.

Geddy gave Lestiko an apologetic look. "Sorry."

He only returned his usual patient smile, which made his dark green face look cartoonish. "It's fine, Geddy. We'll pick this up later. You did well."

"I think I heard Morph in my head."

Lestiko nodded encouragingly. "Good! Same time tomorrow, perhaps?"

— *Ask him.*

— *But–*

— *Verveik can wait five minutes. He's your friend.*

"Sure ... Hey, is everything okay with you?"

He cocked his head curiously. "Why do you ask?"

"You seem out of sorts."

The brainy Basoan let out a long sigh. "Dr. Tardigan hasn't spoken to you?"

"About what?"

Even though they were alone, Lestiko still looked around him before replying. "When he visited me on Basoa, my mind was set, as you know."

— *Now we're getting somewhere.*

"But you were totally isolated. At least here, you have–"

"I wasn't isolated. I never am. And neither are you."

Lestiko was host to a nasty Zelnad called Rai. After years of fighting him for control, Lestiko had finally managed to take the reins through a strict — and nearly impossible — psychological regimen he called the Process. But it hadn't worked for anyone but him and Jel's sister, so he turned his efforts toward safely separating a Zelnad from its host. Every attempt so far resulted in a massive explosion. That was a risk his test subjects were all willing to take. Lestiko was so determined to make it work that he was willing to run the next experiment on himself. Either way, he'd be free.

"I get it," Geddy said. He was never really alone either, but Eli was kind. Rai was an asshole.

"I know you do, which is why I'm telling you what I'm about to tell you."

The way he said it made the hair stand up on his arms. "Okay ..."

He leaned in closer still. "Geddy, you understand better than anyone what we're up against. Without original energy shields and weapons, we will fail. However, I can't design weapons until we know how to store the energy."

"If this is a pep talk, it's not off to a great start."

Lestiko's tone somehow got even more grave. "All I know for sure is that there's enough of this energy held in the bond between hosts and entities to vaporize a large city. It clearly runs between hosts, but my theory is that it's everywhere."

"Everywhere. Like, everywhere, everywhere?" Lestiko nodded. "What does that mean for us?"

"We've been assuming that if Sagacea is destroyed, civilization will follow. I think this is way, *way* bigger than that."

Geddy looked sidelong at him. "How much bigger?"

"If I'm right, I believe the weapon will start a chain reaction that never stops."

He hesitated to ask the obvious question. "How big a bang are we talking here?"

"Big enough to swallow the universe."

Geddy laughed, thinking this was an exaggeration, but Lestiko's expression remained somber. "Oh shit, you're serious."

His blood went cold. Back on Basoa, Lestiko himself said, *They don't have to destroy us. We'll do it ourselves.* But if this new theory was true, then the Zelnads' true intentions were to wipe the slate completely clean. Didn't Eli tell him long ago that "Zelnad" means something like "reset?"

"So that's what they want," Geddy said.

"I believe so, yes."

Lestiko needed to throw him a bone before he lost all hope. "Do you think we can win?"

"I don't know. But even if we figure out how to safely weaponize the energy, I'm not sure anyone could manufacture, test, and implement a brand-new weapons system in time for it to matter."

"What about the Triad?"

He shook his head vigorously. "Not a chance. Retrofitting the fleet, maybe. But not the manufacturing."

"Can *anyone* make them?" Lestiko only stared back, because he knew Geddy already had the answer. "The Xellarans."

Lestiko gave a slow nod. "I don't see another way."

Xellara and Temeruria were the last holdouts for the Alliance. Temeruria was a wild card, but Xellara had already rejected Verveik's entreaty to join. They'd always been secretive, uncooperative, exceedingly weird, and non-participants on the galactic stage. Hell, they might as well be a galaxy unto themselves.

The weight of this horrifying news began to settle on his shoulders. Before he knew it, he was standing and pushing in his chair.

"I should get to the *Gallant*."

"I'm sorry, Geddy. But if there was ever a time to ask the universe for a little help, it's now."

"Who else knows about this?" Geddy asked.

"Just me, Krons, and you."

He paused long enough to consider what he should do with this information. "Shouldn't everybody know?"

Lestiko held out his empty webbed hands like it was a tossup. "That depends. It certainly doesn't look good for us."

He preferred not to think about that, but he didn't disagree. "What's your point?"

"My point? Hope matters, Geddy. In the end, it might be

the only thing that does. If everyone knew what's really at stake, would it harden their resolve or amplify their despair?"

Lestiko made a good point. If the mission was to save Sagacea, did the true consequences of failure even matter? And what would it do to the Alliance's already flagging morale to know what they were? Suddenly, it wasn't so black and white.

"I'll give that some thought," Geddy said. "Thanks for the lesson."

"You'll get it soon enough. You were very close today."

He returned Lestiko's polite smile and departed.

CHAPTER 13

THE PROBE WENT WHERE?

Geddy found Commander Verveik in his huge chair poring over a report on a holoscreen image above his desk. The conversation he'd just had with Lestiko weighed heavily on his conscience.

"Hey chief, you wanted to see me?"

"Have a seat." The big Gundrun flicked off his display.

He sat stiffly in one of the two chairs, unsure what to do with Lestiko's bombshell. Verveik would need concrete proof before he broke the news to everyone else, but there was no such proof. Only a theory.

"So, what's up?" Geddy asked.

"First, Kigantu. Mr. Tretiak has thus far ignored my requests for a debrief."

Until now, Geddy hadn't extended much in the way of empathy for his old boss. But seeing the look on his face when they found the Double A in ruins, and again when he inadvertently destroyed the Tomb had offered a rare glimpse into his internal life.

"He lost his kingdom," Geddy said. "I expect he's still processing that."

Verveik's irritated expression didn't abate. "What happened?"

Geddy explained about the storm, the Zelnad massacre in Aquebba, the Kiganteans, and the unfortunate events that took place in the Tomb.

"You're certain this drone escaped?"

"Yes."

"Then our time is shorter still." He let out a long sigh and rubbed his face as he rose. "Anyway, Kigantu isn't why I wanted to see you."

He gave his head a curious tilt. "It wasn't?"

"I've promoted Ogos to captain of the *Steadfast*."

None of the clones was more capable or had gulped more of the Alliance kool-aid than the one formerly known as Ninety-Two.

"Good. He deserves it."

Verveik rose and came around the desk. "Also …" He produced a stylized metal star made of platinum, and slid it across to him. "… I'm promoting *you* to colonel."

Geddy's mouth hung open while the commander bent down, unfastened his current rank, and clicked the new one into place.

"Congratulations." He offered his colossal hand but didn't smile. Geddy still had no idea what his teeth even looked like.

"Thank you, sir, but … why?"

— *Why, indeed. You're a loose cannon.*

— And yet, I've been succeeding in spite of myself for some time now.

"The fleet's growing by the day. I need a number two, and you, Colonel Starheart, are a perfect number two."

Verveik's lips made the slightest upward bow as he drew himself back up.

"Wait … Did you just make a joke?"

"Apparently not. Walk with me."

He brushed past, and the door slid open for him. Geddy pinched the fabric of his Alliance coveralls and stretched it out to get a better look at his shiny new rank. The pride he felt as he followed the commander into the long, curved corridor surprised him. Verveik turned right and strode at a pace that was difficult to match.

"Going forward, I'm calling this group the war cabinet. Military leadership, the Orneans, maybe even the Committee. This is too big for me to be calling the shots alone."

"Did something change?"

"The probe we sent to surveil the Zelnad base has returned," Verveik said.

Geddy's eyes popped wide. This was the first he heard about it. "A probe, sir? Wouldn't they detect that?"

"The Orneans modified it with a version of the bubble drive that jumps it randomly around the base every couple milliseconds and captures an image. They've assembled the initial set of images into a detailed 3D model."

"Okay, so what're we dealing with?"

"That's what we're about to find out."

Verveik took another right through the doorway that led to the theater, a small auditorium designed for briefings.

The New Alliance's key military leaders had already gathered and turned their heads when the two of them entered. Among them were Balzac, Geddy's old Screvari friend; Queen Tymeri, the former pirate; the newly promoted *Captain* Ogos; Grozuc, the Triad commander; and Arbizander, the Gundrun fiercely loyal to Verveik.

Doc and the other Ornean scientists were huddled together at the front of the room. Lestiko breathlessly entered the auditorium and hurried down the steps to join them. It was clear enough from the Orneans' expressions that they viewed him as an outsider.

"Looks like we're all here," Doc said. "Let's begin."

The oversized seats were barely big enough for Verveik. He, Lestiko, and Geddy sat in the row behind the others as Doc activated a large holoscreen at the front.

"My brother Parmhar's deep scanner puts the Zelnad base near the edge of the known universe, not far from a star cluster we call Thotac 2218." He gestured toward Lestiko and his team. "Over the past few weeks, a stealth probe designed by my colleagues here has used 2D imagery to construct a 3D model of it."

A large image materialized in the shape of a finely textured sphere composed of triangles. A uniform series of colossal concave depressions dimpled its surface. Clearly not a planet.

Geddy leaned forward in his seat. "It looks like a golf ball."

"Indeed," Doc agreed. "We believe it may be similar to a Dyson sphere."

Before anyone could ask the obvious question, Lestiko took a step forward. "A Dyson sphere is a theoretical structure that encases a star so as to harvest its energy. The scanner suggested there was a lot of tukrium, and there is. In fact, it likely represents most of the tukrium available in the entire universe."

"And it has a star inside?" asked Balzac.

Doc jumped back in. "Unlikely. Instead, we think the sphere is designed to gather and store original energy, like a battery."

"Gather it from where?" Verveik asked.

"From everywhere," Lestiko said, glancing at Geddy. He flicked something on the hologram, and it zoomed out from the sphere, adding an overlay of faint purple streaks that called to mind the fluid-like aurora from the Ice Castles on The Deuce. "Now that we can detect it, we believe it pervades the entire universe. In fact, we have reason to believe it's the source of cosmic inflation."

"Where are all their ships?" Tymeri asked.

"Our best guess is that they're housed inside the sphere until needed, perhaps to recharge."

"I see no openings," Balzac said. "How do they get in or out?"

"We don't know yet. But the probe will continue to take images until we have the information we need."

"And the whole thing is shielded, I suppose?" Verveik grumbled.

"That's a safe assumption," affirmed Lestiko.

"How do we blow it the fuck up?" Geddy asked, eliciting an appreciative laugh from the other captains.

"It's too soon to talk about an attack strategy," Doc said. "Additional surveillance is needed."

"You've all done well." Verveik rose from his seat in order to address the whole room. "We know the location of both their base and their target, Sagacea. That's more than we knew a few days ago."

"Is it true they know Sagacea's location as well?" Arbizander asked.

"Looks that way." The gathered shifted in their seats and exchanged worried looks. It seemed as though every bit of good news was offset by more bad.

"I don't understand," Balzac said. "How could they not know it already? Isn't it their home world?"

Lestiko said, "I used to wonder the same thing. My personal belief is that they don't attain true sentience until long after they leave Sagacea. If that's true, then they couldn't know its location any more than a baby knows where it was born."

"How goes our weapon and shield development, Mr. Lestiko?" asked Verveik.

"Everything hinges upon collecting and storing the energy," Lestiko replied. "If we can do that, we can build out a viable weapons system. But then we have another problem."

Verveik's lips formed a line, and his left eye twitched. "Manufacturing."

Doc stepped in to rescue him from the hot seat. "Yes. The tolerances required and the production scale exceeds the capabilities of any world in our galaxy …" He and Lestiko exchanged a meaningful look. "… save for one."

"Xellara," Balzac said, and the air went out of the room.

Had it joined the Alliance, Xellara would've helped end the Ring War much sooner and saved many thousands of lives. It took a lot for Verveik to invite them to the table at the Gundrun Summit and extend an olive branch, but they'd spurned him once again.

He grimaced. "I've reached out repeatedly to the Grand Chancellor. Apparently, he's too busy turning his people into robots to listen. We'll have to find another way."

Of course, they'd already considered other options, and everyone's expressions revealed as much.

Doc gave a deferential nod. "We will do our best, Commander."

CHAPTER 14
DADDY ISSUES

Geddy leaned forward in the captain's chair of the *Stalwart*, frantically scanning the battlefield for any sign of the Zelnad weapon that would destroy the universe if it found its target.

The vastness of the supervoid around Sagacea could only be measured by the absence of stars. Through the front screen, billowing clouds of Zelnad and Alliance ships — millions on both sides, were engaged in a battle too chaotic to comprehend.

Bright purple streaks filled the sky. The tide had turned in favor of the Alliance. But where was the damn weapon?

At the center of the void was Sagacea, a blinding ball of pure energy. The invisible barrier around it could only be marked by the sudden disappearance of ships at its edge.

Nearby, a blizzard of Zelnad fighters formed up like a murmuration of birds, rocketing head-on toward the *Stalwart* as it shifted and swirled. The ship's targeting systems seemed confused, the forward battery barely connecting with any attackers before they unleashed a barrage on the bridge.

Though the original-energy shields held fast against the flurry of bolts, the integrity meter abruptly nose-dived.

The teardrop-shaped swarm split apart before they could fire again and blipped out only to reform behind them, pummeling the rear shield.

"Cap, we're taking a pounding!" Denk warned.

"On screen," Geddy said, forgoing the jokes. They were out of their depth, and things could get bad, fast. The look on Oz's face magnified the gravity of the situation.

The Gallant was in the thick of the battle when this fresh offensive began, and it was dealing with the same brand of attack. Swarming fighters attacked it from all sides, and hundreds of Zelnad battleships were assembling into the weapon Geddy called the supership. Their intentions were clear — take out the Alliance big ships first.

It was much the same scenario that had played out in the Battle of the Deuce, Verveik's ship under vicious attack while the *Stalwart* was far away and dealing with its own problems. Coming to their aid would only bring them deeper into the conflagration. Finding and destroying the weapon was the only priority.

The tables had turned on the Alliance. Geddy had no idea what to do. He was a colonel now. Wasn't he supposed to know?

"What's our play, Ged?" The desperation in Oz's voice bled through her bravado.

— Help me, E. Please.

— *I'm sorry, Geddy. It's all up to you now.*

"I don't …" he muttered, his chest tightening with fear.

Another barrage came, this time from the starboard side. The shields dropped below fifty percent as the ship shuddered.

Doc loudly gasped, and all heads jerked in his direction. His eyes were fixed on his scopes. "Oh, no …"

A blinding flash from the screen lit up the bridge. A wall of bright purple energy was radiating outward from Sagacea at impossible speed, a tidal wave of power that would never stop. Somehow, the Zelnad weapon had slipped through their fingers and had already found its mark.

They'd failed. And because of that failure, everything, maybe even time itself, was about to end.

The wave overtook the *Stalwart*. Flames exploded into the bridge, and Geddy watched everyone he cared about engulfed by it, the world-ending wave sparing his vision just long enough to see it happen. The last thing he saw was his own face reflected in Oz's terrified eyes.

"No!!" he cried.

A hand on his chest shook him vigorously.

"Geddy, wake up!"

His eyes popped open to find Oz's pale, beautiful face hovering over him. In that moment, being safe and warm in bed with his girl seemed so much less real than the dream that he could only stare at her in disbelief. Meanwhile, his heart continued to thud.

— *It's okay, Geddy. You're safe.*

"It's Oz. We're in your quarters. You were having a nightmare."

He sat bolt upright, reorienting himself. By and by, he began to trust his eyes. He ran his fingers through his hair and found it drenched.

"Holy shit, Oz, it was so *fucking real*."

She lightly ran her fingers up and down his sweaty back. "Tell me about it."

He related the details of the battle outside Sagacea, the Nads' overwhelming force, and the apocalyptic explosion that followed.

"What do you think it means?" The desperation in his voice troubled him.

"That you're as worried as the rest of us. Especially with …" She trailed off as a dark look washed over her.

"Especially with what?"

A pained sigh escaped her lips, and she tenderly took his hand. "As long as you're already keyed up, there's something I need to tell you."

A flotilla of troubling thoughts drifted through his head. He kept them at bay just long enough to ask, "What?"

Her eyes meandered down to the edge of the blanket bundled in their laps. "The night before we left for Kigantu, I got a message from my father."

Relief washed over him. Oz's relationship with her family, especially her imperious father, Prince Bransel, was fraught. But he'd expected something much more worrisome.

Temeruria was in bed with the enemy, and Bransel apparently liked to watch. They'd already bought up much of the planet's tukrium deposits, further enriching her ultra-wealthy family while handing the Nads exactly what they needed. He was dead to her.

"What the hell does he want?"

"A few weeks ago, the Zelnads abandoned the tukrium mines without warning. They left behind some kind of autonomous borers that are drilling into the planet. Hundreds of them."

"Drilling?"

"He said the boreholes are spewing gas and dust into the atmosphere and they don't know what to do."

Geddy pulled back, blinking in confusion. "What's that have to do with you?"

"He wants me to ask for the Alliance's help on his behalf."

"Ha! I assume you told him to pound sand."

Her pained expression didn't soften. "I haven't responded yet. He sent another message just last night."

Geddy cradled her face in his hands, looking deep into her

huge yellow eyes in the dim light. "Oz, first of all, this is good news, okay? It means the Nads still don't have what they need. And second …"

She gently took his wrists and pulled away. "What if what happened to Earth 2 happens to Temeruria?"

He, of all people, couldn't dismiss that particular concern. "Can't they just, you know, plug their own holes?"

"They've tried that. There's too much pressure."

"Well, fuck him. In fact, fuck him twice for putting you in this position."

"But Temeruria is still my home. Most people aren't like my family."

She had a point. Plus, the Star Guard, though small, was among the most highly trained fighting forces in the galaxy. Temeruria was famously neutral in conflicts and hadn't been to war for millennia, but the Star Guard would be a critical addition to the Alliance fleet. They could help train new pilots and would bring some needed discipline to the mix.

"Does Verveik know?"

She shook her head. "You're the only one I've told."

He chewed thoughtfully on his lower lip. "Is that why you've been a little … let's say, surly?"

Oz gave a pained smirk. "Probably. Sorry."

Verveik had no love for Temeruria, as much for its dealings with the Nads now as for its neutrality. Once again, the Ring War echoed loudly in the commander's ears.

"What would you do if you were Verveik?"

Her eyes turned glassy. "I hate my father. His choices, his greed … I'm even pretty sure he was behind my uncle's assassination. But Temeruria is worth saving, and we need all the help we can get."

"I'll talk to him. All we can do is see what he says and go from there." Geddy offered, kissing her tenderly on the cheek.

"Okay."

— *You should tell her what Lestiko told you.*
— Not yet. She's got enough to worry about.

CHAPTER 15
WHO 'DIS?

At five a.m., before Ogos and the rest of the clones were even thinking about P.T., Geddy gave the con to One-Twelve, whose name was now Juan Rodriguez for some reason, and got ready for sesehlu. He led the entire crew, including a very reluctant Jeledine, across the hangar to the *Fizmo*, parked in its usual spot in the back corner of the maintenance bay. The *Stalwart's* facilities were state-of-the-art and much nicer in general, but after so many sessions together aboard the *Fiz*, it would've felt wrong to do it anywhere else.

"I'm surprised a *colonel* would lower himself to exercise with us plebes," Oz teased.

"It keeps me humble," Geddy replied.

They were barely inside before Morpho jumped off his shoulder and slung himself up to the rear port vent like a wallwalker going the wrong way. In a flash, he was in the ship's bowels again, making sure her seals held against the sandstorm and that she was still spaceworthy.

In the wake of his troubling dream, their demoralizing visit to Kigantu, and the news about Temeruria, Geddy had plenty on his mind. On a good day, he could focus on one thing at a time. Now, he was simply overwhelmed. And, as Verveik's second, he was directly in charge of thousands of lives. If and when they figured out a way to attack the Nad base, he would lead the Alliance into battle.

Not quite a year earlier, he was wearing the replica Neil Armstrong spacesuit back at the museum, drunk dancing with a bottle of Old Earth to celebrate his last day on The Deuce.

— *I'm glad you're doing this. You need it.*

— Are you saying I'm out of shape?

— *It doesn't need to be said.*

Once they were all inside, Voprot closed the hold doors and scampered excitedly to his spot in the middle of the floor. They all had their places. Oz cinched her hair back and stretched while everyone got squared away.

Doc, always pleased to lead practice, looked like he needed the break himself. He and his team were under more pressure than anyone, and Verveik was breathing down their necks.

"Okay, let's start with a few deep breaths in ... and ouuut ..." Doc said, conducting them like an orchestra. "Again, this time with the words ... maaaahhhhaaaakuuut ..."

With each new breath, they exhaled the word, *maha'kut* — a mantra for the practice called psychic breathing. Geddy closed his eyes, too, hoovering up the negative energy in and around him as though only his soul could filter it out. It seemed absurd at first until he did it over and over, and damned if it didn't put him at ease. He always felt great after sesehlu.

After five minutes, Doc moved on. "Now, the *ovikha-nar*."

Back when they were in space for long stretches, Geddy got pretty good at balancing while opening his heart to the sky. Oz did the variation in which one leg extended forward like a counterbalance as she bent backward, nearly far enough that her leg and her spine were both parallel to the ground. Geddy was happy with half that, which was twice what Denk could manage.

One by one, they moved through the eighteen forms. Each one was a tumbler clicking into place on a lock only you could open. If you did it right, you realigned yourself with the universe. He didn't know about all that. Luck hadn't exactly been on their side lately.

Though the movements were slow and not especially strenuous, they always worked up a good sweat. When they were done, they arranged themselves along the edge of the elevated utility area to cool down.

Geddy dabbed at his forehead with a towel and groaned, "Eli thinks I'm out of shape." His crew mumbled their assent.

"Oh," Oz teased. "Were we supposed to disagree?"

He gave a laugh. "Only when I'm wrong." A faint noise came from outside. At first, he thought it was music. "You guys hear that?"

"It sound like alarm," Voprot said.

To their right, Morph abruptly reappeared, rolling down the wall to the control panel. He opened the doors, and the blare of a general alarm invaded the hold.

"Attention all personnel," came Juan's voice over the P.A. "General quarters. Repeat, general quarters. This is not a drill."

They exchanged worried looks before springing to their feet. Everyone but Denk, anyway, who quite seriously asked, "Who's General Quarters?"

"It means report to your posts." Geddy looked at Oz. "Right?"

"Gold star for you, Colonel," she replied drolly.

Voprot, who had no official duties and nowhere to be, nonetheless bounded through the doors before they'd even opened all the way. Oz wasn't far behind, and the rest of them burst through just as the ramp touched down.

Geddy followed her out, turned left, and bolted toward the bridge. Oz was already halfway across the hangar.

When Geddy and the crew came running into the bridge, he expected his much younger clone to be in a panic, but he appeared perfectly calm as he turned around.

"Hello, Colonel," Juan said. "Good session?"

"Yeah, great. What's going on?" There was more urgency in Geddy's tone than there was in the room.

"A single ship jumped in front of us a few minutes ago."

"Why would you call general quarters for one ship?" he asked, drawing closer to the screen. He knew what he was looking at but couldn't bring himself to believe it. The question had just become rhetorical.

"It can't be," Oz muttered, drawing up beside him.

It was a Xellaran ship called a Rapier, arguably the most breathtaking design in the galaxy. Red, gold, and gunmetal gray, it featured a steeply raked upper fuselage that flared outward toward the stern and curled under to form the wings. It gave the impression of a giant, sinister-looking alien head.

Judging from the looks on the crew's faces, only Oz knew its significance. Rapiers were almost never seen because they were used exclusively by the mysterious cabal called the Samaja. Some thought they were a shadow government, others an ultra-secretive religious cult. Nobody really knew for sure — not even Oz.

"What is it?" Denk asked.

"A Xellaran Rapier," Oz replied. "Designed and built by the Samaja."

"The Samaja are real?" Jel asked.

"As real as a shadow."

"I've only seen photos of Rapiers," Geddy noted. "You?"

Oz had spent her early adulthood fighting with the Xellaran resistance. They opposed the government's autocratic efforts to create a fully cybernetic society. The Samaja clearly had power and influence but stayed above the fray, their agenda unknown.

"Once. It flew over our camp."

"It's as beautiful as they say," Doc observed.

Jel asked, "Yeah, but what the hell are they doing here?"

Juan squared up to Geddy. "They want to talk to you and the commander. Alone."

"Me?" Geddy asked. "Why?"

"I don't know, sir," Juan said.

Geddy stared at the Rapier for a few seconds, his mind racing to figure out what this could be about. He barely even knew any Xellarans. What would the Samaja want with him?

"Sound the all-clear," Geddy said. "And give me the room."

CHAPTER 16
STRANGER DANGER

Oz lingered until the rest of the crew had left with Juan Rodriguez. He already knew what she was going to say. She'd given some of her best years to fighting the Xellaran government. Without knowing what the Samaja wanted or what they stood for, she couldn't trust them.

"Oz, I know how you feel about this, but I need to see what they want."

She gently touched his arm. "I know you do. Just be wary."

"Yes, ma'am." He settled into the captain's chair and opened the comm once she'd left.

A young woman appeared on screen, flanked by two men whose faces were largely covered by golden veils. She was fair but not especially young, with wide, narrow eyes and a tiny mouth. Two vertical slits upon a slight bump served as a nose, and expertly painted yellow arches took the place of eyebrows. Her features, lovely though they were, reminded him of an Easter egg. But she didn't appear to have any cybernetic mods, which was exceedingly rare.

"Geddy Starheart," she intoned, her face expressionless. "I am Kyisa, daughter of the Samaja. I come in peace."

"That's a boring way to come."

She didn't react. "The Samaja-Netri, leader of our sect, wishes to meet with you."

"Well, unless this leader of yours can commit Xellara to the Alliance, we're not interested."

"Once you hear what he has to say, you will be."

"Why me? And how do you know my name?"

"You are host to a Sagacean," she said. "That makes you of great interest to us."

Rader. Oz's old Xellaran boyfriend, who he'd met at the IASS show. That was the only explanation. He sensed the harmonic in Geddy but mistook him for a fellow Zelnad at dinner. How that came back to the Samaja, he couldn't know.

"That doesn't explain what you want from me."

"All your questions will be answered when you accompany me back to Xellara."

"Lady, I only take orders from Commander Verveik, and I rarely follow those. I'm not going anywhere until you tell me what this is about."

The way she shifted uncomfortably in her seat suggested frustration. "You're studying a form of cosmic energy you don't understand, yes?"

Anxiety surged through him. No way the Xellarans could know that. Did they have a mole? Pretty much the whole fleet had the bubble drive now. Some enterprising pirate could jump back and forth to Xellara exchanging information for money and they'd be none the wiser. Then again, only Tymeri was privy to any of Doc and Lestiko's research, and he trusted her. Maybe that was a mistake.

"Go on."

"We can help you understand it."

"In exchange for what?" he asked warily.

"For our survival."

The entire crew of the *Stalwart* save for Denk, who was watching the bridge, gathered in the hangar to watch the breathtaking Xellaran ship land, which was roughly equivalent to seeing a leprechaun. Even Verveik, who had shuttled over from the *Gallant*, regarded it with awe. A number of the clones stationed on the *Stalwart* were there, too.

Xellara was sometimes referred to as the Cloaked World because, except for the tightly controlled and self-contained IASS show, it was poorly understood. Its endless factories churned out the vast majority of the galaxy's electrical components, weapons, and shield systems, meaning it did a lot of business with pretty much every other world. So it had been for millennia. And yet, its mysterious culture might as well have just burst into existence that morning.

Even for Geddy, who had dealings with a handful of Xellaran industrialists back in the Double A days, watching the sleek ship settle onto the landing pad called to mind *The Day The Earth Stood Still*. The iconic first-contact scene had played on a loop at the Old Earth Museum of Space Exploration. It had much that same feel, of seeing something that would change everything, one way or the other.

Beside him, Oz seethed. Fifteen years earlier, she would've shot the thing down and interrogated its occupants. Now, on little more than the vague promise of help, she had no choice but to watch him and Verveik board it.

"It's gonna be okay," he said.

Through gritted teeth, she said, "They've been in bed with the Zelnads since the beginning. Just like my father."

"We don't know that for sure."

"The Samaja are a cult," she replied. "We need weapons, not religion."

— *Hallelujah to that.*

— Yeah, but there's something to this. Call it a gut feeling.

— *And what a gut it is.*

Geddy asked Lestiko to join them, and he eagerly accepted. The science of original energy was of far less interest to him than how it connected him to Rai and Geddy to Eli. Verveik was loath to leave the fleet, but Doc and the Orneans were still busy studying the Zelnad sphere, and he agreed that an offer of help from the Samaja was worth hearing.

The ship settled onto the forward landing pad and powered down. The doors had already closed by then, and overhead vents quickly refilled the hangar with air. Once it stopped, the faint orange scrim of the pressure shield dissipated. The ship's ramp unrolled like a tongue as metal slats self-assembled before their eyes.

— *Okay, that's pretty cool.*

— Don't be too dazzled. I need you on high alert.

— *There's no other way to be with you.*

— Detect anything? For all we know, these could be Nads and that ship could be a bomb.

— *Not yet.*

Kyisa, daughter of the Samaja, descended the ramp like a ghost, her hands and feet obscured by the elegant folds of her golden robes. Flanked by the two guards, who carried no weapons, she glided toward Geddy as though on a moving sidewalk, pulling up a couple of meters in front of him.

She paused to survey the assembled gawkers but didn't appear troubled by their presence.

With a graceful nod, she said, "Thank you for welcoming us aboard. And you, Commander, for agreeing to join us. The Samaja-Netri will be very pleased."

"Let's not get ahead of ourselves," Verveik said gruffly. "Say what you came to say."

— Still nothing?

— *No. They're not Zelnads.*

Her eggy face pinched in confusion. "I do not understand."

"Then maybe you'll understand this," Verveik said. "I don't trust you. You're asking us to come to Xellara, but we don't even know who you are. And if this leader of yours is so intent on meeting with us, why not come himself?"

"My humble apologies, Commander." She gave a polite bow. "I am Kyisa, daughter of the Samaja and scion of the First Followers."

"That's a lot to fit on a business card," Geddy noted.

"The energy you are studying cannot be understood through science alone. But together, we may be able to unlock its secrets. Our very existence depends on it."

"Then join the Alliance and fight with us!" Oz demanded.

"The government and the Samaja are separated by an ideological divide. We have no influence on policy."

"Then you're just as useless to us as they are," Oz muttered under her breath. Kyisa's eyes lingered on her, but she didn't react.

Murmurs traveled through the crew followed by the tight-lipped shaking of heads. The hope that Xellara had a change of heart faded with her words.

Seeing the doubt on everyone's faces, Geddy stepped forward and turned to face the assembled crowd. "We've all seen what the Nads are capable of. Unless we master original energy, and fast, we're all fucked."

"Unfortunately, he's right," Verveik boomed, his authoritative voice reverberating across the hangar. "We're out of time. If there's even a chance the Samaja can help us, we can't afford to ignore it."

Though the doubtful looks persisted, the murmurs tapered to nothing.

Kyisa pivoted on one of her hidden feet and gestured toward the ship. "I am glad to hear you say that, Commander. Shall we?"

While Verveik and Lestiko began walking, Geddy returned to Oz, whose arms were crossed tightly. Her ropy hair had turned a dull maroon. He placed his hands on her shoulders and looked deep into her fathomless eyes.

"Are you gonna be okay?"

"It's not me you should be worried about."

He regarded the blob on his shoulder. "Morph, hang back and keep her company." Morpho dutifully hopped from his left shoulder onto her right one. "We have to do this. I feel it in my bones."

"I really hope you're right."

He planted a firm kiss on her cheek and brushed it with his fingers as he turned to leave.

CHAPTER 17
WELCOME TO THE TEMPLE

Even before the Rapier popped into space over Xellara, Geddy wondered if he hadn't made a grievous mistake. Any trust in the Xellarans was fundamentally blind. But his gut told him Kyisa was on the level. Verveik obviously agreed or he wouldn't be here. Lestiko would give anything to unlock the secrets of original energy so trust wasn't an issue for him. Anyway, they were pretty well committed now.

Xellara had only become habitable through centuries of atmospheric processing. It was the same way they'd turned Myadan, home of the infamous Xeno Xoo, into a tourist destination. The massive processors, now dormant, still dotted the whole planet and were clearly visible from space. It was the galaxy's first spacefaring world by at least a century, and until the Nads came along, the most technologically advanced by far.

No one knew exactly how Xellara had progressed so much faster than the rest of the galaxy. Their deeply insular society was a cipher, the IASS show pure theater. As far as Geddy could tell, all their manufacturing riches merely got converted into more factories. They'd bloomed outward from each of the Seven Cities, the planet's industrial centers, like bacteria in agar and showed no signs of stopping.

"It's been a long time since you visited Xellara, Commander," Kyisa said over her shoulder as they descended. The same two masked guards that had accompanied her onboard the *Stalwart* were at the controls, though the ship seemed largely autonomous.

"Ninety years, give or take," Verveik confirmed.

She got a faraway look in her eyes, the closest thing to a meaningful expression Geddy had seen her make. "For what it's worth, you have always had the Samaja's respect."

"But not its support."

"As I explained, matters of state are—"

"Not your concern. Yes, I know." Verveik cut her off. "Then what is?"

"More important things," she cryptically replied.

— *What's that supposed to mean?*

— *Sex, I'm guessing?*

In anticipation of the usual vibrations, Geddy's grip tightened on the armrests of his sumptuously padded chair. But even as wispy clouds zipped past on the ship's screen, he barely felt anything.

"Impressive dampening," he said to no one in particular.

Kyisa's attention shifted to Lestiko as the ship smoothly entered the atmosphere. "You have me at a disadvantage, Mr. Lestiko. We know very little about you."

"That's the whole point of being a recluse," he responded. "As you know."

She almost seemed amused. "Indeed."

As the ship broke through the clouds, Xellara's bleak industrial landscape opened up before them. Seven megacities, of which Donglan was the largest, covered roughly half of the reddish-brown surface. They were each arranged around colossal manmade lakes not unlike Laguna on Earth 2, formed by drilling into deep aquifers. The sun glinted off their surface in much the same way as it did the unbroken sprawl of factories surrounding them, so much so that it was hard to tell where the water ended and they began.

The northernmost city, Churuma, was strangely flat on the east side where it butted up against a range of rugged mountains. A gradient of snow developed shortly thereafter, growing whiter as it neared the pole. The galaxy's highest peaks by far were found in the frozen North, hundreds of which exceeded fifteen thousand meters.

Their approach vector suggested they'd be landing in Churuma, but then the ship leveled out and headed toward the mountains.

"I didn't exactly dress for cold weather," Geddy noted.

"Do not worry, Colonel, we will not be outside."

As the ship made its final approach, the destination became clear — a symmetrical crater on the side of a colossal mountain.

"I didn't know anything was up here," Geddy said.

Kyisa said, "The Samaja live in isolation."

A narrow horizontal door slid open in the snow near the bottom of the bowl-shaped depression. The ship dropped even with it and glided silently inside. It took a few seconds for his eyes to adjust to the light, but the dark interior soon resolved into a smooth-walled cave, like a giant bubble that had formed within cooling magma. Half a dozen Rapiers were parked in a perfectly spaced row on the left. Otherwise, it was utterly empty and plain.

The ship alighted so softly onto the pad that Geddy didn't even know it happened until the two mute pilots powered down.

"Wow. Like a butterfly landing on a marshmallow."

The ramp lowered automatically, and cool, dry air wafted

inside. Kyisa calmly got up and gestured toward it. "Please follow me."

They followed her down. "What kind of place is this?" Verveik asked.

"It is called Mahalaya, the Samaja temple." Kyisa's flat voice bounced off the smooth ceilings as she again glided across the polished floor.

"Love the decor," Geddy observed, earning a glare from Verveik.

"We have no need for extravagance." After a short walk, they approached a guard posted by an arched doorway and a small table. "Your weapons, please."

Verveik customarily wore a Ring War-era Alliance blaster pistol but hadn't brought it. Lestiko was unarmed as well, so they all watched Geddy draw the long-barreled PDQ from its holster and reluctantly hand it to the guard.

"I feel naked without it," he offered.

— *I've seen you naked with it. Many times, in fact.*

— Yeah, but it brought us closer.

— *How's that?*

— I mean me and the gun.

"This way," Kyisa said, gesturing at the door.

She disappeared through it as the guard set Geddy's pistol on the table.

A short distance in, they arrived at a landing beside a wide cylindrical void with a domed ceiling. A set of steps spiraled down around the outside of it. Kyisa began downward, and they followed. They couldn't even see the bottom. As they descended, they passed an ornate drawing carved into the smooth stone wall using only vertical, V-shaped grooves.

"The Illustrations depict major events foretold by the Asurya," Kyisa said.

"Asurya?" Geddy asked.

"An ancient prophet," she explained. "The Samaja-Netri will explain."

The first carving showed a beautiful planet surrounded by an asteroid belt. Incredibly, the images seemed to shift and animate as they passed. A deep crack formed in the planet's surface.

"They're lenticular," Lestiko said, clearly delighted.

Kyisa said, "Each one is carved by hand, decades or even centuries before the event occurs. They are the cornerstones of our faith."

Indeed, as they descended, each new carving highlighted a particular event. The majority exceeded his knowledge of galactic history. One depicted the signing of the Zihnia Accords, an early peace agreement. Another, the Scouring of Vyeph. On and on they went, hundreds of them, unfolding in brief, but elegant animations. A faint tapping sound met their ears, growing louder as they descended. Near the bottom, Verveik paused before the penultimate drawing while Kyisa waited patiently. Beside her, an old woman whose robes nearly matched the pale gray marble gave tiny taps on a tiny chisel on the last available space, seemingly oblivious to their presence.

Geddy and Lestiko caught up to Verveik. The Illustration depicted three great armies united against a fourth, all within the boundaries of a celestial body instantly recognizable as the Exiod Ring.

The Ring War.

"Please, Commander," Kyisa said softly. The Samaja-Netri awaits." She gestured toward another arched door across the floor from the steps. Geddy peered upward. The top was just a dot.

Kyisa said, "No outsider has ever been beyond this point."

She paused a moment as though waiting for them to react. When they didn't, she stood to the side of the door.

"This is when we find out the only bathrooms are

upstairs," Geddy whispered to Lestiko, the comment resounding much louder than he intended.

The old woman carver, who was standing on a small stool, gave her chisel another couple of taps. She was stooped, her back curved as though she'd spent her whole life bent over her work. Maybe she had. So far, only the upper left corner of the image was complete. It didn't look like much of anything. The partial arc of another planet, maybe.

She cast a brief glance in his direction as though trying to decide whether they were real before returning wordlessly to her labors.

Kyisa lowered her head and pushed the door open.

"Welcome to the Sanctum."

CHAPTER 18

ARE YOU ASURYA?

They entered a pitch-black and seemingly boundless chamber. So unsettling was the effect that Geddy glanced at his feet to ensure something was still under them. The surface was solid, but it was impossible to tell what it was. Stone? Concrete? Before they could get their bearings, the door closed behind them, and the silence was total.

"Now what?" His voice was swallowed like he'd only said it in his head.

— *Geddy, I feel very strange here.*

— How so?

— *There is another entity.*

— Zelnad?

— *I'm not sure.*

A dim purple light about the size of a basketball grew out of the darkness, illuminating their mysterious host but little else. Though he couldn't be certain, he judged the person to be male, though he looked for all the world like a ghost. Like Kyisa, he wore pale robes, so nearly the color of his skin that they bled together. The light touched nothing else.

"Are you the Samaja-Netri?" Verveik's voice sounded uneasy.

This was all too mysterious for his taste, and the boundless room ironically triggered Geddy's claustrophobia. Nervous sweat trickled down the small of his back.

"Yes, Commander, but you may call me Ziksu."

"What the hell is this place?"

"We call it Sanctum, the heart of the temple."

Ziksu approached, and the ethereal light followed him, but it cast no shadows, making Geddy wonder if it was even light at all. The laws of physics seemed malleable here.

"Why did you want to meet with us?" Geddy asked.

"All in good time, Colonel Starheart. The energy you are studying is well-known to us. We call it mahk'ti."

"We call it original energy. I still think it sounds like a sports drink, but that's what the Nads call it, too."

He stroked his chin. "Interesting ... but not inaccurate."

"Kyisa said you understand it," Lestiko said. "Where it comes from? How it works?"

"To the extent it can be understood."

He made a sweeping motion with his hand, and a half-dome of light appeared around them. It continued beneath them as though they were suspended in a bubble. Either that or the floor was some kind of mirror. Particles like microscopic fireflies lit up in the air and gathered into an image, not unlike the star map in the research ship.

The place was unrecognizable, a featureless plain dotted with jagged hills. A string of smoky columns on the horizon suggested volcanoes. It could've been Geddy's imagination, but he thought he caught a whiff of sulfur. Smell-o-vision, maybe?

"Are you familiar with predeterminism, Commander Verveik?" Ziksu asked.

"If you mean fate, then sure," he grumbled. "But I don't believe in it."

He wagged his finger at Verveik. "Ah, now fate is not the same. A chemical reaction doesn't occur because it's fated. Certain conditions produce an inevitable result. The formation of a planet, for example. Gravity. Friction. Matter. Pressure. All working together, or at odds, to create or destroy in ways that are chaotic yet predictable. To a point, at least."

The scene fast-forwarded through time. Volcanoes cooled into mountains. The ground cracked and heaved, and escaping steam turned to clouds. Then came rains, and lakes, and oceans. Thousands of years sped past in a second.

Strange creatures began to crawl out of the water. Fins and tentacles became legs, and a few seconds later, they were standing upright and building villages and cities. Here, the simulation slowed.

"Civilizations change slowly, then all at once," Ziksu declared. "These leaps forward seem to come from another place. Some call it genius. Others, proof of the divine." He locked eyes with Geddy and spoke to him without moving his mouth. *A rare few know the truth.*

— *Ooh, you've got this one!*

— *Sagaceans.*

Their host smiled, having heard the thought. "Like your Old Earth, Xellara once exploited its natural resources for energy. It would've suffered the same fate were it not for a remarkable gift. A seemingly boundless source of power."

Ziksu moved in behind it, and the three of them drew closer in spite of themselves. The orb boiled and roiled as though a storm was taking place within it, yet there was no discernible container.

"You're looking at a thirty-thousand-year-old generator," he said, indicating the strange orb.

"A gift from who?" Lestiko asked, raising his eyes. "Or what?"

"An ancient being known as the Asurya, who our sect once worshipped."

"Host to a Sagacean, I'll bet," Geddy said, weirdly certain of it.

"Yes, and an extraordinary one," Ziksu confirmed. "To our ancient ancestors, he was a god. There could be no other explanation for the knowledge he possessed. "His disciples soon numbered in the thousands."

— How come I'm not anyone's god?
— *Gods don't chew with their mouth open.*
— I do that?
— *Please.*

"What knowledge?" Verveik inquired.

"The future. Not as a vision or a prophecy, but a frighteningly accurate extrapolation based on variables only he could discern."

The orb rose, seemingly under its own power. As it did, threads of bright purple snaked out from it, connecting to unseen points in the velvety darkness like electricity arcing across a gap.

Lestiko's eyes widened at the sight. "This isn't ... it can't be tukrium oxide."

Their host cocked an eyebrow, impressed. "Very astute, Mr. Lestiko. Yes, tens of thousands of years of exposure to mahk'ti has caused the room's walls to oxidize. Unfortunately, its power is nearly spent."

A new translucent scene opened around them. It depicted a man in very similar robes as Ziksu sitting atop an unadorned throne, surrounded by concentric circles of followers dressed much like him, listening intently.

"The future the Asurya predicted for Xellara was bleak. He

convinced his followers that they could change it by connecting to the power hidden within themselves."

"Hidden power ..." Lestiko mused. "You can't mean ...?"

"The entities already inside them," said Ziksu. While the three of them exchanged dumbfounded looks, he continued. "You see, Sagaceans ride waves of Mahk'ti throughout the universe. When it is drawn into living things, so are they."

Only then did any of them notice that the threads of energy emanating from the orb had very slowly coalesced into four bundles that flowed right into them and continued through. It didn't feel like anything at all.

Verveik's face contorted in confusion and disbelief as he took big steps to either side. The bundle followed. The fiercely independent and private old warrior had no idea what was happening.

But they weren't simply connected to the orb. Through it, they were linked to each other. Eli had told Geddy as much when he was floating over Kigantu in the Morpho-bubble at the brink of death. *We are all connected.* It seemed like woo-woo bullshit at the time, but everything was different now, including him.

"Since the dawn of time, Sagaceans believed their purpose was to observe life through our eyes, learn all they could, and move on when their host died. Sometimes, they would provide a spark of insight that moved civilization forward. But generally, they remained passengers. As far as we know, the Asurya was the first Sagacean to seize control."

Lestiko's eyes glittered with curiosity in the purple light. "Why?"

Ziksu held his hands open. "Imagine an immortal being as old as the universe itself, carrying the accumulated knowledge of all its past hosts while watching the same destructive patterns play out over and over."

— *Yeah, just imagine.*

— Right?

"The Samaja believe the Asurya intervened to disrupt these patterns. He taught his followers how to open a channel, so to speak, to their entities and avail themselves of their knowledge."

"And it worked?" Lestiko asked.

"Oh, yes. They soon developed ways to journey into the stars and conquer disease. They even learned how to harness mahk'ti for energy. But some were corrupted by their newfound power, believing it should be used to hold dominion over lesser worlds. It broke the Asurya's heart to realize this truth."

"So what did he do?" Geddy asked.

"He gathered the faithful into his chamber and offered even more power to anyone who wanted it. But it was a test. Those who rejected the offer and fled became the Samaja. The rest were tricked into separating from their entities all at once. The concave depression you saw from the air is the scar of that event. We call it the Virikta."

The display animated to show the large room full of acolytes in a sort of trance, then exploding as one. It went fully white, and then the particles fell like glowing flakes of snow, dissipating before they reached the floor.

"I can't imagine the force ..." muttered Lestiko.

Geddy took notice of this on the way in, wondering how it could've formed. A colossal explosion would've done it. Given the size of the blast from just one of Lestiko's failed experiments, it indeed boggled the mind.

"The Samaja of today are the last living descendants of the Asurya's original followers."

"So what happened to the Asurya?" Geddy asked.

Ziksu seemed pleased by the question. "The answer to that is the First Illustration. And your purpose here is answered by the Last."

CHAPTER 19
ORIGIN STORY

Ziksu summoned a new simulation. The scene that took shape around them this time was a lush, shiny blue and green world. A goldilocks planet like Old Earth or Temeruria, only somehow even more lovely. Twin suns, one nearly white and the other the creamy orange of a dying star made the vast oceans and river deltas sparkle like diamonds.

Geddy didn't recognize it. By the looks on Lestiko and Verveik's faces, they didn't either.

"You're looking at the First Illustration. Before he left our world, the Asurya presented the Samaja with a gift — this orb, which had captured most of the mahk'ti energy released by the Virikta. If it hadn't, the destruction would've been far greater.

"This single orb has powered the temple for millennia. Through the Illustrations, it has continued to reveal the future the Asurya predicted. A future many believe is assured."

"Why show the future if you can't change it?" Geddy asked. "What's the point?"

"That's *exactly* the point. Not even a civilization that knew its future and had the knowledge to avoid it could get out of its own way."

Lestiko nodded at the image surrounding them. "So what're we looking at here, exactly?"

The animated scene unfolded as Ziksu talked, revealing what the orb had shown them long ago.

"It depicts a temperate world at the outer edge of our galaxy that was home to an early civilization. The Asurya was drawn to it. He soon discovered the planet was rich in a type of metal that had entrapped many Sagaceans during its formation. The same metal used to forge the orb."

"Shinium," Geddy said, failing to imagine how it could be formed into such a perfect sphere so long ago.

"Yes. We once believed it comprised all the shinium in the galaxy."

"So what did the Asurya do?" Lestiko asked, held rapt by Ziksu's story.

"He desired to free his kindred from their prison but knew that only the power of Sagacea could do that. Most of it was buried deep in the planet's mantle — far too deep to reach. So, he used mahk'ti to contact the planet's entities. He convinced them that it was time to return all Sagaceans to their home world, including the ones trapped in shinium. That could only happen if they seized control of their hosts."

The animation sped up as the globe spun its way through centuries, becoming duller as it went. The white clouds had caramelized into a sickly yellow. Green lands darkened with the rusty bloom of industry.

"And so they did. Soon, this previously primitive world developed the technology to extract shinium. But drills could only go so deep. To reach the rest required more drastic measures."

The dread that had crept into Geddy's stomach spread its tentacles throughout his body. He already knew what planet this was but couldn't quite summon its name to his lips. It was ripped apart at the seams, the still-glowing core of its hemispheres crumbling as the gravity between them tore shinium-rich hunks of it away.

Verveik beat Geddy to it. "Elenia."

Ziksu nodded. "Its destruction set in motion the Asurya's plan to return Sagaceans home. In so doing, the universe would be born anew."

Dozens of deep-space mining ships shot into view through vagina-shaped purple holes. He didn't recognize the design. They immediately went to work on the chunks of the ruined planet, extracting its bounty of shinium.

Months earlier, Geddy and Doc had observed Elenia's ruined husk from the *Fiz*. Doc shared a theory that the ramrod-straight radial striations visible from space were from drills and that Elenia was plundered of all its tukrium by Zelnads. This meant he was almost exactly right.

"He began accumulating followers throughout our galaxy, calling to Sagaceans to take control of their hosts and join his movement. They referred to it using the ancient Elenian word for 'reset.'"

"Zelnad," Lestiko muttered. "My stars, I never imagined …"

"Where's the Asurya now?" Geddy asked.

"Your guess is as good as mine, Colonel."

"What about the Last Illustration?" Lestiko asked.

Another wave of his hand, and the surrounding display changed yet again to a massive space battle. At the center was a small, blinding white star and a swarm of ships — millions by the looks of it — engaged in ship-to-ship combat.

"What battle is this?" Verveik inquired, his brow furrowing as he struggled to recognize it.

"The Battle of Sagacea," Geddy said. "The one we've yet to fight."

"We call it the Last War."

"Who wins?" Lestiko asked.

"Now that, Mr. Lestiko, is the very question that caused a schism among the Samaja. Almost from the moment the orb revealed it, in fact."

"Schism?" Verveik asked.

"A split, if you will. Most saw a battle that couldn't be won. They took it as a sign that Xellara can survive Sagacea's destruction if it avoids the war and fully transitions to ... inorganic life. That portion of our sect became what you know as the government."

"The mods ..." Geddy muttered. The vast majority of Xellarans were modded out with sometimes grotesque cybernetic enhancements — more each time he visited. He'd always assumed it was to enhance their productivity. Apparently, it was for survival.

"But Xellara won't survive," Lestiko said. "Sagacea's end will be all of ours."

"I agree," Ziksu said. "Which is why we must keep that from happening."

"You said every Illustration has come to pass," Verveik said. "Have any others been open to interpretation?"

"No," replied Ziksu. "But that's religion for you."

"So what's different about this one?" Geddy asked.

"To us, it suggests that not even the Asurya could see beyond the fog of war."

This landed with Verveik, who had personally fought in more skirmishes, battles, and wars than Geddy could name.

"So how do we win?" asked the old man.

"By uniting the galaxy. Anything less, and defeat is assured."

Verveik's aspect darkened, and he regarded Geddy with something between shame and hopelessness. Bringing the galaxy's armies under the Alliance banner was exactly what he'd been trying to do all this time. But that was only possible if Xellara and Temeruria joined the fight.

"Then you know we can't win without Xellara," Verveik said.

Ziksu shook his head sadly. "No. Which brings us to the purpose of your visit. For centuries, Samaja probes have searched for high concentrations of mahk'ti in hopes of finding Sagacea. Recently, they led us to both the Karrea Ion Cloud and Basoa. It stood to reason that you were studying it to match the Zelnads' tech, which you wouldn't be doing unless you were preparing for war."

"So where does that leave us?" Verveik asked, glancing at Lestiko.

"You can't build weapons unless you know how to capture and store mahk'ti. Over the centuries, the orb has shown us how. And, as it happens, Xellara is only good at manufacturing because the Samaja developed the processes."

All three of them could complete the puzzle now. They needed Xellara and vice-versa.

Verveik squinted at Ziksu. "What good is an accord without all of Xellara behind it? That's half the galaxy's warships at least."

"More than half," Ziksu affirmed. "Eight hundred thousand ships, give or take."

Judging from the look on Verveik's face, even he had no idea Xellara's fleet was that big. Together with what they already had, it was more than a million ships.

"How can your government reject galactic unity while standing in its way?" he asked.

"How can you still believe governments act logically?"

Verveik had no rejoinder for that.

"They're too busy turning everyone into robots," Geddy said.

"In their minds, they have no choice."

"We must go on without them," Lestiko asserted. "Tactical parity is our highest priority."

"I agree." Geddy looked to Verveik. "You got shot with the same guns as I did. We need to level the playing field. That's true regardless of who fights with us."

Verveik's jaw worked back and forth for a moment while he turned this over in his head. His gaze returned to Ziksu. "What happens if the government finds out you're helping us wage war?"

He waved his hand and a fresh set of glowing particles assembled before them. This new scene depicted a dead, craggy moon in the middle of nowhere. Tucked deep into the shadow of a sharp-edged crater was a large facility.

"This facility is on one of Xellara's most remote moons, Mikuli. The government has no idea it exists. It was built to answer our most important question — how to produce and store more mahk'ti."

Lestiko drew closer to it, bringing his hands as close as he dared. With no heat coming off it, it seemed almost inert. "And have you answered it?"

He managed a grin. "I'd be delighted to show you."

CHAPTER 20
POWER-UPS

Much to Geddy's dismay, the only way back to the hangar was a long, sweaty slog up the endlessly spiraling stairs, again past the dozens of semi-animated Illustrations. Now, he understood that they were stepping stones on the path between the Asurya's final, desperate intervention on Xellara and the end of all things. Seeing them in reverse, it was quite plain how one event led, directly or indirectly, to the next.

Neither they nor Ziksu spoke as they climbed. Geddy's soaring heart rate was at least as much to blame as the weight of the Temeruria problem. The fact that the Samaja were willing to help the Alliance was a positive development. Now they just needed to convince the Xellaran government that they got the Final Illustration all wrong. But the truth was, not even Ziksu could know for certain that they were.

Upon reaching the hangar level, they boarded the gorgeous Rapier and rocketed into space. From his plush seat, Geddy couldn't quite see the coordinates entered by the two pilots. When they jumped, they came in close enough to the distant

Xellaran moon — one of at least twenty-something in orbit around the planet — that it nearly filled the ship's screen.

"Welcome to Mikuli," Ziksu said.

The secret Samaja facility looked exactly as it had from the hologram inside the Sanctum. No exterior lights betrayed its existence. Buildings were the same dull gray as the surface, making its scale impossible to discern in the shadow of the crater. If he didn't know it was there, he never would've seen it.

"The facility is oriented along the moon's south pole, which runs perpendicular to Xellara and is perpetually in darkness."

"You can make more mahk'ti orbs here?" Lestiko asked.

"Yes, however, the tukrium we need is, suffice it to say, in short supply."

"Tukrium," Verveik muttered. "It's always about tukrium."

Ziksu's face pinched distastefully. "Unfortunately, it's the only material suitable to store the energy."

Verveik asked, "Where do you think it's gonna come from?"

Beneath the surface of the situation on Temeruria lurked two truths — each as cold as the void.

The first of these was that Temeruria boasted vast deposits of tukrium. The Nads needed unrefined tukrium in order to extract the far-rarer shinium they needed to get their weapon past the barrier. They wouldn't have left if it was still there to find, but if anyone would have squirreled a bunch of it away, it was Prince Bransel.

The second, more troubling fact of the matter was that the Nads appeared ready to crack the whole fucking planet in half to get to the rest. Prior to seeing the First Illustration, Geddy couldn't have imagined such a thing could happen now.

— *You have to tell him.*
— *I will.*
— *Now.*

"Sir, can I have a word?" Geddy asked, his eyes darting over to Ziksu's. "In private?"

The Samaja-Netri got up and led them around the corner behind the bridge, where he opened the door to an unpretentious study. Verveik had to crouch low to pass through it.

"Will this suffice?" he asked. "We'll be landing in moments."

Geddy smiled pleasantly. "We won't be long."

Ziksu softly closed the door and Verveik's face hardened. "What now?"

"There may be a way to solve our tukrium problem," Geddy blurted. Might as well cut to the chase.

Verveik's eyes narrowed. "What are you talking about?"

He related what Oz had heard from her father about the abrupt departure of the Zelnads from Temeruria and the strange circumstances that prompted him to reach out.

"How long ago did Bransel contact her?"

"Shortly before we left for Kigantu. She was conflicted what to do about it."

His big, stubby fingers rubbed his closed eyes. "Good. Let that insufferable prick sweat it out."

"That was my first impulse as well, but after seeing the First Illustration, I believe they're about to do to Temeruria what they did to Elenia."

It took Verveik a moment, but he appeared to connect the dots. "You think that's what these boreholes are for?"

"I'm certain of it." Geddy leaned in, his eyes intense as they locked on Verveik's.

The weight of this settled onto the big man, and he scratched his chin. "Partnering with Ziksu is one thing, but now we're supposed to come to *Prince Bransel's* rescue?" The way his lips curled around Bransel's name underscored his contempt.

"Let's find out what Ziksu has to say. But we're gonna need tukrium either way, and Temeruria's got it."

"How are we supposed to get to it if the Zelnads can't?"

"Bransel would make damn sure he was taken care of if things went south. There's a stockpile there, I can almost guarantee it."

"Even if that's true, he's not going to give it to us."

"He might … if it was a condition of the Alliance's help."

Verveik gave him a sideways look. "You're serious."

"If the Samaja are right about the Last Illustration, we need command of every warship in the galaxy. That includes the Star Guard."

"He'd never agree to that."

"He's out of options. If he waits too long, the planet's either gonna become uninhabitable, or …" He didn't have to say the rest.

"What are you suggesting?"

"We've got him by the balls. Let's work up some terms we can live with, then go to him. The tukrium we need will magically appear. We get the tukrium and the Star Guard, he gets to save face, and the Alliance takes credit for saving Temeruria. Win-win-win."

There came a rap at the door, and it opened for Ziksu. "Gentlemen, we're about to land."

"Very well," Verveik said, casting a final look at Geddy as he rose. "Let's see this secret facility of yours."

CHAPTER 21

MAHK'TI FOR TWO

The secret facility's hangar door was covered in the same dull gray rock that surrounded it, the seams invisible until it slid aside. The Rapier eased in, revealing a cavernous space at least five times the size of the hangar in the temple. Only a handful of small transports were parked inside.

"What would the government do if they knew this was here?" Geddy asked Ziksu.

"Our uneasy truce would end. The Samaja would be rooted out. We'd be modded beyond recognition and forced into the factories."

The ramp lowered, and Ziksu rose. The three of them followed.

"How did you even build such a place in secret?" Lestiko wondered.

"We're on the main shipping route to Myadan, and Samaja fly most of the cargo ships. They deliver supplies while the moon is between them and Xellara. They can't possibly detect us."

Geddy chuckled to himself as he scanned the hangar. "Got any wood we can knock on?"

Two guards stood to either side of a vault-like door. It took both of them to unlock and open it as they approached. A short, dimly lit corridor curved to the left.

"As I explained, mahk'ti can be stored in tukrium spheres. Solving that little problem was one thing, but harvesting the energy itself has proven even more difficult."

The passageway, which was just barely high enough to accommodate Verveik, straightened out, and another door slid open to reveal a state-of-the-art laboratory. Three rows of maybe twenty Xellarans each, presumably members of Ziksu's sect, were seated at long tables. Each held shiny metal spheres the size of tennis balls in their fingers, their eyes closed in deep concentration.

"These are volunteers from among the Samaja," Ziksu said. "They are learning how to donate their mahk'ti to the orbs."

"Donate?" Lestiko asked, incredulous. "But the energy is held in the entity bond. It can't be released that easily."

Ziksu pulled back, looking sidelong at him. "Ah ... you *are* him. The Basoan who claimed to help people take control of their entities. Only they never returned."

Lestiko raised a cautioning finger. "I *did* help them. The Process wasn't always successful."

— *That's a bit of an understatement.*

He glared at Geddy.

— *What? I didn't say it.*

"We're well aware of your experiments, Mr. Lestiko. Our probes picked up multiple, massive spikes of mahk'ti from Basoa but obviously, we couldn't investigate."

Basoa was known for engineering and design. They'd long accused Xellara of stealing their intellectual property, but the Intergalactic Justice Commission never found sufficient evidence. Ever since, they implemented draconian policies regarding visitors. There was no love lost between the two worlds.

"It's not possible," Lestiko asserted, tears forming at the bottom of his frog-like eyes. The shame of his many failures clung to him like smoke to leather. "If it was, I would've found a way."

Ziksu gave him a sympathetic look. "The bedrock of science is evidence, yes?" Lestiko allowed a hesitant nod. "Come with me." He led them down a few steps onto the main floor, strolling down the first row of Samaja volunteers as he continued. "As I mentioned earlier, the force of the Virikta should have destroyed Xellara, but it didn't. The vast majority of its energy was captured by the orb."

"How?" Lestiko asked.

"That's the very question we've been trying to answer for a very long time. The Samaja have always known that mahk'ti was drawn to living things. But it's also drawn to tukrium. In fact, in its molten form, it oscillates at nearly the same frequency as the energy itself."

So deep in concentration were the volunteers that they barely noticed Ziksu. Again, there wasn't a cybernetic mod among them.

"Which means shinium doesn't form by chance," Geddy said excitedly. "Molten tukrium is a Sagacean magnet."

"Exactly right, Geddy." Ziksu seemed both pleased and surprised by the observation. "But obviously, the orb isn't molten. It clearly had other properties we didn't understand. When tukrium's crystalline structure is oriented a certain way and formed into a hollow sphere, it easily draws the energy inside."

Geddy, Verveik, and Lestiko seemed to realize at the same time that the Zelnad base likely worked according to the same principle.

Lestiko asked, "Why the different sizes of spheres?"

"You were correct when you said mahk'ti is held in the entity bond," Ziksu admitted. "You're also correct that the host controls that bond. Through practice, one can learn to siphon a small amount into a sphere." He nodded toward the last row, where he now led them.

Ziksu opened an oblong box sitting at the end of the long table. Inside were three highly polished spheres matching those they'd seen. He handed one to Verveik. In his giant hand, it looked closer to a ball bearing.

Verveik hefted it. "It's light."

"And yet, its capacity is astonishing."

Ziksu gave another sphere to Lestiko, who brought it close to his face in order to study its flawless surface. "What happens when it runs out?"

"In theory, it could be 'recharged' in perpetuity."

"By whom?" Lestiko asked.

"By anyone willing and able to learn how."

"But the Samaja already understand mahk'ti," Lestiko protested. "How can you expect the average person to do this?"

"Let's put it to a test." He turned back to Verveik. "Commander, would you care to try?"

Verveik frowned as though he should be the last person to attempt such a thing. Geddy could tell he'd been swayed by what he learned in the Sanctum but was still skeptical. The big man dealt only in the concrete.

"You can't be serious."

"I suspect that only a demonstration will convince you."

The commander's dark eyes swiveled doubtfully between Geddy and Lestiko before returning to Ziksu's.

"All right. Show me."

Pleased by his willingness to try, Ziksu squared up to him. "Hold it in your fingertips. Good. Now close your eyes." Following a final quick glance at Geddy, he did.

"Now, do you accept that mahk'ti flows throughout the universe?"

"Yes."

"And that it flows through you?"

"I suppose," Verveik replied.

"Good. Now focus on the sphere's emptiness. Like a hole yearning to be filled."

— *Geddy ...*

— *It's okay. I'm learning self-restraint.*

— *Since when??*

"Okay," Verveik muttered.

"The very thing that sphere needs is the power you hold deep within you. Some part of you has always known it was there, but you couldn't quite reach it . Even now, it connects you, Otaro Verveik, to the birth of the universe."

An odd calm fell over the commander, his usual scowl relaxing into something more neutral. Peaceful, even.

"All right."

"What do you feel?" Ziksu asked.

"Warmth," the commander replied.

"Where?"

"Behind my eyes."

Again, Ziksu smiled in a way that suggested this was the correct answer. "Excellent. Now gently guide it down your arms and into your fingertips. Imagine it feeding the sphere. Nourishing it. Sating its hunger."

"My stars ..." Lestiko whispered.

Geddy saw it, too. A faint purple light had collected in the old man's fingers where they held the sphere. It drank the energy inside like a sponge.

"You're a natural, Commander," Ziksu said softly. "Now maintain that concentration as you slowly open your eyes."

He did, and they instantly widened in shock at what he saw. Brilliant purple energy still passed through his fingertips and into the sphere — and with it, every cherished paradigm he held about the world.

"Is this a trick?" he asked, still fishing for the concrete.

"No tricks." Ziksu gently took the sphere from Verveik, then returned it to its box and picked it up. "This way."

They continued across the room and into another, much larger one. It was a manufacturing facility, its ceiling-high machines and robotic arms presently dormant. Only a couple of lights were on, suggesting it wasn't in use. Neatly organized bundles of cable gathered above the machines and crisscrossed the ceiling, ending at the top of a triangular device along the near wall. It suggested a power source, though it seemed too small for that. Some kind of step-down converter, maybe?

Ziksu approached it with Geddy and Lestiko right behind him. Verveik shuffled along after them, still in a mild state of shock over what just happened.

"Triangular shapes direct the energy toward the points," Ziksu explained. "In both cases, the manufacturing tolerances must be incredibly precise."

At the center of the triangle was a small concave recess. Geddy gasped. "The Zelnad fighters ... this is what they look like. Most of their ships, in fact."

"I'm not surprised," Ziksu said. "Now watch."

He reached up to the recess and set the little metal ball inside, where it was held within some kind of field. The moment he did, it lit up much like Ziksu's orb had. The machinery around them whined to life, and the lights flickered on.

"I would never have believed it," Lestiko said, an ecstatic look on his face as his eyes took in the sight.

Verveik's jaw hung open as he turned in a slow circle. Geddy had never seen him quite so incredulous. Most likely, no one had.

"All that power ... came from me?" he asked.

"Yes," Ziksu said. "Now do you understand? The power you require is already inside you and your allies."

Verveik nodded slowly. "Can this facility produce weapons as well?"

"Depending on the design, perhaps."

"Then leave the tukrium to us," Verveik declared, glancing at Geddy. "Lestiko, if you had some of these spheres, how quickly could you finalize your designs?"

"In short order, Commander," Lestiko said.

"Good." Verveik extended his giant hand, and Ziksu graciously took it. "We have an accord."

CHAPTER 22
SHOW US YOUR ENTITIES!

Geddy was propped up in Oz's bed against a ramp of pillows. She sat effortlessly cross-legged at the foot, rocking slowly as she listened to his account of the events on Xellara and at the hidden mahk'ti facility.

"I barely believed my eyes. I mean, *Verveik*? The whole factory fired up. Ziksu said that one orb could run it for days. I'm telling you, this stuff is incredible."

"How'd he react?"

"Like he'd just learned that ghosts were real. But I don't think anything less would've convinced him."

"And this orb of theirs has been powering their compound for thousands of years?" she asked.

"Yeah, and it's made of pure shinium, if you can believe it."

Her eyes drifted down to the bed. "Wow."

That they'd struck a bargain with the Samaja was difficult for her to reconcile. Oz ran away from home just like he had, only she was sixteen and not an orphan. She'd become fixated on the plight of the Xellaran rebels and wanted to help bring their decade-long civil war to an end.

Ostensibly, the conflict was between the government and

people who understandably didn't want to get turned into cybernetic worker drones. On that point, the rebels and the Samaja were philosophically aligned. However, the Samaja never got involved. Oz believed they could've turned the tide of that war just like Xellara could turn the tide of this one.

"Look, I know how you feel about all this, but we're pretty much out of options. We need the Samaja's help."

An internal struggle played out on her face. She'd been there with him for the Battle of the Deuce and knew perfectly well how outmatched they were.

"Where are they gonna get all the tukrium?"

"Don't you know?" Oz cocked her head, trying to understand his meaning. It didn't take long. "I told Verveik about Temeruria." He quickly added, "He's willing to intervene."

Her lips formed a straight line. "So he can hand their tukrium to the Samaja."

"Does it matter why?"

Oz's eyes narrowed at him. "Are you really asking me that?"

"We help Temeruria, they join the Alliance. That means the Star Guard fights for us *and* your people are under our protection. So what if we get tukrium out of the bargain?"

She hugged her knees tightly to her chest, her fleshy locks of hair as dark and rusty as he'd ever seen them. A faraway look fell over her giant eyes.

"Can we change the subject?"

"Okay …" he said warily.

"Two things. One, we need to talk about Voprot."

He gave her a wary side-eye. "Is he molting again?"

"No … it's just … I think he feels like a third wheel here," she said. "He needs to feel useful. I mean, Iondra's busy helping Dr. Krezek on Afolos, he's estranged from his family, Kigantu is all but dead …"

"How do you suggest we use his … talents?"

"I'd like to train him on the weapons console."

Before laughing, he wisely read her expression. She wasn't kidding. "As in ... on the *Stalwart*?"

"Just the simulators to start. I think it'd give him something to focus on, y'know? As it is, he sleeps like twenty hours a day."

"So I've noticed."

"Compared to the *Fiz*, it's really not that complicated. And he likes to fight."

"Does he even know how to shoot a blaster? There must be some cans we could line up in the hangar."

She gave him that tired look that meant he needed to be serious. "I just want to keep him busy. Is that okay with you, *Colonel*?"

There wasn't much to consider. Most of the incoming pilots had already trained on the Alliance platforms, so the simulators were generally open. "Sure, knock yourself out."

"Thank you."

"So, what was the second thing?"

Staring at her knees, she took a deep breath. "Umm ... well ..."

— *Uh-oh.*

The blood in his extremities retreated inward. Nothing good ever followed that statement. Last time, it was about her father. What was it now? Some genetic disease? A vow of celibacy?

"Whatever it is, you can tell me."

"You said everybody has an entity in them."

"According to Ziksu, yeah."

"Well ... I have more than one."

The ice that had formed around his fingers and toes hardened, his pulse quickening.

— *Double uh-oh.*

Every word that came to his lips evaporated like a raindrop

on a hot starship. They only trembled silently. The thud of his heart in his ears was the only sound.

"Are you saying you're …?"

"Yeah," she said.

"I … didn't know that was possible."

She stared expectantly at him for a few seconds. "Is that all you have to say?"

So many thoughts swirled in his head that he couldn't grab ahold of just one. Was it a boy or a girl? Were those the only Temerurian genders? Would they live to see their child born?

"I mean … it's a lot to process. How do you feel about it?"

"I don't know yet."

"How long have you known?" Geddy asked.

"A few weeks. But it doesn't change anything. We tell no one, and you don't go into protection mode. You'll want to, but don't."

"I'll do my best. Have you heard from your father again?"

"Twice while you were gone. A third time this morning. He's desperate."

"Verveik called a meeting with the war cabinet about the Temeruria situation, but say the word and I won't support it."

She blinked away a tear. "No, you're right. We're out of options."

He got his legs under him and crawled up to her, leveling his eyes at hers. "Are you sure it's mine?"

It took a painfully long moment, but Oz finally burst into a fit of laughter, which freed him to do the same.

CHAPTER 23
BIGGER THAN YOU THOUGHT, HUH?

"Do you remember what I told you?" Lestiko asked Geddy.

They were back in the Engineering containment room practicing tuning. The lone light overhead cast the long shadows of scientific equipment across the room. Neither of them could sleep.

After Oz dropped her truth bomb, Geddy called on Lestiko, as much for the company as anything. The man had rubbed him the wrong way at first, but they'd developed a kinship. The kind that could only result from knowing what it was like to have a voice in your head that didn't belong to you. Besides, he was enigmatic like Zirhof of Zorr, inscrutable like Sammo-Yann, and a deep thinker like Doc — all people who fascinated or inspired him.

"Filaments surging with the ... what was it again?" Geddy asked.

"The music of the universe," Lestiko said.

Morpho didn't come tonight. Three would've seemed like a crowd.

As before, Geddy closed his eyes and pictured pulsing,

delicate threads of energy, like a loosely twisted rope stretching between him and Lestiko. It was easier this time. Seeing it flow out of Ziksu's orb helped with the visualization.

"Yes, Geddy," Lestiko said softly. "Now ride the waves into my consciousness."

Something about their visit with Ziksu had focused him. Or maybe Oz's news. Either way, he suddenly found it quite easy to do as Lestiko asked.

"Good ... I can feel you reaching through the darkness."

Geddy felt it, too. A sort of tugging at his attention from somewhere inside. Another frequency. The Eli frequency.

— **Welcome.**

"Did you say that out loud?" Geddy asked.

— **No.**

— Holy shit.

— *Hello, Les. May I call you Les?*

— **'Les' try it on for size, Eli.**

— I did it?

— **You did.**

The only other time he'd done this with Lestiko was back on Basoa shortly after they'd met. That time, Morpho had connected them physically and built a psychic space that resembled a physical one. That was like training wheels. This was the real thing.

— **You can open your eyes.**

He did. Looking Lestiko in the eyes didn't break the spell.

— Can you still hear me?

— **Clear as a bell.**

— I'm not sure I love this.

— **You may, in time.**

— Where's Rai?

Lestiko's aspect darkened. Eli and Rai were diametric opposites. "Sequestered."

Just like that, they were back to talking. Geddy could jump

into Lestiko's head if he wanted, but it felt weird. He wasn't in a hurry to do it again.

"What does that mean, exactly?"

He shook his head grimly. "I had all I could take of its foul whispers. I walled it off in a sort of mind prison."

It was hard not to picture an Old West sheriff sitting across the room from a jailed scoundrel who taunted him mercilessly.

"I'm sorry."

"Don't be. It knows the end is near. Rai wants everything to become nothing, just like the Asurya. I won't allow that energy into my awareness."

Looking back, it was no wonder that Lestiko couldn't fathom Eli's goodness. That he and Geddy were a team determined to save the universe seemed like a fairy tale until they met inside Morpho's consciousness and talked. Geddy knew perfectly well what it was like to suffer at the hands of his own inner voice. To stand by as it actively worked against him. But Eli gave him something else to listen to. Something better. Lestiko would never have that.

"If we survive this, what happens to Rai? Or any Zelnad, for that matter?"

"I've long wondered the same thing. Will they be called home? Regroup and come after us again? Have a collective change of heart?" He shook his head as though ruing the unknowable. "I just know I won't endure that dreadful voice in my head any longer."

Geddy knew what that meant. If Doc hadn't convinced him to come help the Alliance, he likely would've sacrificed himself in the name of science.

"I never realized how bad it was for you. Didn't Rai help you make weapons?"

"If I die, it dies. Making and selling weapons kept us alive. It wasn't done out of kindness, believe me."

— *I'm sorry you're in such pain.*

— I know you are, Eli.

The switch back to tuning happened so effortlessly that it momentarily seemed Lestiko was doing a ventriloquist act.

— Me, too.

— I'm now convinced that it's possible for hosts to separate themselves from their entities without a machine. I've given a great deal of thought as to how the Asurya tricked his acolytes into doing it.

— You mean the Virikta.

— Yes.

— *How did Ziksu convince you of that?*

— Good question, E.

— *We* control the energy bond, Geddy. Not Eli, not Rai, not any entities.

— What's your point?

— The Zelnads plan to use hosts as bombs. You and I have that same power.

— So?

— So, if it came to it, would you rather go out with a bang or a whimper?

Geddy hadn't given much thought to Ziksu's story about the explosive mass suicide that cratered a mountain, but Lestiko knew this would resonate.

— How?

— By drawing all the energy you and Eli share into yourself. Quickly and decisively, like snatching a toy from a child.

Geddy slid off his stool and took a deep breath as he paced, arms crossed, rejecting the mere thought of it. He loved Eli, and Eli loved him. They were bound together. Eli said it from the very beginning — *Your end is my end.* To this point, however, he'd pictured it in terms of his accidental or natural death.

"I could never do that."

Lestiko slid off his stool and approached Geddy with a look of paternal patience. "Have you ever wondered why we call mahk'ti 'original' energy?"

"Not really."

"Before it, there was nothing. It doesn't just connect us or flow through us, Geddy. It *is* us."

"Why are you telling me this?"

"Because what we're about to do is scary. Our enemy is far more clever and determined than any of us can know. But you can't let fear keep you from doing what you need to do. We come from the unknowable, and we return to it. Simple as that. The in-between is all we get."

Geddy never believed in an afterlife. He still didn't. But there was something inside him he couldn't explain, and it bound him to the universe like invisible glue. At a minimum, it was a comforting thought.

"What do you think happens? At the end, I mean," he asked.

"Then you brave the unknown. Know what we call that on Basoa?"

"What?"

He gave Geddy's shoulder a reassuring pat and grinned impishly. "An adventure."

In addition to its top scientists, Ornea's contributions to the Alliance included the science vessel *Inquiry*, on loan from the University of Tathé. Among its maze of labs and offices was a fabrication facility where various electronic or chemical components could be made quickly. It was the perfect setup for Doc and his team to help bring Lestiko's designs to fruition.

Geddy, the Alliance senior officers, and Ziksu himself had gathered to see the latest mockups. The Orneans regarded

Ziksu with a mix of skepticism and curiosity. Few had ever seen a Xellaran without mods, and they knew almost nothing about the Samaja.

Lestiko stood behind a long, black table on which a number of 3D-printed components rested. "Thank you all for coming. I know you've all been anxious to see the designs. Please."

They closed ranks evenly around it as Lestiko touched the first object, which resembled a wide, chunky arrow about two meters long. It had no obvious cooling system or cables. "This is a full-scale model of the disruptor assembly. With the help of this universal coupling, it can replace the existing assembly of most any small vessel. The design easily scales to fit the bigger warships."

"It's solid state?" Balzac ran his finger down its length. He knew a thing or two about tinkering and weapons himself.

"Yes," Lestiko replied. "It uses the fewest possible components and with the barest minimum of materials. Everything that can be hollow, is." He nodded at the next largest piece, a flat metal box about the size of a pilot's seat. "That goes for the shield generator here as well. Now this …" he held up an orb the same diameter as the one Verveik filled. "… is its heart. On a full charge, one orb can power both systems for days. Think fast."

He tossed it to Balzac, who almost fumbled it before turning it over in his hands. Its high polish reflected the room so perfectly that it looked more like a bubble in the fabric of reality than an actual object. Dropping a tukrium ball would only damage the floor at most, but it wasn't much heavier than a holiday ornament.

"How is it charged?"

Balzac returned the sphere to Lestiko, who then held it out to Geddy.

"Colonel Starheart?"

Geddy hesitated, not having expected to be put on the spot.

He glanced at Verveik, who gave him a look that said, *Seeing is believing.*

"Right. Well ... here goes nothing."

— No pressure.

He held it lightly in his fingertips, imagining its emptiness as he closed his eyes. He pictured a stream of original energy flowing between him and Eli, then diverted a tiny bit down his arm into the orb.

Balzac and the others gasped. Geddy opened his eyes to find purple lightning dancing between his fingers and flowing into the orb. In a few seconds, he'd charged it completely, yet his bond with Eli remained intact.

"Damn, Starheart," Tymeri said.

Grozuc, the other Screvari who led the Triad forces, leaned in close to look at it. "How are you doing this?"

"Ziksu will teach you," Lestiko said, passing his eyes over the group. "The Alliance will be its own power source."

When all eyes swiveled to him, Ziksu gave a gracious bow. "It will be my honor."

"But we're not like you two," Balzac said. "It's not possible."

"It is," Verveik said from the back. "I didn't believe it either until I did it. And we're more like them than we know."

"Even if I believed it was possible, this work is too fine to be made at scale," Balzac objected. "Especially not with pure tukrium."

"They can, Mr. Balzac," Ziksu said. "In fact, prototypes will be ready for real-world testing within a week."

"But we don't have the tukrium," Grozuc lamented. "Unless you're planning to melt down half the fleet."

"I'm glad you raised that issue, General," said the commander. "All of you, please come with me."

CHAPTER 24
A SPLIT DECISION

The Alliance leaders and the Orneans filed into the *Inquiry's* circular auditorium, speculating with each other in hushed tones about what Verveik had to say about their tukrium problem. Of course, Geddy already knew.

A sound from the back of the room caught his attention. He turned to find Tatiana Semenov, his old flame, enter ahead of Tretiak, Zirhof, Zereth-Tinn, Smegmo, Everett Hau, and the rest of the Committee. Geddy threw them all a hearty wave.

Tatiana spotted him, smiled politely, and shuffled down the row toward him. It was still weird to see her wearing pants, a businesslike blouse, and sensible shoes. They hadn't seen each other since she showed her tits to the clones and changed their lives forever.

"Hiya, Tots."

"*Colonel*," she gave a deep, theatrical curtsy. "I am humbled by your presence."

He rolled his eyes and patted the seat beside him as he shook his head. "Man, what's the point of getting promoted if everyone just makes fun of you?"

She reached over and mussed his hair with pouty lips.

"Aww, is my widdle Geddy-weddy's ego threatened? If anyone should know how to take abuse gracefully at this point, it's you."

"How've you been?" he asked, laughing.

"I've been better."

"Mo' gorodons, mo' problems?"

"And leaks, and supply issues, no tourists, and I'm bleeding cash ... Shall I go on?"

"Sorry to hear that. What're you gonna do?"

"Find a new planet."

His impulse was to laugh again, but it didn't seem like she was kidding.

"Thank you all for coming," Verveik said, and the conversations faded. "Let's begin."

The old man outlined the events of the past week, focusing mainly on the Temeruria situation. Initially, Tati and the others appeared ready to tell Bransel to piss off. However, as Verveik connected the dots between Bransel's predicament and the Alliance's tukrium issue, their attitude visibly began to shift.

Oz was personally invited by the commander but begged off. Not just because Tati would be there, but because she didn't want to influence their decision. It would be hard to be objective with a Temerurian royal in the room.

"... and as you've seen, we now have a solution to our power problem."

Tati's face pinched cynically. "What makes you so sure it wasn't a bunch of hocus-pocus to earn your trust?"

"To what end?" challenged Everett Hau, the flamboyant trillionaire of Caloth. "Besides, we just saw it with our own eyes."

"The Samaja would rather risk exile than be turned into cyborgs," Verveik answered for Tati. "They need us as much as we need them." He looked her dead in her big baby blues.

"But Ziksu's true motives don't concern me. I know what I saw, and he can help us."

"Perhaps I speak only for myself, but I trust your judgment on the matter, Commander," said Zirhof of Zorr, the rich, eccentric uncle Geddy never had.

"Agreed," said Zereth-Tinn, the mysterious Soturian who killed his own half-brother, Sammo-Yann.

Tretiak, for whom the destruction of his empire was still very raw, sat stone-faced in a row by himself.

Verveik placed his big hands on the long table at the front of the room and leaned, making it groan under his weight. "We now have a logistical problem and a political one. Solve them in the right order, and we've got a real shot at pulling this off. But there's a wrinkle."

Zirhof and the others exchanged worried looks. Verveik's words had palpable gravity.

"As I said, the Zelnads abruptly halted their mining operation and vanished, but they left something behind." The hologram of Temeruria rotated to show the boreholes encircling the planet in a crooked line. "Some kind of autonomous drills have dug their way through the planet's crust and into its molten mantle. They're spewing up lava, sulfur and methane just like Earth 2."

"You can't mine anything that deep," said Queen Tymeri, the Ceonian madam-slash-pirate who against all odds had become a loyal soldier and one of Verveik's favorites.

"Correct," Verveik affirmed. "Which is another reason why we believe they're about to do to Temeruria what they did to Elenia."

He let that hang there for a very long several seconds, during which everyone's rapid blinking suggested confusion.

Doc stood and approached the hologram. "My stars, he's right! I didn't see it before, but the borehole pattern runs through Temeruria's major fault lines." He traced the jagged circle around the planet, which resembled a cracked egg.

"Okay, but Elenia?" said Zirhof over the tops of his eyes. "You think the *Zelnads* blew up *Elenia?* That was what — twenty, thirty thousand years ago?"

"More like broke up," Geddy said, and all heads swiveled to him. "Those aren't just drills — they're bombs. At some point, they'll reach some minimum depth and explode with unimaginable power."

"How the hell could you know that?" Tymeri asked. "You're not that smart."

Geddy opened his mouth to answer but realized he couldn't do so without explaining about the First Illustration. That would all be too much for this lot to swallow.

"If that happens," Verveik answered, sidestepping the explanation, "anyone still on Temeruria will die."

"He's right," Doc said. "The atmosphere's already filling with poisonous gases, and the release of pressure will make the planet disastrously unstable."

"As in, earthquakes?" Geddy asked.

"Yes, but that is … too small a word," Doc replied. "Pressure-driven shifts deep within the mantle will cause high-amplitude tectonic shifts. Orders of magnitude beyond a typical earthquake."

"Why the hell aren't they evacuated already?" Tati asked.

Geddy replied, "Bransel was the architect of this Zelnad deal. Ordering a full-scale evacuation would make him look weak."

"I'm sorry …" interrupted Geddy's old friend, the young Ceonian heir, Smegmo Eilgars, who had largely bankrolled the Alliance to this point. "Are we talking about stopping these bombs or forcing the total evacuation of a nonmember planet based on a theory? Because, with all due respect, Commander, I'm not crazy about either option."

"We evacuate first, then deal with the bombs if we can," Verveik responded.

"Does Bransel know about this parallel to Elenia?" Zirhof asked, piling on before Verveik could answer.

"Not yet," Verveik replied. "But he will."

"What would an evac look like, exactly?" Tymeri asked.

Verveik pulled up another animation, this time depicting his proposed intervention as he described it. "At least half the ships on Temeruria aren't jump-capable. We'll send a battle group to Medrikar, the capital. Along with the Star Guard, we'll form a cordon to control the evacuation of conventional ships. One long line from the lower atmosphere into space. There, they'll pair up with one of ours and use the bubble drives to jump both ships to the rendezvous. Jump-capable ships can leave on their own."

"To where?" asked Balzac, Geddy's old Screvari friend.

"Inside the khetaka," Verveik replied, referring to Gundrun's planetary defense system.

"There's no safer place in the galaxy right now," Arbizander added.

"And then what? Bransel just hands over his tukrium?" Hau asked sarcastically.

"His stores will be the price of our assistance, paid in advance," Verveik said. "Every last rod in Bransel's stockpile."

"What if there is no stockpile?" asked Balzac.

"Oz says there is," Geddy answered. "Deep underground. She heard him talk about it when she was a kid."

"But even if the Xellarans can deliver what they promise, we still have to retrofit the fleet," Smegmo pointed out. "It took Zirhof's people weeks just to install the bubble drives."

General Grozuc, the Screvari in charge of the Triad forces, rose. "The Triad has been building ships for millennia. We'll get it done as fast as the Samaja can make the weapons."

Verveik folded his thick arms behind him and stuck out his

chest. "Helping Temeruria is a gamble. We don't know if or when the Zelnads will return. With luck, we'll have the planet evacuated and the tukrium in hand long before then. I don't trust Bransel any more than the rest of you, but we're out of options."

"What makes you think the Star Guard fight for the Alliance?" asked Tymeri.

"Assuming control of their military will be another condition of our assistance," Verveik stated. His eyes passed slowly over the assembled leaders. "Any other concerns?" Everyone exchanged wary glances, but no one spoke. "Very well." His head swiveled to Geddy. "Colonel Starheart, you and First Officer Nargonis handle the negotiations. Ogos and Tymeri, I want you to lead the formation of the cordon and the jumps to the khetaka. Balzac, get us our tukrium."

"Aye, sir," replied Ogos, Geddy's most accomplished clone.

"With pleasure," Balzac said.

"You're really pairing me up with Young Starheart?" Tymeri asked drolly. "Yo ho fuckin' ho." Ogos' face reddened, and she tousled his hair. He immediately reset it.

"If it's all the same to you, I'd like to take my crew, sir." Geddy said.

Verveik paused to glance at Doc. "Very well, but I want Dr. Tardigan to accompany Ziksu back to Mikuli and monitor production."

"I will be with you in spirit, Colonel," Doc said apologetically.

"Why not send Lestiko?" Geddy asked.

"Because he's a civilian consultant," Verveik replied plainly, adding, "No offense, Mr. Lestiko."

"None taken. But I'd be happy to join the Colonel aboard the Stalwart, if he'll have me," Lestiko piped in. "I'm no science officer, but perhaps I could still be useful."

Verveik hemmed and hawed for a moment. "It's his mission."

Geddy and Lestiko exchanged a friendly smile. He always felt better with Doc around. Lestiko had a different, but equally calming presence. "The more, the merrier."

— *It probably is a good idea to have someone smart on board.*

— I'd be insulted if I didn't agree.

"I'll alert the shipyards on Aku, Kailoria, and Ghruk," said Grozuc. "We'll be ready."

"Our work is cut out for us," Verveik declared. "I want briefs on my desk first thing tomorrow morning."

"Are boxers acceptable, sir?" Geddy asked.

— *Oh dear god, Geddy.*

— What? It was a softball! Everyone needs to lighten up around here.

It might've been his imagination, but one corner of Verveik's mouth twitched upward. "Dismissed."

CHAPTER 25

WELCOME BACK DAUGHTER

The *Stalwart* popped into space a hundred clicks from Temeruria's outer marker. The Star Guard was expecting them, but even so, Geddy didn't trust that this wasn't all a big ruse and that Bransel wasn't leading them into a trap. That's how little he thought of Oz's father.

It felt good to be back in the saddle, though. Denk at the controls, Oz at the weapons console, Jel in Doc's place on navcom, and Voprot crouched behind her. Morph was splayed out as always on his left shoulder. Lestiko was in one of the jump seats, seemingly relishing all the activity after so many years in isolation.

Off in the distance, Temeruria's ordinarily dazzling palette had taken on a sickly hue. A faint yellow haze, eerily reminiscent of The Deuce, blanketed the planet.

It didn't mean Bransel wasn't playing them, but something was definitely amiss.

Geddy turned to Oz, failing to resist the urge to linger on her noticeably fuller bosom. Maybe this baby stuff had its perks.

"They're not any bigger than when you looked three minutes ago," she whispered.

"Sorry, just trying to help."

"Help? What are you—"

"Well, Cap— er, *Colonel*. What's the plan?" Denk asked, unknowingly cutting her off.

"We'll take the *Armstrong* from here." Geddy hitched his pants as he and Oz rose. "Stay outside the markers until I contact you. Once the battle group jumps in, we'll meet you over Medrikar and watch over the cordon."

"Aye, aye!" Denk said.

Leaving the bridge, Geddy and Oz proceeded through the open airlock and descended the wide steps into the mostly empty hangar. The *Armstrong* was parked in one of the forward pads, gleaming and gorgeous as ever. Well behind it, in the back corner of the maintenance bay sat the sad and lonely *Fiz*. Morph had spent most of his time the past couple of weeks cleaning it inside and out, but it still looked woefully out of place in the *Stalwart's* state-of-the-art hangar.

"How you feeling about this?" Geddy asked.

She flared her eyes bemusedly. "Look at you, interested in feelings."

"You've infected me," he said with a smirk.

"I'm okay, Geddy. Really."

They boarded the *Armstrong*. Once the seals were all in the green, he gave Denk the order to open the hangar doors. A few minutes later, they were streaking toward Temeruria.

As expected, the Star Guard picked them up shortly after passing the outer marker. They received a hail, and Geddy put it on screen.

"Greetings, *Armstrong*," said the handsome young man at the point of the five-fighter patrol. "I'm Captain Luvimar. The Prince asked me to escort you in."

— Escort? I could turn these dipshits into space dust in like two minutes.

— *Maybe they just want to tell their grandchildren they once escorted Geddy the Great.*

— I like how you think!

"Buckle up, sweet tits. I'm gonna show this kid what a Kemik 1013A drive matrix looks like from behind."

Oz rolled her eyes and buckled herself in. "Comparing dicks would be a lot better for the environment."

"Maybe, but it's too cold outside." While she busted up laughing, Geddy said to the captain, "Say, young feller, what's the record time from the outer markers to the inner? I know you know."

He gave a sly grin. Cocky flyboys were always up for a wager. "With conventional engines? Six minutes, seventeen point two seconds."

Geddy gave a low whistle. "That's movin', no doubt about it. But I can do it in under six without breaking a sweat."

He laughed as though Geddy was kidding, but he wasn't. The *Armstrong* could get up and go. Plus, playing this little game got them there faster. "Yeah, right. Isn't that thing technically an antique?"

"Yeah, and so's the ship," Oz muttered.

Geddy glared at her then returned to the captain. "I'll wait for you at the finish line, okay, kid? I'd hate for Bransel to put in time-out because we got there before you."

The captain allowed a chuckle. "You might beat us, old timer, but you can't make it in under six."

"A thousand credits say I can."

The kid was slurping this up. Geddy almost felt sorry for him. "You're on," he said.

A mischievous grin spread across Geddy's face. "Gimme a countdown." He cracked his knuckles, and leaned into the console. "Oz, time us, would ya?"

Oz groaned and brought up a stopwatch on her floating screen, her finger hovering over it. "Do you even have a thousand credits?"

"No idea."

The Temerurian captain officiously said, "Ahem, high-speed escort maneuver commencing in five ... four ... three ... two ... one ..."

As long as he'd flown the *Armstrong*, Geddy had few reasons to go full-burn. He honestly didn't know how fast it was, but the way the kid said the record time indicated it was a Star Guard ship that set it. And he knew with absolute certainty that the *Armstrong* was faster than any ship Temeruria ever made.

Oz stopped her timer as soon as they passed the inner marker. Five minutes, forty-seven seconds. Even after slowing down, they waited almost a minute for the escort ships to catch up. Once they did, a red-faced Captain Luvimar hailed them.

"Did you get lost? I circled back twice," Geddy teased.

The captain allowed a sheepish smile. "That's some fast ship you've got there."

"Five forty-seven. But I'm sure that's unofficial."

"Very."

Oz gave an exasperated sigh. "Are you two gonna blow each other now or after we land?"

"That depends which of us was more turned on by that display of power," Geddy said. "Please, Captain, lead the way."

He chuckled appreciatively. "Sending the approach vector now. Stay within the green zone or we'll have to shoot you."

"I left my bifocals at home, but I'll do my best."

The vector dictated a leisurely pace, giving them plenty of time to appraise Temeruria's sickly appearance. Not all the boreholes were spewing anything, but plumes of poisonous steam billowed from the ones that did. As they'd seen earlier, none were anywhere near Medrikar or Ganurdan, by far the most populous cities. The more remote settlements were chiefly occupied by natives called the Ophir, whom the ruling class had exploited for centuries. Oz's family's servant, Chafton, was one of them.

"How do we evacuate the Ophir? They don't have starships, do they?" Geddy asked Oz.

She gave a slow, grim shake of her head. "No, which is why we're adding it as a condition."

That wasn't among the terms they were sent to deliver, but she was right. There couldn't be ten thousand Ophir left on the entire planet. It wouldn't take much to get them out.

As they punched through the clouds, Medrikar again came into view. The greenish smog made it appear bleak and industrial, not the shining jewel of a city they'd marveled at during their last visit. Oz's red locks grew even duller, the sadness of it all playing out in her eyes and trembling lips.

Geddy placed his hand on hers. "You still okay?"

"Please stop asking me that."

It was hard to see her like this, but she was here as a representative of the Alliance and had a responsibility to be professional. Besides, her anger, both at her father and the worsening situation here, wasn't something he could assuage.

As they dropped lower, the vector swung them toward the tallest building in the city, Medrikar Palace. It was just a fancy-looking skyscraper and home to the offices of the bureaucrats who actually ran the country.

The escort detail remained in a hover behind them as they descended to the private landing pad at the top of the tower.

Apparently, he wasn't going to get his money from the young captain. Not yet, anyway.

He extended the skids, and they settled onto the roof. They unbuckled themselves while the engines powered down, and Geddy rose with a stretch. Oz had closed her eyes and was taking a series of deep breaths. He gave her a minute, then placed a hand on her shoulder.

"Ready?"

She rose and drew herself tall. "Sure."

CHAPTER 26
HERE'S THE DEAL

Prince Bransel and two of his cronies, one of whom Geddy recognized as the hilariously named Sky Marshal Komfeti, sat together at the opposite end of a long oval table. They rose when Geddy and Oz entered, and Bransel crossed the room with his arms outstretched to greet Oz as though they had that kind of relationship.

"My dear Osmiya," he gushed. "What an unexpected surprise!"

Oz took a step back, prompting him to pull up short and frown. "All surprises are unexpected. And this isn't a social call. I'm only here at Commander Verveik's insistence."

Bransel's icy countenance regarded her with pointed disdain. "Pity. I'd've thought such an urgent matter would demand his attendance."

"It's the smog," Geddy said. "He has to protect his vocal cords so he can yell at me."

He gave a bemused smirk and gestured for them to sit at the near end of the table. "Please, sit." They took two chairs while Bransel returned to his seat. "You remember Brodrik, don't you? And Sky Marshal Komfeti, of course."

"No fetti like cumfetti," Geddy muttered under his breath. Oz covered her laugh with a cough.

An elf-like Ophir servant appeared and set glasses of water down in front of them. The sharp creases on his face, particularly around his tired eyes, suggested a hard, sad life.

"Thank you." The servant briefly met Geddy's eye but quickly averted his gaze.

"Thank you?" Bransel chuckled. "This is Temeruria, Captain Starheart. It is not customary to thank the Ophir."

"It's *Colonel*, and I don't give half a shit about your customs."

Bransel stiffened and his phony smile vanished. He cleared his throat. "Have it your way, *Colonel*. I'm guessing my daughter has apprised you of our ... predicament."

"She did."

"And what is the Alliance's response?"

"We'll help you." He paused to enjoy the looks of relief on the men's faces, then continued. "Evacuate."

"Evacuate?" Bransel hissed. "I hardly think this calls for such–"

"Drastic measures? Don't worry, you will. But first, we have terms."

His beady eyes pinched, and he leaned back in his chair as though he already knew what bargaining chips they'd use. "I assume you mean joining the Alliance."

"Obviously."

Their expressions suggested they weren't expecting more. "Go on," Bransel said.

"Number two, we immediately take command of all Temerurian military assets and personnel."

Sky Marshal Komfeti's face reddened with rage, his gloved hands squeaking as they tightened into fists atop the table. Bransel shot him a look, and he reluctantly relaxed.

"Is that it?"

"Number three, you surrender all tukrium reserves to the Alliance to assist with the war effort."

"War?" Komfeti sneered. "We're not at war."

"In fact, you are," Oz said. "You're just too stupid to realize it."

Komfeti shot up from his chair, outraged by her insolence. Oz struck a fighting stance. "You want to tangle, Komfeti? I'll drop you like a load."

Geddy lightly touched her leg and gave her a look that said, *I've never loved you more, but keep it together.*

"Enough!" Bransel ordered. Oz reluctantly lowered herself into the chair, and Komfeti did the same. He gave Geddy a patronizing grin. "Thanks to the Zelnads, we no longer have tukrium reserves."

"Like hell you don't," Oz said. "You think I grew up in that ridiculous house and didn't eavesdrop? I know about the warehouses."

Through his tightly drawn mouth, he continued, "Will that be all?"

"Not quite." Geddy gave Oz a crooked grin. The evacuation begins with the Ophir."

The men's faces initially registered confusion, then they burst into obnoxious laughter. Bransel sneered, "You can't be serious."

"The borers currently embedding themselves in your planet are bombs," Geddy said. "At any moment, they'll explode and break Temeruria in half so they can harvest whatever tukrium they didn't already find."

Bransel's narrow face puckered in confusion. "I don't believe you."

Oz reached into her jacket and produced a pocket-sized holobar with the planet visualization they'd seen at Verveik's briefing.

"It's happened before." She played an animation of how

Elenia broke apart. "If you don't evacuate immediately, everyone will die." A stunned silence followed. She let it linger for an uncomfortably long time. "While you help the Ophir, we'll form a cordon into space. Conventional ships will pair up with ours so we can jump them away. Jump-capable ships are free to go to the coordinates whenever they wish."

"Then what?" asked Brodrik.

"Then you help us defeat the beings who did this to us."

Her use of "us" was interesting. Was it a tactic, or did she suddenly feel a dormant attachment to this place?

Bransel's expression hardened, and his spiteful gaze fell on Oz. "I should've known better than to ask Verveik for help. This is extortion!"

"You don't have much time." Oz switched the display to show the borers' projected paths in a cross-section, about halfway through the planet's mantle. "We figured you've got three days at the outside before they reach optimal fracture depth. Then …"

"Boom," Geddy finished, making an exploding motion with his fingers.

Oz continued. "As the two halves of Temeruria drift apart, the gravity between them will rip each other's guts out. Then the Zelnads will return in force to harvest the tukrium they need to destroy the universe. Not many people would consider this a tough choice, father."

"You can't prove any of this," Bransel complained. "I'm not ordering a full-scale evacuation on a half-baked theory."

"Proof? How about this?" Oz pulled up another image showing the pattern of the holes. "The boreholes more or less encircle the planet. It appears random, but it isn't." She added an overlay of Temeruria's plate tectonics. "As you can see, they align perfectly with major fault lines."

Finally, Bransel and his counselors appeared rattled.

"The pressure changes will make the crust highly unstable," Oz continued. "The earthquakes that follow will shake anything on the surface into dust. We need everyone in the air before that happens."

"We will ... discuss the Alliance's proposal," Bransel said.

"Yes, by all means, talk amongst yourselves." Geddy waved his hand at them and leaned on his hands.

"I'm referring to the royal council," Bransel said condescendingly. "We need time to convene a full–"

Oz pounded her open palm on the table, giving them all a start. "My stars, how can you be this daft?! You don't have time! This isn't a *discussion!*"

"You're asking me to order the abandonment of our home world — *your* home world, Osmiya!"

"On my order, an Alliance battle group will jump immediately into orbit and see to the safe evacuation of your people." Geddy tapped the communicator on his wrist. "But the clock's ticking."

"Exactly where do you intend for us to go?" Komfeti asked.

"Inside the khetaka. Gundrun will ensure your peoples' safety." They flared their eyebrows at this but said nothing.

Bransel glanced from side to side, presumably looking for any dissenting advice from Brodrik and Komfeti, but they were just as flummoxed as their liege.

Geddy continued, "Well? Do we have a deal?"

Plainly, Bransel wasn't used to being put in this kind of position. Geddy could almost watch the mental gymnastics as he hunted for some way to turn all this to his advantage. But there was none, and his usual uppity sneer dissolved into a hangdog look.

With his thin lips drawn tightly, Bransel said, "Temeruria accepts."

"Good." Geddy gave the table a celebratory slap. "Now give the order. We've got a lot of work to do."

Again, Bransel smirked as though Geddy was kidding, but

he quickly realized he wasn't. "Sky Marshal Komfeti, please oversee the immediate evacuation of Temeruria." His nose wrinkled distastefully. "Beginning with the Ophir." His eyes slid back to Geddy. "I trust freighters will suffice?"

"They're not freight, they're people," Oz objected. "Use transports."

"We may not have enough to evacuate the cities, let alone …" Komfeti grimaced and trailed off. "They aren't equipped to land in settlement terrain."

Oz looked to Geddy for verification. Unfortunately, he was right. Freighters weren't made to carry passengers, but they could land pretty much anywhere. He nodded to her.

It was clearly a bitter pill, but she capitulated. "Fine. Just get them off-world safely."

"As you wish, my princess," said her father. When he noticed Komfeti hadn't left, he added a sharp, "What are you waiting for? Go!"

The sky marshal stiffly rose and shot daggers at Geddy and Oz as he strode out.

"Brodrik, inform my family I'll be along soon," Bransel muttered.

The adviser gave a quick nod and also hurried off, leaving only the three of them in the large room.

"Now that we're alone, I have a condition of my own," Bransel said.

"I can hardly wait." Geddy batted his eyes.

"You have a gunship. I would feel safer if you escorted me and my family into space."

Oz had thoroughly disowned him and her mother, Nandra. As far as she was concerned, they were strangers. But keeping an eye on Bransel until he jumped away to Gundrun didn't seem like a terrible idea. Besides, once the fleet arrived, there wouldn't be much for them to do.

"Fine," Geddy said. "But don't dawdle. Nobody's gonna want to be here if the shit hits the fan. Feel me?"

"Indeed, Colonel. Now … I'd imagine Verveik is eager to collect his spoils, yes?" Bransel said, pushing away from the table. "Come with me."

As they began to walk, Geddy raised his wrist and activated the encrypted channel that went to Verveik's office. "We're all set here, Commander."

"Good. So how do you suppose he's gonna burn us?" he asked, likely knowing that Bransel was within earshot.

Bransel gave him a look that was supposed to pass for sincere, and Geddy smirked. "I'm already counting the ways, sir."

CHAPTER 27

BOOTY CALL

The *Armstrong* skimmed the treetops across a vast and unbroken forest west of the city. The battle group had jumped in and already formed its cordon. Two heavy cargo ships of Ghruk origin, led by Balzac, followed from well above. Bransel sat behind Geddy and Oz looking as though he might throw up at any moment.

A plume of pale green gas spewed from a borehole about five clicks east, forming a dome-shaped cloud over it. Geddy couldn't take his eyes off it. Bransel pretended it wasn't there.

"What does the Alliance plan to do with twenty thousand cubic meters of refined tukrium?" asked the prince.

"That's classified," Geddy said.

"But we're all on the same team now, are we not?"

"Once this op is complete, I'm sure Verveik will bring you up to speed."

He gave a bemused grin. "You don't trust me, do you, Colonel?"

"Gee, whatever gave you that idea?"

"As I recall, I saved your ship from pirates, repaired it for free, and invited your entire crew to a royal feast at my home," Bransel said. "How did I betray your trust, exactly?"

"By sleeping with the enemy," Oz hissed.

"It was good business, while it lasted. I've no love for the Zelnads."

"I remember you saying you had nothing to fear from them," she said. "In fact, wasn't that right after we warned you about them?"

The distant borehole passed beyond the edge of the front screen, and Bransel finally raised his eyes to the horizon. "Ah, Osmiya. What a pleasure it must be to live in such an ... uncomplicated world." He pointed at a nondescript rock formation, a sandstone cliff peeking out just above the trees. "Toward that outcropping."

Geddy gave the stick a gentle bump to align them with it.

"Open a channel to 168.33 megahertz," Bransel said. When Geddy hesitated, he rolled his eyes and added, "It's clean."

Geddy keyed in the frequency and verified the encryption, then nodded at him. "This is Prince Bransel on approach. Authentication JQ175."

"Confirmed," came a male voice on the other end. "We weren't expecting you, your highness. Is everything okay? I'm hearing chatter about an evac."

"All in good time, Captain. Open the cargo entrance, please. These are our new friends from the Alliance."

An oval area of trees below the outcropping began to unfurl like a colossal set of jaws, calling to mind the cleverly hidden entrance to the Samaja temple on Xellara.

Geddy brought the ship into a hover over it, and they watched through the belly camera as the huge door slid aside to reveal a massive cargo dock and a large elevator rig. He eased the *Armstrong* down past the bewildered operator inside a control booth. He reached for the controls, but Bransel stopped him.

"Leave the door open, Captain."

"Sir?" he asked, nervously eyeing the ship.

"Our new overlords have come to collect their tribute."

The shadow of the big cargo ships fell over them, and the captain's eyes swiveled upward in awe. Geddy set them down on one of five landing pads, waited for the pressure failsafe to run its checks, and extended the ramp.

"Balzac, you're clear to dock," he spoke into the comm, suppressing a giggle.

The cargo ship's umbilical deployed from three hundred meters overhead and lengthened toward the connector. A boxy cab emerged from beneath the nose and descended along the cable, its blue jets keeping it level as it entered the breech. Inside was a smattering of Ghruk, Kailorian, and Screvari engineers handpicked by Balzac to handle the logistics. It gently settled onto the landing pad beside the *Armstrong*.

The cab's doors slid open, and its occupants hurried over to assist the Temerurian dock workers with the tether. Meanwhile, Balzac strolled toward Geddy and Oz as they came off their ramp.

"Boy, no wonder they didn't know about this place." He and Geddy embraced, and when Balzac pulled back, he regarded Bransel's robes with unmasked contempt. He gave a phony little bow. "Your eminence."

"This is Balzac," Geddy said. "He'll gently cradle your tukrium."

A chunky sound drew their attention, and an electric whine indicated the tether had connected. One of the Ghruk gave Balzac his version of a thumbs-up, and an electric motor began drawing it taut.

"Speaking of which …" he began. "Where's our cargo?"

Bransel jerked his head over his shoulder. "This way."

They followed him toward a rectangular vault door locked in place by beefy cylinders in the surrounding frame. He signaled to the captain up above, who activated something in his booth. One by one, hidden motors retracted the cylinders, and the door slowly swung open. It had to be at least three meters thick, maybe four. As it opened fully, lights switched on inside.

— *Oh, my.*

"Holy hell," Geddy muttered.

As a kid, they only had one tukrium item — a chef's knife given to his parents by his maternal grandparents as a wedding gift. After each use, his mother dutifully returned it to a safe in their bedroom. It must've been worth five or six thousand credits at the time, but it would be at least twice that now.

The warehouse inside was at least ten times larger than the one where they'd discovered the clones beneath the Myadan xoo. Metal platforms designed for loaders were piled two meters high with identical tukrium rods, perfectly bound together. They stretched almost as far as they could see.

"We're gonna need a bigger ship," Balzac noted.

"Make it happen," Geddy said. "I don't care how you do it, but every last gram's leaving with us."

"Aye aye, Colonel." Balzac spun and barked at the engineers, who were awaiting further instructions. "Look lively, people! We've got work to do!"

By the following day, the full-scale evacuation of Temeruria was well underway. As promised, Bransel dispatched freighters to collect the Ophir. Most, Oz explained, had never even been in a starship. Even her family's servant, Chafton, had only been allowed aboard the family's Hovensby once. That was only because they were hosting diplomats from Zihnia and needed him to serve tea and coffee while they gave an aerial tour of the city. Since the freighters were jump-capable, they could leave as soon as they were full.

So far, the cordon had worked according to plan. Along with the Star Guard, Ogos and Tymeri quickly orchestrated the gauntlet leading into space, and the pairing off of conventional vessels with Alliance ships was already underway. The *Stalwart* was serving as overwatch.

But the controlled chaos over Medrikar was thirty clicks away in the valley, and the crew of the *Armstrong* was in the highlands, above the layer of green smog. If you didn't know what was going on, you'd think it was another nice, if cooler-than-average day on Temeruria.

However, Geddy already wished he hadn't agreed to escort Bransel off-world. He'd envisioned them throwing their valuables into a few crates, quickly loading them, and heading out in a couple of hours. Instead, he and Oz slept in the *Armstrong*, which was parked on the sprawling, manicured grounds of the Nargonis mansion while Bransel and Nandra apparently packed all their belongings into the Hovensby. Geddy only slept fitfully, and Oz not at all.

They sat in the bridge with their feet propped on the console, both drinking coffee as they watched hundreds of jump-capable ships throughout the valley streak into space on their own. Had they known that this would take so long, they might've checked on the Ophir to make sure they were safely away. But they got regular updates from Khetaka Central Command about how many had jumped inside, and things seemed to be going as well as could be expected.

Oz hadn't talked much since the operation began, but her inner turmoil was apparent. She'd made peace with never seeing her family again, but now here they were. Her home world likely faced an apocalypse. As if that wasn't enough, they were expecting but couldn't even tell anyone or make time to be happy about it.

"I wasn't allowed to play in this yard," she mused, her hands interlaced behind her head. "My father had an area cleared in the woods for that."

"I'm sorry," Geddy said.

"No, it was good, actually. I preferred the woods. I felt more connected to it than to my family."

"I never set foot in a forest until I was twenty-six," Geddy said.

"Bullshit."

He shook his head. "Trees didn't grow on The Deuce. Or Kigantu, obviously. I just never had the opportunity. But the first time I met Zirhof, he basically made me visit the northern woodlands on Zorr."

Oz's mien, which had been sour since the moment they'd arrived at the palace, sweetened. "And?"

"It blew my mind that trees could grow so tall. After everything I'd seen and done, I'd never witnessed anything so improbable to me as a fucking tree. And I've wanted to get back to one ever since. A forest, I mean. Not the trees. But I see the fucking trees now."

She gave him the sweetest smile he'd seen in days. "Then I guess we'd better get our fill while we can."

CHAPTER 28

THE FOREST FOR THE TREES

The perfectly manicured lawn had been painted white by an overnight frost, the tips of the blades already softening with the sun. The ramp retracted behind Geddy, and he gave his NASA jacket a fluff, enjoying how slowly his breath drifted through the hazy sunshine.

He found Oz already waiting.

"Oh, hey. How long have you been up?"

"A few hours. I couldn't sleep."

"Me, neither," he said. "Story of my life lately."

"You ready?"

"Why else would I be up this early?"

She took exaggerated steps through the perfect grass, slamming each foot down against the frozen blades. Over her shoulder, she said, "In a few days, these'll be brown footprints."

In a few days, everything would be brown and dead, suffocated by the vacuum after the atmosphere dissolved.

He caught up, and then they clumsily did the Eleven Steps of Kigantu across with her, inflicting as much damage as he could while his boots became slick with water. Oz laughed and joined him, two stumbling idiots ruining all that meticulous work, because why not?

A thick stone wall defined the edge of the property, but an unlocked metal gate, overgrown with thistles, provided access to the forest beyond. Oz led him through and they started across a grassy area dotted with bushy trees in symmetrical rows. The branches were laden with dark orange fruit.

"Escilots," she said, plucking one from a random branch and tossing it over her shoulder at him.

"Whoa, really?"

He snatched it out of the air and studied its leathery, bumpy rind. Escilots were one of those ingredients you'd only see on the menu at some ludicrous restaurant like that place on Pretensia. Maybe at a hipster market on Eicreon for the cost of an entire meal elsewhere. Once picked, it went bad within a day.

"It's on the house," Oz said as she backed away down the row, picking another for herself as her boots crunched beneath her.

With some difficulty, he peeled the vaguely rust-colored rind and exposed the nearly white flesh inside. It grew as a cluster of bean-shaped segments stuck lightly together. They were so easy to pull apart that the fruit seemed designed to be enjoyed one delicious bite at a time.

He popped one in and bit. The brightest, fruitiest juice in the galaxy filled his mouth, and he groaned with pleasure. "Holy shit."

"You've never had it?"

"Only in these fancy jams mom used to get. But fresh? Forget it. How big is this grove?"

"A thousand trees at least," she said. "It's how my father pays the help."

"Don't these go for like twenty credits each in the city?" Geddy asked.

"Twenty-seven, last I heard. The landscapers get to take home all they can carry."

"They must make out pretty good."

"Well, considering the annual harvest is only about three weeks long, it's eleven kilometers to the nearest Ophir settlement, and they walk both ways, I'd say it's …"

"A Bransel-esque arrangement?" he offered.

"Yeah."

The trees he'd seen on Zorr were scraggly, with thick, rough bark that locked in precious moisture. Others were more papery and grew taller, but with thin, wispy leaves that didn't provide much shade from the punishing Zorran suns. The trees on Verdithea — the godforsaken planet that almost got him killed — were more like very long cocktail umbrellas.

Now this was a proper forest.

Just beyond the escilot grove, the forest grew thicker still. As they crunched through a blanket of ice-dusted twigs and seeds, his head craned back to take it all in. All manner of trees grew here, even the dark green ones with needles. The soaring canopy was thick with leaves, some the size of his face, but they still permitted streaks of yellow sunlight through so they could dance on the ground — as entertaining and fascinating a display as he'd seen this side of Stemir, all powered only by the sun and a building westerly breeze.

— *Damn.*

— Well said.

"Welcome to the *real* woods," Oz said, giving a half-twirl to face him. "The tallest ones are called shroves."

"Does that make this a shrove grove?"

"Gee, you're the first one to think of that," she teased.

"What's this one?"

He pointed at a delicate shrub that was almost perfectly symmetrical and in the shape of a flattened sphere. Yellow and white flowers the size of his thumbnail stretched wide to collect the sun.

"Terakina," she said, smiling. "Rich people treat it like a weed, but to the Ophir, it's sacred. They make tea from it. I told the landscapers they could take all the wanted of that, too. The clippings'll grow just about anywhere."

He leaned against one of the shroves and found it reassuringly sturdy. It saddened him to imagine it turning to ice and shattering in the vacuum after Temeruria broke apart. At least it wasn't too bad yet.

"Thank you for bringing me here, Oz."

She cozied up next to him, running her fingers lightly down the tree's smooth bark. "I'm glad I got to see it one last time."

The communicator on his wrist gave a soft beep, and he raised his arm to look.

"It's Jel," he said to Oz, then opened the channel. "Hey, Blondie. What's up?"

"Where are you guys?" She asked anxiously, squinting as she studied his surroundings. "Wait — you're still on the *ground??*"

"We're still waiting on his princen–" A distinct, long rumble traveled up through his feet. Reflexively, he grabbed hold of the tree. "Whoa. Was that what I thought it was?"

"I've been monitoring seismic activity since we got here, and it's increasing, fast. You need to get in the air, like, *yesterday.*"

"It's happening already?" The evac wasn't done yet. Lots of people remained in the cities.

"Gas gets released, stuff moves around. Usually not on your schedule. I shouldn't have to tell *you*," Jel said.

"Fair enough."

"Look, just get out of there before it gets too gnarly, okay? We're leaving the hangar open for you."

"Roger that. See you soon." He clicked off and met Oz's expectant gaze. "Time's up. The earthquakes are about to hit."

Oz let out a long sigh. "If they're not ready, we're leaving without them."

"Works for me." Before he took off back toward the ship, he glanced down at one of the Ophir's sacred bushes. "Do *you* like that terakina tea?"

"It's okay. Why?"

He stooped down and smelled it. It had a subtle, but distinctly lemony scent. "Is it the leaves or the flowers?"

"Both." He broke off a thick bouquet of wispy green fronds as she sidled up to him. "I thought you hated tea."

"I do, but you should keep some around. Someday, it'll remind you of a happy time."

He'd barely risen when Oz embraced him and squeezed tight. "Two happy times."

So many ships were clustered around the Medrikar spaceport waiting to enter the Alliance cordon that they resembled a dark-gray cloud. Only the royal palace's spire poked out through the top. Between that and the condensing gas that filled the sky with urine-colored clouds, the beauty of the planet that had so dazzled them now looked every bit as pre-apocalyptic as it was.

From the North, a handful of freighters streaked skyward.

"Are those the last of the Ophir?" Geddy asked Oz.

"Let's hope so."

Bransel, Nandra, their pilot, Aibry, and their servant, Chafton, were following the *Armstrong* in the family Hovensby, which they'd spent hours filling with whatever treasures they couldn't live without.

Geddy opened the channel back to Jel aboard the *Stalwart*, and she answered immediately.

"About time! Tell me you're on your way."

"Yeah, we're airborne. Have you heard from Balzac?" he asked.

"The two heavies we brought have jumped back. A third had to jump in from Doxx-Mora. I guess that one's almost full."

He let out a relieved breath. "Good. How many ships away so far?"

"Six thousand and change. A few hundred conventionals to go, plus the Star Guard." Jel said. "Another forty-thousand jump-capable ships are already outside Gundrun."

— *This is good news, Geddy.*

— I know. We might actually pull this off.

"Do we have enough ships left to pair up?"

"We'll be short by a few dozen. I asked the old man about sending some ships back for a second jump, but he said to just take 'em in the *Stalwart*."

Verveik wouldn't be crazy about sending anybody back for a second trip, especially once they were safely inside the khetaka. He didn't want to be here to begin with.

A slow drip of vessels rocketed skyward toward the cordon, one every few seconds. Considering how abrupt the evac order was, it could've been a lot more chaotic.

He turned to Oz, nodding over his shoulder to indicate the Hovensby. "They're awfully quiet back there."

"Hey Jel, can you hack an encrypted military channel?" Oz asked.

Jel gave a bemused laugh. "Puh-leeze. What's the frequency?"

"Theta 990.4," Oz said. "It's the royal family's private channel."

Jel briefly turned away from the camera to tap and swipe her way through a series of screens on her console. She chuckled to herself. "They must not be as paranoid as I thought. Just gimme two shakes ... and ... donezo. Passing the feed through."

Oz's screen lit up with a waveform, and official-sounding voices filled the bridge.

"... sending you the coordinates now, sir."

"Got it," came Bransel's unmistakable, nasally voice.

Geddy's head spun toward Oz, who scowled. "What's he talking about? They've had the coordinates since yesterday afternoon."

"You're certain this went to everyone on the list?" Bransel asked.

"Yes, sir. Your security detail is waiting at the rendezvous."

"Good work, Captain. We'll see you there."

The transmission went silent. Oz's pale face reddened with rage as she fought back tears. "That miserable bastard!" She shook her head in disbelief. "They weren't packing — they were coordinating their own escape. They're not going to the khetaka."

"They're not?" Geddy asked.

"Whoa, holy shit!" Jel exclaimed.

"What's wrong?" Geddy's head spun back to the front screen.

"I've been monitoring the University of Medrikar's sensors. Seismic activity just shot through the roof."

"Scan terrestrial emergency channels," Geddy said.

Jel worked her magic with the holoscreens and zeroed in on a frantic transmission from spaceport traffic control. "The planet's going to pieces! Everyone to your ships now! Go! Go! Go!"

"What about the cordon?" asked a female voice.

"Are you kidding me?! Just go!"

At the edge of the city, maybe two kilometers ahead, was a water processing facility with two rows of tall filtration silos. Geddy sucked in a breath as one of the silos broke from its base and toppled into another. Millions of gallons of water spilled from the bases as they tumbled like dominoes.

Below them, a series of cracks tore across the grassy plain surrounding Medrikar. If it kept going like this, the bombs wouldn't even need to go off.

"Jel, tell Ogos and Verveik what's happening. Keep the hangar open until we get th–"

Oz gasped, her eyes popping wide. "What? Son of a bitch!"

A flash of movement hit Geddy's peripheral vision. Bransel's Hovensby had broken away and was speeding skyward without them. He'd played them for fools.

"Just say the word and we'll catch him before he reaches the stratosphere." She only stared at the screen like she hadn't heard. "Oz!"

When he followed her horrified eyes to it, he couldn't blink, either.

The battlement of skyscrapers in downtown Medrikar rocked violently in widening circles, none more so than the palace. A crack shot across its north side, and the windows exploded. The top swayed back the other way, and as though in slow motion, the top one-third of the tower twisted free and fell, wrenching sideways as the last threads of steel snapped. It pinwheeled as it plummeted to the ground, clouds of dust billowing from the impact. It was surreal to watch from the air where they couldn't feel or hear it.

"No ..." Oz muttered.

— What do I do?? I don't know what to do.

— *Flying into space seems like a good idea.*

— But we need to know where Bransel's going.

— *We have bigger problems.*

Eli was right. Bransel was in the wind. They'd have to deal with him later.

"Buckle up," he advised Oz. "We're getting the hell out of here." With tears streaming down her face, Oz complied.

After cinching his own restraints, Geddy nosed her up and punched it.

CHAPTER 29
WHO'S THERE?

The *Armstrong* broke through a wispy layer of low, greenish clouds that had settled over the valley as it rocketed spaceward, the engines sending deep vibrations into their backs. Soon, the sky darkened, and stars filled the front screen.

Geddy hailed Verveik, who answered right away.

"Colonel," said the big man. "Is the evacuation complete?"

"Almost, but the quakes are tearing her up. Medrikar's basically rubble. Anyone still on the ground isn't gonna make it. Tell me Balzac made it back to the fleet with our tukrium."

"He just jumped in," Verveik confirmed. "Order the Star Guard to jump to the khetaka and get the stragglers into the *Stalwart*. We're done here."

Telling him that Bransel was MIA could wait. There was nothing they could do about it, and it would only enrage him.

The moment Verveik blinked out, Geddy hailed the Temerurian battleship *Urangalia*. Sky Marshal Komfeti soon appeared on screen.

"Colonel." He looked strangely calm. "I've been expecting to hear from you."

"Sky Marshal, it's time for the Star Guard to jump to the rendezvous."

Komfeti gave an obedient nod, his tone a bit too accommodating. "Of course. I will give the order immediately."

He blinked out. The *Stalwart* lay ahead, well above the U-shaped formation of Star Guard ships at the top of the cordon, its hangar sitting open. The nearer he drew to it, an odd sensation crept up his spine like they were being watched.

— What am I feeling here?

— *I am not sure, but I feel it as well.*

— If I didn't know better, I'd think …

From the corner of his eye, the Star Guard ships blipped away, leaving only Tymeri's ship, Ogos' Berzerker, and a handful of Chimeras.

The stars up ahead didn't look quite right to him, as though an invisible line separated them. Before he even knew it, he'd spun up weapons and shields.

Oz whirled toward him, her brow furrowed. "What are you doing?"

He barely heard the question. The scopes on the side of the screen were empty, and yet he felt certain they shouldn't be. His targeting reticle had nothing to lock on to, so he placed it just left of the invisible line he'd noticed and fired one of his missiles. It detached from the right wing and sped, seemingly, toward open space.

"What the fuck, Geddy??" Oz demanded.

He was too focused on the bright white spot as it shrank in the distance. After a few seconds, it disappeared from view.

But then the missile exploded against something solid, a balloon of light quickly swallowed by the vacuum. The space around it shimmered and rippled like he'd just thrown a rock into a pond.

Oz said, "What the hell?"

Before his eyes, the very fabric of space bent into angles

and unfolded into a colossal black half pyramid, a Zelnad destroyer. A moment later, a handful of others materialized, then freighters, asteroid breakers, mining drone carriers, and ore processors — so many that they filled his vision.

"Oh, *shit!*" Oz cried.

He slapped his palm on the breakthrough frequency. "All remaining Temerurian ships, this is Colonel Starheart. Proceed immediately inside the *Stalwart*. As fast as you can!"

"Where the hell did they come from?" Oz asked.

No Zelnad ships were moving except the mining vessels and ore carriers. They didn't seem to care — about the missile or the ships. The destroyer was the only visible support.

"I dunno, but something tells me they've been here a while."

"Why aren't they attacking?" Oz asked.

Geddy didn't even have time to speak before a flash from the aft camera caught his eye. A monstrous ring of purple shot out of the planet on a diagonal, radiating outward with the blinding power of a celestial blade. Geddy and Oz reflexively shielded their eyes and turned away.

The calamitous explosion would soon tear Temeruria in half, yet only silence filled the bridge. Through his fingers, Geddy noticed the brightness dissipate, and he lowered his hand.

At first, it almost seemed like nothing had happened. Temeruria looked exactly as it had when they left it. But then bright orange cracks spiderwebbed across its surface as the planet's molten inner beast punched through. A chunk of it with a scythe-shaped northern peninsula drifted away.

Soon, the main fracture line widened into a crescent and the smaller half broke off, opening a gap between them like a clamshell. One of its suns shone clear through.

Oz had become a statue. There was nothing to say.

They had to get to the *Stalwart*. But before they could, a

blast from the destroyer slammed into them, and they tumbled out of control through space. Alarms blared, and Geddy's eyes and brain both struggled to focus.

As though in a dream, he felt Morpho leap from his shoulder, and a moment later, the Armstrong righted itself. When his focus returned, Morph had seized the controls, and they were zooming toward the *Stalwart* at a full burn.

Their old-school shields were already down to thirty percent. One more direct hit and they were goners.

Up ahead, the handful of remaining Temerurian ships were filing en masse into the *Stalwart's* hangar. Blue-white flashes came from the port plasma cannons as Denk provided covering fire. The streaks sailed past the *Armstrong* in a blink, but he didn't need to look at the aft view to know they'd splashed harmlessly off the destroyer's impenetrable shields.

"Cap, Oz!" came Denk's frantic voice over the comm. "Are you guys okay?"

Geddy glanced down at Oz's stomach, thinking how stupid it was to put her in this situation. His blood boiled, and he yanked the controls away from Morpho. "We're fine but comin' in hot. Be ready to jump the second everyone's inside."

"Way ahead of you, C–"

A purple streak from behind them slammed into the *Stalwart's* port side, causing her shields to ripple. She rocked to starboard, and a bank of lights around the impact zone flickered out. Based on Verveik's experience on the *Gallant* over Earth 2, three or four hits were the most they could handle.

"Denk!" Geddy yelled, angling for the open maw of the hangar.

"Holy crap, that thing is powerful!" Denk said, picking himself up off the floor.

Up ahead, the last of the Temerurian ships abandoned their single-file line and frantically crammed themselves inside with Ogos and Tymeri bringing up the rear.

Another jarring impact slammed Geddy's head against his seat back. Sparks caught his eye to the right, and he smelled smoke. The shield integrity showed zero. Only two of the five engines were still online. His yaw control was wonky, but that wouldn't keep him from entering the hangar.

Oz's eyes peeled wide in terror, her fingers white from where they gripped the armrests. "We're not gonna make it!"

"Not with that attitude."

The Armstrong sailed through the open doors, just clipping the back of Tymeri's ship, and he hit the retros hard.

"We're in, Denk! Get us out of here!"

The doors began to close just as the Stalwart took another direct hit. Again, she listed hard to starboard nearly ninety degrees. Temerurian ships that had already landed slid across the floor, clanging off each other like pinballs.

"C'mon! Let's go! Let's go!" he yelled again, struggling to keep the ship steady.

"The bubble drive's offline!" Jel said frantically on screen, her long white hair covering half her face. "We can't jump!"

"That destroyer's headed right for us," Denk warned. "Everybody hang on!"

Denk hit the thrusters, and the *Stalwart's* engines surged to life. But the doors were still open, and artificial gravity wasn't engaged. A couple of the Temerurian ships slid out through the gap when he accelerated. The others slammed into them as they closed. Zero G was a real bitch sometimes.

Geddy glanced at the scopes. The destroyer was lining up for another shot. Denk was taking evasive maneuvers.

"Geddy!" Lestiko's face pushed into the edge of the frame. "There's a way to expand the jump bubble on a Berzerker enough to envelop the *Stalwart*!"

"What are you talking about?" Geddy asked.

Oz gasped, having snapped out of her daze. "Sammo-Yann

jumped a whole asteroid to Gundrun, remember? The Xellarans said it was just a matter of power."

"But where are we gonna get that kind of ...?"

He didn't have to finish the thought. Lestiko was going to separate from Rai and release a nuclear-scale burst of energy into the shield generator. But the *Armstrong* was too fragile to risk it.

"We're too banged up," Geddy said.

"My ship isn't." The other face that popped up on the flickering screen belonged to Ogos. "Lestiko, meet me at the front of the hangar! Denk, reopen the doors!"

"Ogos, no!" Geddy protested. "There's gotta be another way."

But he didn't respond. His Berzerker emerged from the pile of ships at the back and floated toward the front, passing through the pressure shield and skillfully hovering before the upper airlock. Meanwhile, the hangar doors worked open again.

If Lestiko was successful, the bubble would whisk them away in the nanoseconds before the explosion. Either way, he and Ogos wouldn't return.

Lestiko leapt across the small gap from outside the bridge into Ogos' open cargo hold. While it closed, he spun the Berzerker around and rocketed back through the pressure shield toward the doors. Geddy's head whirled as they passed, just catching a glimpse of his determined clone through the front shield.

Another blast rocked the *Stalwart*, and she began to tumble.

"They hit the engines!" Denk said. "Shields are down! I can't control her! We're dead in the water!"

"Did Ogos get out??" Geddy asked.

His answer came in the form of a blinding white light that seared his retinas. It was gone as soon as it flashed. But no explosion followed. Nothing did. The ships in the hangar still clinked off each other as the *Stalwart* rolled lazily through space.

The scopes were so full of signals that it appeared as a single mass. As their uncontrolled tumble continued, Geddy caught a glimpse of a giant red planet through the open hold doors.

Gundrun.

CHAPTER 30
FREE FALLIN'

For five tense minutes, the *Stalwart* continued to tumble, accelerating as Gundrun's epic gravity reeled them in. Once they realized they'd made it out from Temeruria, Morpho squeezed his way out of the *Armstrong* and into the guts of the battle cruiser to see if he could bring its propulsion and artificial gravity systems back online. Meanwhile, Khetaka Central Command held an emergency meeting to figure out how to slow her down without causing further damage.

Geddy could easily discern the terrified faces of Temerurians through the front shields of their ships as they tried to keep from slamming into each other in the endlessly rotating, gravity-free hangar. One family of five or six had crowded into the forward cabin and were just holding each other, desperate for this nightmare to stop.

Oz stared blankly ahead, unable to fully process what had just happened. It was a strange enough feeling to barely escape one dire situation and land right in another. Her particular cocktail of emotions, however, had to be crippling.

Temeruria was gone. So were Lestiko and Ogos. There would be time to grieve later.

— Any bright ideas?

Twenty Gundrun trade ships were waiting to fire a barrage of novaspheres and open an old-school jump gate if it came to that. At least they wouldn't crash. But even that would require absolute precision, and it would still leave them in an uncontrolled tumble until the ship could be repaired or stopped in a safer location, which might take hours or days.

A Gundrun Commandant named Norgut, who had taken Arbizander's place over Khetaka Central Command, had been keeping them updated. His stern face appeared on screen.

"Okay, Colonel, here's what we're gonna do," he said. "Every Gundrun commercial vessel with a tractor beam has been pressed into service. That's about sixty in all. Working together, they should be able to arrest your spin enough for all of you to safely get out."

"Okay, well, the engines should be back online any second. My best guy's already on it."

"That doesn't matter now," he said grimly. "You can't overcome Gundrun's gravity. My priority is to get everyone out of there so we can jump it away empty."

As much as he didn't like the idea of abandoning ship, Norgut's plan was a good one. The sooner they got out, the better. They'd deal with the ship later.

"Thanks, Commandant. Keep us posted."

Norgut nodded and blinked out. Geddy turned to Oz, who was looking a bit green from all the spinning.

"You don't look so good."

In lieu of a reply, she undid her restraints and sprinted out of the bridge with her hand over her mouth. A moment later, he heard her retching in the small galley.

The scopes showed an arrangement of trawlers and deep-space rescue ships lining up behind them. Soon, their endless tumble began to slow. As it did, the amplitude decreased, and the free-floating ships in the hangar had an easier time keeping their distance. When Denk appeared on the screen, the ship's wobble was only slight.

"Cap, I'm gonna open the doors. Norgut says we've got three minutes before we hit the ionosphere."

"Okay. As soon as you do that, you and Jel get to the *Bogart* and abandon ship."

The hangar doors slid apart. Geddy opened the emergency short-range channel. "Attention civilian craft, this is Colonel Starheart. Please proceed in an orderly fashion through the doors."

Naturally, they did precisely the opposite, jamming through the gap all at once. Some paint was traded in the process, but they all got out in less than a minute. He gestured toward Tymeri for her to follow them out.

A peculiar noise came from the back somewhere, followed by the reassuring sound of Morpho's sticky parts swinging across the ceiling. Geddy smiled as he plopped down on his shoulder.

— No luck?

— **The fusion converter housing is badly damaged. Without it, the engines are inoperable.**

"I appreciate you trying. We're gonna jump her away for now."

— **Thanks for not leaving without me.**

"Oh, like I would."

Morpho and a team of Kailorian technicians were patching up the *Stalwart* over Afolos, where Khetaka Command had temporarily jumped it. The goal was to patch up the bubble drive first then jump it back to the fleet where it could be fully repaired. Meanwhile, Verveik had joined the crowd inside the khetaka using Commandant Arbizander's corvette. He wanted a full debrief from Geddy and Oz about what went down over Temeruria and to personally appraise the evacuee situation.

After docking the *Armstrong* at the back of the corvette, they followed the big man down a long hallway toward Arbizander's quarters at the front. As they walked, Oz kept her arms folded tightly about her, staring at the floor and not quite keeping up.

Verveik threw Geddy a look over his shoulder that said, *Is she going to be okay?* Only he didn't know, so he just shrugged in return.

When the door opened for them, Verveik gestured them inside, doing his best to appear empathetic. Geddy gently touched Oz's arm as she shuffled in ahead of him.

"We can do this later if you'd prefer," the big man offered.

"Let's just get it over with."

Arbizander's quarters were spacious but spare. Six gigantic chairs were arranged around a handmade Gundrun steel table in the middle with an ordinary desk against the right wall. A large window was the only adornment.

Oz took one of the chairs near the door and settled gently into it. Less than two hours ago, she watched her home world crack in half. Her discomfort was palpable.

Geddy chose the seat next to her and Verveik went across to the other side. As he sat, he gave a heavy sigh and folded his hands in front of him on the table.

"I'm very sorry, Osmiya," Verveik offered, his tone as tender as Geddy had ever heard it. "I truly am. And I wish we didn't have to do this now, but–"

"My father ran away," she cut him off. "He left his people, and he took the Star Guard with him. Right?"

Verveik nodded silently for a couple of seconds before answering. "It looks that way."

"What about the Ophir?" she asked pointedly.

"What do you mean?"

She got up and went to the window, peering out at the cloud of Temerurian ships. They were spread too far and wide to see them all, but a cluster of boxy freighters would've stood out among the thousands of transports and private vessels. The longer she searched, the tighter the knot in Geddy's stomach became.

Evacuating the Ophir wasn't among Verveik's terms. He didn't know she'd added her own. "I made my father get them out first. I just want to know they're safe."

She looked as though she could burst into tears at any second, but she never would. Not in front of the Commander. Maybe not even in front of him.

The look on Verveik's face telegraphed his anger, but she couldn't see it. Geddy watched him swallow it.

"What kind of freighters?"

"I don't know. They all look the same to me. Big, boxy cargo ships. There'd be dozens."

Verveik's eyes met his, and he gave his head the tiniest of shakes. The air went out of the room. Oz must've sensed it because she immediately spun back to face them.

"They're not here either, are they?"

The commander couldn't bring himself to turn around. "I don't think so."

Her lips formed a tight line, and she returned to the window. "I knew it. I *fucking knew it in my bones.* He didn't rescue the Ophir — he only rescued more tukrium. The quakes would've buried it if he hadn't. An entire race is extinct because of *greed!* Maybe the Zelnads have a ..." she wisely trailed off.

"But the warehouse ..." Geddy said.

"There were more stashes," she sniffed, quickly wiping her eye on her sleeve. "Of course."

The commander gave a pained sigh and wrung his hands. "Any idea where they could've gone?"

With her back still to them, she shook her head. "No."

— *Ziksu said it would take the whole galaxy.*

— *I know.*

— *What are you going to do?*

"We did all we could. He knew what was at stake," Geddy said. "So what now?"

"Nothing changes," Verveik stated. "We fill the orbs, retrofit the fleet, and prepare for war."

"But the Last Illustration …" Geddy began.

He raised his eyes. In them, Geddy saw something unfamiliar — worry. "What choice do we have?"

As they spoke, the Nads were having a free-for-all with Temeruria's shattered remains. It was only a matter of time before they refined all the shinium they needed to complete their weapon. Even working at full capacity, retrofitting the whole fleet with new weapons and shields by then would be a Herculean task. Perhaps impossible.

Verveik's eyes drifted down to the table, his jaw set. "Thank you — that will be all."

"It's been a long couple of days," Geddy said as he rose. "We're gonna go back."

The commander nodded okay but didn't raise his eyes. Oz abruptly about-faced and strode through the door. Geddy gave a final glance at Verveik before following her out, but he still couldn't look up.

CHAPTER 31
GOING IN CIRCLES

Three days later, Geddy woke from an insufficient sleep and checked the clock. It was just shy of four a.m. He and the crew were in temporary quarters aboard the battle cruiser *Steadfast*, whose command Verveik had only recently awarded to Ogos. The *late* Ogos.

Shit.

Clone number sixteen was in charge now. What was his name again? Choclo? Chucky? Something like that.

— *You should try to sleep some more.*

— What's the point?

He got up, threw on a set of Alliance-issued PT clothes, and wandered out into the hangar. The usual background hum of the engines and the vents was the only sound at first, but soft footfalls soon approached from the near left corner of the jogging track.

— *Who's running at this hour?*

— Oz.

— *Oh.*

He waited for her beneath the stairs that descended from the *Stalwart's* command deck, giving his legs a halfhearted stretch. Ten seconds later, she came around the bend at an enviable clip, her long red locks gathered behind her and her face slick with sweat. She showed no signs of slowing as she approached. The clones did PT on their own time now, but this was still how she blew off steam.

— *You're gonna have to run.*
— *Oh, I know.*
— *Are you sure that's a good idea?*

Shaking his muscles awake, Geddy lined up in the adjacent lane. The moment he accelerated to her pace, he realized he'd better talk fast. Her eyes remained fixed on the track like he wasn't there.

"I'm not slowing down for you."

"I'd be disappointed if you did."

Halfway around, his heart was already working overtime, seemingly baffled as to why he was exercising at such an hour. Or at all.

"Do you need to talk?" he asked.

"No. Do you?"

"I mean … maybe."

"Then talk."

"This isn't your fault," he said.

She'd ignored her father's overtures for weeks. Had the Alliance intervened sooner, perhaps everyone, including the poor Ophir, could've been evacuated. He knew her well enough to know that's all she could think about.

"The Star Guard'll turn on Bransel before long," he assured her. "Their families are among the evacuees, right?"

"Yeah."

Bransel's decision to abandon his people wasn't overly surprising. Whether out of shame or self-preservation, it fit his M.O. But the Star Guard, not so much. Geddy's best guess was that Sky Marshal Komfeti had replaced the Alliance's jump coordinates with new ones. They likely didn't even know where they'd gone.

Geddy ran in silence beside Oz for a lap and a half, during which he thought he might actually die.

— *Is your heart going to explode?*

— Quite possibly.

— **Then you should stop.**

He'd heard Oz clearly, yet she hadn't spoken.

— Oz?

— **You see anyone else around here?**

— You can tune to me?

"I've been able to for a while," she said aloud. "It's not that hard."

At first, she could only get a vague sense of what Eli was saying in Geddy's head. Lately, though, she heard everything. She used to swear up and down she couldn't read his mind. Hearing his conversations with Eli wasn't quite the same, but it was close enough to make him a bit uncomfortable.

"Did Lestiko teach you?"

Oz abruptly pulled up and stopped. Geddy doubled over, panting with his hands on his knees. "What's ... wrong?"

"When were you gonna tell me the Zelnads want to blow up the entire fucking universe?"

A shot of nervous adrenaline sent his heart into overdrive, and he drew himself up in front of her. "Lestiko told you?"

"Once I learned how to tune, I could feel his despair like it was my own. I coaxed it out of him."

Oz was an empath. Tuning would bring her even closer to people's emotions than she already was. Hell, maybe she always knew how to tune.

She defiantly crossed her arms. "Answer the question."

"I was going to tell you, but ..."

"But what?"

"I didn't want you to lose hope."

"For what?"

"For a real family. The kind neither of us got to have."

She took a step forward, her big yellow eyes staring uncomfortably deep into his. "How many times have I told you, Geddy? It's not your job to protect me. Especially not from the truth."

It wasn't quite that simple. Yes, everyone had a right to know what was truly at stake. But in the end, did it matter? Protecting Sagacea was still the mission.

She'd essentially done the same by waiting to tell him about Temeruria. Maybe that's why she wasn't more upset.

"I didn't tell you because I'm fucking terrified. And if I'm being absolutely honest, Oz, I'm not sure we can win anymore, and that scares the shit out of me because it would mean I won't have a future with you."

— *Oh, Geddy ...*

— Not now, E.

Oz searched his eyes for any glint of insincerity, but she wouldn't find it. He couldn't have said the real reason why he'd kept it from her until that moment.

Her gaze softened, and her sweaty hand brushed his cheek. "I'm scared, too."

"It was comforting to think we could afford to lose, y'know?" he said. "I figured that even if Sagacea was destroyed, we wouldn't live long enough to see the consequences. But now ..."

She nodded sympathetically. "I know. I thought so, too."

"I should've told you, and I'm sorry. Look, we're testing Lestiko's prototypes on Mikuli tomorrow. Assuming they work, we'll plan the attack. I'll tell Verveik and the war cabinet then."

Oz took his hands in hers. "I'm sorry, too. I kept the truth from you about Temeruria, and I shouldn't have. If I hadn't, maybe—"

"Hey, you two!" came Denk's voice from down the track. "You weren't gonna do sesehlu without us, where you?"

Voprot, Jel, and Doc entered the hangar behind them in their workout clothes, all looking bleary-eyed. Geddy gave Oz a, *We good?* look and got a tiny nod in return. They made their way to the others. It felt good to clear the air, but he dreaded the moment he'd have to the awful truth to Verveik and the cabinet.

"Sorry," Geddy said. "We were just deciding whether we had time for another twenty laps. Guess not."

Jel threw her head back and laughed. "Ha! Starheart, you couldn't do twenty laps around the bridge."

"I agree," said Voprot. "You are fat and slow."

"Love you guys, too. Doc, you care to take any potshots?"

They set out together across the empty hangar toward the *Fiz*.

"You are my superior, Colonel. It wouldn't be appropriate," Doc said. "But if you need to stop and rest, just let us know."

Even Oz laughed at that, and it was the most beautiful thing he'd heard in a long time.

CHAPTER 32

FINALLY, WE GET TO SHOOT STUFF

Ten days later, Geddy and the rest of Verveik's cadre took two Berzerkers to the Samaja's remote facility on Mikuli to conduct the first test of Lestiko's designs. Geddy flew one and Tymeri the other. They'd jumped from the edge of the ion storm to just above the crater and immediately entered the narrow hangar so as not to risk detection by the Xellaran government.

News of Temeruria's destruction and the disappearance of both Prince Bransel and the Star Guard saw public opinion galvanize around the Alliance. The last few holdouts, notably Gethenia, Knetos, and Nichu, finally sent what few military assets they had, about four hundred ships in all. Other worlds that had no armies dispatched police vessels, transports, and supplies, including cargo vessels full of donated tukrium trinkets and keepsakes like the knife Geddy's mother had.

The fleet now numbered nearly two hundred thousand ships, and Zirhof's people were equipping them with bubble drives the moment they arrived. The knowledge that Xellara had multiples of that sitting useless on the ground had become a popular topic in the news, and pressure was mounting for them to act. But if any world had shown a capacity to ignore the rest of the galaxy and do its own thing, it was Xellara.

Meanwhile, a probe similar to the one that had taken surreptitious photos of the Zelnad base was sent to monitor their mining operation on what was left of Temeruria. Massive cargo ships were jumping in and out almost daily, heavy with tukrium ore. The undertaking was now guarded by ten destroyers and hundreds of fighters, which suggested, at least to Geddy, that the Nads took the Alliance seriously.

Ziksu appeared the moment the hangar re-pressurized wearing his simple Samaja robes. A few eyebrows were raised as he greeted everyone in turn — the Orneans in particular, who had no time for religion and prophecies. But this wasn't about that.

"Is Mr. Lestiko not joining us?" he asked, scanning the contingent for him.

"You didn't hear?" Geddy asked. He shook his head no. "He ... ah ... separated from his entity in order to save the *Stalwart*. I wouldn't be here if it weren't for him."

"It was a hero's death," Verveik agreed.

Ziksu's face fell. "I am deeply sorry. Come." He motioned for everyone to follow. "Perhaps what I have to show you will raise your spirits."

They followed him to a table bearing fully realized versions of the mockups they'd seen aboard the *Inquiry* and a power orb. Beside it was one of the Alliance Chimera fighters, which had been delivered as a reference platform along with the tukrium. They formed a semicircle around it.

A length of flexible conduit ran between the two pieces, connecting to a concave housing that held the orb.

Smiling, Ziksu said, "As you can see, we were able to produce Mr. Lestiko's designs with very few modifications. He was quite ingenious."

"It looks small," Queen Tymeri noted.

— Please don't say size doesn't matter.

Ziksu, who could hear Geddy's thoughts, allowed a smirk. "Looks can be deceiving."

Verveik ran his fingers along the top of the boxy part. "This is the shield generator?"

"Yes, Commander. As with the disruptor, it's a simple replacement, with power being delivered through the conduit. Now, if you'll accompany me over here …" They shuffled over to the Chimera. Ziksu pointed out the two disruptors inset in the wings. "This fighter has already been retrofitted with the new system."

General Grozuc of the Triad squatted to study it. It would fall to Aku, Ghruk, and Kailoria to handle the large-scale operation.

"How long to swap out the systems?" he asked Ziksu.

"We did it in half an hour. I am certain your people will do it in far less, General."

He rose and crossed his thick arms. "We'll do it as fast as you can make 'em."

"How many can you manufacture in a day?" Verveik asked hopefully.

"Five hundred full assemblies per day, maybe six."

The number hung in the silence like a fart. Geddy and the others exchanged grim looks. That was a lot, but not nearly enough. Not even close.

"That's more than a year to upgrade the whole fleet," Geddy muttered.

Verveik turned to Ziksu. "Is there any way to make them more quickly?"

He looked apologetic. "I'm afraid not. Not in this facility, at least."

"Mmm," Verveik muttered. "One problem at a time. Have you test-fired them?"

"Yes, but only in a very controlled environment. Ziksu

turned to him. "Colonel, I understand you're quite the pilot. Would you like to put it through its paces?"

A broad grin split Geddy's face.

Despite being surrounded by them all day and standing by while the clones trained on the sims, Geddy had only flown a Chimera a handful of times. A number of Samaja technicians had moved it into a gigantic service elevator and up into the hangar where the Berzerkers were parked. He put on his helmet and climbed inside while Ziksu waited.

"All right, so how's this gonna work?" he asked.

Ziksu's head appeared above the edge of the cockpit. "Your targets are three training drones equipped with their own mahk'ti weapons and shields," Ziksu said. "They're small, but they've been programmed to act like Zelnad fighters based on the data you've shared. The crater rim is your operating ceiling. Anything above that risks detection."

"Got it."

"Good luck, Geddy. We'll all be watching from the observation area. Your comm is already tuned to it, so if you need anything, just talk."

Ziksu hurried away through the airlock, and Geddy closed the canopy. His ears popped as it pressurized, and he yawned to clear them as the hangar doors slid aside.

He fired up the VTO thrusters and eased the ship through the narrow opening, then zipped across the crater, reorienting himself in the Chimera's cockpit. As Ziksu promised, his scopes immediately warned of three small bogeys closing fast from dead ahead.

Geddy activated the new shield and rocketed toward them. Ziksu wasn't kidding about the size. They were spherical, a bit more than a meter wide, and nearly the same dull gray as the moon's regolith.

Their formation tightened as they neared on a collision course.

— *Are you gonna shoot them or crash into them?*

— Neither. I need to know we can trust the shields.

— *Uh, maybe there's a better way?*

His mouth went dry. The memory of the *Armstrong* and the *Stalwart* being pummeled by the Nads was still fresh.

The ships unleashed a volley of purple bolts. Geddy fought the instinct to evade them and winced as they slammed into him, half expecting to be enveloped by flames. The shields deflected the shots, but the force of the impact spilled his velocity by fifteen percent, and the ship wobbled briefly as he righted it. The drones broke off and disappeared.

"Very instructive," he said into his helmet.

"That looked like it hurt. How's your shield integrity?" Verveik asked over the radio.

His eyes darted to the lower right corner of his HUD.

"Ninety-three percent." The drones had turned around and reformed behind him. "Before, I would've been on fumes."

— *Can we shoot back now?*

— Watch and learn, pal. I call this one the Silent Storm.

Geddy nosed the Chimera down and dove. The key was to let the enemy move into firing position, which meant pulling back on the thrusters. The moment the drones lined up for a shot, he sprayed purple bolts at the dark gray regolith below, ripping holes several meters deep as a massive cloud of the stuff kicked up.

He plunged inside, then pulled up and hit his retros just as they fired. They passed right under him, skimming the ground, and when they emerged, he was ready. The Chimera's independent targeting locked onto the two trailing drones as he sped after them.

— Let's see if this works the other way.

He pulled the trigger, sending a volley into the formation from overhead. The rear two drones' shields held, but the force of the blasts sent them crashing into the ground, sparking and rolling as they tumbled across the moon's stark surface, kicking up still more regolith.

— *How about that?*

— What?

— The shield's less effective against a collision.

The remaining target quickly spun around and reversed direction, firing at him but missing as he banked right and gunned it, climbing toward the rim of the crater.

— *Is this called the Ignoring an Important Request?*

— No, this is the Rim Job.

The Chimera was thusly named for its gimbal-mounted cockpit. Both it and the armature ring — basically the rest of the ship — could rotate and tilt independently of each other. Thus, the pilot could face any direction, as could the weapons.

He had it floored, yet the little drone was gaining on him. A couple shots slammed him from behind, and his shield dropped to eighty-two percent. Just short of the rim, Geddy locked on and hit the trigger. The armature ring spun around in a flash and blasted the target until it popped like a blister in the void.

— Whoa. That didn't take many hits.

"Well, Colonel, your reputation is well-earned," said Ziksu in his ear. "Go ahead and return to the hangar."

"I dunno, I'm having a good ol' time up … here …"

He slowed the ship to a stop, barely below the rim, as a bright spot lit up on his scopes. It was a big signal. A cluster of smaller ones came in behind it.

"Hey Zikky, we've got company."

Swiping to the next screen, he found the transponder

analysis and gasped. The ships approaching the Samaja's secret moon base were Xellaran military.

CHAPTER 33
WHO CALLED THE COPS?

Twelve Xellaran Darkstars, the fighters that had bedeviled him on Verdithea, approached the remote moon escorting a ship he'd never seen before. It was elegant and beautiful like the Rapier but much larger and newer, with the distinct red and gold accents that gave away their make. Geddy hovered just below the rim of the crater, the hangar doors a good seven hundred meters straight below him.

"Ziksu, I don't think this place is a secret anymore," he said.

"It's the Grand Chancellor's ship," Ziksu replied in his helmet. "Return at once."

While the armed escort passed overhead, Geddy plunged the Chimera straight down, glancing frequently up through the canopy to watch the ships slow to a stop over the center of the crater.

— *Is this bad? It seems bad.*

— How'd they find this place? Especially now?

The hidden door opened as he neared it, and he eased the ship inside. Ziksu, Verveik, and the others were waiting behind the airlock window. Geddy settled onto the pad. A few seconds later, a gleaming drop ship similar to the Rapier darkened it and slowly entered. The hangar closed behind it, and its skids touched down. Just looking through the window, it was hard to gauge anyone's reaction.

The hangar re-pressurized, and Geddy popped the canopy. Meanwhile, the airlock door slid open, and Ziksu led the others inside as Geddy ambled over to meet them.

"I swear I didn't go above the rim," Geddy said to Ziksu. "Unless you count me dunking on those drones."

Ziksu appeared more baffled than worried. "I know, Colonel. Something tells me we were betrayed."

The ramp opened, a puff of condensed air escaping as it did. Six soldiers from the infamous Golden Guard emerged first. Per their monikers, they wore bright gold body armor over red undergarments and carried long polearms, the likes of which Geddy had never seen. They marched down in sync, their heavy footsteps suggestive of numerous cybermods. A few meters short of Ziksu, they parted to reveal a small man in a crisp military uniform.

Like Rabhu, who had represented Xellara at the Gundrun Summit, his eyes were mirrored orbs that reflected Geddy and the others like a funhouse mirror.

He marched right up to Ziksu with his hands folded behind his back, wearing an expression so imperious it made Bransel look like a eunuch.

"Grand Chancellor Ranimus." Ziksu gave a courteous bow. "What an unexpected surprise."

It wasn't returned. The Chancellor moved his not-quite-a-nose to within a centimeter of Ziksu's, his face reflected in those unsettling eyes. "Spare me the theatrics, brother. You respect nothing. But I'm not here for you."

"Then why are you here?"

Verveik took a giant step toward Ranimus, drawing even with Ziksu. "Because I told him about this place."

Geddy gasped at the admission. Why would he do such a thing? This whole operation depended on absolute secrecy.

Now Ziksu's confused expression turned grave. "I don't understand."

"I knew this would get his attention," he growled, casting an accusatory look at the chancellor.

He took a small step back, craning his neck to look him in the eyes. "Commander Verveik. We've not had the honor."

"Do *not* talk to me of honor, Chancellor!" The sharpness in Verveik's voice gave everyone a start. "I'd say ignorance is more your area of expertise!"

If he was intimidated, he didn't show it. In fact, he looked up at him with a smile, which somehow made the ball-bearing eyes even creepier. "And if *you* were a man of honor, Commander, you would accept Xellara's clearly and repeatedly stated position regarding your Alliance."

Verveik's eyes squinted at him like he was trying to decide which limb to rip off first. "You don't know what's at stake."

"Oh, but I do. We have no interest in your …" as he fished for the words, he looked sickened by them, " … grotesque charade."

For reasons he would never understand, Geddy stepped directly between them. He extended a hand to Chancellor Ranimus. "Hi! Geddy Starheart." He regarded his hand like it was a fresh turd. "Sorry, you didn't strike me as a hugger."

"Colonel, you're out of line," Verveik warned.

— *What are you doing??*

"Yeah, probably." Geddy wagged his finger at the Commander — another thing he'd never get over. "*However*, I think I can save us a lot of time here. There's something you all need to know." Only Doc knew what he was about to say.

"Another time," Verveik said through clenched teeth.

"Nope, gotta be now. Should've been sooner, but a lot of shit was going on."

"Starheart ..." the Chancellor began, thoughtfully scratching his chin as his weird eyes passed over him. Geddy got the feeling he was being scanned. Ranimus suddenly scowled. "You destroyed my Xoo."

Myadan had always been a Xellaran settlement. "Ah ... You mean the Xoo that was developing super-ranses and growing clones of me right under your ... " he hesitated because whatever organ was in the middle of his face, it hardly qualified as a nose, making the metaphor less punchy. "Without you knowing about it. The point is, the Nads have been playing us all for fools."

"That can't be difficult," the Chancellor said.

Geddy let out a long sigh. "Practically everything they've done to this point has been a big distraction. While we've been chasing our tails, they've been building a weapon capable of destroying Sagacea. Only that's not their ultimate goal. It's not civilization they want to wipe out — it's the entire universe."

"You'd better start making sense, Colonel, and fast," Verveik said.

"If Sagacea blows up, it'll start a chain reaction that never stops."

"What do you mean, never stops?" Verveik asked.

"Earth 2's atmosphere was full of methane, but you could light a match and nothing would happen. A big enough explosion, however, set the whole thing off. That's what'll happen if Sagacea is destroyed."

Verveik's gaze slid over to Doc, who stepped forward to join them. "The Colonel is correct. If we fail, the resulting cataclysm will consume all matter and energy in our universe. It was a theory of Lestiko's, but the science agrees."

Ranimus scoffed. "Nonsense! Sagacea's end is merely a new beginning. Xellara was chosen to create a better future."

Now he scanned the faces around him. "Your failure in this pointless endeavor is assured. But all your cultures, your collective knowledge, the terrible lessons you've learned ... we will bear them into eternity. Indeed, it is our sacred duty to do so."

"We saw the Last Illustration, too," Geddy said. "It's ambiguous. Not unlike your whole red-and-gold motif. It's, like, *this close* to not working for you."

The Chancellor's reflective eyes narrowed murderously at him, his head swiveling back and forth between Geddy and Ziksu. "What could you possibly know of the Illustrations?"

"It doesn't matter!" Verveik barked. His chest thrust forward, his muscled arms flexing like he might rip the Chancellor in two. "I will not see the light of this world extinguished because of your cynical interpretation of a damned *painting!*"

"The Asurya's meaning is clear. For a new and peaceful history to be written, the old and violent one must end," he asserted.

"Not if we are united!" Ziksu pleaded. "Don't you see? This isn't about Xellara or the Alliance. It's a test of our resolve! We've finally harnessed mahk'ti. It could change our entire galaxy for the better, but without the skill and strength of our people, we cannot prevail. *That's* the Asurya's lesson. *That's* our challenge."

Geddy still wasn't sure about all this "chosen" stuff, but if it helped change the Chancellor's mind, so be it.

"We can stop this," Geddy interjected. "But only with Xellara at our side. It's as simple as that."

Verveik's expression finally softened. "He's right. Xellara and the Alliance have had their differences over many years, but if ever there was a time to put them aside, it's now."

Ranimus clearly was blindsided by all this, however, he didn't appear unswayed by it either. "I respect your desire to survive, Commander. If you believe that open war against the Zelnads is the only answer, then we won't stand in your way. The same goes for you, Ziksu. If the Samaja casts their lot with the Alliance, that is your choice. But war is not Xellara's destiny."

A deathly silence followed his words. Geddy's heart sank. Verveik was expressionless.

"Ranimus, please ..." Ziksu pleaded.

He held up his hand. "I was not finished. I said we won't stand in your way. Xellara is still open for business. If it's manufacturing you need, then our factories will help equip your fleet."

"In exchange for what?" Verveik asked.

"Your technology."

CHAPTER 34

A MAN WITH A PLAN

Between the war cabinet and the Orneans, it took several days to devise a battle plan to stop the Nads. Geddy was part of those meetings, and it gave him a new appreciation for the planning that goes into your standard military operation.

Nobody yet knew where Bransel and his cronies had gone with the Star Guard, or if they truly intended to let the Alliance deal with millions of evacuees. Fortunately, they were still safe behind the khetaka, and supplies were flooding in from around the galaxy. It had been proposed that they re-settle on Myadan, much of which was terraformed but unpopulated. Xellara never bothered to develop it beyond the walls of the Xoo. Now Geddy understood why. They were hunkered down waiting for the world to end so they could build a new one.

He walked shoulder to shoulder with Oz down the curved hallway that led to the *Gallant's* small auditorium. Her grief and anger were being expressed as silent brooding, which was an improvement from the morning's touchy conversation. When he told her that Xellara would help equip the fleet, she barely reacted. Of course, her relationship with them was complicated.

"It's cool that the Temerurians are filling power orbs for us."

Teaching New Alliance pilots how to donate mahk'ti for the war effort had proven more challenging than expected. But the Temerurian evacuees, aggrieved but bored, jumped at the chance to help. They were damn good at it, too.

"Yeah."

They reached the door to the auditorium. He gestured her inside, pausing to let her descend the steps ahead of him.

— I'm dyin' here.

— *She just needs time.*

— Not enough of that to go around these days.

The rest of the war cabinet was waiting for them. Oz chose the fourth row and left the aisle seat for Geddy.

Verveik and Doc got up. "Now that we're all here, let's take a moment of silence for Ogos and Lestiko."

He lowered his big head, and everyone fell silent. Lestiko was an enigma and seemed to like it that way. But they'd gotten close in a short time, and Geddy couldn't help but wonder if he knew the man better than anyone. As for Ogos, at least he went out on his own terms. That might be the best any of them could hope for.

He found Oz staring absently at the back of Arbizander's seat. Meanwhile, Verveik dimmed the lights and activated the hologram of the Zelnad base they'd seen earlier, now with greater detail.

"As we speak, the Xellarans are shipping thousands of disruptor and shield systems to the Triad worlds. They're being installed as fast as they arrive. General Grozuc, Balzac — your people have risen to the occasion, and they have our gratitude." The two Screvari gave appreciative nods. "Our battle plans are based on new intel, which I'll let Dr. Tardigan present."

Verveik took a step back while Doc zoomed in tight on the colossal Zelnad sphere, again revealing the pattern of interlocking triangles that formed its surface.

"We no longer believe the structure is a Dyson sphere, however it does store energy," Doc said. He swiped the image of the Zelnad sphere to the side and brought up another set of images from the ruins of Temeruria. Now it was Oz's turn to squirm. "Our probe caught this ore carrier just before it jumped away from Temeruria." He zoomed in on a huge ship that was there one moment and gone the next. "This was taken a few milliseconds later." It reappeared right outside the sphere.

A ragged hole had opened in the superstructure that roughly matched the carrier's shape. When Doc swiped again, it had closed and the ship was gone.

Arbizander got up, his face nearly level with the floating image, and leaned in for a closer look. "What kind of door is that?"

"It is merely an opening," Doc replied. "They could open anywhere in the structure."

"I don't understand."

Doc zoomed in tight, and Geddy gasped. "Holy shit. It's made of ships."

The opening appeared ragged because it was merely a space between ships. The sphere's textured pattern wasn't part of any superstructure. It was formed entirely by Zelnad triangle fighters.

"Yes, Colonel. Like pieces in a three-dimensional puzzle. Each time ships move in or out, the sphere adjusts to maintain its integrity."

He panned around the image to reveal much larger

isosceles triangles mixed in among the fighters. The half-pyramid destroyers he called schnozzes.

Doc continued, "Indeed, we've measured continuous increases in its diameter as the mining vessels have returned."

"How many ships are we talking about here?" Tymeri nervously inquired.

"One point seven million, give or take," Doc said. "We can't know how many more might be inside. We suspect the weapon is there, too."

All the air went out of the room. Their combined forces comprised the largest fleet ever seen. Even so, they only had a fraction of that many.

"How are we to win against such a foe?" lamented Grozuc. "It's suicide!"

Verveik stepped forward, his expression grim but determined. "Perhaps, General, but so is inaction."

— Here we go.

The military leaders exchanged wary looks.

Doc calmly folded his hands in front of them. "We know the Zelnads are using hosts as the payload for their weapon. Based on Lestiko's readings of the energy released during separation, we now believe that Sagacea's destruction will cause a catastrophic chain reaction."

He brought up another image of a glowing celestial body that resembled a star except it was bright purple — almost exactly like what Geddy had seen in his dream.

"The energy pervades the universe. If Sagacea is truly its source, then an explosion of such magnitude will result in a sudden expansion." An animation showed the purple star ballooning outward. "It will consume everything in its path."

"How big will it get?" asked Arbizander.

"Big enough to swallow the universe," Doc said. The same words Lestiko used. His eyes met Geddy's.

"Bioweapons, clones, the Coalition — all distractions," Verveik said. "This has been their endgame from the beginning."

"But how?" Tymeri asked. "If we were outnumbered two to one, maybe three, we've at least got a fighting chance. But by a factor of eight or nine? It's not possible."

"Maybe we can improve our odds," Verveik said. "It'll require perfect execution and more than a little luck, but it could work."

"Now this I've gotta hear," mumbled Balzac.

Verveik brought up a new hologram of the Zelnad sphere. "After jumping in, a small force will attack the sphere directly, concentrating all fire on one spot like a dart." A cloud of ships came into view and opened fire, their blasters converging on a single point. "If we can punch our way in, we'll hit the weapon with this." A rotating diagram of a standard torpedo housing appeared at the upper right corner. "Before he died, Lestiko designed a torpedo that works similar to a bubble drive. We've got sixteen in all, distributed among our biggest ships. If all goes well, we jump it away to where a third group will be waiting to disable it and rescue the hosts inside."

"Sounds like an awful lot of 'ifs,' Chief," Tymeri sneered.

The Battle of the Deuce saw mostly pirates leading the first wave of their attack on the mining facility. Verveik and Arbizander made those plans, and Tymeri's privateers paid a heavy price.

"Which is why we'll take volunteers to start, then hold a lottery if necessary."

Tymeri's cynical sidelong glance didn't abate, but she remained silent.

"I volunteer," Geddy quickly said. "The *Stalwart* will lead the attack."

— *What?*

"What??" asked Oz.

All heads turned toward him.

"No one's got more experience fighting these assholes. Tymeri's pirates led the attack on The Deuce, it's only fair I lead this one. I'll train the attack group myself."

Maybe Verveik hadn't envisioned this, but he knew in his bones that no one else could pull it off.

"Very well, Colonel," Verveik said, and the matter was settled. The others returned their attention to him, but Oz's eyes were still burning a hole in the side of Geddy's head. He turned to meet her stare, finding a curious mix of anger, sadness, and admiration. The decision to join him would be up to the crew. But Oz wouldn't be there this time. It was too risky.

"As I was saying," continued Verveik, "we might get lucky and find the weapon inside. If we don't, then we have to assume they'll jump it to Sagacea immediately. The rest of the fleet will be waiting to pounce."

The sphere blipped out, and the blazing purple star again appeared.

"The second our scopes detect the weapon, we'll form up between it and Sagacea — shield to shield like a net so it can't get past us." A pulsing, elongated shape appeared, and the Alliance fleet formed a wall in front of it.

Grozuc protested, "But we don't have enough ships! Besides, how do we know these torpedoes will work on such a large vessel?"

"The torpedo can make a jump bubble five clicks wide, maybe more," Verveik replied. "Any Zelnads within that diameter will go along for the ride. If that happens, we'll be ready."

"I'll start training the attack group right after the lottery," Geddy announced. "There's a remote moon almost the exact same size as the sphere. Quite a few structures on it for targets."

Verveik said, "Good. Arbizander and I will oversee training for the rest of the fleet. Any questions?"

Again, doubt and fear crossed everyone's faces.

General Grozuc turned his scary, soulless Screvari eyes on Geddy. "What remote moon?"

CHAPTER 35
OH, SPEAR ME

The moment Verveik adjourned the meeting, Oz leapt over the back of her seat and left the auditorium in a huff. Geddy chased after and caught her in the curved hallway that returned to the hangar. They'd shuttled over together, but it seemed they might return separately.

"Hey, slow down, would ya?" he called after her, half-jogging to catch up. "You want my heart to explode?"

"Geddy Starheart, the tip of the spear!" she spat over her shoulder. "Aren't you gonna make a 'just the tip' joke?"

"I mean ... not anymore."

"Bet you can't wait to tell the crew about their suicide mission."

"I just said the *Stalwart*. Whether they go or not is up to them."

Oz abruptly stopped and whirled to him, her heavy red locks flopping behind her. "Like they won't be first in line! You know perfectly well they'll follow you anywhere."

"It's still their choice."

"Good grief, you're naïve sometimes." She about-faced, shaking her head, and continued striding down the hall.

— She's upset you made this decision without her.

— Yeah, I picked up on that, E.

— Well, sometimes you need a clue.

"Stay out of this, Eli!"

— Sorry, Oz.

Again, he hurried to catch up. "I can't train the damn attack group but not lead the charge, Oz."

"That's not it and you know it."

"That's not what?"

"You don't have to train them. You don't trust anyone else to do it. It's late in the game, and you want the ball."

What he said in the meeting was true. No one knew the Nads' capabilities better, so it should be him. But she was right, too. Firing the first shot in a battle for the universe appealed to his ego.

Oz turned left down the wide hallway that led back to the hangar. The doors parted, and a wall of recycled air hit them.

"It's no less risky than Verveik's part of the plan."

"That's not the point!"

The *Gallant's* hangar was nearly full of Chimeras and Berzerkers awaiting deployment to Kailoria and Ghruk, where the retrofitting was being done. Several dozen pilots, mostly clones, were milling around the perimeter looking bored. Oz's raised voice echoed loudly, drawing their attention. She breezed past them like they weren't there, but they kept staring anyway. Who wouldn't?

"Don't you have something better to do than watch us fight, one-seventy?" Geddy asked.

"Not really," he replied.

"His name's Ashley," Oz said over her shoulder. "Or do they all look the same to you?"

"Oh, come on ..." Geddy protested. "I'd ask how you tell them apart, but I'm not sure I want to know."

"Cute." Oz pointed at the clone. "Ashley, you're a Berzerker pilot, right?" He nodded. "Care to give a girl a ride back to the *Stalwart*?"

He hesitated briefly then caught up with her, looking back anxiously at Geddy as though conflicted about what to do.

"Don't be ridiculous," Geddy said. "Belay that command, Ashley."

"It wasn't a command — it was a question. Where's your ship?"

The clone pointed to one of the Berzerkers lined up on the left. "Over here."

"Okay, look ..." Geddy drew even with her. "I probably should've talked it over with you first, but it wouldn't have changed my decision. I get the crew I get."

"Really? So you'd be okay charging into the breach with a bunch of randos? Please."

Ashley dashed ahead to his Berzerker and opened the ramp as though he couldn't allow Oz to break her stride.

"Come on," Geddy protested, pointing toward the back of the hangar. "The shuttle's right over there."

"We've both got shit to do." He pulled up as she approached the bottom.

"Oz, stop!" She did and turned around expectantly. "I'm sorry, and I'm here for you. No matter what."

She managed a weak smile. "I know, Geddy. Don't worry about me."

Ashley, who was just in his coveralls and not a flight suit, hesitated as she headed up ahead of him and looked anxiously Geddy's way.

He gave an indifferent wave of his hand. "It's fine, Sergeant. Just get her there safely."

The clone gave a hasty salute and hurried up the ramp, then closed it behind him. The glare off the front shield made it impossible to see Oz inside. A few moments later, the spinning red lights came on overhead and the decompression alarm sounded.

"All personnel, please clear the flight deck," intoned the computerized female voice.

"Fuck me," Geddy grumbled.

— *You're not the only one who's scared shitless, Geddy.*

— I know.

— *You're all she's got left. She's afraid of losing you.*

— I know!

The Berzerker's engines whined to life as he about-faced and returned to where the other clones were, behind the thick yellow line that demarcated the safe zone. A few seconds after he crossed it, the faint orange pressure shield activated. Once it did, the alarm stopped its *whoop-whoop* and the fans overhead reversed, loudly sucking out the air.

Soon, the hangar doors engaged, and the Berzerker lifted off the deck, retracting the skids and coming around. Geddy bit the inside of his lip as it passed through and jetted off toward the *Stalwart*.

"Everything okay, Colonel?" came a voice behind him.

The clones all wore concerned expressions. The one in front had presumably asked the question.

Geddy patted him on the shoulder as he passed. "All good, Fifteen. Thanks for asking."

"Sixteen. But my name's Leslie now," he said.

"Oh, for fuck's sake," Geddy muttered on his way out.

CHAPTER 36
GONE, BABY, GONE

Geddy didn't bother returning to the *Stalwart*. Instead, he and Eli spent all night in an empty workroom aboard the *Gallant* planning the details of the attack. He welcomed it. At least it kept him from ruminating over what happened with Oz.

The hard truth was that she had every right to be upset. Once Verveik outlined the plan, he knew he had to be out in front. So did she. But he hadn't considered her, and he should've.

Their risky visit to Old Earth months earlier revealed that the moon base, Selene, was home to human-sized tardigrades who were also Zelnads eager to join the cause. As baffling as that was at the time, it made sense now. That was how they'd acquired intelligence and evolved to where they could build jetpacks, speak, and even briefly imprison the mighty Voprot.

It had been a very strange year.

Selene base offered an array of small targets and was nearly the same size as the Zelnad sphere. And since they'd mapped the route, it was possible to jump straight to it.

The *Stalwart* would form the center of a multi-layered cone comprising five thousand ships. Every ship needed to focus its fire on a single area, which should keep the formation tight. The ships near the middle would carry Lestiko's torpedoes. Gundrun battleships, Ghruk Vanquishers, Screvari Broadswords, and Kailorian Juggernauts would join them there.

When they jumped, though, they'd have to be in formation and hauling ass. They'd also have to be wingtip to wingtip so their shields overlapped just like Verveik's wall. That would give them the best chance. The Nads didn't appear to patrol their base. It was nothing more than a spherical parking lot for their triangular ships, all of which fit neatly together. In theory, they'd have several seconds to inflict damage before the Nads reacted.

At some point, however, all hell would break loose. Thousands upon thousands of fighters would leave the sphere in its defense, and those that remained would ripple into the gaps.

That's why concentrating their fire was key. If they could make a wide enough hole by the time they reached it, then maybe the *Stalwart* could slip through. Then it would be a race to find the weapon, hit it with a torpedo, and get out before things got too hairy. If they couldn't punch through, or if they didn't find it in time, they'd just jump to Sagacea and join Verveik's last stand.

— What are the chances of this working?

— *Very low.*

Before he knew it, his comm cuff was giving him little taps in a repeating pattern — the one that meant urgent. His lead lay atop his folded arms, and a puddle of drool had collected on the table. At some point, he'd fallen asleep, and it was suddenly four ten in the morning.

He rubbed his face to wake it up and was immediately reminded that he needed to shave. The message was from Denk. He picked up. "Denk, why are you awake?"

His pudgy young pilot looked more worried than usual. "I just got alerted to a depressurization in the executive hangar."

The executive hangar was a much smaller space, accessible from the bridge via elevator. It was mainly intended to house the command crew's personal ships. Under the old Alliance model, they would be on a six-week rotation and return home while another crew relieved them. Presently, it only housed a couple of Chimeras and Jel's ship, *Bogart*.

"Who left?"

"Jel."

Jeledine was the wild card in all this. She was technically part of the crew but had no interest in being a soldier. Her sister, Ori, was back on Stemir trying to manage an uneasy truce with her entity. Maybe she was having a hard time and needed Jel there. It was surprising, but not shocking that she would leave without notice. She'd always been flighty.

"Why do I get the feeling that's not all?"

"Before I contacted you, I figured I'd better see if Oz knew anything about it."

Geddy rubbed the bridge of his nose. "Yeah, and how'd that go over?"

"She's gone, too."

Now that got his attention. Oz didn't just leave like that. "Did you page her?"

"Multiple times."

A sick feeling sprouted in his stomach, extending its icy fingers deep into his chest. "Did you do a chip count?"

The translator chips they all had embedded in their brains acted like little personnel transponders that the bigger Alliance ships could track.

"Of course. She's just not on board, Cap."

— *Oh, shit. Did Oz run off with Ashley?*

— No!

— *You sure about that?*

In light of their recent conflicts, it wasn't crazy talk. But he already had a pretty good notion where she and Jel had gone.

"Sit tight. I'll be right there."

Geddy's return to the *Stalwart* didn't magically make Oz reappear. Not that he believed it would, but some part of him wondered if she was just blowing off steam somewhere. Once it became clear she and Jel weren't taking a joyride, he had to reckon with the more likely explanation.

She'd gone to find her father.

Now that he thought about it, Oz almost certainly had a notion where he'd go if the shit hit the fan. She'd feigned ignorance so Verveik wouldn't be tempted to hunt him down.

Fretting over it didn't do him any good. He couldn't know where she was or when she was coming back, so he had to trust her judgment. He told Verveik that Jel had a family emergency on Stemir and Oz went with her for support. The commander seemed irritated, but he had plenty else to worry about, and Geddy had an attack group to train.

They didn't even need a lottery. Lestiko's chain-reaction theory spread quickly through the fleet. Loss equaled annihilation. He had his five thousand pilots by late morning, including twenty-eight clones. They comprised every world, race, and age in the New Alliance. Their ships were prioritized for retrofitting.

It got done in less than two days.

Oz was right, of course. Denk, Voprot, and Doc volunteered immediately. Voprot's presence on the bridge had been largely ornamental to that point, but Oz had spent the past week training him up on the ship's weapons console — further proof that her sudden departure was premeditated. He took her usual place to Geddy's left as the cone formation eased its way out of the ion cloud and prepared to jump.

The collective anger over Temeruria and fear over losing everything had morphed into a powerful resolve. Pilots who had never flown together and barely understood what Sagacea was were suddenly ready to die for it.

"Voprot, if you're on the fence about this, now's the time."

"No," he said determinedly. "I ready."

"Okay, then. Doc, open the attack group frequency, please," Geddy said.

"Open, Colonel."

"All right, everyone, this is Colonel Starheart. Listen up. You've all read the mission brief. On my command, accelerate to mark fifteen point seven. I'll count down the jump. We need to keep the formation tight.

"Our training ground is a distant moon about the size of the Zelnad sphere. It's home to an abandoned base with a large central dome. That's our initial target. The moment we come out, concentrate your fire on the top. Every second counts. We're gonna kick up a whole lot of regolith, so trust your scopes. At the end of our run, we'll jump to the rendezvous, regroup, and do it all over again."

The squadron leaders all checked in that they understood and were ready. By the time they were done, they'd left the ion cloud and entered open space.

"Accelerating to mark fifteen point seven in three ... two ... one ... now."

Denk accelerated to their attack speed. Geddy glanced at the scopes and was pleased to see the formation held pretty well.

"Looking good, people." Voprot's giant claws hovered in front of the weapons console. "Be ready for anything."

"Like what?" Voprot asked.

He ignored the question. "Jumping in three ... two ... one ... go!"

CHAPTER 37

GOODNIGHT, MOON

The attack group jumped in a hundred clicks outside Old Earth's lonely moon. Voprot immediately led the volley as though he'd done it a thousand times. The purple streaks from all around them formed their own cone as they converged on the central dome of Selene base.

Immediately, a cloud of regolith rose to obscure the base from view.

"Whoa, lookit that!" Denk remarked.

It wouldn't be enough to simply turn Selene into another crater. Anyone could hit a static target. This had to be as accurate a simulation as possible. For that, he'd turned to Ziksu.

Just a few seconds after the formation turned Selene's once-famous atrium into a divot, a hundred of Ziksu's training drones shot out of the regolith cloud and started shooting back.

"What the heck?!" Denk exclaimed.

"I said be ready!" Geddy reminded him, a bit too pleased with himself about the idea. Only Doc knew that was going to happen. Someone needed their finger on the kill switch in case something went south.

Much to his relief, the first barrage of fire from the drones was absorbed by their upgraded shields. But then they started ramming directly into ships in an effort to break the formation. Just like the Nads would the moment they caught on.

The shield-to-shield contact sent dozens of ships spinning out of formation, colliding with each other like protons in an accelerator. Each collision created ten more.

— *It's too tight.*

— Now that's something I've never said. But you're right. Unfortunately, that's not our only problem.

— *How so?*

— Tymeri's right. This is a suicide mission. But maybe it doesn't have to be.

By the time the formation was almost to the moon, nearly half the ships had been knocked out of the cone and were being chased by the little drones. Not enough fire was still concentrated in the same place, which would allow the Nads to easily close any hole they could make.

Geddy shook his head. "This isn't gonna work. Doc, call off the drones and open the group channel again." Doc nodded that he was back on the group frequency, and their surprise attackers immediately disengaged. "Everybody cease-fire. That's it for our first run. Jump to the rendezvous and wait for us there."

One by one, they broke off and jumped away to the other side of Old Earth over what used to be called Europe. Geddy turned back to Doc. "Get Ziksu and Verveik. I've got an idea."

Geddy knew they were watching his tactics from the *Gallant*. Before he could adopt his new tactic, he needed to know it would work.

"I've got them, sir," Doc said. "On screen now."

Verveik and Ziksu appeared together in Verveik's office. "Well, Colonel, that was an inauspicious start," Verveik observed.

"Yes, but I might have a better way. Ziksu, how many of those drones do you have?" Geddy asked.

"You're looking at all of them. Why?"

"Focusing our attack on one point will only focus their defenses. What if we used that to our advantage?"

Geddy decided to use a time-honored method and shut up so Verveik could work out what he was proposing. After a moment, understanding crossed his face.

"Use the drones as a diversion," Verveik said, giving a slow nod, "then attack elsewhere."

"Not just elsewhere," Geddy said. "If we had enough drones, then *two* columns could attack nearby points on the sphere. It should create a soft spot in between. Like an open pair of legs. Which, to be honest, is what gave me the idea."

— *I think you could've omitted that detail.*

— Yeah, but it helps with the visualization.

"Spread their knees and hammer the center," Doc said, impressed. "Famously spoken by King Herkimer the Younger before the Battle of Tymuid. You know your Knetosian history, Colonel!"

Though he understood none of that, Geddy nonetheless pointed at Doc and winked. "You know it! Also famously spoken by me to my tag-team partners at Tatiana's New Year's Orgy. The second one."

The best part of this plan was that it didn't require the real attack group to change tactics. It merely gave them a better chance to succeed.

Verveik turned to Ziksu. "Can it be done?"

"It depends. How many drones are we talking?"

"At least as many in each column as our attack group, so … ten thousand?" Geddy asked, fully expecting to be laughed at.

Instead, Ziksu said, "I'll speak with Chancellor Ranimus."

"Remind him what's at stake," Verveik affirmed. "Good

thinking, Colonel. Continue your training, and keep us posted."

Praise from Verveik was pretty rare, so Geddy paused a moment to revel in it. "Yes, sir. Starheart out." Doc cut the feed, and Geddy met his smiling eyes. "Ya hear that? 'Good thinking,' he said. And all I had to do was think about sex."

"I knew you were the right man for the job, Colonel," Doc said with a wink.

———

Three days passed without word from Oz. Since they left, Geddy had distracted himself with the training. But now that the attack group knew its job and could scramble into formation at a moment's notice, little remained to do but fret about Oz's whereabouts and watch the newly retrofitted ships jump back.

Entire sectors of Xellaran factories were repurposed to make the Alliance's weapons systems and, now, the drones. At the same time, the Ornean probes were continuously returning images of the Zelnad sphere in case they made a move. There was still no way to know what, exactly, was inside.

Geddy had just entered the mezzanine level of the *Pompadour*, Everett Hau's lavish party ship that had become the fleet's unofficial entertainment venue. It was basically a mobile version of Caloth itself but with more gambling — a place for the Alliance's rank-and-file to blow off some steam.

Why Verveik, of all people, wanted to meet there, he didn't know.

The mezzanine was a ring of overstuffed lounge chairs and tables set apart by hand-carved half walls like semiprivate party areas. Bars ran down both of the long sides with shelves of liquor stretching to the ceiling. It formed the upper perimeter of the main entertainment space everyone called the

Oval. Everything was dark save for the soft green lights behind the bar, leaving the rest of the area in thick shadows.

Geddy found Verveik sitting at the bar with a drink in front of him, which was so out of the ordinary that he wondered if it wasn't actually Arbizander. But no, it really was the old man.

"Evening, Commander," Geddy said.

"Is it evening already?" Verveik laughed. "Time has no meaning anymore." Geddy settled onto the chair beside him, and Verveik slid the drink over. He already knew what it was by the color. "Old Earth whisky, right?"

Flabbergasted, he brought his fingers to his chest. "My stars, thank you! How'd you know?"

"Everybody knows."

"None for you?"

"Never had much affinity for drink," Verveik admitted. "I guess I prefer a clear mind."

"Well, there's your problem." Geddy took a sip and closed his eyes, letting it bathe his grateful tongue, and swallowed. "Ahhhh. Mother's milk."

"Still no word from your first officer?" Geddy shook his head. "She where I think she is?"

Of course, the perceptive bastard already knew. "Probably."

He nodded knowingly. "For what it's worth, I wouldn't have gone after Bransel. That's up to the Temerurians."

"Speaking of whom, how are the evacuees holding up?"

"As well as can be expected, considering."

Geddy pointed at his glass and studied Verveik. "Wait — is this a test?"

"No, Colonel. It's a gift."

"A gift for what? For the spread legs thing?"

He actually laughed aloud, a sound so unnatural that Geddy did a double take. "You really don't know the date, do you?"

He really didn't. The last date he remembered it being was the twenty-fifth of February, the date Temeruria broke apart.

"I dunno. March something."

Verveik rose shaking his head. "Come with me."

"Am I in trouble? You're sure this isn't a test? Because yeah, things got a little out of hand with the Kailorian gin over Kigantu, but it really didn't, y'know …"

Geddy followed him to the top of the wide staircase that led down to the dance floor. Verveik reached over to a nearby pillar and flipped a switch, which activated a single light over the middle of the floor below.

He gasped. "… compromise my NO FUCKING WAY."

Parked in the middle was the *Penetrator*, as gleaming and shiny as the day he finished it. He stared at Verveik with his jaw hanging open, the questions piling up so quickly that he couldn't pick just one.

The commander gave a sly grin. "Happy birthday, Geddy."

CHAPTER 38

RESTORATION

It's March fourth already?

Geddy slowly descended the carpeted staircase, unable to take his eyes off the ship he and Eli built together. It didn't seem real.

— Apparently.

A lone light, directly overhead, left the rest of the place in darkness. Geddy stepped into its cone and reached out to touch the sleek ship's nose. It had to be a hologram, right?

Nope.

He turned to Verveik, who had quietly followed him down. "This can't be shinium."

"According to Ziksu, it is."

"Ziksu?"

The slightly built Xellaran stepped out of the shadows. "Happy birthday, Geddy."

"I don't understand. How did you get this much …?" he trailed off, suddenly realizing exactly where the nearly unworkable metal must have come from. "The orb??"

He smiled. "Its power was nearly depleted. There was just

enough to fully clad your old ship. We even threw in a bubble drive. You know — for the resale value."

Geddy chuckled but kept his fingers on it, tracing its sleek shape as he moved toward the back. "Holy shit, sir. I mean, damn. But ... why?"

"It's like I told the clones, Geddy ..." came a sultry voice from behind him.

Tatiana Semenov, his old flame, slinked out from the direction of the bar carrying her own glass of the same silky, caramel-colored liquid currently warming his throat. She wore a slinky blue dress with a touch of sheen that almost perfectly matched her eyes. It plunged to a depth many had seen, but few had ventured. Except for that one New Year's.

"... sometimes we need to be reminded what we're fighting for."

"Aren't you gonna make that point the same way you made it to them?"

She gave a full-toothed smile and nodded at his glass. "You already seem to appreciate the finer things in life."

He pointed at the ship. "Did you do this?"

"Ha! Like I'd have the time. No, this was all Oz's idea. That girl must really love you."

The guilt hit him like a sledgehammer. After all their recent tensions, she'd somehow managed to wrangle this. He glanced at the cockpit, hoping Oz might pop out of it wearing only pasties, but it was empty.

"I wish I knew why," he said. A soft ruffle leaked out of the shadows, giving him the impression they concealed a great deal more than just Tots and Ziksu.

"Oh, somebody get the lights, already," she said with a mischievous grin. "Let's get this party started."

The lights came on, and hundreds of people who had been pressed silently to the walls threw their hands up.

"Surprise!!"

You could've blown him over. Geddy Starheart getting a surprise party? That wasn't a thing in any objective reality. But there it was, and so was the *Penetrator*, even prettier than he remembered.

— Holy shit, E ... did you help plan this?

— *Very funny, Geddy*.

His jaw hanging open, Geddy made a slow turn as more people emerged from the room's recesses and onto the dance floor. The whole Committee was there. Tretiak. Zirhof. Smegmo. Tymeri and all the lieutenants. Even Doc, Denk, and Voprot were there, Morpho on Denk's shoulder.

"What is even happening right now?" Geddy asked.

"You idiots, the lights were your cue!" Everett Hau yelled toward the small stage.

A moment later, the curtain slid open and an Eicrean band fired up a rock song. Hau was wearing a tuxedo, which looked natural on him but out of place otherwise. He raised his own glass for Geddy to clink.

"Happy birthday, Geddy. In lieu of a gift, I've cleared your outstanding balances from Caloth. Including the four-thousand credit tab you ran up on this very ship."

He took a welcome sip of the whisky and paused to savor it. "Does that mean I can run up another one?"

"Well, Starheart, much of this war has been paid for by me already," Hau said with a wink. "The least I can do is improve morale."

"Not to be confused with morals," Geddy quipped.

"Never."

CHAPTER 39
GET PUMPED

Commander Verveik stood at the front of the holding platform in the *Gallant's* hangar, wearing his Alliance dress uniform and looking like the kind of guy you'd want to follow into battle. His determined visage swept across the tightly packed crowd as though he meant to look everyone in the eye. The five thousand pilots of Geddy's attack group had gathered to hear his big speech. They comprised virtually every race in the galaxy, from Afolosians to Zihnians and all worlds in between that had pilots to commit.

Geddy, Arbizander, Grozuc, Balzac, and the other leaders stood along the railing to either side, also in their Alliance blues. The speech was being simulcast to the entire fleet.

Denk, Doc, and Voprot were at the very front, just below the platform, with their hands folded behind their backs. It was weird to see them but not Oz and Jel, who were still MIA. Geddy had tried his level best not to worry, but at this point, it was impossible. A million things could've happened to them, none of which were good.

All he knew for sure was that they weren't here and neither was the Star Guard. In a few hours, they'd be in the fight of their lives against a superior force with a much deeper bench. The Last Illustration said only a united galaxy stood a chance, and they didn't have it. Not by a long shot. The only thing they had going for them was the element of surprise, and they could wait no longer. All Zelnad ships had departed Temeruria and rejoined the sphere, which could only mean they had what they needed to finish the weapon.

"All right, listen up!" Verveik bellowed, and the crowd fell silent. No microphone necessary. Even the pirates shut up for once. "In a few hours, our plan to end the Zelnad threat once and for all will begin. You'll say goodbye to your loved ones, you'll get in your ships, and you'll do your jobs. This is what we've all trained for. Whether you *feel* ready or not, you *are*.

"Our galaxy and untold others face annihilation. If we fail, history itself will disappear in an instant. Everything that ever was will be erased, and our world will return to darkness. But we matter. Our existence *matters*. And we're gonna fight like hell for it."

A cacophonous war cry burst from the assembly and boots stomped on the metal floor like an army on the march. It gave Geddy goosebumps.

After a moment, Verveik continued. "Our enemy is ancient, highly advanced, and determined. But they are not infallible. In fact, they're afraid of us. How do I know? Because the only real tactics they know are misdirection, misinformation, and trickery. They may have seen war through the eyes of their hosts, but they've never fought one as an army. In battle, they're sloppy and arrogant. I don't just think we're better prepared for this — I know we are. We *can* win, and we *will*!"

The crowd exploded in cheers. While he waited for it to die down, the big man's hands twisted on the metal railing with a tight squeak, and his aspect turned somber.

"The Old Galactic Alliance began as little more than an experiment. A dream that unity and peace could triumph over tribalism and hate. But we weren't ready. A simple trade dispute expanded into the Ring War, and many died. Some were your fathers or mothers. That Alliance failed them. It haunts me to this day.

"But this is a new day, and we are the New Alliance!"

The excitement that had built to a fever pitch ached for release. Verveik leaned over the railing, spittle flying from his mouth as he shouted his final exhortation into the din.

"There *will* be a tomorrow! Our civilization *will* survive! Together, we will shine such light into the darkness that nothing can extinguish it! Now get your asses to your muster points and get ready to show these motherfuckers who really controls your destiny!!"

Geddy had never heard anything like the red-faced, full-throated roar that followed. It filled every corner of the hangar. Even Doc was clapping and shouting. Tears streamed down little Denk's face as he thrust his fist defiantly in the air again and again. Voprot's neck sacs inflated as he stomped on the floor, an otherworldly screech emanating from his toothy maw.

Verveik turned away from the railing and stared down his XOs, all of whom looked appropriately puffed up. Arbizander's heavily muscled arms were ready to rip somebody's head off. Tymeri shifted her weight from one leg to the other like a title fighter at a weigh-in.

Geddy's nipples could've pierced Gundrun steel, though it was unlikely it would come to that.

"You all know what to do," Verveik said. "Whatever happens, it's been the honor of my lifetime to serve with you."

"You, too, Commander," Balzac said.

Verveik offered Geddy his giant hand and smiled. "Good luck, Colonel. Now go do what you do best and hammer that soft spot."

Geddy snapped his heels together and saluted. "I won't let you down, sir. Or the soft spot."

For the time being, the bridge was empty and quiet. Denk, who almost never left it unattended, had done so on this occasion. Even if he hadn't, Geddy would've ordered him to. There was nowhere more important to be than with the men, women, and genderless aliens who would effectively be shielding the *Stalwart* and a handful of other big ships from the Zelnad onslaught in a couple of hours.

Morph was perched on his shoulder as always. The others would be back at any moment. Geddy closed his eyes and pictured the threads, singing with the music of the universe Maybe it was his focus in the present or an abiding desire to somehow reach out and touch Oz wherever she was, but it worked almost immediately.

— You're there.

— **Yes,** Morpho replied. **You did it.**

— It was easy this time.

— **Your mind was quiet.**

— It doesn't feel quiet.

— *It's not,* Eli said.

— **Hello, Eli.**

— *Hello, my friend.*

— **You're thinking of her.**

— Not just her, Geddy said.

— **Yes, of course.**

— I'm gonna be a dad.

— *What will that make me?*

— The cool uncle?

— *You think I'm cool?*

— Well, you are made of energy. Besides, I wouldn't let some loser entity live in my head.

— **How are you, Geddy? Really.**

Truthfully, he didn't know how he was. Now that the

moment had arrived, he wasn't terrified anymore. In that awful dream he'd had about this day, Oz was there. She watched him fail, and the pain in her eyes was the last thing he saw. Only that couldn't happen now. Maybe that was a sign that the dream wasn't as prophetic as it felt and that he'd see her again. Not just at the end, but after.

— I'm ready.

The door hissed open, and Voprot entered ahead of Denk and Doc wearing an actual Alliance uniform and carrying a custom-made EVA suit.

Oz's instincts were right. The lizard had a flair for the weapons console. His reflexes were peerless, as was his vision. Besides, the only weapons worth using now were the disruptors and of course their single bubble torpedo. It was one button and a joystick.

Geddy squared up to them as they entered. All three of them gave an asynchronous salute.

"Senior Science Officer Dr. Krons Tardigan, reporting for duty, Colonel."

"Major Denk Junt, at your service!" Denk said.

"Major?" Geddy asked, amused.

"Since we might not make it through the day, I thought you might be willing to pretend. Sir."

He gave Denk a big smile. "I can roll with that. Major."

"Corporal Voprot of Kigantu here."

"I can see that, Corporal. You sure you don't want to be a command sergeant major or something just for fun?" Geddy asked.

"No, Vop– er, I am okay being corporal. I salute Denk now?"

"You can salute Denk until he walks funny for all I care." Not getting the innuendo, he and Denk machine-gunned salutes at each other. He paused to frame up a mental snapshot of that moment. "So, I guess this is it."

"It feels strange for Osmiya and Jeledine to not be here," Doc observed, "though part of me is glad they are not."

"I'm with ya, Doc."

"They went to find the Star Guard, didn't they?" Denk asked.

"That's my best guess, buddy." In the wake of Verveik's speech, Geddy couldn't imagine saying anything more inspiring, but he had to take a stab. "Y'know, guys, we've been through a lot together. I've put you in danger again and again, yet here we are. I just want you to know how very proud I am of all of …" Voprot started huffing, his claws forming fists at his sides like he was overcome with emotion. "You okay there, big guy?"

"I wish to talk."

"The floor is yours."

"Before you find me in desert, I was alone. My father want me to learn old ways and take over clan. But I not want to. I want to learn new ways and see galaxy. You think I am strange and dumb, but you teach me. I make friends. I find female of mating age. Now I help save everyone." He regarded Doc affectionately. "Doc, you always patient and kind with me. Teach me to talk better. You not deserve exile. I am grateful to you."

Doc sniffed, his eyes turning faintly glassy, and he patted Voprot's upper arm. "Thank you, my friend. I have learned a great deal from you, as well. In the figurative sense, of course."

Voprot turned to Denk with a smile that revealed all his teeth. "Denk, you my best friend. I not know how big heart fit inside puny little body. You glue that hold crew together. Crew glue."

Denk, who had begun sobbing the moment Voprot got emotional, lunged forward and hugged his upper thigh, resting his cheek on Voprot's groin like it was a mother's breast.

"You're my best pal, too, V. And you're not strange or dumb. You're just Voprot. That's all you ever need to be, ya hear me?"

— *You know you're next, right?*

— I'm already steeling myself.

— *Is it working?*

— Nope.

After Denk finally released Voprot's leg, the big lizard stepped up to Geddy, who had to crane his neck to look him in the eye.

"Geddy, you give me chance. If I stay on Kigantu, I never see anything. You show me the universe. You save my life. You believe in me. You are a good, good man. Starheart the right name for you."

In that moment, all pretense fell away, and Geddy saw Voprot in an entirely new light. Maybe himself, too.

"*Is* the right name for me," Geddy said, smiling.

Voprot laughed, a high-pitched wheezing sound that fell somewhere between a dog toy glued to a bicycle tire and a runaway train.

"Look," he said, his voice starting to crack. "They say the universe is infinite, but it really isn't. It's you and the people in your orbit. That's what we're fighting for. The rest is just … space. Whether we win or lose, there's nowhere else I'd rather be and nobody I'd rather be with. 'Stalwart' means strong and brave. And that *is* the right name for our ship."

There wasn't a dry eye on the bridge. But Geddy didn't allow himself to lose it. He couldn't. They had a job to do. The time for maudlin sentimentality had officially passed.

"Now let's do what we do best and fuck shit up."

CHAPTER 40

WE'RE GOING IN

Geddy's Garrison? Starheart's Squadron? The great armies, battalions, and brigades from Old Earth all had cool names. But maybe they could only be forged in the fires of battle, and even then, somebody either had to witness its feats or live to tell the tale.

Unfortunately, the only witnesses to this raid would be them and the Nads, and there was a very good chance none of them would make it back.

As the attack group emerged from the ion storm, Geddy's mind wasn't on the op so much as the fact he might already have seen Oz for the last time. If there came a point when he knew he wouldn't survive, would he be thinking about their awful final exchange or about the million exceptional moments that preceded it?

— *You're thinking about Oz.*

— Duh.

A looping message had been playing across Jel's private channel on the Band of Thieves with Sagacea's coordinates and the time of their attack. He could only hope it was received.

The last ships had cleared the storm. Two thick columns of

Ziksu's training drones, all ten thousand, all equipped with new weapons, led the way. They would jump in first, followed one minute later by ... Maybe just The Five Thousand? That had a ring to it, like the Three Hundred in ancient Greece. Five thousand hoping to strike a fatal opening salvo with trillions of lives were at stake? It worked until he had a better idea.

Denk's stubby fingers gripped the *Stalwart's* controls like a lifeline, but the kid's determination was palpable. Doc was in his usual spot to Geddy's right, the sphere's coordinates already loaded into the bubble drive. His normally implacable expression had become hard. Voprot was ready at weapons control.

"All right, everyone, it's just like we drilled. Form up and keep it tight, like a miniskirt on a big g–"

— *Are you thinking anything specific about Oz?*

— That I might not see her again.

— *Don't think like that.*

— My life's been in danger before. Too many times to count. And I knew it, too, but ...

— *There was always going to be a tomorrow.*

— Something like that.

— *This will work. I know it. It's a good plan.*

— Y'know, I've never asked you ... why do you have hope for the world and the Nads don't?

— *I suppose mine just hasn't run out yet.*

The ships in the formation drifted together into the tight cone they'd rehearsed, forming a cluster of smaller ships around the torpedo carriers at the center. Soon, he'd give the command to accelerate to attack speed.

— What's your earliest memory, Eli?

— *That's a strange question to ask now.*

— Suddenly, I'm dying to know.

— *I became aware, and I saw the stars. Too many to conceive.*

— Did you know what stars were?

— *Yes, but in a way that I would describe as academic. That they were made of gas and light and power beyond imagination.*

— So you don't even know your origin story. Not really.

— *I knew what I was. But not why I was.*

— Do you know now? Why you are?

— *I believe so.*

— And?

— *Like Ziksu said, my role is to observe life through your eyes. I've swum in an ocean of your thoughts, your fears, your many loves. I've been a part of you, yet still apart. I am incorporeal, yet bound to you until the end. Why would that be my fate unless my purpose was to know exactly who you were?*

— Do you remember anything else?

— *A ... longing to know.*

— To know what?

— *Everything.*

"Everyone accelerate to attack speed, mark fifteen point seven. Watch that spacing. Doc, send in the drones."

The two drone swarms blipped away. The balance of the fleet had already jumped to the edge of the supervoid around Sagacea. The Orneans figured energy concentrations would interfere with communication, so until Geddy and the Five Thousand joined them, they'd likely be out of touch.

The video feed from the probes surveilling the Zelnad sphere was a few minutes behind at one frame per second. The drone swarms would appear in about a minute, and they would know what the Nads' defensive response was. Assuming everything lined up, he'd give the order to jump.

— So did you?

— *Did I what?*

— Learn everything?

— *Everything I needed.*

— Everything you needed to what?

— *To hope.*

— I *taught* you hope?

— *Obviously.*

A pool of tears formed at the precise moment the first probe image came through. It was taken just as the drone columns appeared over the sphere, great in number but no bigger than a sperm was to an egg. The next several images would tell the tale.

The formation had accelerated to attack speed. Another composite appeared, stitched together from thousands and relayed to the *Stalwart's* front screen. The drone swarms were working! Triangle fighters swarmed around the two-pronged onslaught, and tiny cracks had formed in between. A faint light emanated from within.

"Doc, what say you?"

"It looks good from here," Doc replied.

"All right, gang, we've got our opening. Get ready to pound that soft spot like there's no tomorrow. Because there might not be."

One more image. Either the gap would open more, stay the same, or shrink. The first two were easy calls. The last, not so much.

He muted the group frequency and turned to Voprot, who actually appeared as nervous as he should for once. "Remember, save the jump torpedo until you've got a clean shot."

"I know, Geddy. I will do good."

"Denk, if we don't punch our way inside, nobody will."

"Aye aye, Cap!" Denk's knuckles were pure white.

— Oz, I know you can't hear me, but I sure hope I see you again. E, it's been real.

— *This will not be our end. I'm certain of it.*

The next image appeared, and Geddy gasped. The crack had widened to the point where he could almost, but not quite see inside.

"Here we go, people!" Geddy shouted into the comm.

"This one's for all the marbles. Which, now that I think of it, is an unrelatable reference for most of you. But you get the gist. Give 'em hell."

Mutters of, "You, too, Colonel," percolated through the channel.

"Jumping in three ... two ... one ... now!"

CHAPTER 41
THE HOLE ENCHILADA

The battle group jumped in with a head of steam over the Zelnad sphere, an inconceivable distance from the ion cloud, to find the drones already under a full-scale assault. Countless thousands of triangle fighters swarmed the two columns like angry bees defending their nest — so thick that the drones themselves were completely obscured.

The sphere was noticeably smaller than the moon on which they'd practiced. As a result, they came out of their jump further from the target than they wanted. The number of fighters that had left the formation to defend it must've reduced its diameter by quite a bit. Still more had formed a sort of callus where the drones were concentrating their fire, thickening the sphere's skin against the onslaught. But in between, it was thin enough that bright purple light leaked through.

There was no time to lose.

"Weapons free! Fire! Fire! Fire!!" Geddy cried, and the attack began. The first volley appeared to slip right through the weak spot, but it quickly tightened like his sphincter.

The mad flurry of purple bolts from their ships, whose

disruptors were much more powerful than those of the drones, seemed to catch the Nads off-guard. Still more layers of triangle fighters peeled off the sphere and zoomed toward them while others rushed in to reinforce the weak spot, but it was too blistering of an attack. Small gaps still appeared, and they kept pounding away.

That was when the destroyers entered the fray.

Scores of the large black half-pyramids boiled up off the surface like solar flares as fighters formed up around them, a wall of death heading straight for the cone. The first wave of purple bolts slammed into the outer layer of ships, but the shields held, and so did the formation.

That didn't last long.

The moment the Nads figured out that the Alliance had mahk'ti weapons, the fighters broke away from the destroyers and started hurling themselves into the attack group like kamikazes. From the *Stalwart's* perspective, it appeared as though the layered phalanx of ships would collapse in on them. As more fighters poked holes in their formation and struck the inner ships, their shield monitor registered dozens of impacts all along the ship's length and the integrity began to drop. Not alarmingly fast, but fast enough.

"Uh, Cap?" Denk's voice filled with panic.

— *Kinetic energy is more effective against these shields! Like when you ran those drones into the ground on Mikuli!*

If that was true, then their best defense was to turn theirs into missiles, too, just as he'd done when he bailed out of the *Penetrator* and rammed it into Tretiak's ship. But that vessel was unmanned. He couldn't give such an order, but their window might close fast. Every second might see the destruction of a hundred more ships.

"All ships, prepare to jump to Sagacea on my mark. We're gonna take our shot right now."

The attack group tightened even further, and with it, the

precision of their shots. There was a small gap where they were concentrated, and it wouldn't get any wider. They still had to make up for the time they'd lost by jumping in too far away.

"Mr. Junt, we're jumping ahead to the target," Geddy said. "Doc, do the math."

"The target, Cap?" Denk asked over his shoulder.

"You heard me." He switched to the open channel. "We're going in. Stay focused on that gap and be ready to jump away if it's too hairy."

"Oh jeez, oh jeez, oh jeez," Denk squeaked.

"Coordinates plotted, Colonel," Doc said.

"All right, everyone, when we jump, you jump. Ready, Denk?" He nodded, his finger hovering over the bubble drive screen. "Jumping in three … two … one … now!"

They jumped ahead just as the gap narrowed dangerously. Behind them, the rest of the cone blinked away, leaving only a smattering of functioning drones to either side. Denk had to tilt her forty-five degrees to port to scrape through, but it worked, and the *Stalwart* barreled into the sphere like a sperm into an egg.

The sphere's inner surface shimmered and pulsed so brightly with mahk'ti that they had to shield their eyes until the screen adjusted. Once it did, the central structure became visible.

Conduits of purple lightning collected in the sphere and traveled through space to a massive, complex central matrix of scaffolding. Huge, boxy structures that must have been for the refinement of tukrium were attached to it, along with dozens of smaller nodes that seemed to route energy throughout it. The scaffolding itself was crawling with so many gray synthetics like Eveth that it looked like a spider nest.

At the very center, barely visible through the metal framework, was a vessel shaped like a flattened oval. Its outer surface was so highly polished that only the distorted reflections at its edges betrayed its shape. The scopes indicated it was almost four kilometers long and half as wide. Assuming it was full of hosts, there had to be at least a million of them. A torpedo hit would have to be precise to envelop it.

"That's it!" Geddy pointed excitedly. "That's the weapon! Voprot, ready the torpedo!"

"I ready!" Voprot replied.

He could already see the problem. The gaps between the surrounding scaffolding, probably tukrium, were small. The torpedoes were independently guided but couldn't possibly navigate something so complex.

Their view of the structure was short-lived. More fighters detached from the sphere and raced inward, causing its diameter to shrink around them like a rapidly deflating balloon.

"Doc, if the torpedo hits that scaffolding, will the bubble be big enough to transport the whole thing?" Geddy asked.

"Possibly," Doc said.

"Then we make a hole. Voprot, give her everything we've got."

Voprot's lizard lips curled into a relishing sneer, and he unleashed the forward disruptor bank on the structure. The mahk'ti beams sliced through it like a knife, and bits of it tumbled away.

Meanwhile, the fighters that had broken off from the inside focused their assault on the *Stalwart* as it hurtled toward the weapon. The bolts were already flying, and the shields held well against them, but once they started ramming it again, they'd plummet fast.

"Voprot, tell me we've got a firing angle," Geddy said.

The targeting computer flashed and displayed a bright red line to indicate the torpedo's plotted trajectory.

"Yes, Geddy!" Voprot said.

"Then fire!"

Voprot tapped the launch button, and a white flash shot from the *Stalwart's* belly. It steered around a few chunks of scaffolding and streaked toward the hole they'd opened with the disruptors. With each passing second, Geddy's heart thumped harder in his chest.

Come on, baby.

A fraction of a second before it reached the demolished edges of the structure, a wall of fighters jumped right in front of it.

"No!" Geddy pounded his fist on the armrest.

The torpedo veered hard left but struck the wall anyway. The faint purple warp bubble it created expanded instantaneously but collapsed just as fast, taking a big chunk out of the scaffolding and leaving a void that almost but didn't quite reach the weapon.

They'd missed.

Meanwhile, the sphere continued to contract. Triangle fighters smashed into them from all sides like a hailstorm as the ship shuddered. Shields were already down to thirty-two percent and falling.

— *Jump away, Geddy!*

— There's got to be a way. If we can get close enough, maybe–

— *You can't. It's too big.*

"Colonel?" Doc asked.

As more ships joined the fray, the scopes became confused. The sphere continued to collapse. Whatever happened next would be up to the fleet.

He'd just opened his mouth to order the jump to Sagacea when the impact of bolts and ships immediately ceased. The purple blasts and dark triangles that had filled the screen were replaced by a Ghruk battleship that they were about to hit.

"Denk! Evasive maneuvers!" he screamed.

"Oh, shit!" He'd never once heard his young pilot curse.

He fired the aft landing jets and the retros and yanked back on the controls, the Ghruk ship so close that they could see inside. Geddy sucked in air between his teeth and waited for an impact, but it never came. The rear view showed it receding behind them, and he heaved a sigh of relief.

"What the hell just happened?" Geddy asked. "I didn't give the order to jump yet!"

The answer awaited them at the far left side of the screen, a white-purple glow the size of a small star. Light emanated from it in pulsing waves, giving the impression of a liquid. Only it wasn't.

It was Sagacea.

The feeling that hit him was almost impossible to describe, like going to sleep alone in your bed and waking up in the middle of the ocean. It was the same thing he'd felt over Temeruria, only a million times stronger.

"It seems the Zelnads took us with them," Doc said.

"Then where are they?" Geddy asked.

"Look!" Voprot said.

They didn't even need the scopes to see it. A portion of the sphere had contracted around the weapon, forming a thick, protective shell the size of a planetoid that was already accelerating toward Sagacea. The rest, including several thousand of the big destroyers, unfolded into a wall in front of it so large that they couldn't tell where it ended.

"Aw, fuck me," Geddy muttered. The Nads had just done what Verveik intended to do.

Over the next few seconds, elements of the fleet blinked in around them. The wall of Nads didn't fire, but as they closed ranks and linked their shields together, it became harder to see the fighter-encrusted weapon as it accelerated, a ragged silhouette receding in the distance. Eventually, it disappeared from view entirely.

"Colonel, it seems they intend to inject it into Sagacea like a capsid does a virus," Doc said.

"Then we'd better get to it before that happens. "Denk, prepare to jump to the other side of that wall."

"We can't," Doc warned. "We don't know where the barrier begins or even if the drive will work properly here. Energy readings are off the charts. We'll be lucky to have comms."

Geddy sighed. "Which means we have to break through this damn wall, too."

"I don't see another way."

He glanced at their shield integrity. Only eighteen percent remained, and the battle for the universe had barely begun.

CHAPTER 42
REINFORCEMENTS

By the time all the other battle groups popped in, the scopes were already on the fritz. The only way to gauge how big the fleet was compared to the Zelnad wall was to look outside, but everything was too spread out to even comprehend.

The green ring around the front screen illuminated.

"It's the commander," Doc said.

"Tell him I'll call him back," Geddy joked.

Verveik's stern gaze appeared, albeit with with heavy interference that made him difficult to see. His voice was garbled, too.

"What the hell … pened?" he asked.

"We managed to break through, but barely. We missed our shot at the weapon. The Nads used their ships like missiles. It depletes our shields faster."

"So much for our blockade," Verveik mused.

He could almost hear the big man thinking how they might do the same and whether he could order anyone to throw themselves against the wall. There had to be a better way.

"Maybe a torpedo can open a hole," Geddy offered. Each

battle cruiser and destroyer other than the Stalwart still had a torpedo locked and loaded. "What are your orders?"

"Your shields are almost gone," Verveik said. "Hang back and guard the flank. You did well."

That was the last thing Geddy wanted to do, but for the sake of his crew, he acquiesced. "Aye, sir. What about the rest of the fleet?"

"We'll try the torpedo. If that doesn't work, we'll just have to hit one spot with everything we've got."

The screen blinked out.

Above the *Stalwart*, the barrage began, focused on a small area in the wall that the Nads immediately reinforced. A big Gundrun battleship fired its torpedo at the spot, a white streak slicing through space. It was barely halfway when a Zelnad destroyer blew it to bits.

— Well, shit.

The green ring lit up again. "Who's it now?" Geddy asked.

Doc's toothy grin was all the answer he needed. Oz's beautiful white face appeared on screen, her big yellow eyes locking with Geddy's as her locks flared bright red.

Geddy planted his hands on the armrests and leaned forward, a broad smile splitting his face. "Oz! Boy, are you a sight."

"You, too," she said.

Jel leaned into view. "Permission to board, Colonel?"

The moment the executive hangar re-pressurized, Geddy squeezed through the airlock door while it was still opening and sprinted across the deck to the *Bogart* as it powered down. Oz bounded down the short ramp toward him. They collided, and she gave him the most delicious kiss of his life. Morpho wrapped himself around them in a deeply weird group hug that was quickly joined by Jeledine.

When Geddy finally pulled away, he looked Oz over from head to toe. "Are you okay?"

"We're fine," Oz assured him. "But I need to talk to Verveik right away."

"All right, then come on!" Morpho gathered back into a ball on his shoulder as Geddy trotted across the small hangar and into the waiting elevator that led to the bridge.

"Thanks for the birthday present. It's gonna be hard to top," he said.

Running alongside him, she smiled. "I know."

"What happened? How are you here?" Geddy asked, his tongue tripping over the million questions he wanted to ask.

"Long story. What's our status?"

"The weapon's still in play, and it's already on the other side of that giant Zelnad diaphragm. We're about to hit it hard."

The elevator reached the bridge, and the doors parted. "Don't do that yet." Oz strode through.

Jel frantically tapped away on her wrist comm. "What are you doing?" Geddy asked.

"Sending an encrypted message," she replied.

"To who?"

"To *whom*," Oz chided over her shoulder.

Jel finished her message and followed Oz as she approached Doc at the navcom station.

He rose, smiling. "Osmiya! We're so heartened to see–"

"Hold that thought," Geddy said. "Hail Verveik again."

"Why? What have you–"

"Just trust me," Oz assured him. While Doc hailed the commander, she said, "Hey Denk. Voprot."

They gave an awkward wave hello as the Commander appeared again. "First Officer Nargonis? How did you–"

"Commander, listen ... hold off on your assault for ..." her head spun toward Jel.

"A minute and a half."

"A minute and a half," Oz repeated.

His eyes narrowed. "Why? What happens in a minute and a half?"

"It's a surprise."

"We don't have time for games," Verveik cautioned.

"No games, sir. You need to break through that wall, and I'm here to help you do it."

The wall neither moved nor fired. They didn't need to.

"One minute," Jel said.

Oz acknowledged her and kept talking. "I lied to you, Commander." She turned to Geddy with shame in her eyes. "I had a pretty good idea where my father and the Star Guard went."

"So we figured," Verveik said, his tone prickly.

"While we waited on Temeruria, I put a tracker on his ship. I had a feeling he wouldn't keep his word, and I was right."

Geddy had found her already up that morning on the Nargonis estate when she showed him her secret woodland refuge. She must've snuck up to the house during the night.

"Thirty seconds," said Jel.

"So you found them?" Geddy asked anxiously, continually checking the screen. "The Star Guard is coming?"

She grinned mischievously. "That was the easy part. Luring the Chancellor off-world so they could help us surround his ship ... now that took some doing."

Jel raised one hand and said, "You're welcome, by the way."

"You used the Star Guard to compel the chancellor's cooperation?" Verveik asked, incredulous.

She shrugged. "I can be pretty convincing."

Jel consulted the device on her wrist. "Right about ... now."

As though by magic, the screen filled with more ships than Geddy had ever seen. Red and gold Xellaran Dark Stars, Rapiers, and hundreds of larger warships that no one, likely including Verveik, even knew existed, interspersed with light gray Javelins and Paladins from the Star Guard.

Oz thrust out her hands in a *ta-da* pose. "Surprise!"

CHAPTER 43
THIS OLD THING?

"Good goddamn, it's like starship bukakke out there," Geddy said, marveling at the sight of an Alliance fleet numbering more than a million.

"Do I even want to know what that means?" Oz asked.

"It's best you don't."

"Guys, something's happening with the wall," Denk warned.

Indeed, there was. All across it, the big half-pyramid destroyers were drawing closer, angling the pointy ends toward the attacking fleet. Because of the Gundrun Incident, everyone knew what that meant. They were forming superships powerful enough to turn a planet-sized asteroid into dust. It was scary to imagine what they'd do to a ship, mahk'ti shields or not.

"Oh, shit," muttered Geddy.

Verveik's expression hardened. "All ships, fire on those destroyer formations! Don't let them come together!"

As awesome as it was to behold the full onslaught, it immediately became clear it wouldn't be enough. Instead of firing on one spot, they were firing upon hundreds.

"What are we doin', Cap?" Denk asked. "Are we hanging back like Verveik said?"

"Hanging back?" Oz asked. "Are you serious?"

"Our shields are low," Denk replied. "Verveik ordered us."

Oz's eyes settled on Geddy. "You really plan to watch the big game from the bench? Come on."

His eyes swept across his crew, searching them for any sign of hesitation. He only saw determination. They were in this together until the end, however and whenever it came. And that was the problem.

"Everyone into the Armstrong." The crew exchanged baffled looks but didn't make any move. "Right now."

He switched control of the ship from Denk to him and turned her toward the wall, giving power to the thrusters.

"Hey!" Denk objected, realizing he was no longer the pilot.

Geddy strapped in. "We may not have another torpedo, but we've got a hole to make and a big-ass ship. Now go!"

"Oh, hell, no," Oz said. "We do this together or not at all."

"This isn't a discussion. I'm ordering you to abandon ship!"

Still, no one moved. But another familiar voice rang in Geddy's head.

— **Let me.**

— Forget it, Morph. You're going with them.

— **I am expendable. You are not.**

A light flashed amid the hornet's nest of Alliance ships near the top of their screen. A Kailorian battleship had exploded, its pieces sparking as they flew apart like shrapnel, taking at least two Chimeras out with it.

How many hits could it have taken? Three? Maybe less?

The wall held fast against the full Alliance. Five minutes of withering fire still hadn't opened a gap. Five more, and the weapon would be out of their reach. Maybe it already was.

The *Stalwart* maybe, *maybe* could take one hit from a supership. The odds of Geddy making it to the wall intact were nil, but maybe it didn't need to be intact. It just needed to be moving fast.

A colossal explosion rocked the ship, throwing Geddy so hard into his restraints that it knocked the wind out of him. His eyes peeled wide as he struggled to refill his lungs, but they saw nothing. For a terrifying moment, he thought he'd gone blind only to realize the bridge had gone completely dark.

Some decisions get made for you.

"What hit us?" Geddy gasped. "Is everyone okay?"

Murmurs of *yes* traveled through the bridge.

"We're a dead stick, Cap," Denk said. "Hydraulics are offline."

"The aft hull's been breached," Doc said. "We're on emergency power only."

The escape pods had independent power with mechanical releases if it came to that. But they'd just be cannon fodder. Not an option. Better to take their chances in the *Armstrong*.

Certain critical systems like life support, medical, and doors also used discrete power systems. A glance over his shoulder to the right of the main bridge door showed a green light on top. That meant the airlock was still intact, thank goodness. But the corresponding light underneath it was red, which indicated negative pressure on the other side.

The front screen, normally filled with data, was now just a window. As the ship tumbled out of control toward the wall, the raging battle passed from left to right, followed by a slice of Sagacea, then more ships and debris. They were in a flat spin more or less parallel to their vector.

Debris pinged off the tukrium hull, so loudly it made them jump. The severed left wing of a Darkstar spun past the window.

Shields were gone, too.

"That's weird," Denk said, pointing at the screen. "Do you guys see that?"

"See what?" Geddy asked.

Again, the ship's lazy tumble brought the battle back into view, and a bigger slice of Sagacea. Among the pieces that drifted across the screen was the entire stern of an Alliance battle cruiser. Geddy only caught the last few letters of the name emblazoned on the side, but they were enough.

W-A-R-T

Oh, no. Geddy gasped and unbuckled, then dashed to the window at the back of the bridge.

The hangar looked like a clean bite had been taken out of it from the starboard beam to the port side of the now-missing doors. That included the executive hangar where Jel's ship was. The *Armstrong*, which had been parked on a pad at the front, was gone.

The others joined him at the window. As the ship made another turn, Sagacea practically blinded them as it shone through the open aft portion of the ship, then cast hard shadows at the edges when it passed.

"The *Armstrong* …" Jel mumbled. She turned to Geddy, her eyes pleading and frightened. "And *Bogie*. What're we gonna do now?"

In that moment, he really didn't know. At best, they would keep drifting through the fringes of the battle and collide with the wall. More likely, they'd run into one of their own ships first. Escape pods might be their only option, though they wouldn't last long in the chaos.

"Wait." Voprot squinted into the darkness. "*Fizmo* still there."

"Bullshit," Geddy said.

The maintenance bay on the aft port side of the main hangar was largely in shadow, even through a full rotation, but just enough light made it through to briefly illuminate a corner of their old ship.

"Not bullshit," Jel said, hope creeping back into her voice.

Geddy sucked in a quick breath and drew himself tall, pacing toward the front of the bridge. An idea so beautifully crazy hit him that he needed a moment to make sure it held to logic.

"What?" Oz asked.

He spun on his heels like a detective about to reveal the murderer's identity. "The *Stalwart's* headed straight for the wall. If it makes a hole, the *Fiz* could slip right through. To the Nads, it would just look like debris."

"Wouldn't they just blast us like they did that torpedo?" Denk asked.

"Maybe not with enough covering fire," Geddy said.

"We should be able to adjust our rate of rotation so the back of the ship hits the wall first," Doc said. "It could make the gap the fleet needs to go after the weapon."

A long silence ensued.

Denk let out a long, cleansing breath. "For Durandia."

Voprot said, "For Kigantu," and high-fived Denk with his tongue.

"And Stemir," Jel said.

"And, with mixed feelings, Ornea," Doc said.

Geddy locked eyes with Oz. They felt much the same way about where they'd grown up It was a bit more complicated.

"For home," he said. "Wherever and whatever it is."

"Or *whom*ever," Oz said with a wink.

CHAPTER 44
MISSILE ME?

The full crew had never been suited up at the same time. Seeing all of them lined up at the airlock door in their EVA suits made Geddy think of the NASA footage that played on a loop at the Old Earth Museum, crew after crew making that walk out of the building and heading out to the launch pad. Those nerds probably would've relished the challenge of making a suit for an eight-foot-tall lizard with a huge tail.

"I'll go first," Geddy said. Morpho sat on his shoulder as always. "Remember, just line yourself up and push off the edge of the railing. Watch your velocity or it'll be hard to catch you."

The crew nodded, and they entered the airlock. Once they were all inside, he closed the door and waited for the pressure to equalize. About ten seconds later, the light came on, and he opened the outer door.

He gave everyone a thumbs-up, then grabbed onto the railing and gingerly threw his legs over. With his feet firmly planted on the edge, he aimed himself like an arrow at the *Fiz* and pushed off. He sailed across open space, glancing to his left just long enough to see how close they were to the Zelnad blockade. At about the two-thirds mark, his helmet lights picked up *For Sale Make Offer* painted on the starboard side of the old trawler.

That relief became mild anxiety when he realized he would miss by a couple of meters on the high side and smash into the wall. He felt a twinge in his shoulder from the last time he'd done it.

"Morph, I could use an assist."

Morpho snapped out a sticky arm and latched onto the roof of the *Fiz*, then gently drew Geddy down to where he could lock his magnetic boots to the hull. Denk came next, followed by Voprot, Doc, and Jel. Being last, Oz aimed perfectly and sailed right into Geddy's waiting arms.

Once they were all on top, they clomped across to the upper hatch, not far from the crew-sized escape pod Morph built for them.

Geddy opened it and let the others slip inside first. Once they'd descended into the maintenance shaft, he closed it and followed them down the ladder to the crew quarters. Doc, who had led the way, sealed the open airlock door while Denk powered her up and activated artificial gravity.

Pausing by the airlock, Geddy gazed out at the *Fizmo's* hold. As always, it was empty save for the newly restored *Penetrator*. The lights glinted off its polished shinium surface, which had no discernible seams. Damn, she was beautiful.

"Don't bother pressurizing." He turned away from the window. "This thing'll be over long before we run out of O2."

Doc was the first to sit down and immediately hailed Verveik. When he came onscreen, his expression was desperate.

"Colonel, thank the stars!" he said. "When we lost your transponder signal, I feared the worst. Wait — where are you?"

"The *Stalwart's* half the ship she used to be." Geddy

explained what happened. "But she's not out of the fight just yet."

"What do you mean?"

He walked the old man through his crazy idea, noting that the ships in the blockade might be too distracted by the assault to notice a clearly disabled ship drifting lazily toward it.

"Hmm ... That's actually not terrible." Verveik said. "How long before you reach it?"

"Doc says six minutes, forty seconds."

"What do you need from me?"

"We're a dead stick and no shields," Geddy said. "We'll need a clear path and plenty of cover once we get close. If you can concentrate all fire on our contact point, it might hide our approach."

"Good. We'll line up the torpedo ships right behind you," Verveik confirmed.

Geddy nodded. "Let's just hope the weapon hasn't crossed the barrier already."

"Say this works, and you make it through. You'll be defenseless against the counterattack."

The crew exchanged looks of grim resignation. This was the unspoken truth of it. The *Fiz* wasn't part of the retrofit. Why would it be? Despite a few upgrades, it was still a damned antique. *If* this plan worked, which was already a big *if*, there would be no miraculous escape. At least they'd be together.

"If I can't find a way, I'll make one," Geddy replied. "Hannibal said that."

The big man sighed. "If you make it through, we'll do our best to protect you."

"I know you will, sir."

"I'll inform the fleet," Verveik said. "Good luck, all of you."

He blinked out, and a heavy silence followed. They all knew this was probably a one-way trip, but it hadn't really sunk in until then. Their whole long, weird journey together may be about to end.

Oz's eyes met his through their helmets, following his gaze as it drifted down to her abdomen. She reached across to him, and their gloved hands touched. Words weren't necessary.

Geddy smacked his hands together. "All right, people, let's get our game faces on. Doc, how's our rotation?"

"We will be under-rotated by twenty-one degrees when we make contact," Doc said. "A precisely timed burn should speed us up just enough so the stern hits first."

"You heard the man, Mr. Junt," Geddy said. "Dead stick, my ass."

Denk released the magnetic restraints that locked the *Fiz* to the *Stalwart's* deck then tapped the VTO jets to lift off.

Doc pointed at a spot along the port wall where two big panels met. "That joint is precisely four hundred meters from our center of rotation. Put the nose tightly against it."

"But gently," Geddy reminded Denk. "Any speed at all, and this thing could crumple like an aluminum can. Because that's basically what it is."

The little Durandian gave the stick a series of tiny taps using just the landing thrusters to align the ship with the magic spot, then eased her forward so slowly that it seemed they were barely moving. It took a couple of minutes for the nose to make contact with the *Stalwart's* fuselage.

"That's some delicate flying, amigo," Geddy said. "Well done."

— *He's every bit as good as you are.*

— Yeah, because I taught him everything I know. The good parts, that is.

Denk glanced over his shoulder with a self-satisfied grin, always grateful for Geddy's validation.

Consulting his computer model on the nav screen, Doc

said, "That's perfect. Now, on my mark, we need a ten percent burn for exactly five seconds. I'll count you in."

"Roger that, Doc." Denk's right hand curled confidently around the thruster lever.

Geddy glanced at the scopes. They'd nearly reached the no-man's-land between the fleet and the Zelnad wall where no ships dared venture.

"Executing burn in five ... four ... three ... two ... one ... now," Doc said.

Denk nudged the thruster forward, hitting ten percent on the nose.

"Stopping in one ... two ... three ... four ... five ... stop."

Denk pulled back, and the model adjusted accordingly. It had them making contact with the wall at almost a perfect right angle.

"Holy shit, Dude." Geddy made worshipful bows. "The apprentice has become the master." Denk's face lit up. "Now bring us about, but keep her in the shadows. Front shields up."

As ordered, Denk slowly backed away from the wall and positioned them at the edge of the shadow that blanketed the maintenance bay, finishing pointed outward.

The blockage was close enough now that they could discern the outline of individual fighters against the backlight of Sagacea as they continued to rotate.

"Sending our latest contact point coordinates to the fleet," Doc said.

Just a few minutes remained. Any moment now, the Alliance would renew its assault, hopefully making the disabled *Stalwart* all but invisible. Just another piece of debris that would bounce harmlessly off their wall.

A few rotations later, the onslaught began. Tens of thousands of ships at the front of the battle concentrated all their firepower on the spot where they would hit the wall. The

Zelnads finally returned fire with equal zest, but it was unfocused.

All Geddy and the crew could do was watch and wait.

"Contact in thirty seconds," Doc warned.

"Whatever happens, guys …" Emotion overwhelmed him. This could end badly. At least it would be instantaneous.

"We love you, too, Geddy," said Voprot.

— This might be it, pal.

— *Perhaps. But I don't think it will be.*

— Just the same …

— *I know. Me, too, my dearest Geddy.*

Another slow rotation, and the light became so bright that they all shielded their eyes. One more to go. Morpho's sticky body tightened on his shoulder.

Geddy shot his hand out for Oz to take. She did, squeezing it so desperately he thought she might break his fingers. He returned her weary smile by flashing her a devil sign, sticking out his tongue, and jerking his head up and down.

She laughed at him, but seriously, *could it get more rock n' roll than this?*

If her giant yellow eyes were the last things he saw, that would be okay. But fuck, he'd wanted to meld with her one last time. In all the ways.

— **See you on the other side,** she said in his head.

— I hope so.

As the open stern of the *Stalwart* made its final turn toward the wall, the light of Sagacea blazed inside, and no shadow remained to hide them.

CHAPTER 45
PUNCTURE WOUND

The sensation of seeing utter destruction unfold around you without feeling it was disorienting. It only lasted a second, if that. The *Stalwart* crumpled as the neatly severed edge of its sharp, shortened stern pierced the wall, only to instantly disappear behind them as the *Fiz's* momentum propelled them through the opening with admittedly shocking speed. After that, it was like nothing had happened.

Geddy pried one eye open, then gasped. "Holy shit, that *worked*? Doc, damage report."

"The front shield took a small hit, but that's all," Doc said, coming dangerously close to a smile.

"Look!" Jel shouted excitedly as she pointed at the rear camera view.

The still-intact *Gallant* exploded through the crumpled husk of the *Stalwart* like a battering ram, disruptors blazing. Half a dozen more torpedo-carrying ships barreled through right behind it. The moment their blockade failed, the Nads collapsed the wall around the hole, forming a funnel shape. As it did, it constricted like thumb cuffs around the Alliance ships as they streamed through. Meanwhile, the *Gallant* and the other torpedo ships that got through first now surrounded the *Fizmo* to protect it.

As the funnel of Zelnad ships swallowed the first wave, they gathered into a needle-shaped formation that quickly gained on the torpedo group. Thousands of Alliance ships pursued them, both sides exchanging a blur of disruptor fire in both directions even as they sped up. As the full fleet unleashed its fury on the crumbling blockade, it turned into a wall of flame and debris that made it impossible to tell who was who.

"Doc, tell me you've got the weapon," Geddy demanded.

He shook his head. "There's still too much interference. I'm trying to filter it out."

"See if Verveik's got it!"

The torpedo ships surrounded the Fiz like a suit of armor, firing backwards at the mass of advancing Zelnads. But they wouldn't be able to hold them off for long. Denk had her wide open, but she just didn't have the horsepower of a modern warship.

"Uh, Cap?" Denk said. "Balzac's protecting our flank, but he's taking a pounding. He's the only thing between us and the Nads."

Oz covered her face shield with her hands and shook her head with a heavy sigh. Her eyes met Geddy's. "Oh, god, just get it over with."

A bolus of adrenaline sent Geddy's heart into overdrive. Never had such a golden opportunity been teed up for him, yet he couldn't summon the perfect punchline. "My whole life has led to this moment," he rasped. "Now that it's here, I can't help but wonder ... What if the setup *is* the joke?"

The light over the front screen lit up to signal a hail. "It's Verveik," Doc said.

"Wow, talk about a whiff," Oz laughed. "And to think I'm

having a kid with …" She closed her eyes and sunk into her chair. "Shit."

She caught herself too late. Not that it mattered now. The crew stared at her, incredulous. Apparently, she hadn't even told Jel. The Commander's appearance broke the spell. "Ahem, Colonel?" Oz wanted to crawl into a hole and die, but Verveik remained focused on Geddy. "That hunk of junk is slowing us down. Get inside the Gallant so we can put some distance between us and the assholes on our tail!"

Verveik's ship had already lined up in front of them and was opening the hangar doors.

Geddy wanted nothing more than to be in the bigger, faster, more powerful ship, but slowing down even more put the whole torpedo group at mortal risk. "Are you tracking the weapon? Our sensors are struggling."

"We just picked it up. We're nearly in torpedo range. You've gotta move!"

"I'm tracking it now, too, Colonel," Doc said.

The heaviness of Oz's accidental reveal still hung in the air when the sharp clang of metal on metal rang from the stern. It sounded like two colossal swords clashing together.

Geddy gave an alarmed gasp. "What the hell was that??"

He unbuckled and hurried as best he could to the airlock in his suit, half expecting to find the rear half gone. It wasn't, but a jagged chunk of a Screvari battleship had pierced the hold doors like an axe. Whatever air remained inside hissed out through the breach. It meant their old-school shields were already depleted.

Balzac, his crotchety old frenemy, had just died protecting the *Fiz*. If the other ships didn't get within torpedo range, and fast, they'd miss their window.

He spun on his heels and marched back toward the screen, where Verveik still was. "What just happened?" asked the commander.

"Balzac's gone," Geddy said. "But a piece of him's still embedded in our ass, so to speak."

That visibly stung. Balzac was one of his most loyal and capable lieutenants. "All the more reason to get it inside!"

"Negative." Voprot and the rest of the crew exchanged looks with each other, then him. He didn't need to ask if they agreed. "The weapon's all that matters. Go chase it down."

Verveik equivocated briefly, then grimaced. "Good luck, Colonel."

"Just go!" Geddy said.

With the hangar doors still open, the Gallant's engines flared bright blue and it pulled away, leaving only a handful of ships to defend the Fiz against the determined swarm.

"The torpedo's away!" Doc yelled.

The scopes showed a fast-moving projectile launched from the *Gallant* and streaked toward the unidentified signal up ahead of them.

C'mon, baby …

But a moment before it found its target, the signal vanished.

Doc looked up, and horror surged through Geddy's body. "It's the barrier. The weapon's already through!"

Verveik reappeared on screen. "All ships, evasive maneuvers! Now! Now!"

The torpedo group broke off. Denk was about to do the same when Geddy stopped him. "Belay that, Corp– er, Major." He spun to Doc. "How long before we reach it?" Geddy asked Doc.

"One minute, fifty-two seconds at our current speed. We can't afford to slow down."

There wasn't time to dally. Geddy shot to his feet and started a one-minute, forty-five-second countdown on his cuff. "Steady as she goes, Mr. Junt."

"But we're naked out here!" Denk protested. "One hit and we're toast."

"Then make yourself as hard a target as you can."

"Where do you think you're going??" Oz asked after him.

She only needed a look from him to know the answer. Only one option remained.

"Aw, hell ..." she mumbled.

"Denk, open the hold doors as soon as I'm inside the *Penetrator*. Everyone into the escape pod as fast as you can. Right now."

The sight of Denk's somber face broke his heart. "Aye aye, Cap," he said weakly.

Oz's big eyes turned glassy, but she nodded that it was okay. He took a mental snapshot of her face and hurried back to the airlock. The moment he opened the inner door, he stole a glance over his shoulder. The whole crew understood. There wasn't time for tearful farewells.

Geddy stepped inside the airlock, then performed the necessary overrides to open the second door to the compromised hold. Once it finally slid aside, he clomped across the floor as fast as his heavy boots would allow toward the *Penetrator*.

A hidden button extended the small ladder and opened the canopy of the svelte one-seater. He bounded up into the cockpit, hoping against hope it wasn't too tight a squeeze with the suit. The key was still in its slot where he left it. Had some part of him known this would happen? Had Ziksu?

While the canopy closed over him, he consulted the timer. Just under a minute remained. The hold doors started to open, but the embedded chunk of Balzac's ship stopped them from opening all the way. While the motors whined in protest, a purple bolt shot through and ripped the jagged piece of shrapnel away.

It also pierced the outer airlock door.

Another shot struck the stack of empty cargo boxes right next to him and bored through the starboard hull, leaving a perfectly clean hole with glowing edges.

When his eyes shot to the opening, all he saw was a rapidly shrinking cluster of Nad ships being ripped to pieces by a huge swarm of Xellaran Darkstars and Star Guard Javelins.

But Denk couldn't slow them down now. He ran to catch up with the rest of the crew, already en route to Morpho's custom-built escape pod. Oz paused just long enough to touch her glove to the airlock window.

Go, he mouthed to her.

He lifted free of the deck, spun, and shoved the thruster forward, hoping like hell her shinium-clad outer hull could withstand a couple of hits.

The moment he shot through the narrow opening, he dove beneath a renewed flurry of bolts and turned, inverted, back toward Sagacea. When he righted himself, he looked up through the canopy just in time to see the *Fiz* hit the barrier and vanish.

He gasped. "No!"

The last few Zelnads chasing the *Fiz* got torn up by the cloud of Darkstars, which immediately veered in all directions like a school of fish avoiding a diver. In this case, avoiding a barrier that could zap you into some random place in the galaxy.

Geddy urged the *Penetrator* right toward it.

— This had better work.

— *It will.*

As he accelerated, Geddy could almost hear the Sagacean souls trapped inside the shiny metal enveloping him. There were too many to make out.

All he could do was trust to hope.

He closed his eyes and whispered a wish to the universe

that he'd survive. That Oz and the crew were still alive and that he'd see them again soon.

For a moment, he imagined being hurled through the front shield at twenty-eight thousand kilometers per hour, disintegrating when he got jumped into the side of a mountain on some alien world. But that didn't happen.

The back of his eyelids were dark, and then they weren't. A light too powerful to suppress sliced right through them, and his eyes reflexively popped open.

What had been empty space was now filled with brilliant purple-white light. What had been black was now filled with threads of energy as crisp and detailed as a painting. Some kind of celestial hair waved sinuously like seaweed in a current. It was a physical manifestation of Lestiko's tuning method.

Images surged into his consciousness of life and death, war and peace, love and loss. All at once. And voices, too, pumping through his veins. A powerful sense of belonging fell over him, like he was supposed to be here. Like he'd just given the correct password to the doorman at Tatiana's First New Year's Orgy.

More than anything, he felt like he'd come home.

CHAPTER 46
THE EXPANSE

— *Hurry, Geddy!*

It took him a moment to comprehend that he was far beyond the bounds of established knowledge. He was looking at the cytoplasm of the universe.

He mindlessly shoved the thruster forward, and the too-big MPD drives from an old Kemik AS-322 pinned him to the seat. The threads blurred as he rocketed toward what he could only assume was the center of Sagacea. The nucleus, where a weapon made of people was also headed.

Not surprisingly, the *Penetrator's* old, secondhand scopes didn't work here. The power of this place wouldn't allow it.

"I have no idea where I'm going."

— *Then make your way.*

It took him a moment to ponder what Eli meant. "You mean ... tuning?"

— *If you can't do it here, you can't do it anywhere. Just concentrate.*

— **We will help you.**

He'd been so awed and overwhelmed by sights and feelings that he'd forgotten that trusty little Morpho was still on his shoulder. They'd only just learned to tune. But then, hadn't he done it with Oz for a moment?

Geddy took a long, deep breath and focused, Lestiko's visualization made real all around him. It was like listening to a radio when you were in the same room as the transmitter.

— *Do you remember what I told you when the three of us were floating in space over Kigantu?*

"When my brain was starved of oxygen and I was about to die?"

— *Yeah, that's the one.*

"That we are all connected?"

— *Yes. That includes the people inside that weapon.*

Geddy closed his eyes and concentrated. If he could connect to even one person, he should be able to follow the thread right to them.

The voices in his skull were indistinct and incomprehensible, like a billion simultaneous whispers in as many alien tongues. His translator chip only worked with sounds.

He shook his head. "I can't. There are too many."

— **We must focus on a single one.**

"But I don't know anyone on that ship."

— **You sure about that?**

He paused, doubting his instinctive response. "You can't mean Colonel Pritchard."

— *Why not? He's a puppet like the rest of them. He was just playing a part.*

Geddy didn't want to believe that. Until recently, Pritchard was the public face of the Zelnads, such as when they announced the short-lived Coalition of Independent Worlds at the IASS show. But no one had seen him since Geddy and Jel rescued Oz and Dr. Krezek back on Stemir. If Pritchard was merely a host, then who had he hated all these years? Who could he blame for his parents' deaths? And if the Asurya created the Zelnads, then where was he now?

"How do I zero in on him?"

— *Picture him in your mind's eye. His face. His voice.*

Again, he closed his eyes and pictured the stern-faced officer. He wasn't big, but he was solid, square-jawed, and exuded authority. Geddy could plainly remember him say, *Have a seat, young man. I'm afraid your parents were involved in an accident.*

For reasons that exceeded his understanding, Geddy got a strong sense that the weapon was close, but still ahead and below his position. As though guided by an unseen hand, he nosed the *Penetrator* down.

— **Good, Geddy.**

In a way, it reminded him of a metal detector, only there was no electronic beep to tell him he was on the right track.

A minute later, he reopened his eyes and noticed that the threads of energy had become turbulent, swirling like eddies in a stream.

"The weapon came through here. That's what caused these disturbances."

— *I think you're right. Shinium would disrupt the flow.*

He followed the vague trail for a few minutes, making minor adjustments as he found and lost whatever connected him to Pritchard. At a certain point, the wispy threads faded, and a void opened before him.

An indeterminate distance ahead was a bright orb that was either small but close, or colossal but distant. Instinct pointed to the latter.

"Is that ... the origin?" Geddy asked.

— *It must be.*

A glint caught his eye on the starboard side, almost out of view. He banked to get a better look. Had it not been for the reflections on its polished surface, it would've been indistinguishable from the surroundings.

There was still time!

— *Perhaps I should've asked earlier, but what exactly is your plan here?*

Eli might as well have asked this rhetorically. Geddy had no idea whether or how he could keep such a huge vessel from reaching its target. The only good news was that he had the faster ship and didn't need to deal with any attackers.

The closer he got to the weapon, the more immense he realized it was. Within the Sphere, its mirrored surface made its size difficult to discern. Now, he figured the flattened oval was at least as long as three battle cruisers and fully twice as wide. The amount of shinium needed to cover it boggled the mind. It must've taken centuries to build. Maybe longer.

"Well, I guess knocking it off-course is out."

It had no visible openings. It was just a surfboard-shaped bomb bigger than any ship in their galaxy. Like the other Nad vessels, it had no visible thrusters. It seemed to pull itself along using mahk'ti like a rope.

He could turn the *Penetrator* into a missile again and hit it going as fast as he could. But he was far too small for that, and the last thing he wanted to do was kill any hosts.

Maybe there was a way.

He swiped past the nav screen to the bubble drive interface. Why would Ziksu have taken pains to install one? And why had he been willing to use the Samaja's sacred orb to restore its shinium skin? Could he have known it would come to this?

"E, I've got an idea, but you're not gonna like it."

— *You want to jump it away.*

"Yes."

— *Like Lestiko and Ogos did.*

Not only had Lestiko used the power of his mind to sever his bond with Rai and channel the energy into a jump bubble that saved the *Stalwart*, but he'd told Geddy how to do it.

Eli's heartbreak, his anguish, unfurled in Geddy's consciousness like a black umbrella.

"Do you see another way? Because I sure don't."

— **He's right, Eli.**

— *I know.*

If it worked, Geddy would lose Eli, Morph, *and* Oz in one fell swoop but save the universe. His kid would grow up without an old man, but with any luck, he'd still have a badass, army-gathering force of nature for a mother. On balance, not a bad deal.

Urging on the *Penetrator,* he descended and drew even with the weapon's perfectly smooth and symmetrical form, settling directly over it. He could sense the people inside, if not their thoughts. Pritchard was in there somewhere.

Up ahead, the core of Sagacea, whatever it was, grew larger but not large. It was still a weird optical illusion. Could it really be as small as it looked?

Sagacea's structure wasn't like a cell. It was an atom — a tiny nucleus, an energetic shell, and a space between that nobody fully understood.

"What happens if this works?"

— *Our bond will be severed.*

"Yeah, but I mean after."

— *We can't know.*

— **You don't have much time.**

The full, terrible gravity of what he had to do settled onto his chest.

"Morph, I …"

— **It's okay, Geddy. Just set the jump coordinates and focus.**

The screen had begun to flicker so badly that he worried the drive might not work at all. Doc had even said as much.

Geddy entered the coordinates to the safe zone, where a detachment of a hundred warships and civilian vessels eagerly awaited the weapon. They included tractor beam-enabled ships to slow it down. Transports and cargo ships. Hospital ships and the Ornean science ship, *Inquiry*. They would attend to the hosts and see if the the Zelnads' spell over them broke with their failed plans.

"How does this work, exactly?"

Morph had helped Dr. Nilsson develop the miraculous drive that saved humanity so many years ago. No one understood its mechanics better.

— Once the bubble forms, the energy release will expand it like breath into a balloon. As long as it expands quickly enough, it should take the weapon along.

"That's it?"

— That's it.

Geddy raised his eyes, squinting against Sagacea's incredible brightness. The birth of the universe took place right here, yet there wasn't so much as a commemorative plaque. Of all the times to forget your camera.

He heaved a sigh and swallowed hard. "You ready, E?"

— Ready, Geddy. You pull, I'll push.

"I hope this isn't the end."

— As do I.

"I love you. You, too, Morph."

— I love you, Geddy.

— Do it now!

Before he closed his eyes, Geddy took a final look at Sagacea. It reminded him of the embers at the heart of a fire, fragile yet seething with power. As close as he was, he still couldn't have said if it was solid, gas, liquid, or plasma. Whether space itself emanated from it or was being drawn into it.

He activated the jump bubble. *EXECUTE POINT TO POINT?* was barely readable on the scrambled screen.

Geddy concentrated on the energy that surrounded him,

flowing between him and Eli like an unseen river. For the first time, he felt its full power. It was too much for just one. Maybe that was the point.

Like cutting a cord, Lestiko said. *Quickly and decisively.*

He exhaled, then sharply inhaled, imagining he was stealing Eli's nonexistent breath. Only it wasn't stolen. It was given, and everything turned purple.

CHAPTER 47
AFTER HOURS

Time couldn't end because it had no beginning. Space couldn't end because it was infinite. Reality wasn't real because nothing was. And Geddy wasn't Geddy anymore. He wasn't even Eddie Kepler. He was neither corporeal nor immaterial nor anywhere in between.

And yet, he *was*.

He had no eyes with which to see. He had no nerves, no brain, no biochemistry. There was no death or life, and no fear.

Was he standing? Floating? Was it cold? Warm? Absence and presence were abstractions. Everything and nothing could and did exist at once.

All he knew for certain was that, for the first time since that fateful day in the tunnels, he was alone in his own head. But *something* was there with him. He could feel it.

Quite suddenly, a solid and tangible scene resolved in front of him. He was standing just outside the Old Earth Museum of Space Exploration back on The Deuce. Gravity tugged on his feet like always, which was to say, a bit more than he would prefer.

What the actual fuck?

It was dark and chilly, but the rarefied air and lack of light pollution made the stars especially brilliant. This was before the methane and sulfur clouds formed. The dense band of white, purple, and red painted diagonally across the night sky was the disk of the Eionus Galaxy. The Deuce's two moons, Trebek and Sajak, hung overhead like a pair of sleepy gray eyes. The crescent of Laguna still burned brightly.

The museum was closed, but the doors were open, and a faint voice came from within. He wandered cautiously inside. The sound emanated from the back right corner, a tunnel made of fake moon rock where all the NASA footage and news clips played on a loop. It only activated when someone tripped an infrared sensor at the entrance.

Geddy cautiously made his way from the gift counter to the space exploration timeline that read, THE LONG ROAD TO THE STARS over the entrance. He entered and followed the curved tunnel until he arrived at the display that recounted the first moon landing.

A little humanoid boy with four eyes in an upside-down U shape stood in front of it with his mouth hanging open. Not a single hair graced his gangly, narrow-limbed body. His skin was dark gray and mottled, and he only had three fingers on each hand. Like Zihnians and Vyephs, his knee joints bent backward like a cat's, but otherwise, he didn't resemble any species Geddy had ever seen.

Grainy footage showed Neil Armstrong making his way down the ladder of the Apollo 11 lander.

"July 20, 1969," Geddy said, testing his ability to speak. "A long, long time ago."

The startled boy's head spun toward him just as Neil hopped off onto the moon.

"Aren't you going to make a sixty-nine joke?"

The kid's voice was no less familiar than his own.

"Eli??" He resisted the urge to hug him.

The boy stared at Geddy for a long moment, confusion crossing his face. He raised his hands in front of him, wiggling his narrow fingers in fascination.

"I have ... form."

"Yeah, and it's weird as hell. No offense."

"And you're even fatter than you look in a mirror."

"That's one small step for man ... one giant leap for mankind," came Neil's voice across the scratchy connection.

Geddy took a step forward, extended his finger, and poked him in the shoulder. It was solid. "Damn."

"What?"

"I was hoping you'd say, 'I'm a real boy!' and dance around."

"Something tells me we're not al–"

A faint but distinct echo rippled through the museum's vast inner space. A man's voice. It sounded like it was coming from the second floor, which was exclusively dedicated to Project Rearview.

"What's that?" Eli asked.

"The Rearview display. Upstairs."

While Neil described the moon's regolith to NASA, Geddy led Eli out of the tunnel to the wide stairway that spiraled its way around the 1:2 model of the Saturn V rocket, the tip of which nearly scraped the top of the atrium. As they climbed, the hovering, animated timeline of the project that allowed humankind to leave Old Earth loudly played through. It was an AI-generated voice loosely based on Walter Cronkite. That was his mom's idea.

"... but not all world leaders attended the summit, leaving those that did with no choice but to proceed without them. An unprecedented international effort began in which the world's best minds led teams, each with a specific role ..."

When they reached the top of the spiral stairs, the timeline came fully into view. A woman in a white lab coat meandered around the circular exhibit with her hands folded behind her back. She paused at a life-sized hologram of Dr. Birgit Nilsson, the Swedish-born scientist credited with discovering the natural wormhole that let the Rearview ships here. In fact, she had developed the bubble drive in secret with the help of a Sagacean — Morpho.

He and Eli looked at each other as they crossed into the exhibit, both realizing that the fifty-something woman looking at her hologram was wearing the exact same clothes.

She slowly turned toward them, looking every bit as confused as they were.

"Morpho?" Geddy asked.

It seemingly took her a moment to fathom what was happening, because she only stared back at first.

"Geddy? Eli?"

Geddy reflexively felt his empty left shoulder, Morph having been perched on it almost every day. He was there at the end, too, helping to pull him and Eli apart. The blast would've vaporized him, too.

"You're hotter than I expected," Geddy offered.

"Hers is the last form I inhabited. As I suspect Eli's was."

"I remember now," Eli said. "Eli was the boy's name."

"How could you not remember?"

"It was seventeen million years ago. You can't remember what you did yesterday," Eli said.

The two of them moved deeper into the exhibit while AI Walter Cronkite elucidated the mining and recycling effort required to build the massive transports.

"Most of the world's aluminum, titanium, copper, and gold went into building Rearview One, Two, and Three. Buildings were demolished and stripped of their wiring and plumbing. Cans and even airplanes were broken down for their aluminum …"

"Do you know what's happening?" Geddy asked.

"I'm afraid not." It was odd to hear Morph's normally androgynous voice sound like a human female tinged with a Scandinavian accent. "My guess is that we've entered some kind of temporal envelope."

"Oh, well that clears things up."

"Sagacea's power must be enough to distort spacetime," Eli offered.

Morpho took in the museum's vastness with wonder. "Dr. Nilsson would've been humbled by all this. She was a quiet, brilliant woman. We made a good team, she and I."

"You remember Project Rearview?" Geddy asked.

"Oh, yes. It was a time of both spectacular achievement and profound despair." She nodded toward another part of the timeline, some fifteen years later between the Asian famine and the Northern Migration. "Especially the lottery."

Ostensibly, everyone selected to board the Rearview ships besides the crew was random, at least among those who met the age and health requirements. That was how it was presented here, but Geddy's mother told a different story — one in which deals were struck behind the scenes that favored the wealthy and connected. That aspect of Old Earth had accompanied them beyond the stars.

"Yeah, well, that's ancient history now," Geddy said. "It doesn't explain why we're here or what we're supposed to do."

Quite abruptly, the displays shut off along with all the lights except for a few small canisters in the ceiling. It became startlingly silent — enough to discern heavy footsteps ascending the stairs and a rhythmic swish of synthetic cloth.

"You guys hear that?" Geddy wondered aloud.

The three of them left the now-dark display and moved together toward the sound. A single light illuminated the landing. As they watched, a shiny white dome came into view, then a gold face shield. A few seconds later, a man in a full Apollo

A7 pressure suit reached the top and stood perfectly still as he stared at them, his appearance completely obscured by the thin layer of gold.

"I don't know what this is, but I am so fucking here for it," Geddy muttered.

The name patch, sandwiched between the NASA logo and Apollo mission insignia, read ARMSTRONG.

CHAPTER 48

NEVER MEET YOUR HEROES

Neil Armstrong stared silently at them, and they stared silently back.

Geddy exchanged confused looks with Eli and Morph, no longer certain what was real or imagined. When Neil finally spoke, it was in the same tinny voice that everyone knew — the one made possible by a once-miraculous radio connection to Houston five hundred years earlier.

"There's a human expression I always liked. Can you guess what it is?"

"Just do it?" Geddy ventured.

"It's that those who don't learn from the past are condemned to repeat it," Neil said.

"Damn! That was my second guess."

Neil's helmet swiveled toward Morpho. "I wonder if it was on Dr. Nilsson's mind when she boarded Rearview One."

"She wasn't thinking about the past," said Morph. "She only ever cared about the future."

"That's precisely the problem."

"Who are you?" Geddy inquired. "Or is it *what*?"

"The more relevant question is what *you* are, Geddy Starheart."

"You know my name?"

"All too well."

Geddy narrowed his eyes at the mysterious being animating the space suit. "You're the Asurya, aren't you?"

"I was called that once, yes."

"Were you ever called Neil Armstrong?"

"No. The energy suggested this form to me."

"Thanks for the consideration. Where are we? And don't say the museum."

"We're at an intersection of time and space where neither holds sway. The point from which the energy first manifested and forced the universe to unfold."

"That's cool, but I meant, like, on a map."

A void instantly opened between them, swallowing the space between them even though Geddy could still feel the gravity on the soles of his feet. Pure black stretched in every direction save for a tiny dot of pure white light hovering between them.

"You're witnessing the birth of a universe. There are an infinite number, all born from sentient energy."

What happened next wasn't an explosion per se. It was more like the plastic globe toys sold in the gift shop downstairs that expanded as you pulled the corners. The light passed through them as it rushed outward, threads of it balling into stars as space grew around them, swallowing the entire museum.

"Each universe has something to teach us. Because the energy is driven to learn all it can, it divides into an infinite number of individual beings to observe its evolution. We are those beings."

The white dot stretched and morphed into a cloud of molecules that collided, linking and growing until it took the shape of a single-celled organism.

"Given enough time, the formation of life is a statistical certainty. From the moment it begins, we are drawn to it, binding us to living hosts. Over the ages, our sentience and knowledge passed into them."

"The seeds of knowledge," Geddy said, echoing Eli's own description of what Sagaceans are.

"As intelligent life flourishes, it makes copies of itself and civilization develops. Our very presence allows it to advance and grow."

As the Asurya described this, the organism divided, reassembling itself into a crab-like creature that crawled from a pool of water, building itself a little house from pebbles. More followed. In seconds, the arrangement of pebble houses grew into a little community.

"But the same patterns always emerge. The desire for knowledge becomes a hunger for power and dominance. Once that occurs, civilization collapses. Again and again, in a constant loop.

"I began to wonder if it wasn't our role to break the cycle. I revealed myself to Xellara, your most evolved society, as a 'god' who could deliver their salvation."

"The Illustrations," Eli said.

"Yes. When that failed, I understood that the lesson of this universe was one of self-extinction. I became determined to destroy it so another could manifest. The only way to do that was to return as many of my kindred as possible to Sagacea. Like overloading a circuit, if you will."

"But what about the Last Illustration?" Eli asked. "You couldn't see beyond that, could you?"

His big, helmeted head gave a slow shake. "No, because there was a variable I hadn't considered."

"Why?" Geddy asked. "Or was it X? Heh, see what I did th–"

"It was you, Geddy. You and your resurgent Alliance."

"Me??"

"Every decision you've made, every action you and Eli and the others have taken has defied the pattern. That made me very curious about you."

Geddy's initial reaction was to reject this. He had acted selfishly time and time again and almost got himself and his crew killed as a result. But he never lost sight of his goal.

"But why me? How does a being like you even know about me?"

"As you know, shinium is rather difficult to find. Even for us. We have scoured the universe for it. We detected it on your home world and hired a freelancer to locate its source, which he claimed to have done."

"Sammo-Yann," Geddy said under his breath.

"Only he didn't find a shinium deposit. He found your ship. When he tried to sell it, we bought it. When you took it, we took it back. Only then did you, Geddy Starheart, enter my awareness."

"So the creatures, the Gundrun Incident ... the clones ... that was all misdirection?"

"More like rabbit holes I expected you to follow. Instead, you followed the shinium," the Asurya said. "And now, here we are."

"Does that mean we saved the universe?" he asked hopefully.

"It means that, in this infinitesimally small moment, you are both alive and dead," he said. "As is the universe itself."

"Like Schrödinger's cat?" Geddy asked. The famous thought experiment illustrated a paradox of quantum mechanics called superposition.

"Not bad for a guy who got a C in physics."

Geddy heaved an exasperated sigh. "I always knew that would come back to haunt me."

"The end that I foretold is no less certain than the future for which you've fought," said the Asurya. "That's why we are here."

"So if we're both alive and dead, how do we push the needle toward, you know, alive?"

"Convince me I'm wrong."

He'd fantasized about this moment ever since Sammo-Yann stole the *Penetrator* from this very museum. He and Eli helped Verveik finally the Alliance and defeat the evil Zelnads. Only the Zelnads weren't necessarily evil and they might not have saved shit.

"Jeez, no pressure."

"And yet, you seem to relish it."

"I think you learned the wrong lesson about the universe," he offered.

"Explain."

He turned to regard Eli, whose current form was no taller than Denk, and it all became very clear. "Before Eli, I was ..."

Once again, he thought of Tatiana.

He hadn't repressed the memory, exactly. Or had he? The night before Eli first spoke to him, Tati had thrown one of her lavish, booze-soaked parties at the penthouse that loomed over Laguna Luxe mall. While the music thumped against the walls and the party raged on, he wandered alone out onto the veranda — the same one he'd been standing on years later when the building collapsed under him and he fell into the lagoon.

Nobody was around. In the distance, he could just make out the lights of the military spaceport on the far edge of town. He and Tots had just gotten engaged, but love wasn't the right word for what they had. It was more like they'd fallen off a ship, clinging to each other as they drowned because it was easier than swimming toward an indeterminate shore. For a few significant seconds, he very sincerely thought about jumping. The only thing that stopped him was realizing that it wouldn't matter. Not to him, not even to her.

"Before Eli, I was alone. So was he. Morph, too." They both nodded their assent. "In fact, maybe we all are. That feeling you had when you didn't see a future? It's despair. It's what made it possible for you to take over hosts. But there's an opposing force that's every bit as strong."

The empty space contracted again until the museum reformed around them. The Asurya didn't speak for a long moment.

"You mean hope," he said, his tone suddenly less assured.

Geddy nodded. "It's why Dr. Nilsson created the bubble drive. It made me jump on a damned space elevator in a replica of that suit you're wearing. It kept my crew — my family — together. You might even say it united the armies of the galaxy. Without hope, there is no future. *That's* the lesson of this universe."

The Asurya's helmeted head turned to Eli, then Morph, who asked, "Do you see a future now?"

Silently, the Asurya about-faced and started back down the stairs. Geddy frowned and regarded his companions with grave concern.

"Hey, wait!" he called after him. "Where are you going?! Where's Oz and my crew? What are we supposed to do now?"

He bolted forward, but as he did, the floor fell away under his feet and he found himself adrift in space, arms flailing. It got very cold very fast, and though he craned his neck to see Eli and Morph, they were nowhere to be seen.

CHAPTER 49
POD PEOPLE

Stars again filled Geddy's vision. The lights of the *Penetrator's* console still glowed. His right hand was on the stick, his left, the throttle. The colossal, sleek Zelnad weapon sailed through space right beside him just as it had when he separated from Eli.

Sagacea was nowhere to be seen, nor was the fleet, but the scopes indicated a large number of vessels inbound. The ship's sensors were cobbled together from what he could find in the repair bay of The Deuce's spaceport. They couldn't do much more than track the signals and display transponder data, but in this case, it was enough.

Leading the small armada closing in on their position was Queen Tymeri's ship, *Athua*.

"What the hell just happened?" he muttered.

— *We must've jumped to the safe zone.*

"Eli! You're still with me?!"

— *As always, my friend.*

Nervously, his eyes drifted down to his left shoulder. The familiar black blob was still there, too.

"Morph!"

— **Hello, Geddy.**

"Hey, were you guys just in the museum with m–"

An incoming hail from the *Athua* cut him off. He opened the channel, and Tymeri's face appeared on the *Penetrator's* crude HUD. The last time he was so thrilled to see a face like hers, it was on a bed of perfectly cooked linguini.

"Holy shit, Starheart! I mean, holy fucking shit! You made it!"

"Tymeri? Is this the extraction point?"

"What do you mean? Of course, it is."

He was so disoriented that he'd forgotten the original plan. Thanks to Lestiko, no one in the galaxy had a more powerful tra*ctor* beam than Tymeri.

"Has anyone heard from Oz and my crew?"

"I haven't. I just know what's left of the fleet is already back at the Karrea Ion Cloud. I can't wait to hear the story. Even if you're the one telling it."

The big ship hadn't lost any of its previous velocity. If anything, it was going even faster. The *Penetrator* was nearing top speed.

"Are you sure we can stop this thing?"

"Eventually," Tymeri said. "But there's no point in trying until we can shut down its engines. Does it even have engines?"

— **I can do it.**

"Please hold." He cut the feed. "Are you sure?"

Morph knew the guts of ships better than anyone. He could easily survive the vacuum, and he could squeeze through impossibly tight spaces.

— **Open the canopy.**

"Morpho's gonna take a crack at it," Geddy said to Tymeri. "Sit tight."

It took Geddy a moment to realize he still had a suit on and a solid twenty minutes of O2. Though he had to override the ship's pressure maintenance system to do it, he raised the canopy just enough for Morph to slip through, then quickly closed it behind him.

Against the backdrop of space, Morph was pretty much invisible. Geddy only caught a brief glimpse of him after he'd leapt across the small gap between the *Penetrator* and the smooth, windowless missile. He found what must have been a hatch and disappeared. Geddy could still sense Pritchard inside along with many others.

"Hey, were you just in the Old Earth space museum with me, Morph, and the Asurya?" he asked Eli.

— *I don't know what you're talking about.*

Geddy's mind instantly raced for answers, one of which was that he was crazy. "Uh …"

— *Just kidding.*

Relief washed over him. "That's hilarious. So what happened? Where did the Asurya go?"

— *I suspect he had some way of influencing our quantum state.*

"So we were dead and alive, and he nudged us toward alive."

— *My best guess was that he saw a different future.*

"So we really did save the universe?"

— *So it would seem.*

"Too bad we can't high-five. Or in your case, high-three."

Morpho next appeared at the top of the sleek weapon. Geddy got as close as he dared and cracked the canopy once more. Morph flung himself up and crawled inside.

"Any luck?"

— **Yes, I was able to disconnect its propulsion system.**

Geddy reopened the link to Tymeri and smiled at her. "It worked. That just leaves momentum or inertia. Possibly both."

"All right, people, let's see if we can slow this damn thing down."

The hundreds of salvage vessels formed a large ring and

activated their tractor beams, focusing them on the back of the ship. It was funny to think that Tymeri's beam was the same one that had snatched Oz away on Verdithea. That seemed like twenty years ago.

Oz, who may or may not have gotten out before the *Fiz* hit the invisible barrier. Or the escape pod.

"Thanks, Geddy," Tymeri said. "I think we've got it from here. You'd better get your ass back to the fleet. I'm pretty sure Verveik thinks you're dead."

He couldn't know for sure whether the bubble drive still worked considering how much power he and Eli just pumped through it. But once he switched it on and entered the coordinates to the edge of the ion storm, the familiar prompt appeared.

EXECUTE POINT TO POINT?

Geddy made the jump with a jubilant heart, pleased that he and his Sagacean companions weren't dead and that they'd saved the universe. But it didn't last.

Near the edge of the Karrea Ion Storm, the remainder of the mighty Alliance fleet had gathered to lick its wounds. It was impossible to tell how many they'd lost, especially with the *Penetrator's* limited scanning capability. Interference from the storm made it that much worse.

An incoming hail appeared, and one of the larger ships on the scopes flashed to indicate its source. Geddy's heart leapt when he saw it was the *Gallant*.

Even in victory, Verveik looked like he'd just jettisoned a puppy into the vacuum. "Colonel! Are you all right? What happened in there?"

"Yeah, we're all okay. It's a long, strange story I can't wait to tell you, but right now, all I want is to find the escape pod."

"Escape pod?" Verveik asked. "What escape pod?"

"From the *Fizmo*," Geddy explained. "The crew got out just before ..." He couldn't say the rest aloud because he had no way of knowing if it was true. "Someone scooped them up, I'm sure of it."

His already pained expression fell even more. "I'm sorry, but I haven't heard anything about an escape pod."

The comment knocked the wind out of him. His jaw hung dumbly open. He gave his head a vigorous shake. "But it's got to be here somewhere."

"You saw them eject and steer clear of the barrier?" Verveik asked. "You're certain?"

Of course, he wasn't. The last he saw of them was when they were headed up to Morpho's pod. That didn't mean they got away. Plus, it would've been going as fast as the *Fiz*. If the pod's small engines couldn't spill their velocity, momentum would've carried them straight into the barrier. If that happened, they could be literally anywhere.

"No." Geddy's mouth was a desert. "Not certain."

A tiny blip of light in the near distance caught his eye, and he glanced up. No more than twenty clicks away, a vertical rift opened in space, tinged purple. It parted, looking as vaginal as it ever did. A fargate opened by an old-school novasphere.

The ship that squeezed through was large and rust-colored. Geddy gasped. It couldn't be, yet it was. The *Red Raven*, the *Fizmo's* rival trawler captained by the odious Beebit Tompanov.

"Sorry I'm late," came his grating, nasally voice over the comm. Jabbing a scalpel directly into his eardrums would've been preferable. "Did I miss anything?"

Maybe he shouldn't have saved the universe.

"Leave it to you to show up during the credits, Tompanov," Geddy replied.

"Starheart, you're alive!" exclaimed the blue-headed Kailorian, then turned to his off-camera pilot. "Sorry, Steve, better re-cork the champagne."

"Don't you ever get tired of being a mustache-twirling villain? It's so clichéd."

"I am the hero of my own story." He gave a melodramatic flourish.

"What do you want?"

"I merely came to assist with slowing down this pretty silver thing. You'd think there'd be a better way to stop a runaway ship, but it appears our– er, *my* trade never ceases to be useful."

Geddy shrugged. "You want to be useful? Stop the *Raven* right in front of it."

He acted hurt, and he didn't act well. "Tsk, tsk. Always threatening violence, even when I come to offer help."

"Cut the crap. Why are you really here? I don't remember Commissioner Gordon flashing the dipshit signal."

"I came to barter, of course."

"I'm not interested in anything you have, including and especially your face. I'm Geddy Starheart, and I just saved the universe."

"You mean the Battle of Sagacea?" Tompanov asked. "Interestingly enough, I came from there. Did you know Commander Verveik gave me exclusive salvage rights to any tukrium debris I found?"

"That's because he thought the world was ending."

"No it wasn't, Colonel," said Verveik, whom he'd nearly forgotten was still on the comm. "If he wants to take the risk, he can be my guest."

Geddy sighed and gave a hard roll of his eyes. "Fine. As long as it takes literally forever."

"Are you sure you don't want to barter? I have something in the hold I think you'll be very int–"

A giant set of green, scaly hands gripped Tompanov's

shoulders and lifted him clear out of his chair and off the top edge of the screen. His protests to be put down immediately quickly faded, and Oz took his place, shaking her head.

"Man, that guy never shuts up."

He gasped and bent forward so his face was right next to the little screen. "Oz?!"

"I'm going to exit this conversation," Verveik said. "Welcome back, First Officer Nargonis." He blipped out.

"Morpho built us one hell of an escape pod," Morph tightened on Geddy's shoulder and gave her a crisp salute.

"I'll bet he did."

Her brow furrowed in concern. "Are you okay?"

"I'm great now. You?"

"A little banged up, but otherwise we're fine."

Doc, Jel, and Denk leaned in around her, all wide-eyed at the sight of him.

"Holy heck, Cap, you made it!" Denk said.

"My heart is full," said Doc. "It is so very good to see you, Geddy."

"This oughta be one helluva story," noted Jel.

"Back at ya."

"Geddy, Geddy!" Voprot said, leaning his giant snout over Oz's shoulder as she wrinkled her nose. "I put blue pointy-headed man in hold."

"In *the* hold." Geddy said. The emotion that poured out of him was shapeless and raw at first, but quickly gave way to laughter when they heard Tompanov pounding on the door to his own hold, demanding to be let back in.

CHAPTER 50

THE ROAST OF GEDDY STARHEART

Geddy had been to some epic parties, many of which were thrown by Tatiana herself. This was decidedly less fancy, but infinitely more fun. The central atrium of the *Pompadour* was once again crammed with people. And, as before, the now-famous *Penetrator* was proudly displayed in the middle of the dance floor. Only this time, it was the centerpiece of a lavish buffet comprising the most iconic foods from around the galaxy.

He and the crew, along with Smegmo, Zirhof, Zereth-Tinn, and Balzac, had gathered into a corner of the mezzanine level with puffy lounge chairs. It was the perfect place to hold court and tell the tale that would soon become legend. He sat on a velvety loveseat next to Oz, whose head occasionally lolled over onto his shoulder. She was dog tired but insisted on coming for some reason.

"So I'm looking at Eli in this weird gray body of his, Morpho in his Swedish milf getup, and we're like, 'What the shit?' All of a sudden, some cat in an Apollo space suit shows up at the top of the stairs, and guess who it is? Neil Fucking Armstrong!"

"No way!" Denk said, sucking up the dregs of his pink squirrel. "Who's that?"

"One small step for man, one giant leap for mankind?" Geddy replied, as though this was common knowledge throughout the universe. "Apollo Eleven? Armstrong!"

"We had a ship called that!" Denk noted excitedly, adding, to no one in particular, "What are the chances?"

Everyone stared as if expecting a punchline. Everyone except Zirhof, that is, who was a student of Old Earth history.

"Only it wasn't him," Zirhof said with a profound yawn.

Geddy snapped his fingers. "That's right! It was the main Zelnad. Like, the one responsible for the whole damn mess. We're talking the Asurya, like, the head vampire of Zelnads. The don, chief, the grand poobah …"

"Wait, so Neil Armstrong was the head Zelnad and his name was I-sue-ya?" Smegmo made the intergalactic standard sign for a blown mind.

"No, no," Geddy corrected. "*Asurya*. He was just wearing Neil's suit. Well, the replica one. I think. Because my energy told him. Or something like that. Anyway, then I go …"

He could already see by the way everyone's eyes were drifting over him, across the room, that the story wasn't as exciting as it played out in his head. Plus, he'd had at least six glasses of Old Earth whisky and was omitting key details. He may or may not have been slurring his words as well.

"Doesn't matter. Long story short, Eli and I gave the Zelnads hope and saved the universe. The end." He made a farting noise.

"Wow, great story, Ged," Oz teased. The whole lot laughed. She, of course, was stone-cold sober. Moms-to-be had it bad like that.

"You know what? Fuck you guys. Not you, Oz, but everyone else." He held up his glass and gave it a shake as though the ice inside would rattle, but he wouldn't dream of contaminating Old Earth whisky with water. "Empty!"

Voprot returned from the buffet carrying an entire chafing dish full of nyaptomurk poppers, which apparently represented the very best Caloth had to offer.

"Want some?" asked the lizard. "Nobody eat. I eat all giant Kigantean sand weevils."

"I'll try one!" Denk grabbed a tiny fried lizard as Voprot settled onto a padded bench. He chomped into it, a thoughtful look crossing his face. "Damn, V, you're right. The claws really add a satisfying crunch!"

Geddy's stomach turned at the sight and he looked at Voprot, nodding at the chafing dish. "For all you know, those are distant cousins of yours." He downed the rest of his glass and hoisted it toward the bartender in the corner, jabbing his other finger at it. "Yo! Another round for Mr. Universe here!"

"I'd keep what remained of my wits if I were you, Geddy," Zereth-Tinn cautioned, a sly grin spreading across his face. "It's almost showtime."

"What're you talking about?" he slurred. The hiccups were coming on. "The show's already in prog (hic) … prog (hic) … He's already played like ninety songs. (hic)"

No less a celebrity than Simpop Smythe, who had played at the Sumbakh festival on Zorr, was the night's musical guest. He and his band finished the song they were playing, thanked the crowd, and walked off stage with instruments in hand.

"Hey, what the hell?" Geddy yelled to no one in particular. "He didn't even play that one I like!" He turned to ask Oz what it was called, but at some point, she'd left.

— Am I in (hic) trouble?

— *Well, you're hiccuping inside your head now, so …*

"Simpop Smythe, everyone," said an amplified voice from stage left. Tretiak, nattily dressed in a gunmetal tux, ascended a set of steps where a spotlight picked him up. "Everyone having a good time?" A big cheer exploded from the revelers. "Good, good, because this is your night, and we've got a special surprise in store. Colonel Starheart, get your ass up here."

A pair of spotlights swung across the partygoers and landed on Geddy, who shielded his eyes against the blazing beam.

"I don't know what's happening. What's (hic) happening?" he asked in a mild panic.

Zirhof rose, smoothed his royal blue jacket, and offered his hand. "C'mon, I'll help you."

Still baffled, he searched the eyes of his crew, all of whom looked much too innocent. Whatever this was, they were in on it.

— *Just roll with it.*

— What do you know, E?

— *I know nothing.*

Tentatively, he took Zirhof's outstretched hand. As he shakily rose, the crowd offered extra encouragement. The bartender swapped his empty glass for a full one, and he followed Zirhof across the mezzanine and down the steps of the rapidly spinning room. As they approached the stage, Tretiak ushered him toward a chair that someone had just brought out. He'd never been so happy to sit in his life.

"What is this?" he inquired.

"Overdue," he said with a wink, then returned to his microphone. "Colonel Starheart, everyone! Tell me, who better exemplifies the highest ideals of the Alliance tonight, huh?"

A hearty laugh came, and Geddy's bafflement only deepened.

"I've known this man longer than any of you. Since he was thirteen, in fact." He quickly added, "And no, I don't mean in a creepy-uncle sort of way." More laughter. "He showed resourcefulness right off the bat, too. Not every kid could hold his own against a bar full of space pirates, but Geddy never budged ... until they were done."

That one killed. The room practically shook with release.

— Good goddamn, E. Am I being roasted??

— *If so, when's my turn?*

Tretiak delivered a couple more zingers at Geddy's expense, then transformed back into an emcee.

"We've got a full slate of roasters tonight, but none with a bigger axe to grind than the Colonel's ex-fiancée, Tatiana Semenov!"

— Oh, shit.

Tati sashayed up to the stage with a martini in her hand, the liquid perfectly level as she did. She'd finally ditched the sensible pants and blouse in favor of a sequined silver dress so slinky, it could've walked down the stairs on its own.

When she passed him in the chair, she whispered, "How drunk are you?"

"Not nearly drunk (hic) enough."

"You've got that right," she said with a wink, and took the mic from Tretiak as he exited stage right. "Good evening. Just to clarify for everyone, yes, I'm *that* Tatiana Semenov. Chair of the Earth 3 governing board, heiress to the Semenov empire, legendary socialite, swimsuit model, yadda yadda." She thumbed over her shoulder at him. "And I *still* dated this guy — and not for why you think, believe me. My question is, does that count as charity work?"

— This isn't going to end well, is it?

— *I'm enjoying it.*

"Ladies, it *is* true what you've heard about him." Tati nodded across the crowd. "He carries a *hug*e pistol. You know what they say about men who carry big guns? Well, I'm here to tell you it's true. They are *massively* insecure."

"But I'm working on it!" he shouted. Like Eli said, he might as well roll with it.

"Not everyone knows this," she continued, "but he has an alien in his head. Can you imagine? All that space out there, and he sets up shop in *Geddy Starheart's* brain? Apparently, he needed a place where he could really stretch out."

— *Okay, that's pretty good.*
— What do you know?

It went on like this for a long while. It seemed just about everyone got in a pot shot or two, during which time Geddy's glass became maddeningly empty. Nobody came to his rescue.

Zirhof: "I made Geddy's acquaintance because he said he dealt in antiquities. Only later did I realize he was referring to his jokes."

Even Verveik, who rarely even smiled, let alone said something funny, got in on the fun.

"The Colonel's a real 'shoot first, ask questions later' kind of guy. Which helps explain how the Zelnads got his DNA."

After about forty-five minutes of this torture, Tretiak came back onstage. "Ladies and gentlemen, we've all had a bit of fun at Colonel Starheart's expense, but the time has come to turn things over to the people who love him the most. Which is to say, at all. Please welcome Osmiya Nargonis, Denk Junt, Krons Tardigan, Jeledine Berwynd, and ... Voprot — the crew of the late, great *Stalwart!*"

Everyone howled as the old gang took the stage, each of them smiling devilishly at Geddy except Doc, who looked deeply uncomfortable.

— This is what I get for saving the universe?
— *Imagine if you hadn't.*

Oz took the first shot.

"As many of you know, I'm expecting." She patted her abdomen. A thunderous ovation followed as she grinned at him. "Thank you, thank you. I've got a feeling the baby's gonna look just like Geddy. Which is great, because I don't have to remember which clones I slept with."

When they discovered the clones on Myadan, he'd joked that it was a perfect opportunity for Oz to indulge in her gang-bang fantasy. It seemed less funny now.

The whisky had reached critical mass, as had the applause. His head swam. By the time it was Voprot's turn, his stomach had become deeply unhappy.

The big lizard had to raise the mic all the way, and even then he bent almost in half to speak into it. When he finally started talking, it was halfway inside his giant mouth. "Geddy try teaching Vo– er, *me* how to talk better," his voice boomed. "That go about as well as his other missions."

— I need to get off this stage, pronto.

— *Aww, but they love you.*

— No, I mean I'm gonna be sick.

"Geddy not like Kigantu very much," the big lizard continued. "He say it not rain, but like woman, it only dry when he around."

Voprot lowered the mic all the way and angled it at the ground for Denk, who had to stand on his tiptoes.

He was clearly terrified but soldiered on. "Cap's nothing if not humble. Like, did you guys know he won Ponley Point?"

As though on cue — indeed, it probably was — the entire crowd said, "Yes!" in perfect unison.

"Well, that's my time," Denk smiled sheepishly at Geddy as Doc stepped up and cleared his throat.

"There is little I wish say in jest about my friend, Geddy Starheart. He always checked with me before doing something stupid. Then he'd do it anyway."

More laughter. Doc let it die completely down.

"Seriously, though, he stood up for me when no one else would. On the off chance he can stand now, maybe he'd like to share some of his trademark humor with all of us. Colonel?" He stepped back and gestured at the mic.

— Oh, boy …

— You've got a tight five in you, right?

As the crowd welcomed him, all the roasters moved off to the side. Geddy slowly got out of his chair, hanging on as long as he could, and tottered up to the mic. The applause died down, and the silence was deafening.

"Thanks, everyone, for making fun of me. I 'serve and 'espect it."

As his eyes fished for focus, he couldn't tell whether there were five hundred people there or five thousand. Both hands clung to the metal stand like it was a high-rise ledge.

"I dnnn't come prepared. Big surprise. But I can improv with the best of 'em." He gestured off-stage. "Get ready, you assholes, because I'm about to … to …"

It happened so fast. You'd think after all these years, he'd know better. At least half a bottle of the galaxy's rarest hooch had sloshed around in his stomach for the past couple of hours waiting its turn to raw-dog his liver.

It could wait no longer. The bilious mix vaulted up in his gullet, and when it spewed forth onto the microphone, an electric *pop* met his ears, and the floor seemed to yank him toward it like asteroids to Gundrun. The last thing he remembered was a massive green hand catching him at the last moment and being carried off stage to a smattering of bewildered applause.

CHAPTER 51
CHANGE IS INEVITABLE

The mogorodon's orange-yellow eye seemed to stare straight into Geddy's soul. The thick shell of indestructible graphene laminate between them didn't necessarily make him feel safe. Earth 3's endless ocean was the creature's domain, and it always would be. Mogues, Tatiana called him.

The tubular passages that connected the Bubbles were largely empty now, as were the underwater domes themselves. The tourist utopia Tati envisioned would never be. People came once, if they came at all. Between the many fatal accidents during the very challenging final approach to the spaceport and the constantly leaking seals that made it seem like the whole thing could fill with water at any minute, it was too much risk for too little reward.

Tatiana had invested much of her personal fortune into making Earth 3 into a destination, but between the mogorodons, winds, and leaks, it seemed the planet didn't want to be settled. Years of costly engineering problems and an uncooperative ecosystem were enough for most. The vast majority of Earth 3's residents had already gone. Tati was still trying to sell off the troubled planet's assets.

"Whatever possessed you to take this thing as a pet, anyway?" Geddy asked her.

This wasn't technically a social call. Several investors from New Alliance worlds were interested in purchasing the facility, likely to turn it into something else. He'd volunteered to take them since he knew how to handle the tricky approach. Plus, he wanted to check in with her one last time before they left for New Earth.

"He was taken by poachers," she explained. "Jaret and his port security team caught them before they could get away. I figured he had to be an orphan and couldn't bring myself to just release him back into the ocean."

Mogorodons were prized for their various body parts, including and especially their admittedly tasty anal polyps. Tati had done her level best to crack down on illegal poaching, but there was too much ocean and too few mogorodons. The fish they ate had become scarce. Either they'd settle into an equilibrium or they wouldn't.

Tati had previously sold Mogues to the Xeno Xoo, of course, to help ease her burgeoning cash-flow problems. Once the Zelnads' phony bioweapons program was exposed, she had him returned to Earth 3 at eye-watering expense.

"When did you become such a softie?" Geddy inquired.

"I don't know if it's that," she said, leaning against the side of the tube with her arms folded. "In a way, I think he reminded me of you."

An orphan, estranged from his home world and forced into a life he never wanted? Yeah, that tracked. The difference was, Mogues still had a home world to go back to.

The investors had already met with Tati and were now being shown around other parts of the facility by her engineering team. He'd meet them at the ship in twenty-five minutes.

"I should probably make my way back," he said.

She checked her watch. "Yeah, I suppose." Her manicured fingers ran lightly down the side of the tube as though saying goodbye to Mogues.

The two of them strolled back toward the spaceport, Geddy in his blue flight jumpsuit and Tati in a businesslike skirt and jacket.

"So, assuming you're able to get out from under this place, where do you think you'll go?" he asked.

A pained expression crossed her face. "We're looking at some land on Afolos, but they want a mint for it. We'll figure something out."

"You always do."

"What about you?"

"Oz is pretty busy with the resettlement program, but we're heading to Thegus soon for some R and R."

"Good for you. Congrats, by the way." She formed a thin smile. "I never imagined you being a dad."

"You and me both."

They reached the tube that led to her palatial residence, which sat upon one of the lone little islands in the shallow sea.

"Listen, I need to freshen up and check my messages," she said. "But if you're interested ... I'm down to my last few bottles of Old Earth."

"Thanks, but I'll pass. I still can't look at the stuff."

"Suit yourself." Tati sashayed away, her perfect ass swishing from side to side in her fitted skirt. She cast a glance back over her shoulder and caught him staring, but only gave a knowing grin before continuing down the hall.

"He's gonna die," Oz said.

"You already sound like a mother," Geddy replied. "He knows what he's doing."

The crowd at the finish line of Ponley Point was easily four times larger than it had been when Geddy nosed out Zereth-Tinn to become champion. Ever since Thegus joined the Alliance, the race had gone from a poorly kept secret to just one stop in a sanctioned series of starship races across the galaxy. But Ponley was still the most prestigious.

Denk and a handful of mechanics from the *Gallant* had spent the last few weeks modding out the *Dominic*, the *Fizmo's* old dropship that Verveik had taken to the IJC while Geddy looked for Oz. It had been parked in the *Gallant's* executive hangar this whole time, which the crew was delighted to discover. It was much faster and more maneuverable now than it had been when Geddy won.

Voprot and his Kigantean girlfriend, Iondra, sat in the bleachers beside them sharing a giant bag of chili-lime Thegan nutbats. Thankfully, the smell couldn't sicken any other spectators because they'd been given one of the VIP boxes. Being a universe-saving past champion had its perks.

"Want some?" Voprot asked, reaching across Iondra to shake the bag of dried brown flying mammals in Oz's face.

She was already getting sensitive to certain smells, and this one clearly hit her wrong. But, not wanting to make him feel badly, she pressed her lips tightly together and said, "I had a big lunch."

Voprot reached even further across them to Doc and Jel, who were on Geddy's left. "Doc? Jel? Nutbats?"

"They are all yours," Doc said politely.

"I'm trying to quit," Jel said.

"Morpho?" Voprot asked the blob on Geddy's shoulder. He shot a tendril into the bag, withdrew a nutbat, and flung the offending thing directly into the trash can.

"There he is!" Oz said, pointing at the barn-sized holotron hovering over the finish line. Denk had a comfortable lead heading up to the Moonshot Gate, but the *Dom* still wasn't that great a climber, and an overpowered Kailorian speedship was right on his tail.

— *Suicide Plunge is next, right?*

— You know it.

Races were won or lost there, but the pile of wrecked ships at the bottom was a testament to how often it was lost. Denk knew how to do it, but shit happened. Geddy's chest tightened with worry.

The moment he slipped through the Moonshot, he angled the *Dom* straight down, and they began to count.

"One ... two ... three ..."

Even from the stands, Geddy worried that Denk was going too fast. You had to reach the ninety-degree turn at the bottom before your competitors, but you couldn't wait too long to invert and hit the thrusters. Six seconds would put him in the dirt.

"Four ... five ..."

— Now, Denk!

He sucked in a breath and squeezed Oz's hand just as the camera switched to the bottom of the plunge. It filled with orange-white flames as Denk spilled his velocity, and he couldn't tell what happened. But then, the smoke cleared, and the *Dom* leveled out before squeezing through the gap into the Devil's Transcending Colon.

They all heaved a sigh, exchanging nervous laughter as Denk built upon his lead. The rest would be a cakewalk.

Meanwhile, the chyron at the bottom pleaded for more salvage workers to help clean up the mess around Sagacea. Beebit Tompanov couldn't handle it all by himself, which Verveik must've known from the get-go. The Triad wound up taking over the operation, retrofitting old Ghruk ore processors to separate the materials. Those were making daily deliveries to Aku and Kailoria, whose shipbuilding and weapons industries had found new life.

General Grozuc had led a bloodless coup against the deeply corrupt Screvari Circle — yet another sign of a resurgent Triad. They'd also been given the rights to mine Temeruria's remains, and Grozuc offered half the proceeds to help the Temerurian Resettlement Program.

Denk shot out of the DTC and into Shoelace Canyon. He didn't need to take the more dangerous straight route, but Geddy had advised him to trust his gut. Not surprisingly, the kid angled for the first eyelet and accelerated.

The unchecked speed with which Denk navigated the eyelets took Geddy's breath away. He never would've taken them that fast, and not because the *Dom* was a slower ship. Denk just had a bigger pair of balls, as one did at his age.

By the time he shot up over the canyon rim and leveled out en route to the finish line across the nameless flat, the race was all but over. The Kailorian pursuer didn't even come into view until Denk was close enough to be seen from the stands. The six of them leapt to their feet and screamed as he got the checkered flag.

"And it's Denk Junt with a new Ponley Point track record!" the announcer cried.

"Geddy, that much faster than your time!" Voprot yelled, spilling nutbats as he celebrated.

"It sure is, Voprot, thank you."

Oz gave him a warm smile. "You taught him well."

He returned it and pulled her close. "Maybe a little too well."

CHAPTER 52

SIX YEARS LATER

The bite suit's material was puncture-proof to the point where none of New Earth's known insect species could even dream of getting at Geddy and Denk's tasty flesh. But knowing that and making your peace with dozens of fist-sized beetles trying to eat you alive were very different things. And the multi-layered material breathed as well as a plastic bag, which made it that much more distasteful that they had to go check this particular probe hit on this particular day.

Doc's team had mapped and explored about seventy percent of New Earth's livable surface, which was mostly limited to a narrow band between the tropics. The rest was fresh water, predominantly in the form of swamps that stretched for thousands of clicks in any direction. That, plus the planet's high concentration of oxygen, created the perfect conditions for giant insects.

The first colony was called New Medrikar in honor of the Temerurian capital. Roughly half the evacuees now lived here alongside many former residents of Earth 3 — the last dregs of humankind. But other than insect season, a two-month period near the end of the summer, it actually wasn't bad. There were hundreds of edible native plants and more being tested every day. It was hot and humid during the day but cooler and drier at night, with moonlight so bright that most outdoor activities took place after dark.

But not today.

One of Doc's survey probes detected a large deposit of metal near the eastern edge of an unoccupied plateau on the far side of the valley. Most of the time, it turned out to be a chunk of meteorite. On another occasion, it was a spare fuel cell that fell out of a skimrover and tumbled all the way down a cliff.

Geddy was driving. He thought Denk drove too recklessly down the switchbacks that led to the valley floor, which surely meant he was getting old. Just because the vehicle would keep them upright if it rolled down the mountain didn't mean he wanted to do it.

"So, Cap, how's the memoir coming?" Denk asked.

"Oh, still just jotting stuff down as I think of it," Geddy replied. "I just need to figure out how to structure it. To tell the whole story well would take, like, six books."

That was partly true. Geddy did decide to write a memoir, and he did make a note when something popped in his head. But tying a loosely connected set of anecdotes together into a cohesive story seemed like a superpower that only real writers possessed.

Upon reaching the valley floor, he enabled hover mode and urged the skimrover faster across the grassy plain.

"How's Pyna doing with this place?" he asked Denk.

After everything went down, Denk returned to Durandia to help Minister Napthar restore order in the Underground. Along the way, he reconnected with his old heartthrob, Pyna, and made her his bride. He'd convinced her to come to New

Earth six months ago, but she shared his affability, so it was hard to tell how she really felt about it.

"She's comin' around, I think. The greenhouse keeps her busy."

Together, Denk and Pyna ran one of New Medrikar's biggest greenhouses. It was the best way to grow and harvest food without worrying about the giant bugs.

Geddy and Oz were happy here. Oz was governor of New Medrikar and its representative on the Resettlement Oversight Commission. Their son, Neil Armstrong Kepler, was almost five and about to start school. He was a curious, determined, and effortlessly funny kid who Geddy was more than happy to look after while Oz was working.

It wasn't a picnic by any stretch. To this point, everyone still lived in surplus Xellaran terraforming habs and would continue to do so until Doc's ten-year planetary study was complete. Tatiana was New Earth's provisional ambassador to the Alliance and, as such, was keen to avoid the mistakes of Earth 3. Much about life here was akin to group camping. It was a lot of work and probably always would be even after permanent structures could be built.

The rest of the crew was scattered. Doc split his time between New Earth and Ornea, where he'd established an intergalactic exploration company. Morpho flew survey missions for them. Voprot lived with Iondra on Afolos. Jel commissioned a custom ship from the Kailorians to replace the *Bogart* and later returned to Stemir, where men were slowly being reintroduced into the wild. She was a freelance security consultant who did some work for the Alliance.

Still led by Tretiak, now likely a career politician, the Committee had morphed into the Alliance High Council. Zirhof and Smegmo were still on it, representing Zorr and Ceonus, respectively. Most of the other military leaders, including Tymeri and Grozuc, were training the next generation of soldiers. The *Penetrator* was on permanent display outside the Alliance's new headquarters on Thegus, where Kriggy had decided to set up his new tattoo parlor.

Verveik, however, had fought his last war. Commandant Arbizander had taken the reins shortly after the Battle of Sagacea, and Verveik now lived somewhere on Gundrun.

But he likely didn't live alone. As more people learned how to tap into their mahk'ti, they built connections to the Sagaceans they never knew were there. Oz, Denk, and Pyna all had, along with the majority of Temerurian settlers. It stood to reason that Verveik had done the same.

It took about half an hour to cross the valley. Occasionally, one of the beetles would bounce off the rover's steeply raked shield with the force of a foul ball and leave a mark. Otherwise, the only animals that crossed their path were rodent-like creatures and the occasional armored lizard.

When they reached the plateau, Denk leaned over with the tablet and pointed at the pulsing dot. "Okay, it should be about a hundred and fifty meters up."

Their skimrover had a vert package. It could hover and maneuver but wasn't really designed to fly. Geddy engaged the VTO jets, and they began to climb up the plateau's steep side.

As they rose, the geological history of New Earth unfolded before them. Intense volcanic activity. Centuries of flooding. A colossal lake. A desert. Rough shrubs still clung to the soil in places, stretching as far as they dared to collect the sunlight.

"Okay, should be right up here," Denk said.

Geddy glanced up. Indeed, something was sticking out of the mostly smooth cliff. Not far, but far enough to prove it wasn't a meteorite. Against the clouds, it was impossible to tell.

After a few seconds, they drew even with it, and Geddy's mouth dropped open.

"What ... the ... heck?" Denk asked.

It couldn't be, yet there it was — the upper right corner of the *For Sale Make Offer's* boxy hold. It was canted at such an angle that the nose was just to the right and probably seven or eight meters deep.

They stared at it, then each other as though this was some kind of elaborate prank played on them by Doc. But if there was one thing Doc didn't do often, it was joke around.

The last time he'd seen the *Fiz*, Geddy was in the *Penetrator* looking up as it raced toward Sagacea's invisible barrier. He couldn't see the escape pod launch and jet away from it, but he did see the old ship make contact with the barrier-bubble and blink away.

Upon realizing that the barrier was, in fact, a jump bubble created by Sagacea's awesome power, Geddy had asked Lestiko where it would transport something that hit it. He'd said, *It could be anywhere in any galaxy. Space, a planet, a star ...*

A planet. This planet.

But it was too big a coincidence. So, too, had been the appearance of the Zelnad research ship in their previous galaxy. Could the Asurya have seen far enough ahead to know this was where they'd end up? Could Sagacea itself have known? Despite all they understood about original energy, much of it was still a mystery. All Geddy knew for sure was that they were destined to find it. If there was a lesson to be learned, he couldn't know what it was. Not yet, anyway.

"Call it in," Geddy said.

EPILOGUE
SIX MONTHS LATER

The Fizmo Theater became New Medrikar's first permanent structure. It took weeks to finally chisel it out of the rock and dirt on the uninhabited side of the valley, whereupon it took a Gundrun heavy freighter to cart it across to the colony. It wasn't remotely flyable anymore, of course, but Geddy wasn't about to let it become a fossil.

It was Oz who thought it might serve as a temporary community center. The terraforming habs were modular, so there was no way to make a large indoor space with them. Until Geddy and Denk discovered the old trawler, community matters were either taken up outside at night or in the stifling maintenance tent that housed their heavy equipment. Though the *Fiz's* flying days were over, her climate control system was largely intact. After she was lowered into her final resting place at the end of New Medrikar's main road, Denk and a handful of Temerurian techs got the system up and running within a few days.

Geddy thought that it might eventually become a museum of some kind, perhaps using many of the same human artifacts and displays currently gathering dust in a warehouse on Afolos. But that was a long ways off.

It had since become the venue for a few colony meetings and two wedding ceremonies, but it hadn't seen a grand opening. One evening, while struggling with his memoir, Oz half-jokingly suggested that Geddy start small and write it as a grade-school play. The opportunity to work on such a project with Neil and his classmates held great appeal, and so Geddy had spent the last couple of months writing and directing his original play, *A Song of Sagacea*, as the first official production of the New Medrikar Children's Theater.

Pretty much everyone besides Verveik had made the trek. Most of the Committee was there, and Tatiana was on her way. Doc and his research team had come and were sitting next to Voprot, Iondra, and Dr. Krezek. Jel and Ori came all the way from Stemir. Not only had Tymeri come, but she brought two dozen of the clones with her. In all, nearly three hundred people were packed into the *Fiz's* former hold to watch the show.

Geddy and Oz were still posted up on either side of the slightly open hold doors, which now formed the main entrance. They'd greeted everyone who came and handed them programs. Their seats were still open at the back, but Geddy was too nervous to sit.

Neil stood between two other kids, one a couple of years younger playing Eli and another slightly older who was playing Morpho. The younger kid wore all black throughout the show like a stagehand and followed Neil around offering advice. But for the penultimate scene, at least, he got to wear a different costume. While they took in their surroundings at the museum, a fourth kid in a NASA costume made mostly from white flexible ductwork entered stage left. Geddy never appreciated how hard it was to come up with set and costume materials until he had to figure it out himself.

"Are you the Asurya?" asked Neil as Geddy.

He'd gotten Oz's Temerurian "hair," though it was shorter and less indicative of his mood. Somehow, he'd gotten the best parts of them both. On stage or off, he was fearless, funny, and endlessly curious.

"Yes! Look upon me and tremble!" The Gundrun kid playing the Asurya was only ten but sounded like he was in his early thirties.

— *I see you ignored my notes.*

— I thought it sounded punchier that way.

"Where are we?" asked the kid playing Eli.

"At the intersection of space and time where you are both alive and dead."

"Like Schrödinger's cat?" Neil inquired.

"Yes," intoned the post-pubescent kid. "You clearly have a solid working knowledge of physics."

Oz grimaced and rubbed the bridge of her nose, whispering, "Ugh, I can't believe you left that line in."

— *Me, neither. Talk about your revisionist history.*

"Creative license," Geddy said in his defense.

"Your trials have led you here, where the fate of the universe will be decided."

"What do we have to do?" asked the kid playing Morpho.

— *Sheesh. If his acting was any more wooden, he'd be a baseball bat.*

— It's a remote colony. The talent pool's even more shallow than I am.

"Convince me that your universe is worth saving," intoned the Asurya, gesturing grandly. "What say you?"

Oz chuckled under her breath and reached for his hand. This was Neil's big speech, and he'd worked so hard on it that a mistake would be devastating.

The door jostled, and Tatiana poked her platinum blond head in. Geddy gestured for her to quietly enter.

"Sorry," she whispered. "I came as fast as I could."

"Speaking of which, you're just in time for the big climax," he said, earning a glare from Oz.

Tati tiptoed past him and leaned against the back wall a few meters away.

"We have come far to find and stop you, great Asurya. We have bravely battled sky snakes, ranses, and crypsids. We learned the secrets of the bubble drive and mahk'ti. And we have even made multiple trips to Kigantu, the galaxy's worst planet."

Voprot spun in his chair and gave Geddy a full-toothed smile.

"But through it all, my friends and I have remained steadfast and true. Because we never lost hope, I am able to give it to you."

Neil reached into his Alliance jumpsuit and withdrew a shiny gold star fringed with tinsel. When he handed it to the Asurya, more than a few people in the crowd said, "Aww."

"You see, hope is what gives the universe power. Without it, there can be no future."

The Asurya regarded it with awe. "You are right, Geddy Starheart, and I am wrong. You are a great hero for changing my mind and saving the universe. The galaxy owes you its undying gratitude and definitely a statue someday. And also a generous monthly stipend."

"I know," Neil said. "Now go in peace and return us to our friends so we may repair this broken world together."

All four of them turned to the audience, clasped hands, and raised them in the air. In near-unison, they said, "Long live Sagacea and the Alliance!"

The curtain closed on them, and the crowd leapt to its feet in raucous applause. Tears came to Geddy's eyes as he turned to Oz. "That's the best thing I've ever seen. Let's go congratulate him."

"Did you forget about the epilogue?" Oz asked.

"What epilogue?"

The curtain parted again, and Neil was seated on a chair stage left, his head lolling back and forth with a glass of what Geddy hoped was just caramel-colored water in his hand.

— Oh, no. No, no, no …

— *These folks are really getting their money's worth.*

— Did you and Oz plan this?

— *I'll never tell.*

A kid from the stage crew came onstage dressed as Tretiak and pointed at Neil in the chair.

"Well, folks, we had a lot of fun at Geddy's expense tonight. Let's ask him to close out the show."

He began to applaud, and the rest of the crowd joined in. Neil got up, pretending to be drunk, and tottered up to the microphone in the center.

"You all have kept my colossal ego in check, and I appreciate it. I just want to say … I want to say …"

He made a retching sound and brought his hands up around his mouth. When he opened them, multicolored confetti poured onto the mic, and the stage lights flickered out.

Again, laughter and whistles burst forth from the crowd, and they continued as the cast and crew came out for their curtain call.

Geddy looked over at Oz, a shit-eating grin spread across her reddening face.

"I bring the parade, you bring the rain, is that it?" he said.

She gave a sheepish shrug. "It's still a happy ending."

He smiled and turned to look at his boy, who kept bowing as he drank in the adulation. "I do like those."

Her grin broadened into a dazzling full-toothed smile. "Speaking of which …"

DISCOVER THE CYTOCORP SAGA BY C.P. JAMES

www.vinci-books.com/dome-six

In a world where safety means everything, two unlikely heroes uncover a truth that will shatter their reality.

A young technician and his uncle stumble upon a mysterious signal, igniting a dangerous quest for answers. As they delve deeper, they face a chilling question: Is there life beyond the sanctuary of Dome Six?

Turn the page for a free preview…

DOME SIX: CHAPTER 1

A hundred and twenty meters overhead, the man in gray dangled from a safety harness Owen wouldn't have trusted to hold up his pants.

Tosh stood beside him, staring intently at the tablet in her calloused hands, the edges of its rubber housing worn thin by use. The feed from Nathan's helmet cam confirmed what they already knew about the relay — a failed seal allowed moisture inside, corroding the wires where they entered the relay housing, and probably the housing itself.

"I'd say we found our bad relay," said Nathan.

Owen gave silent thanks. They'd been looking for the damn thing since morning. Why was it always one of the last ones they checked?

Tosh heaved a sigh. "We see it, Nathan. Stand by." She turned to Owen and raised her eyebrows. "What should I tell him, Tech Apprentice Welsh?"

Nearly two years had passed since he received his Placement from IDA, the Dome's ubiquitous AI that decided such things. He got Technician, just like he wanted. But then he found out his apprenticeship supervisor was his own adoptive mother.

He had to keep reminding himself she was the best Tech in the city, but boy, she could be a pain in the ass.

"He has to pull out all the wires, remove the box, snip off the corroded wire, re-strip each one before connecting them to a new relay."

"But ...?"

He recognized her tone. Like so many other things on the job, it was a test. "But ... we're out of new relays, so someone's got to rebuild this one." She cocked her head, implying his answer was still incomplete. "*I've* got to rebuild it."

Tosh smiled and pressed the button on her radio. "Nathan, you're gonna have to pull every wire out of that housing and very carefully remove it. We need to rebuild it and replace the seal." She released the button and muttered, "With what, I don't know."

"I was afraid you'd say that, Tosh," replied Nathan.

She looked sideways at Owen, smirking. "I'll put my best man on the rebuild. But in the meantime, that zone's gonna get pretty balmy. I know you're already feeling the heat up there but take your time and do it right."

"Roger that. I wouldn't stand under me unless you want a flop-sweat shower."

She chuckled and shook her head.

The power grid for the massive air Exchangers dotting the Dome's graphene-paneled superstructure ran through the aluminum lattice frame. The major conduits ran along the same vertical ribs as the the maintenance crawlers, but the ocean of sensors and diagnostic circuitry that monitored them an horizontally, like lines of latitude.

Since crawlers couldn't move sideways and such repairs were supposed to be extremely rare, one member of the Maintenance team had to clip into a motorized sled and hang from it while they performed the repair. Their harness was clipped to both the sled and a hand-cranked backup.

That would be fine if this kind of thing only happened once a decade.

Further down the Rad, the Infrastructure ground crew stood around the gigantic airbag, occasionally interrupting their animated conversation to glance up at the repair. Each ten-meter Rad ran directly below a crawler track, but if they ventured more than a few meters to the side, there'd be nothing under them but buildings.

According to Tosh, whoever designed it either failed to account for this or placed inordinate trust in the safety gear. It was a hard point to argue.

A small crowd gathered around the barriers encircling their crew on Rad 60, craning their necks to gawk at the operation overhead. Anything remotely out of the ordinary drew attention. Owen recalled doing the same when he was little, before his dad disappeared. Now, as the end of his apprenticeship drew near, such repairs had become old hat. How tedious would it be when he'd done it as long as Tosh?

He'd have plenty of time to think about that when he was rebuilding the relay.

"Watch him," Tosh said, handing Owen the tablet. "I'm gonna see if any new tickets came in from the Directorate."

Owen unfolded his yellow plastic stool and held the tablet between his legs as he watched Nathan, who was so far away that the tedious work of pulling wires out made it appear he wasn't moving at all.

As he watched, the feed flickered and glitched, turning the image blocky. Neither of them could figure out what caused it. He gave the tablet a firm bump with the heel of his palm.

"What's going on?" asked a boy behind him.

Owen wiped the sweat from his forehead and glanced over his shoulder. A boy of eight or nine steadied himself on the barricade, resting his chin on the top with his toes balanced on the bottom. Owen was about to ask why he wasn't in class when he checked the time projected overhead — 6:18 p.m. The kid probably just came from the cafeteria.

Good god. Had he really been there for four hours?

"Just a routine repair," Owen said, smiling.

"Does anyone ever fall?"

"Owen, focus!" Tosh barked

He immediately returned his attention to Nathan's feed. "Sorry," he muttered, exaggeratedly staring at the fuzzy image to prove he was paying attention. He rose, slid his stool further from the barricade, and looked apologetically at the kid. "Not in a long time, buddy." Tosh returned a moment later. "Anything?"

"The train on Rad 48's got a braking issue. Once we're done here, I'll deal with that while you start the rebuild."

"But it's already like 6:20."

"Oh, I'm sorry. Have you got someplace to be?"

Owen sighed and held up the tablet. "I can hardly even see what he's doing, this thing is so flaky."

She crouched beside him and frowned at the static in the feed. "More interference?"

"You really don't know what that is?" he asked.

"No one does. It's even worse with the stupid radios."

The fancy handheld devices they used to use conked out before he was even born, adding to a long list of high-tech junk they'd abandoned to the Boneyard. They used the backup system of old-school radios exclusively now. They worked okay, but were even more susceptible to interference than the tablets.

"Dek thinks it's RF," added Owen.

She sighed. "Is that what my brother the junkie janitor

thinks? There is no RF in here because there's nothing to generate it."

"I know, but—"

"Hey guys?" asked Nathan.

Tosh picked up the radio. "Go ahead."

"Any idea what this is?"

She leaned closer to the tablet and studied the feed from Nathan's helmet. Hidden beneath the bundle of wires, molded to the inside of the housing, was a tan piece of material Owen didn't recognize.

She shook her head, frowning. "I'm not sure. Insulation, maybe? Some kind of heat shield?"

"Hang on, I'll see what it's made of," Nathan said. He removed a knife from his utility belt, poked it into the material, and carefully removed a pea-sized piece. He brought it up to his face, too close for his helmet cam to focus. "It's pliable." He sniffed at it. "Smells a little like oil."

Tosh activated the radio. "Don't worry about it, Nathan. Just keep working on the relay." She released the button. "What is it with men and distractions?"

"You seriously don't know what that is?" Owen asked.

"Don't know, don't really care. I just want him done and back on the damn crawler." She pressed the button. "Byron, switch to channel four." She switched hers and gave him a few seconds to do the same. "You there?"

"I'm here," said Byron, his voice weary. He'd been in the crawler since morning.

She turned her back to Owen while she spoke with him, her tone softening. They worked together fairly often, on the same shift, and had begun seeing each other socially. Tosh shunned relationships while she raised him and it was good to see her relatively happy. More than that, it was nice to have her attention directed elsewhere for a change.

"How you holding up?" Tosh asked.

"Sweating my balls off next to a broken crapper," he said. "How about you?"

Owen chuckled, the radio making it impossible not to eavesdrop. The big, heavy Crawlers moved so slowly that they had their own toilet system. Unfortunately, they, too, broke frequently.

"Do you know what that molded piece is?" Tosh asked Byron.

"My tablet's out of juice so I can't see the feed. What's it look like?"

"It's just thin, tan material molded to the inside of the panel. I thought it could be insulation. He said it's pliable, so maybe the humidity degraded it."

"Hm. Your guess is as good as m–"

The boy behind Owen gasped, as did several others in the gathering crowd. They craned their heads back to see Nathan swinging wildly back and forth. Owen leapt to his feet.

"Byron! What just happened?! Switch back to three." She changed her own channel and anxiously tapped her fingers on the radio.

Byron's voice came back on. "Nathan's primary just broke. I'm gonna go get him."

She shoved the radio into Owen's hands while he stared dumbly at the swinging gray form overhead. "Call it in!" she commanded.

He gathered his wits and switched to channel six. "Infrastructure, this is field unit two. We've got a code red on Rad 60, requesting emergency response team."

"Copy that, field two. We're on our way."

"Come on!" Tosh yelled.

Owen tucked the tablet under his arm and followed her through the barricade at a dead run. They pushed past the young boy and ran toward the two men standing idly beside the big blue airbag, a small motor keeping it inflated. They saw

Tosh and Owen running and looked up, suddenly realizing there was a problem.

"Where are your damn radios?!" Tosh yelled. Owen passed her and shoved the barricade aside while the two men stared, wide-eyed, up at Nathan.

She held the radio back up. "Nathan, we need to know your position on the ground. Are you able to drop a marker?"

"I'll try," Nathan said, his voice frantic. A few seconds passed. "Marker away."

Their eyes scanned the air overhead. A bright orange marker trailing a wispy ribbon fell from Nathan's position, landing on the ground right next to the building with a thin plop.

Tosh pointed at the airbag. "Okay, this needs to be tight against the building. It's gonna be close." She activated the radio again. "Byron, hurry. We're not in a good position here."

Infrastructure had sent the two young safety workers to set up the airbag, which took them nearly as long as it took Byron and Nathan to reach the junction in the crawler. The four of them lined up in the narrow space between the edge of the bag and the building and gathered up the nylon fabric in their hands.

"On three!" Tosh said. "One, two, three!"

They yanked the airbag as one. As they did, the seam above Owen's knuckles ripped, and air blasted his face. When he turned away, he saw it had ripped in other places, too. The airbag began to deflate faster than it could refill. Panicking, he tried to grab the top flap and roll it closed, but as he did, he heard a scream over the rush of escaping air.

"He fell!" came Byron's voice, loudly enough to hear without the radio. "Look out!"

His eyes shot upward. Nathan's body plummeted toward them, limbs flailing. Owen unconsciously did the math. When he landed, he'd be going more than 220 kilometers per hour. They had seconds.

"Get back!" cried Tosh.

Owen turned and ran until he was well clear of the airbag, turning back just in time to see Nathan crash through the roof of the building like a bullet, just wide of the mark.

DOME SIX: CHAPTER 2

The morning after Nathan Graser fell to his death, Tosh found herself seated at the end of a well-worn boardroom table in the Council chambers adjacent to the Administrator's office, hoping none of the six Directors tried to engage her in small talk. Real wood covered the walls, each with a single piece of dull corporate art hung precisely in the center.

Several dozen citizens witnessed the accident, after which the Dome's hyper-efficient rumor mill kicked into high gear. Everyone knew what happened, more or less, and the Authority had egg on its face yet again.

How many times had she been here to debrief the Council after a preventable accident? Half a dozen times, at least?

She already knew how this would go. They would pepper her with questions, vaguely imply it was somehow her fault, and then do nothing.

The Directors averted their eyes while they waited for Administrator Elle Travers to arrive, save for Luther Downing from Security. Ever since he caught her brother, Hideki, making and using psychedelic Macros as bribes last year, he regarded Tosh with suspicion. When Dek got demoted from

Bioprinting all the way down to janitor as a result, she thought that would be the end of it.

Elle's approaching footsteps finally broke the pregnant silence, and she entered in a huff.

"Sorry to keep you all waiting," she said, closing the door behind her. "I just met with Nathan's family and offered the Authority's condolences."

Like a warm blanket, I'm sure.

"Thank you for being here for this debrief, Toshiko. I know you have plenty to worry about."

Her childhood friend's square shoulders were pulled back as tightly as her long, blond hair, which spilled out over her crisp blue Authority jacket in a long, sleek ponytail. Frown lines carved into the corners of her mouth were more pronounced now, her eyes a bit darker, yet she maddeningly retained her youthful face.

How long had it been? Seven years? More? She'd never called her anything besides Tosh, her preferred nickname, until that moment. Almost no one did except her parents, and they'd been gone for nearly twenty years.

"Actually, *Administrator Travers*," Tosh began, parroting Elle's formal tone, "this incident is precisely what I worry about every day."

Elle settled into her chair and leaned in, resting on her elbows. "We all read the incident report, but maybe you could walk us through the repair up to the point Mr. Graser's safety equipment malfunctioned."

"It didn't malfunction. It failed," corrected Tosh. "Twice. First the clip on his primary harness and then the backup strap–"

"Infrastructure is well aware of the harness issue," said Downing, cutting her off and nodding to Director Harrison. "If you could limit your remarks to the facts, that would be great."

Tosh stiffened and shifted in her seat, taking a deep breath to calm her ire. "Infrastructure diagnostics reported that all Exchanger nodes in zone eleven were throwing a code 9A. That means a communications error with the sensors that monitor RPMs, heat, that sort of thing."

"And had you seen this code before?" asked Harrison.

"Yes, many times. Lately, especially. I confirmed the code with Infrastructure and they dispatched a crawler team so we could get a look inside the zone's main sensor relay, which was the logical place to start. We already had a good idea that a failed seal caused it to corrode."

Harrison checked his tablet. "And that team was the victim, Mr. Graser, and his supervisor ... Byron Wallace, with whom you are romantically involved. Is that correct?"

Tosh narrowed her eyes at him. They knew because IDA knew. IDA knew everything. "How is that material to the discussion?"

Harrison held up his palms. "We're just establishing the full context."

Elle gave him a cautioning look. Tosh continued.

"Anyway, when Nathan removed the outer cover of the node's access panel, it confirmed what we suspected. A faulty seal caused extensive corrosion to the relay housing and the wires going into it. I instructed him to remove the wires, followed by the housing."

She briefly considered mentioning the molded material, but if she and Byron didn't recognize it, they certainly wouldn't.

Elle cocked her head. "You personally provided that direction, not your apprentice, Owen Welsh?"

And there it was, the fishing for blame. If they could chalk it up to human error, they could avoid accepting the truth indefinitely. To try and pin this on Owen or his training was beyond the pale.

"I asked him for the correct way to proceed, which he gave

me, then I repeated the instructions to Nathan. I was only testing his knowledge."

Harrison leaned back and folded his hands across his stomach. "What was to be Mr. Welsh's role in all this?"

"I was going to have him rebuild the relay."

"I'll bet he looked forward to that," said Downing, smirking.

"It's tedious work, but it wouldn't be necessary if we had spares, which we don't."

"Everyone's aware of our supply shortages," said Downing with a roll of his hawkish eyes. "What happened after Mr. Graser began the repair?"

"We monitored his helmet cam on a tablet and were in constant radio communication. That's when—"

Downing cut her off. "I'm sorry to interrupt, Miss Yamamura, but the logs indicate you switched the channel on your radio in order to have a separate, private conversation with Mr. Wallace. What was the nature of that conversation?"

Tosh's brow furrowed and she looked to Elle, whose shrug indicated it was a fair question in her view. "I was checking up on him. He'd been up in that stupid crawler for fourteen hours."

"So, for a time, he was distracted and channel three was unmonitored," said Harrison.

Tosh gave him an indignant stare. "What are you implying, Director?"

Again, Harrison innocently held up his hands. "It just seems to me Mr. Wallace was distracted for a critical few seconds, during which he might have been able to respond ."

Elle cleared her throat and glared at him. "Please continue, Toshiko. No one will interrupt you again."

Tosh gritted her teeth and recounted the events that culminated in poor Nathan's death. The failure of the airbag's seams, in particular, she wrapped in loving detail.

"Thank you, Toshiko," said Elle with phony concern. "As always, we certainly appreciate your time and candor. You should go home and get some rest. I've asked Director Harrison to redirect your tickets for a couple days."

"I'm sorry," said Tosh through a tight smile. "I didn't know I was done."

"With due respect, I think we have all the information we need."

"All the information you need to do what, exactly?"

"I'm sorry?" Elle asked.

Tosh jabbed her finger into the table. "I mean you're not getting it! I don't think the Council understands what's at stake here."

Elle narrowed her eyes at Tosh and gestured deferentially with her hand. "Then please continue."

Luther rolled his eyes and leaned back, interlacing his hands behind his head. "Here we go ..." he muttered.

Tosh took a deep breath and folded her hands in front of her. "The air Exchangers that keep us alive are caked with a hundred years of grime, making them heavier. The added weight has put increased strain on the motors. Meanwhile, the system that monitors them is supposed to be protected from the humidity by seals that are now failing.

"The Dome's superstructure depends on air pressure to help support its immense weight. If the Exchangers go down, we lose much of that pressure, putting undue strain on the frame. Strain them enough and the panels will start to crack. If that happens, we'll lose both the UV shield and our solar capacity. Backup power is rated to last six weeks, but considering the system's age, I'd put it at half that.

"We have no replacement parts, which means we have to do rebuilds or print the parts we need. The safety equipment in the crawlers is hardly the only junk made by the lowest bidder in this godforsaken place, further evidenced by an airbag that won't even hold air.

"You don't see the condition of this place every day, but I do, and I'm telling you in no uncertain terms that it's falling apart."

The Directors' faces wrinkled in faint concern, but said nothing. Tosh looked pleadingly at Elle.

"Thank you for your assessment, Toshiko. We'll reach out to you if we need more information."

Tosh's eyes roamed across the table of bureaucrats, none of whom had ever so much as held a wrench in their entire, IDA-determined lives. She knew their histories intimately. With the exception of Elle, each one had a family member in the Authority.

This is what happened when generation after generation of so-called leaders with meritless Placements repeated the same mistakes.

Something dark bubbled up and overtook her. She slapped the table with her open palm, jolting them back to attention.

"No! The Dome itself might stand for a thousand years, but the systems that keep us alive won't. We need to have a serious conversation about what happens when these systems finally fail, because they will. Not if, but when."

Downing broke the awkward silence that followed. He jutted his chin toward her. "Most of you didn't know Ms. Yamamura's father, but he was a talented Technician in his own right." He pointed at the door that led to Elle's office. "He sat right there in Administrator Keane's office and gave us the same exact lecture — that no one would listen to him and we were all gonna die. That was twenty years ago."

"No one believed the day would come when half of California splintered off into the ocean, either. How'd that work out?"

"The Fifth Epoch is our priority right now," Downing said,

nodding to Elle. "After that, I'm sure we'll take a closer look at these maintenance issues of yours."

Now Tosh understood what this was really about. Every twenty years, the Authority hosted a celebration called the Epoch, at which they read the latest sensor readings. Cytocorp, the company that initiated the Dome Project, believed it would take a century, at least, for the outside world to stabilize and recover from the deadly climate event called the Burn. At each Epoch, the data improved slightly, but never to survivable levels.

Unfortunately, it seemed the Authority's focus on the Epoch came at the expense of all else.

No one wanted to confront the fact that they hadn't been contacted by Cytocorp, the other Domes, or anyone from the outside world in almost ninety years. Not since cyberterrorists took down the internet. Their only connection to the Time Before was the Cache, a snapshot of the web based on pages viewed by Dome citizens during its first decade of operation.

Anyone who had been to an Epoch eventually came to see it for what it really was — a way to give a younger generation a tiny bit of hope. If they rode that wave of optimism through their most productive years, then the Dome would get the best of them before they realized it was all bullshit.

"Look," Tosh said. "No one is coming for us. We need a concrete plan for what comes next. Send a team to either find help or–"

"Or what?" Downing asked. "Or build a camp in a windswept desert that can sustain a hundred thousand people? Learn how to grow food and find water in the scorched earth? This facility is our lifeboat. You want to jump overboard and wind up like your parents, be my guest."

Tosh seethed at the reference to her parents, who died during the Fourth Epoch as a result of a harebrained search for the exit. Her brother, Hideki, tormented himself by believing it wasn't an accident, but she'd processed her grief and moved on.

The future was what mattered now, not the past. If the Authority didn't do something about the failing Dome, and soon, Owen's generation would be the last.

"Okay, let's all cool off," cautioned Elle, a thin rebuke considering Downing was her not-so-secret lover. "Toshiko, you've given us a lot to think about, but this debrief must conclude. Again, please take a few days to decompress. We'll reach out if we need more information."

Tosh rose from the table, glaring murderously at Downing as he held the door open for her.

"Say hi to your brother for me," he said.

Tempting though it was to unleash a string of obscenities at him, she decided to save it for another day. If the Authority wouldn't act, then she'd have to. But if Downing locked her up out of spite, she couldn't do anything at all.

She cast a final look over her shoulder at Elle, who met her eyes for a brief moment before suggesting they move on to other business. Before she did, she thought she might've mouthed *I'm sorry*.

Grab your copy…
www.vinci-books.com/dome-six

ABOUT THE AUTHOR

C.P. James writes cinematic sci-fi with humor and heart. He lives in the magical country of Ecuador. His first novel, *The Perfect Generation*, was published in February 2018. A dystopian trilogy, The Cytocorp Saga, was released in 2020. Reassembly, a humorous space opera, was launched in April 2021.